Kill the Dragon

Being the first part of
Lake of Dragons

E. Michael Mettille

TMR Books
PO Box 510886
Milwaukee, WI 53203
www.themikereynolds.com

All images provided by Deposit Photos

Cover Artwork – © 2021 L.J. Anderson of Mayhem Cover Creations

Published by TMR Books 05/15/2021

ISBN 978-0-9975571-3-8

DEDICATION

For Shelia…thank you.

CHAPTER 1
CHILDHOOD'S END

Maelich leaned against the mighty oak crowning Keller's Hill. The spot was a favorite of his, a place to ponder both days gone by and days yet to come. This particular occasion was similar to most. After a full day of rigorous training his mind often had a tendency to chase concepts rather than relive memories or form new ideas. Of all the concepts he mulled over while leaning against the rough bark of the great oak, mother earned the lion's share of his attention. Of course, he knew what the concept meant. He simply had no experience with one. His died shortly after he was born. All he had were stories, and they were vague at best. There was something about a young woman and a great power. None of it was anything tangible. Nothing more than loose concepts and generic ideals.

"Hey there, lad," Ymitoth's voice shattered the quiet. "It be time for your feeding."

Maelich waved his response, collected himself, and tromped on down the hill. Pink clouds caught his attention, painted by the sun setting behind him. He must have lost track of the hour. His stomach grumbled loudly as if to confirm the idea. He quickened his pace down the hill.

Admiration swept through Maelich as Ymitoth glanced back at him. His stern mentor looked like he had jumped right off a painting Maelich had seen once. It was an image of valiant men standing tall against a horrible dragon. Ymitoth could easily stand among heroic men like that. He was massive, a half-head taller than most and broad about the shoulders. The wind caught hold of his hair. It danced about the breeze glinting like rusty gold in the failing light of the setting sun. He was every bit the hero in Maelich's eyes. There wasn't a man who stood mightier.

Then something about Ymitoth's expression changed. It was odd and unfamiliar. It resembled a smile the way it parted his beard from his mustache and plumped his cheeks out, but it didn't quite fit, like a dwarf seated on a giant's throne. Normally the sharp lines of his face looked like something that could cut stone. Accompanying the strange smile-like thing twisting up his beard was an uncustomary wave. The warrior almost looked…happy.

Maelich grinned and quickened his pace all the more. He puzzled only briefly over Ymitoth's odd behavior as he worked to catch up to the man he had grown to know as father. There was a concept far more readily available to him. Ymitoth had always been very clear about the fact he and Maelich shared no blood. However, as far as Maelich could tell, his teacher, mentor, and trainer accepted him as a son. And, of course, Maelich loved and admired Ymitoth as he imagined any lad would love and admire the one teaching him to be a man. Ymitoth wasn't one to fall victim to bouts of affection and show anything which might be construed as weakness. There were times, though, times when the rough and tough would crack just enough for Maelich to catch a hint that Ymitoth cared for him. The odd smile combined with the awkward wave equaled one of those times. Those brief moments were enough for Maelich. They had to be.

Every day was the same for him. Rise with the sun, take in the morning feeding, run the pastures with Ymitoth—who seemed to get slower as Maelich grew—and then bathe in Yester's Pond. All those things were considered by Ymitoth to be, "the warm-up." After the warm-up came sword training. Sword training always seemed to last forever. By the time it was finished he could barely lift his sword. He didn't mind too much as he was but a lad of twelve summers and already close to being Ymitoth's equal. The fact made him feel powerful. Stories of his master's conquests spread as far as Maelich had ever been.

After sword training was complete it would be time for the midday feast, the nucleus of the day. Every other activity was planned around it, even the short nap that followed. Maelich's workday ended with his book lessons, when he learned about how the world came to be and how to make your way through, "The great journey of life," as Ymitoth called it. Once all his daily tasks were complete, Maelich was allowed a bit of time to himself before the evening feeding, which brings us back to where we began.

The warmth of the fire seized Maelich immediately when he entered the hut. He shook the chill from the winds of the hill off himself and took his spot at the table. A large sweet cake sat at the center of it, decorated as if it were meant for some sort of festival. Then he inhaled the savory scent of roast tubberslat, his favorite.

"Are we expecting guests, father?" he asked, confused by the ado over the evening feeding. Normally it consisted of bread and sweet jelly, maybe a little stew but never anything as extravagant as roast tubberslat.

"No lad, just us," Ymitoth responded with a grin and a slight giggle as if he were enjoying a joke all by himself.

"Why the feast?" Maelich continued, still a bit taken with the great meal placed before him.

Ymitoth laughed out loud at his pupil, "Ah, my lad, you're still so simple. A bit of roast tubberslat and a sweet cake and ye be having us at a feast. It weighs heavy on me heart, lad, but this day be a very important one to ye, and on this night I be telling ye why."

Ymitoth's strange behavior kept Maelich off balance as he continued his line of questions, "What of this day be so special that makes it different than any other?"

"Today be a celebration, laddy!" Ymitoth boomed as he swept Maelich up and embraced him.

"Father, ye be scaring me," he could barely get the words out. Ymitoth had never acted in such a way. Perhaps the grizzled, old soldier had lost his mind. "What we be celebrating?"

Ymitoth eased his grip and took a step back, still holding onto Maelich's shoulders. "Today be the end of your twelfth year, lad," his voice trailed off and he looked as if he might cry. Instead, he continued with bit more strength behind his words, "Today we be celebrating your success."

Maelich's head was swimming. He had no idea what had happen to the man who had raised him, taught him and trained him. The jovial fellow standing before him looked almost…

"I be quite proud of ye, lad," Ymitoth finished Maelich's thought. "This part of your journey be complete. Tomorrow ye be starting off on a new adventure. On this day, I call ye a man," Ymitoth's cheek moistened as a tear raced down it to mingle with the course hair of his beard.

Maelich couldn't speak. This must be exactly how a father swelling with pride at his son's accomplishments would act.

After the feast and some fun chatter Maelich was unaccustomed to, Ymitoth said, "Maelich, join me in a pint of ale."

"Ale?" he couldn't believe his ears. Ale is what men drink, not young lads.

"Maelich, today ye be a man. Ye've trained hard since ye could lift a sword and read a book. Ye've finished the first part of your journey. Tonight, we share a few pints. Tomorrow we forget the sun and sleep till our bodies be ready to wake!"

The two men drank and shared laughs about things they had done together over the years. Maelich got to see a side of Ymitoth he never thought existed. Not that Ymitoth wasn't a caring father to him, laughter and fun were just not part of the normal routine. Maelich thought it quite possibly the best night of his life.

"Tell me more about me mother," Maelich said after finishing a laugh about a laugh he had some years back at Ymitoth's expense. The mighty Ymitoth had been showing him a sword technique used on horseback that required two hands and an agreeable horse. In this particular instance the steed was not so agreeable and managed to lose his rider, Ymitoth, in quite an abrupt fashion. Maelich was unable to contain his laughter. The outburst earned him a harsh scolding and proper punishment for his disrespect. On this night, however, Ymitoth had a great, booming belly laugh at the memory of the incident.

"Ah, your mother," Ymitoth started with a sigh. "Truth be told, lad, I never did get to meet her. All I know of her are the stories, and those I can share with ye now. They say she was of unrivaled beauty, hair golden like sunshine, eyes deep and brown. The likes of which can enchant a man and have him forgetting his name. They say she had pale, soft skin and her voice was even softer. She'd be singing with song birds of the morning as the sun peeked his head over the mountains. Anyone who ever heard said her song was sweeter than any song a chorus of song birds could sing." He paused and lost himself in a thought staring into the fire.

"So she was pretty?" Maelich broke in desperately wanting to know more.

"Pretty? Did ye here what I said? Pretty wasn't the word. They say the word beauty was created only to describe this woman. Though the word itself came long before your mother, she was what that word be trying to describe."

"What kind of person was she?" Maelich continued.

"Aye she was a kind, gentle lass. They say she never had a cross word for anyone. The type of lass who would listen to a little child's story as if it be the most important news she'd ever heard."

"Did she ever marry? What of me father? I mean ye no disrespect, father, but ye've said we share no blood. What of me birth father?" He pressed on, prying for more. All of these questions he'd been carrying around and asking but never getting straight answers. Finally, Ymitoth seemed ready to tell him all.

Ymitoth's smile faded a bit, "That question be a bit harder to answer. Ye see, son," Maelich was taken a bit by surprise. Ymitoth had always treated him as a son, but he had never actually referred to him as such. The father in him noticed the surprise on the young lad's face and continued, "Ye've had a hard life. Ye wouldn't know it because it be all ye know. For as long as ye can remember, every day be training. Aside from a few adventures all ye've known be..." he paused, searching for the right word, "preparation. It be true, I've never called ye son. I be greatly sorry for that. I've always thought of ye as me own though," he paused again.

"I know ye be keeping me in your heart, as any father does," Maelich helped, prodding him to continue.

"That be true, son, I do. I thought if I didn't call you me son this day might be easier. I tell ye it ain't. What about your real father though, that be your question." He shook his head a bit and made a weak attempt at putting the smile back upon his face, "This may sound a bit confusing, but your mother never knew a man in that way."

Maelich's brow wrinkled up as he digested the tidbit. He knew enough about life at this point to know how babies were formed and that a mother needs the assistance of a father to create one. "How could that be?" his words dripped with doubt.

"Ye see, son, it ain't me place to be giving ye all the answers right now. That task belongs to another. All I can really tell ye about your father, or lack of, is that ye've a very important role to play in the shaping of our world. In the very survival of our race, your role is key. Ye..." He stopped suddenly and looked up at the low ceiling of the hut, "Did ye hear that?"

"I didn't hear a thing," Maelich replied and then, feeling a bit bold from the ale, added, "I think ye're dodging me question."

"No, no lad, there be something on the roof."

Ymitoth leapt to his feet. He cleared the small table sitting before the fireplace and snatched his sword from the mantel in one smooth motion. His eyes were slits as he cocked his head to one side and listened hard for the noise to repeat itself. Maelich hadn't heard a thing and thought perhaps Ymitoth was having at him with a prank of some sort. Though a prank wouldn't fit his usual cold demeanor, he was acting a bit odd being all full of the ale. A slight sneer crept onto Ymitoth's upper lip. The muscles of his face flexed as he set his jaw tight. The room was completely silent. Ymitoth stared at the ceiling and Maelich stared at him. Maelich jumped out of his chair. This time he heard the noise, a light scratching on the roof. There was something up there trying not to be heard.

"Grab your sword, boy. Time to test your training," Ymitoth growled through clenched teeth.

Maelich did as his master said without knowing what exactly he would be dueling with. He couldn't stop staring at Ymitoth who seemed to be getting bigger with every tense breath. He wasn't, but as he stood hard like stone, ready to face the danger slithering around on the roof, the man looked like a giant. Right at that moment, Maelich felt a great swell of pity for whatever poor creature was about to be slain.

They both strained hard through the silence, waiting for the sound to repeat itself. There was nothing. Suddenly, the door of the small hut crashed in. Splinters filled the room with a large gray shape racing in behind them. Before Maelich could raise his sword, the beast was on him. Mouth open, long, jagged teeth dripped saliva onto black lips. The thing slammed Maelich to the floor yanking his head back by the hair and exposing the soft flesh of his neck. He howled as if a chunk of him were already missing and slammed his fists down against the beast's head. Then he stretched his own head back trying to get his throat as far away from its mouth and those nasty fangs as possible. Before his fists had another chance to strike, Ymitoth was on the beast. They crashed through the table and rolled across the floor. Ymitoth wound up on top. Without pause, he began pummeling the beast.

The battle lasted only moments. Maelich watched in awe as his master fought like a wild animal. He was an animal. Snarling and grunting, he pounded the beast's face with his fists, his elbows, and his head. The thing didn't have a chance. After a few moments, Ymitoth snatched the back of its head with one hand and its chin with the other. With one quick twist, he snapped its neck. A loud groan poured from the thing's slobbery mouth as the beast twitched, trembled, and then stopped moving completely.

Maelich stood motionless, stunned. He couldn't believe what he had just witnessed and had no idea what kind of creature the dead thing on the floor might be. His mind raced along without slowing, a series of questions for which he had no answer. As his mind fumbled along trying to make sense of everything, the roof came crashing down with another of the beasts riding the eaves to the floor. Once it hit, it dipped into a deep crouch and then leapt up into the air. Quite instinctively, Maelich slashed at it with his sword and relieved the thing of its head. In one smooth stroke, he deposited that gruesome head into the fireplace and dropped the pale, thin body to the floor in a heap. Maelich gazed at the dying beast for the briefest of moments before leaping away to avoid having his boots saturated in the black ooze pumping out of the thing.

"Congratulations, son," Ymitoth started, slapping a hand on Maelich's shoulder. "Ye've seen your first real battle and survived. This place no longer be safe for us. We must go."

Before Maelich could add voice to any of the multitude of questions dancing around his mind, Ymitoth quickly started packing some essentials into horse sacks. Obviously, they'd be in the elements that evening. Maelich stared first at the head burning in the fireplace, then at his blood-stained sword, and finally at Ymitoth. His young mind struggled to process everything he'd just seen along with what he had just done.

"What were those?" his whisper was barely audible.

"Those were amatilazo, me boy, and they always be traveling in packs of ten or more. These two be scouts. They must have been too hungry to wait for their kin," Ymitoth replied in his normal matter of fact tone, as if they hadn't almost been killed.

"What be amatilazo?" Maelich asked. This time he had a better command of his voice.

"The amatilazo be parasites that live on the blood of men. They walk like men but they ain't a mind for thinking. Their hunger be all they know. Make haste, lad. There will be more," Ymitoth continued to pack, leaving Maelich to work at getting his wits back about him.

Once all they could carry was packed and loaded on their horses they mounted and rode north into the night. The moon offered ample light for travel. Maelich expected they would make good time through the evening and stop for a nap when the sun rose. His theory proved false when Ymitoth abruptly halted their horses a mere two hundred yards from their hut.

"The pack be near," Ymitoth whispered, eyes scanning the tree line. "They have our scent and will be giving chase if we try to elude them. Tonight, we hunt. There be ample light. We should be filling our quarry quickly."

The cool evening and all the action back at the hut had eliminated the fuzziness from Maelich's head. Along with that, his years of training were serving him well. He was prepared to follow his master's lead and go on the attack. Ymitoth's sureness, along with his own instinctive dispatching of the creature in the hut, had his confidence soaring. On this night, his training and his mentor's confidence would finally be tested.

"Look there, lad," Ymitoth whispered and pointed with his sword to a small group of trees about one hundred yards to the east of their position.

"Aye, I see them," Maelich whispered just as quietly, catching sight of two sets of yellow eyes staring at them from behind the brush.

"I'll be riding straight at them," Ymitoth began, again whispering, "Ye'll be following a bit slower, catching any that may be trying to flee to the north or south. They move quick. We'd be no match on foot, but they can't outrun our horses."

With that Ymitoth slammed his heals into his horse's sides and started off at a mad gallop straight at the trees. Maelich did as he had been instructed. He followed about twenty feet behind. None of the creatures tried to flee, however. Instead, roughly twenty nasty beasts, just like the ones they had faced in the hut, poured out of the trees like bees from a hive. They climbed over each other, racing to reach Ymitoth whose sword was out and ready to spill their blood. Maelich quickened his pace to help his master dispatch the wicked, mindless demons descending upon him. The three leading the charge attacked Ymitoth in unison. All of them leapt high, at least fifteen feet in the air, and dove straight down on him. Ymitoth pulled out a dagger with his left hand and fired it at one of them, lancing its eye. It screeched like a horny witch. Almost simultaneously he swung his sword with his right arm and slashed his other two immediate attackers in half. Maelich started for his sword then opted for his bow. Another of the beasts was airborne and soaring toward Ymitoth. Maelich fired an arrow. It sliced the air before piercing the thing's heart. He quickly killed two more in the same fashion. By that time, he was too close for his bow to be effective. He tossed it to the side and pulled out his sword. A few of the beasts took notice of his speedy approach and turned their attention to him. They sped toward him almost as fast as he sped toward them. Once they were within striking distance, the first two leapt high in the air while three more circled around behind. His horse reared back kicking one of them out of the air and losing his rider in the process. As Maelich hit the ground, he saw the second airborne amatilazo slash Gildrah's throat with razor-sharp claws. He cried out as he scrambled to his feet and slashed the beast's belly open with his sword, spilling its insides out on the ground in a steamy lump. He growled at its falling corpse as he relieved it of its head before it hit the ground. A moment of mourning was all he had time to offer his fallen friend. A gift from Ymitoth, Gildrah was the horse he had learned to ride on and cared for since he was a young lad.

Before a tear could trickle down his cheek, rage filled him. Fire burned in his soul and with an agonizing howl he spun to face the three monsters that had managed to get behind him. Four menacing claws sailed past within inches of his face. He kicked the beast that slashed at him hard in the mid-section. Then he brought his sword down on the back of its skull, cracking it open and exposing the wee scrap of a brain that lay inside. The other two went just as easy. Then he turned his attention to the rest of the pack attacking Ymitoth.

Ymitoth was off his horse as well, but he had removed himself jumping off to kick one of the beasts out of the air. Now he was battling with six of them amidst the bodies of those already fallen. Maelich sprung into the center of the melee and the two warriors quickly dispatched the rest of the foul horde. The battle ended as the last of the amatilazo fell. Impaled through the throat on Ymitoth's sword, it whimpered like a beaten scrod.

Both warriors looked around at all the corpses and then at each other. Then Maelich looked back at Gildrah. He felt Ymitoth's heavy hand on his shoulder, "Go ahead. This be the last time ye can cry, lad."

Maelich wept for about half of an hour while Ymitoth consoled him. He was in a big hurry to get the mess they made cleaned up and make camp, but he knew this was the end of Maelich's childhood. A childhood which was anything but ordinary. The lad needed a chance to let all this emotion out. He let him cry until all the tears were gone, and then the two men got started.

In silence they hauled the bodies into a pile and then set them ablaze. The stench of the burning carcasses was thick and foul. It saturated the air, almost dripped from it, the kind of odor that could choke a grong. It would, however, scare off any would-be attackers and allow the men to catch some rest. They had a long journey ahead of them. At least two weeks on horseback, it would be a bit longer being they were down one horse.

CHAPTER 2
THE JOURNEY BEGINS

When Maelich finally woke the sun was at its highest point. His skin was good and warm from being cooked under it until midday. He took a deep stretch and looked out across the horizon. Long, rolling fields reached for miles before him dotted here and there with small groups of trees and settlements. He slowly rose to his feet turning to look back toward the hut where he had spent his life up to that point. Perhaps he would never see it again. From his vantage point, however, all he could make out was the tall oak crowning Keller's Hill. In his mind he said a brief good-bye and watched a stream of memories dance through his head. He would miss his hill, his tree, and yes, even bathing in Yester's Pond, which at this point was on the other side of the hill.

All at once he realized he was alone. Ymitoth had gone. The packs were gone. Rumallah, Ymitoth's horse, was gone and all of the food was gone. The hair on the back of his neck stood as a chill shot quickly through his body. He'd never been alone before. Worse than that for him right at that moment was the fact Ymitoth had abandoned him. After everything he'd been through the night before and everything that had happened between he and Ymitoth...

His thoughts trailed off and he fell to his knees lamenting his situation. 'Why would Ymitoth leave me?' he thought. 'He seemed so proud and I fought so strong. Why would he be leaving me?'

He continued torturing himself for just a short time before gathering himself back up. He took one last look at his only friend the oak, and one last scowl at the pile of carcasses still smoldering, before

11

heading north. The night before, Ymitoth was leading them in that direction toward the river. The great kingdom of the north had always been a favorite topic of Ymitoth's. He spoke of it incessantly. Perhaps he had left to return there. It lay far beyond the river. According to Ymitoth's stories, if Maelich kept the rising sun over his right shoulder and the setting sun over his left, he should eventually find himself within that great city. There was no way to be certain Ymitoth indeed travelled to the great city which was such an object of his fancy, but it was all Maelich had to go on. It was as good a chance as any. With the sun just passing overhead, he did his best to quiet his mind and focused on the trail.

As he trod along, his mind proved unable to remain quiet for very long. He tried to reason why Ymitoth would leave him. After a while, he decided it wasn't anything he had done wrong. Ymitoth had been acting quite strange the night before and spoke of someone else having the task of telling Maelich the remaining mysteries of his past. Perhaps this was another test. Perhaps their little party the night before was the end of a chapter in his life and saying good-bye was too much for his mentor's heart to bear. Maelich held on to the last one as it was his hope. Whatever the future might hold for him he wished to stand tall in Ymitoth's eyes and linger long in his heart. Ymitoth was the only father he had ever known. The only father he'd ever had, according to him.

He pulled out his sword and slowly went through some of the techniques he had learned through his lifetime of training as he walked along. It occurred to him this was the first day he could remember not training, aside from Kallum's day. The last day of the week was set aside to pay respects to Kallum for his generosity and all we have. There was no training, no work and no food on Kallum's day, only worship, praise and teachings of Kallum's word. He thought of asking for Kallum's help but didn't have the energy to come up with the words just then. Anyway, he didn't want to think about Kallum or the book. He really wanted to be training, going through his sword exercises with Ymitoth. He wondered if he'd ever get to do that again.

As he walked along he came upon a small wooded area off to his right. It wasn't quite a forest, but it would provide a bit of shelter for him to rest for a while. It was a good time to take a break and maybe snack on some berries. A few yards into the woods, he found a nice tree to sit under right next to a blackberry bush. Though not much of a meal, it was perhaps the best he would do that day. The spot he had chosen would also provide a bit of shelter from the wind which had picked up while he was walking. It would have to do.

The berries were quite tasty, but definitely not enough to fill him. Due to his late start, the sun was already low in the sky and he was getting hungry. On top of that, he felt as if he might be experiencing what Ymitoth referred to as a hangover from all of the ale he had drunk the night before. He would need some meat and another good night's rest. If he were to successfully complete the journey he had no choice but to take, he would need to be both physically and mentally prepared. The state he was in just then was a far cry from that. Ymitoth had left Maelich's bow and quiver behind and, under his tutelage, Maelich had become quite the hunter. Dinner, unlike the rest of his life at that point, would not be a problem.

He found a good spot under a tall pine sitting atop a small ridge. A narrow brook curved back and forth through the valley below. Judging from the abundance of trail, it was quite a popular watering hole. He readied an arrow and sat completely still. The only sound was that of leaves dancing on the wind high up in the trees. Barely half an hour past before a good-sized fallon strode up to the brook to drink. Fallon were swift, graceful and strong, but not difficult to take down if your mark was true. He slowly raised his bow, drew back, took a deep breath and fired an arrow. His mark was true. His arrow whistled through the air and slipped in between two of the fallon's ribs piercing the animal's heart. With a grunt it fell where it stood.

It wasn't long before the beast had been quartered, cooked and Maelich had fed. After the meal and his emotionally taxing day, he decided this would be a grand place to make camp. He gathered more branches, worked the fire enough to earn a healthier flame, and then built a small shelter under the protection of a fallen tree. His belly full, he was ready to sleep and attack tomorrow with a clear head. Sleep came easy and there were no dreams to disturb his slumber. He slept like the dead.

After a good night's rest, Maelich woke with the sun. Big, fat glistening droplets of dew still dangled from every blade of grass, and the fog had yet to burn off from down in the valley. He felt physically refreshed, ready to attack the road before him. With a clear head, he was ready to start the rest of his life. He packed up his bow, as much fallon as he could eat before it would spoil, water, and some berries.

He started off north again toward the river and the great kingdom promised in Ymitoth's stories. He was sure this great kingdom had a proper name, but for him it was only the great kingdom of the north. That was the only way Ymitoth had ever spoken of it. The river, he hadn't a name for it either, would be about two day's journey on foot. However, as good as he felt physically, the morning run seemed a grand idea. Perhaps that's why Ymitoth had him run every morning. Preparation, that's what Ymitoth had said his life had been up to this point. He started off at a fast jog and didn't stop until midday.

He ate what was left of the fallon and moved along. He slowed a bit after his meal but he still made pretty good time considering he was on foot. By midday the following day he was approaching the edge of a small village resting along the bank of a mighty river. He had hoped to re-stock his supplies there. Unfortunately, the place seemed quite deserted. He slowed his pace and drew his sword. At the same time the day before he could faintly see the smoke from the villager's cooking fires drifting up into the sky. Now it was empty. At midday the streets should be bustling with people hurrying home to their feast, but there was nary a sound.

Uneasiness swept over him as he neared the main gate of the small village. It was too quiet. There should have been something, a child playing or a man coming home late for the feast. Something. Anything. There was nothing. The entire town appeared asleep. Warily, he continued.

As he approached the first hut within the main gate, he noticed the door had been smashed in. He slowly strode inside. The stench of rotting flesh hung in the air. It seized him immediately when he entered and tugged at his attention while he quickly surveyed the room. One body, the body of a man of relatively large stature, lay sprawled out across a table occupying the center of the room. A large chunk was missing out of the poor bloke's neck. The wound was rather dry and the corpse's skin quite pale as if the body had been drained of all its blood. 'Amatilazo', he thought. A woman's body lay curled around that of a small child in the corner. Her head lay a few feet from the rest of her. Her face grabbed his attention. It was frozen in a look of terror like none he'd ever seen in his short life. He looked back to her body still clinging to her baby's lifeless carcass. He considered their embrace for a moment, frozen in death. She died trying to protect her own. Perhaps she could have escaped as her husband was being drained of his life's blood but she didn't. Instead, she gave of herself in a desperate attempt to save her child. It was a completely selfless action. How strong must be the love of a mother.

His thoughts drifted to his conversation with Ymitoth about his own mother. He learned early on she died shortly after he was born. He didn't have any details about her demise, but he knew he spent no time with her. He wondered if she had ever held him the way the courageous woman lying in front of him clung to her child. Did she ever cradle him in her arms, brush his hair back and sing to him? Ymitoth said she had a song sweeter than a chorus of songbirds. Had he ever heard that song? If he had he would never be able to recollect, as he would have been but a babe. A strange emptiness began in his belly as if there were a hole right through his mid-section. His head swam as dizziness swept through it and he thought he might lose his feet. He stumbled out of the hut and fell to the ground in a heap. If only there were someone to embrace him, someone to tell him everything was all right. His eyes burned as they filled up, but he fought back the tears. He struggled back to his feet. 'Feeling sorry for yourself won't do any good,' he thought. He pushed back against the hopeless, empty feeling threatening to consume him and forced himself to move on.

He went back into the hut, ignored the carcasses, and gathered all of the supplies he could carry. He ate what was to be the meal of the slaughtered family he was sharing the hut with and then moved on to the other huts in the village. Apparently, amatilazo do not have a taste for horses or other livestock, as there were a good number of them scattered about the town. He took the sturdiest horse as his new steed. He named him Validus. Validus was packed and ready to ride when Maelich heard noises coming from a hut down by the river's edge. It was a hut he had yet to check. It almost sounded like a cry for help, but muffled and without the voice.

He approached the hut slowly, cautiously. Over the past few days, he'd seen some things he'd never seen before and had no idea what to expect. What kind of beast or monster could be lurking behind that door? He slowly pushed it open and was immediately met by the vicious bark of a very unhappy scrod. His sword instinctively slipped out of its scabbard, but the scrod did not advance. It stood its ground, brazen and unafraid. Maelich had no desire to unnecessarily spill any blood, even if it was just a scrod. He pulled his sword back and offered his other hand.

"It's okay, laddy," he said in a soothing voice. "Relax. Just relax."

Then he heard a whisper, barely audible. It came from under a pile of rubble in the corner behind the scrod. The pile began to shift and a small shape crawled out. It was a little girl of about five or six summers. Bright, blue eyes peered out of a grubby face behind dirty, golden hair. She spoke again.

"Please don't hurt Jom," she could barely squeak the words out. Apparently, she'd done some screaming during the attack that had fallen upon this village.

"Jom? Who's Jom?" Maelich asked. "I be meaning ye no harm."

The little girl moved in front of the scrod as if to protect him. She stood as tall as she could make herself.

"Is this Jom?" He asked, trying hard to sweeten up his voice.

She nodded her reply, as Jom's bark became a low growl. Maelich lowered himself to one knee and held out his hand. The scrod warily crept from behind the little girl who was still trying to stand tall and protect him. He continued his low growl as he gingerly approached Maelich's outstretched hand. Then he scrutinized it with his nose. Apparently, Maelich's hand had a pleasing odor as Jom's tail quickly began to wag. Before long his head was nuzzled into Maelich's chest. Maelich pet Jom and received some sloppy, wet, affectionate kisses for his trouble. The little girl seemed to relax a little as well when she saw Maelich had yet to slay her scrod. After a time, she spoke again, at least as much as she could without a voice.

She told Maelich her name was Perrin and her village was attacked during the evening feeding by these monsters with long claws and sharp teeth. She said her papa went outside when they heard the screams and never came back. She told him the monsters came in her hut and her mama had run at them with her cooking blade. She said one of the monsters popped her mama's head off like a dandelion. When Jom came running in from the yard barking, the monsters started howling and squealing like they were hurt or scared. She hid under the table screaming and Jom never left the spot he was in when Maelich had arrived.

They talked for quite a while before Perrin started dozing as she spoke. Maelich laid her down on a cot in the corner and let her sleep. Then he and Jom went outside to start a fire. He burned up all of the carcasses in the village. The stench of rotting flesh was already strong in the air, and it wasn't a healthy odor. Jom didn't leave his side as he went through hut by hut, "cleaning up". By the time he was finished, he was quite weary and the afternoon had fled away.

He prepared a meal for Perrin and him, and planned to spend an evening there in the village before getting back to his journey. He also gave some thought to his new dilemma, Perrin. She was a lass of, by his best estimation, about five summers. She would slow him down. On top of that, he was relatively certain she wouldn't want to leave Jom behind. That would slow him down even more. Perrin he could prop up on a horse and tow along with a rope. Jom would be traveling under his own power. The scrod would be setting the pace.

Maelich looked down at the animal and said, "Ye'll be slowing us down, scrod."

Jom replied by jumping up, placing a paw on each of Maelich's shoulders, and licking his face. He couldn't help but laugh as the two fell to the ground wrestling and playing. Jom's unbridled affection was, besides being wet and slobbery, very therapeutic for Maelich. The past few days had been quite grim and playing with Jom gave him a few moments of peace. It gave him a chance to forget the calamity his life had become of late. The two boys played for a bit and then Maelich got back to his meal preparation. As he finished up he looked down at Jom who sat obediently at his feet. He decided having him on the journey would be worth the time they would lose because of him.

When the meal was ready, Maelich roused Perrin from her slumber and they ate. He could tell her head wasn't quite straight after the horror she had witnessed the night before. How terrible it must have been for her to watch her mother be slain by some beast. He himself felt such a great sense of loss just knowing he had a mother but she was gone. He couldn't imagine watching her die, especially in such a violent fashion. Perrin wasn't crying, whimpering, or even whining. She sat quiet, staring off into nothingness. Maelich wondered how far away from the small hut was her mind just then. He let her be as they ate in silence, two children who had just had their lives ripped apart and of no fault of their own. He found himself staring off into the nothing just as she was.

After the meal, Maelich decided to break the silence, "So, Perrin, I be on a journey right now. Will ye be joining me?"

"Where ye be going?" she asked without breaking her stare.

"I be headed to the great kingdom of the north," he replied.

She held her stare, "Sure, I'll come. Me papa took me to that place once. It's far the safe way."

"The safe way?" he asked.

"Aye, the safe way," she appeared in a trance.

"What be the safe way?" he pressed on.

She finally broke her stare and looked him in the eyes, "The safe way be the road what leads down the river and around the Sobbing Forest. That way be at least twice as far as the other way, but it's safe."

Maelich had never heard of the Sobbing Forest. He knew there was a great forest beyond the river but it never had a name for him. "What be the other way?"

"Papa say the other way be too dane...dane..." she couldn't say the word. "...too scary."

"Too dangerous?" Maelich helped.

"Aye, that be the word papa used. He say they be calling it the Sobbing Forest because them trees always be crying for the men what die there. There be terrible things, monsters and evil men who be hiding there, waiting for travelers. All them trees moaning be to warn people not to come in. I've heard them trees moaning at night. Papa says that be how trees cry. Did ye ever hear them cry?" she finished with a quizzical look.

"No. No I ain't, but I be thinking we should go that way if it be saving us that much time. Besides, Jom will be watching over us," Maelich replied with as much confidence in his voice as he could muster. Truthfully, he was a bit concerned as he had no idea what to expect out of the forest. His desire to complete the journey was far greater than any of his fears. He also felt a bit of confidence knowing the amatilazo were afraid of Jom. The scrod was sturdy. He should prove quite helpful in a battle.

Perrin just nodded. She was very confused, too confused to even be afraid of going through the Sobbing Forest. The next day she would be starting a journey through a place her father had taught her to be terrified of, and she would be going with a complete stranger. The thought didn't trouble her in the least bit. There were far too many other demons torturing her mind just then. Before her journey was done there would be more.

Maelich talked a bit more about where they would be going. Most of it was lost on Perrin. Her mind was elsewhere. She lay down for the night and Maelich found some more horse sacks. He filled them with what he guessed would be enough supplies to get them through their journey. When he had first packed up Validus he had only been packing for one. Now he had two more mouths to feed and his journey would last a few days longer. After he had everything prepared, he turned in as well. Sleep didn't come easy on that night, and his slumber was less than peaceful. As he slept his head was full of terrors, visions of things to come.

CHAPTER 3
THE SOBBING FOREST

When Maelich woke, the sun was just peaking over the horizon. Perrin was already awake. She sat on her cot with her knees pulled tight to her chest and her arms wrapped around them. Long, golden, dirt-streaked hair hung about her face in clumps. She looked as if she were staring at the wall, but Maelich knew she was staring far past it. She rocked back and forth mumbling. He couldn't understand what she was saying. She appeared to be in some sort of trance. He went to her and sat beside her placing his arm around her shoulders.

"Are ye alright, lassie?" he asked in as gentle a tone as he could muster.

She didn't answer. Her weight slumped against him. She buried her face in his chest and wept. He didn't say another word. He just held her, stroking her hair and rubbing her back. He really had no idea how to handle this type of situation. He remembered how he felt at the loss of Gildrah, the emptiness and the rage. Compassion for Perrin filled him as he squeezed her just a bit tighter. He decided he would hold her until the tears were done.

Perrin wept for most of the morning. By the time she was finished, Maelich's shirt was good and wet and her cheeks were streaked with clean spots that rivers of tears had eroded in the dirt there. She sat up and looked him in the eyes, as she wiped her own. Her expression reflected how terrified and alone she felt. Questions floated behind her pretty blue eyes that had become red and swollen from her tears. She looked as if she'd been beaten by a strong man who knew nothing of mercy. What would happen to her now that she had no mother? Where would she go when Maelich's journey was finished? Would she be alone? He could see her little mind was starting to focus on the present and beginning to process the depth of her situation.

"Perrin," he began, before she asked the questions he knew she had, "I won't be leaving ye alone. I'll be watching over ye as if ye were me own. I won't be letting anything happen to ye."

"How could I be your own?" she asked. "Ye're not old enough to be me Papa. Who will be taking care of ye?"

He had no proof for her that he could take care of her. He knew he could keep her safe, alive and fed, but he really had no idea how to raise a child. True, he was well trained for a battle and survival in the wild, but what did he know about little girls? He decided to fake it as best he could.

"It be true I still be a lad myself, but have ye ever had a brother?" he asked, quizzically raising one eyebrow.

"No," she shook her head.

"Fine," he said, raising his hands as if to say voila, "I be your brother then. And if we don't be finding a nice couple who want to be raising a beautiful, little lass like yourself, ye can stay with me."

"Ever your path leads?"

"Ever me path leads. Ye'll never be alone, Perrin. I promise ye that."

He knew she was completely dependent on him. The truth was, he really needed her too. He felt invigorated, like he had a purpose. When he had merely been looking out for himself he felt scared, alone. He hadn't a goal. Now, he had to keep this little lass alive and deliver her to a place where she could live and grow. That alone was reason enough to go on. He was ready to attack the road, conquer the Sobbing Forest, and finish his journey, wherever his path led him.

By the time he had convinced her that everything would be as all right as it could be, given their current circumstances, the sun was already high in the sky. They had lost most of the morning. In fact, the hour was close for the midday feast. However, Maelich didn't want to lose any more light. He gave Perrin some flat bread and kept some for himself. She wrinkled her nose up. They had missed the morning feeding and she was quite hungry. Even still, she didn't fuss. Deep down she wanted to get away from the emptiness the place now held. There wasn't anything left for her there. Her path followed Maelich's and she would follow where he led.

Maelich strapped Perrin onto a good, solid horse. She told him the horse's name was Grinner because he always looked like he was smiling. He had belonged to Master Kelsho from down the road. She told Maelich that her papa had told her to stay away from old man Kelsho because he was a kook. She thought he was funny though. He was always nice to her, and he always let her play with Grinner. That was great news for Maelich because she felt completely comfortable riding the horse. He tied a rope from Grinner's saddle to Validus's saddle and they were off. Jom took the lead. They crossed the river on a bridge that Perrin said her grandpapa had helped build long before she was born. Once they reached the other side, Maelich stopped them. He told Perrin to say good-bye to her old home, as she would maybe never make it back this way again. She turned, looked back at her village, and offered one last tear as her good-bye.

The Sobbing Forest was but one hundred yards from the riverbank and the path they would take went straight toward it from the bridge. It did have an ominous look about it. Maelich couldn't be certain that it would have the same ominous look had Perrin not warned him about it. Still, the thought of going east and taking the large, well-traveled, "safe" road that led along the river and around the Sobbing Forest did cross his mind. However, Ymitoth had taught him, "The straight path always be the best path." He would say, "That be why we train, lad. There be no one or no thing that'll be giving us cause to stray from the path we choose. Let any man or any form of beast try denying me destiny and let them taste the full range of me fury". Ymitoth's might and fury would be well welcomed by Maelich just then. Alas, this journey was his and Perrin's and even Jom's. Into the Sobbing Forest and a thick tangle of trees they went.

Even with the sun at its highest point, the path was dark and gloomy. It was scarcely traveled, by the looks of things. The trees seemed to crowd in around them. Jom even seemed to sense there was something overbearing about these trees. The forest was dense, just a few feet in and it looked to be more about twilight than midday. The trees whispered. They weren't moaning or sobbing or anything of the sort. It seemed as if they were quietly discussing their new intruders as they closed in tighter and tighter on the weary travelers who had ventured into their domicile. Maelich began thinking way too much. Ymitoth had always assured him fear was his biggest enemy. There was nothing Maelich could not defeat. No end that could find him unless he allowed himself to be found. He quieted his mind, lifted his head, and with a strong voice said, "Jom, hup!"

With that command Jom quickened his pace. The trees continued to scrutinize the travelers and whisper back and forth about them, but they also seemed to back off a bit. It even appeared as if there was a hint of sunshine slipping between leaves and branches and making its way down to the path. Perhaps the trees had decided the little caravan was no threat. Or perhaps they had been expecting them. Ymitoth had always hinted about Maelich's great purpose. Perhaps the trees recognized him. Whatever the case may have been, the way was definitely getting easier. That was just fine with Maelich. The group continued to travel in silence and, all things considered, made relatively good time.

Meanwhile, someone else had become quite interested in Maelich's journey. It was someone unknown to him, someone elsewhere. In a place far to the east of where he now traveled, even farther than where the maps don't go, yes even farther still than the lost wood, someone watched. Kaldumahn watched Maelich and his small crew as they made their way through the Sobbing Forest. What the trees saw, he saw, and what they spoke, they spoke to him. He sat upon his throne in a trance-like state as he listened and watched with his mind. He had great power and a great knowledge of Maelich's purpose. He also had a great stake in the lad's journey. After a time, he let the vision pass and told the trees to keep watch over Maelich. He needed him alive. Much of their world would be affected by Maelich, including Kaldumahn. This fact boded well for Maelich. As long as Kaldumahn found him to be useful, he would find clear paths to travel for much of his journey.

"Maelich has made it to the Sobbing Forest!" Kaldumahn boomed.

"Excellent! Order the trees to strike him down and save the last Dragon!" Moshat replied with gritted teeth and clenched fists.

"Don't be foolish, Moshat," Kaldumahn said as he shook his head and waved off the idea. "Maelich's fate must play out. His journey is just beginning and he has much to do before he can be judged. Would you have him cut down before his choice is clear? The effects on our world could be cataclysmic. Surely you must understand that, Moshat. At this moment there is nothing more important to the balance of our world than this lad. The prophecy must play out."

"Kaldumahn," Moshat continued, "the prophecy he seeks to fulfill will bring ruin upon our world. You know this. The war is not over."

"Dear brother, it is not our place to cut him down, not now. We must at least give him the chance to choose his path," Kaldumahn replied, almost pleadingly.

"What if he chooses wrong? Then what for our world?" Moshat pressed on.

"Coeptus have set this play into motion. We must have faith in them. Without Maelich we have no chance. While he still breathes, there is hope. Trust me, my brother, please," he emphasized this last point by taking Moshat's hand and looking him in the eye, "Please."

"Fine," Moshat replied, "For now we do it your way, for now."

Back in the forest, the trees made a grand path in obedience to Kaldumahn's order. It certainly seemed the way through the Sobbing Forest would be much easier than Perrin had described. The group continued to trod along as the whispers of the trees became fainter and fainter. Perhaps they were dying down, or perhaps Maelich was growing accustomed to them. Either way, he feared their intent less and less as they traveled.

The group was making much better progress than Maelich expected they would. By the time the sun was getting low enough that he wanted to stop for the night, they were well into the forest. He found a good spot to make camp, and, by some strange twist, found that a small pile of perfect burning wood had been left right in the same spot. The wood was good and dry and needed no cutting. 'Perhaps I be finding favor with the trees,' he thought. He dismounted Validus and made camp.

Jom stretched out by the fire as Maelich and Perrin shared a bit of chatter while they fed. They ate quite well. Ymitoth had taught Maelich that being prepared was always more important than the speed in which you arrive. "It be doing ye no good to arrive dead for lack of supplies, lad," Ymitoth had always said. Maelich paid heed to this warning and his group had just what they needed to make it through their journey. He made sure to point this fact out to Perrin, as he felt like he was her mentor now. She looked to him for guidance and he intended to do his best to prepare her for, "the great journey of life".

Sleep didn't come easy for either Maelich or Perrin that night.

They both had demons terrorizing their dreams. The trees offered some comfort. They seemed to crowd in a little tighter as the night grew darker. It was almost as if they were protecting Maelich and Perrin. Even Jom, Validus, and Grinner felt completely safe from anything that might be creeping around in the shadows. Maelich noticed the trees were moaning though, just as Perrin had said they would. Not the ones closest to them. Those kind of hummed, almost like a lullaby. The song actually did help ease their minds a bit. The trees farther off were moaning or sobbing. It was hard to tell, but it only kept Maelich's attention for the briefest of moments. He had other thoughts to process. They would find sleep easier in the nights to come, but their dreams would still be filled with horrible, bloody images and lost, lonely feelings.

The days danced by quickly in the forest. The group continued to make good time and after five days was roughly three quarters of the way through the forest. Maelich's estimations were a little less, but he was very close. The trees continued to offer comfort to the group so Maelich offered them a song as they rode. It was more of a chant really. He sung to the tune of a battle song Ymitoth had taught him. At the time he had said that he and his men had sung this song whenever they went to battle. Now the tune was the same for Maelich and the trees, but the words were different. He sang:

> Oh the trees stand mighty and tall by day
> And they knock ye down and they block your way
> Be there darkness in your heart
> But when ye come in peace and hear their cries
> They'll make way and they will spare your lives
> Be there goodness in your heart
> Oh the trees they cry and cry by night
> They shed tears for those who're without light
> Lose their lives in the forest deep
> But they sing to ye sweet lullabies
> If ye see with your heart and not your eyes
> They keep ye safe in the forest deep

He sang the tune over a few times. The trees seemed greatly pleased he was honoring them. They sang back to him, and Perrin joined in. Jom even howled a few notes here and there. For the briefest of moments, they were having fun. It refreshed their spirits and put a sprint in Jom's step. They charged along as they sang amongst the trees who answered back with hymns of their own. They danced a sway making music with the rustling of their leaves and the whistling of their branches. Maelich was so swept up in the moment, as were the trees, Perrin, and Jom, he never noticed the hooded man step out onto the path. By the time he did, Jom was but fifty feet from the dark figure. The scrod noticed the man just after Maelich. Maelich called him to heel as he pulled back on Validus's reigns.

Maelich wasted no time. He could sense from the trees that this man was dangerous and meant to do his group harm. The trees, for their part, seemed upset they hadn't noticed this dark figure before he stepped out onto the path. They had been so caught up in Maelich's song that they let their guard down. Nervousness drifted from branch to branch and leaf to leaf. Fire rushed through Maelich's veins. He was unafraid. There was nothing that would get by him to harm Perrin, nothing.

Jom stood his ground growling as Maelich sized the man up. His face was covered in a shadow from the hood which hung down just past his eyes. He was large in stature and his cloak covered his entire body. The cloak itself was brown and dirty. The man had his arms folded behind his back. 'He won't fair so well against me sword from that stance,' Maelich thought as he drew his weapon.

"Make way!" he ordered the man, surprising himself with the deep authority his voice carried. Perrin even winced a little.

The man didn't respond. Instead, he began to advance toward the group. As he did, he brought his hands up to his face and removed his hood exposing a wild mop of orange hair and a menacing grin buried under a nappy snarl that served as his beard. His eyes were what caught Maelich's attention though. They had no color at all. They were like two hunks of coal, black and dead.

"Make way or taste the full fury of me sword!" Maelich demanded once again. Yet the man, or whatever he was, still advanced.

Maelich leapt from Validus's back. Before his feet hit the forest floor, however, he was caught by a branch and pulled up to the safety of the loftiest point of a tall tree. At the same time Perrin, Jom, Validus, and Grinner were all scooped up in the same fashion. This threw their would be attacker into a mad fit of rage. He stomped about wildly as he cursed the trees. Then two more men clad in the same fashion ran out from behind trees and began stomping about in the same manner. They cursed Maelich. They cursed the trees. They said nasty things to Perrin that Maelich wasn't sure he even understood. He burned inside though. He fought against the tree's grip to free himself. He desperately wished to dispatch these wicked, heartless men who would do Perrin harm. Jom fought to free himself with the same vigor but to no avail. As the two helpless heroes watched, however, the trees exacted their own vengeance.

A vine whipped out from behind a tree and wrapped itself around the first cloaked man's neck. It quickly tightened as his face turned first pink, then red, then purple. A silent scream twisted up the features of his face, but no sound came out. The trees growled in unison as the man's black eyes bulged from their sockets. They burst in a thick spray of blood just before his head popped. Perrin closed her eyes and hid her face, but Maelich watched. He watched as heavy branches sprung from far above their heads and crushed the other two cloaked men. Their screams lasted only a moment and there was silence. The trees heaved a collective sigh and lowered the group back to the ground. They could sense Maelich's anger and he could feel their apology. They had been caught off guard and reacted to save he and his group. He looked at the ground, took a deep breath, and then looked back up at the trees forgiving and thanking them.

The whole ordeal had the group far wearier than the trail had in all their days upon it. It was there they made camp for the night. Sleep came easy. They would be in the forest for three more days, according to what Maelich could sense from the trees. That would go quickly. Being they were all on guard now, it should go safely as well.

CHAPTER 4
PURPOSE

The path out of the Sobbing Forest poured into a great field of unkept wheat seated upon rolling hills that climbed steadily upwards. It was a pale-green, waist-high sea of flowing waves dancing about, motivated by a mild north wind. Maelich took a deep breath inhaling the sweet perfume of the field. He squinted against the brilliance of the mid-day sun. It was much too bright since his eyes had become accustomed to the darkness of the forest. Perrin covered her eyes and giggled. A feeling of security rushed over her. The fresh north wind peeled the grimy, matted hair from her dirt-streaked face. The crisp, clean air of the field was invigorating after the stale, dead air of the forest. Jom charged off into it snapping at little bugs and rolling about the tall grass.

Maelich sensed sadness from the trees. They had grown fond of his little group. They knew he had to leave, but they would certainly miss him. He thanked them in his mind for seeing him through safely and promised one day to return with a new song to share. Validus and Grinner carried Maelich and Perrin up the hill away from the Sobbing Forest. As they did the trees hummed Maelich's song after them with the energy of a choir in full throat.

After a few hours Maelich and Perrin had crested the hill. As Maelich looked back, he could still see the Sobbing Forest behind them. The trees subtly waved back and forth. It could have been the wind, but Maelich didn't believe that. A broad smile expanded across his face.

"Perrin, look. The trees be waving us goodbye," he said as he nudged her.

She turned and waved. "Bye trees!" her shout careened down the hill, her small voice sounding quite large as it boomed and echoed through the valley.

Maelich nearly lost his wits, laughing like he had just heard a dandy of a joke. Perrin's face reddened as she realized why Maelich laughed so heartily, and she fell into a fit of laughter of her own. It had been a good while since either of them had laughed, so it lasted much longer than the joke deserved. That was okay. The trail had been stingy with happiness.

Maelich turned his head back to the north and saw a great valley sprawling below them with a mighty hill rising up on the other side. The path they were on opened into what appeared to be a well-traveled road, branching off in many directions down in the valley. Huts popped up here and there and the land appeared cultivated. The population seemed denser up the hill on the other side of the valley. His eyes scanned it and then, at the top, there it was. A mighty castle with towers that scraped at the sky perched on the hill. 'The great city of the north,' he thought. How magnificent it was. This was what Ymitoth was always talking about. No wonder he had always longed to return, it was beautiful.

Eyes wide with excitement, he turned to Perrin and said, "Hold on tight. We be making some time before we lose the light."

Perrin nodded in agreement as Maelich put his heels to Validus's sides. Hooves tore into the trail as the horse responded. Grinner followed suit. The animal had little choice tied fast to Validus's saddle. Jom had all he could handle just trying to keep up. Maelich kept his eyes on Perrin, watching her fear slowly turn into something close to excitement. After a time, she loosened her grip on Grinner's neck and even sat up a little straighter as she bounced and swayed in the saddle with each of his long strides.

The group had made it about halfway down the hill into the valley before Maelich realized Jom had fallen quite a good distance behind. The sun was getting rather low, perfect time to stop for the night. A large, flat boulder with a massive tree at its southern edge alongside the trail looked to be just the spot. He halted the horses, dismounted, and got to work. By the time Jom finally arrived, Maelich had built a small shelter and a cooking fire. The scrod fell in a heap next to the small blaze, whipped by the trail. Maelich prepared a bowl of water for him and some dried tubberslat. That would help him to get his energy back, that and a good night's sleep.

Maelich sat down next to Perrin by the fire, handed her a few hunks of dried tubberslat, and asked, "So what did ye think about that ride?"

Perrin shoveled a hunk of food into her mouth before replying around it, "It was scary at first," she swallowed a bit and splashed some water down before finishing, "but only a little. Then I be flying over the field."

"Aye," Maelich chuckled, "it be a freedom ye can't hardly describe, butterflies all brawling in your belly, and the ground racing past faster than anything ye ever seen."

Perrin silently nodded as she stuffed more food into her face and stared at the fire.

"How about them trees, all waving and smiling," he asked.

"Aye, and me big voice down the valley," this time she laughed. After the chuckle had a chance to dance off into the darkening sky, she looked up at him and added, "I ain't never been on no journey like this before."

Maelich nodded down at her and then turned toward the western sky, gazing into last bits of pink the sun had left behind. "In that, we are the same," he agreed.

They sat mostly in silence as they finished eating their dried meat and a bit of bread. A sharp snore from Jom broke up the silence and earned a good bit of giggling. The scrod didn't move despite all the laughter. The road had done a number on the poor animal. Perrin dozed shortly after she finished eating. Maelich allowed himself to follow suit once everyone else was settled in.

The night was still very young when Maelich woke to Jom's growls. The fire was dwindling, but the sun was still far from rising. Maelich stoked the fire and threw on some more wood to give himself a bit of additional light. Though the moon was good and full, shadows covered the field as if in defiance. Jom had stepped out onto the path and was growling at a dark shape approaching along the trail from the south. Maelich readied his sword and lit a torch before stepping out onto the path next to the agitated scrod.

"Hey there!" Maelich called to whatever was approaching. "Who're ye that be traveling alone in the darkness?"

The shape didn't respond but did continue advancing toward the camp. It was still a good one hundred yards from them when Maelich decided to meet whomever, or whatever, it was before it reached the camp and Perrin. He stalked toward the shape. Jom trotted along beside him, keeping pace.

"Identify yourself," Maelich commanded, the authority his voice had in the forest was back. The shape failed to slow in the least. The space between Maelich and the unknown traveler quickly shrunk. It wasn't long before Maelich realized the approaching shape was the same manner of man they had met in the Sobbing Forest. He raised his sword as Jom's hackles shot up. The scrod's low growl turned to an angry, threatening bark. Right at that instant, the cloaked figure removed his hood and Maelich recognized that it wasn't simply the same manner of man they had faced in the forest. In fact, it was the same man who had confronted them in the forest. The man, or whatever the creature was, let out a hellish howl as he sprinted toward Maelich and Jom. Jom answered the charge and he and the wily vermin were instantly upon each other. White fangs flashed as Jom lunged for the man's throat. The beast of a man was too quick and snatched the scrod out of the air by his throat. Jom snapped at the man's face but could only manage to come within an inch of it. Instead of tearing into flesh, he yelped under the weight of the man's grip. The sound was brief and sharp, and then Jom lay ten feet west of the trail, tossed to the side like a handful of seed. The scrod wasn't moving, and Maelich felt the man's dead, black eyes back on him.

Maelich didn't wait to see if Jom would regain his feet. He charged the man like a wild mountain scarra running down a fawn. Once in range of his target, his sword arced toward the cloaked man's throat. The velocity of his blade would have easily cleaved the head clean off a full-grown tubber. However, when the weapon shattered helplessly against the cloaked man's forearm rather than lopping the head from his shoulders, Maelich realized his quarry was no fawn. Dumbfounded, he stared down at the handle of his broken blade. A chill wind blew off the black field, shivered down his spine, and raced off into the night with his confidence. Maelich had precious little time to ponder what kind of monster wore skin capable of withstanding the might of his blade or what black forge in the pit of some dark, forgotten hell could spawn a thing with bones that wouldn't shatter under its force. He barely had time to question his own might before the man's right arm slashed out in a backhanded, uppercut and launched him helplessly through the crisp, evening air. His jaw began to tighten and swell even before the ground leapt up to meet his careening carcass. No one had ever hit him like that before.

Doubt is a mad titan on the battlefield, and it took to knocking Maelich's wits around, had him questioning instead of acting. By the time he finally got out of the way of his instincts, the dead-eyed man was on him again. He managed only to get back to his knees before the beast's iron grip closed around his throat, hefted him easily off the ground, and squeezed. His hands shot up and yanked at the stranger's fingers. He might have been trying to pull a mountain up off the ground for all the good it did. The iron grip wouldn't budge. He kicked at the man's legs instead. They were like thick tree trunks, solid and unmoving. Maelich's face flushed as white dots flashed and darted before his eyes, and his burning lungs hopelessly searched for air. Just as consciousness began to flee on a hazy, purple cloud, the grip loosened. He landed back on the ground in a heap, barely aware of the dead-eyed man howling and launching vile curses. Laced among those pained shouts was Jom's growl, a song sweet to Maelich's ears. The faithful scrod had returned to the fight.

Maelich's wits slowly returned as he watched the dead-eyed man dance in a circle and kick his leg in a vain attempt to free his ankle from Jom's death grip. His howls filled the night sky as he fell to ground and flopped about. He kicked Jom's head repeatedly until the scrod was dazed and could hold him no longer. Just then, Maelich had an epiphany. The dead-eyed man was not invincible. The steady gush of some blood-like liquid pouring from the fresh wound Jom had inflicted on his leg proved as much.

The dead-eyed man jumped up and gave Jom a solid kick to his ribs. The valiant scrod yelped and then lay whimpering. A fire burned in Maelich as he leapt to his feet and charged the stranger. His shoulder found the man's mid-section and drove him to the ground. Instinct grabbed hold of the reins again and his fists were no longer waiting for directions. They pounded the man's face while Maelich grunted and growled like a hungry beast in the wild. The assault was short-lived. Mere moments passed before the man managed to free an arm and bring his fist down on the side of Maelich's head. The blow knocked Maelich to the side. Both combatants quickly scrambled to their feet, Maelich woozy from the shot to his head and the dead eyed man nursing a limp from Jom's bite. The cloaked stranger charged Maelich who managed to narrowly avoid the attack and pull out his dagger. When the dead-eyed man turned back around to face him, it was too late. Maelich grabbed him by the hair and slammed his dagger into his black, dead eye. Fresh howling bellowed from the man's twisted face as black blood poured from the empty socket. Good sense finally prevailed over ego and Maelich quickly retreated. He grabbed Jom and dragged him back toward camp.

Just over one hundred yards away, Perrin lay sleeping soundly, completely unaware of the trouble she was in. Once Maelich made it back to camp, he quickly loaded up the horses, roused Perrin, and tied her, along with Jom, to Ginner's saddle before mounting Validus. He was still a bit woozy and unsure if he could finish the dead-eyed man off. They would have to flee. As unattractive as the prospect of traveling in the darkness of night was, the alternative seemed even worse.

Just as Validus and Grinner stepped out onto the path, Maelich heard a howl. When he glanced back, the dead-eyed man was back on his feet and limping quickly toward them. Much to Maelich's dismay, the vile thing was no longer alone. Two more cloaked men accompanied him, probably the same two who perished—or so he had thought—with the first among the trees. He drove his heels hard into Validus's sides. The horse responded, launching into a mad gallop. Grinner followed suit and, though Perrin was terrified, she and Jom were both tied down and safe, at least from breaking against the hard trail.

The dead-eyed men gave chase, sprinting after Maelich and Perrin but losing ground. Maelich paid them no attention. He kept his eyes on the path. When he finally did look back, it seemed his mind might be playing tricks on him. Otherwise, these monsters were even more frightening than he thought. They appeared to be flying close to the ground with their dirty cloaks flowing behind them. He gave Validus another shot in the sides and their speed increased. He didn't look back again until the sun was in the sky.

By the time Maelich felt comfortable taking a break they had made it into the valley and found a place to water the horses. The motley crew he led quickly earned the attention of a good number of curious eyes. He felt scrutinized as the townsfolk did little to hide their interest. Under the watchful eyes of nosy townsfolk, they ate quickly. Then Maelich strapped Perrin and Jom back on Grinner's saddle and got the group back to the trail. He scanned the hill behind them but found no sign of pursuit. The path was clear back up the hill. Had those dead-eyed beasts still been back there, he would see them. A clear trail wasn't quite enough to comfort Maelich. Though he hadn't spotted the trio chasing them, he couldn't be sure where they had gone.

The road grew wider toward the great city. It was also well traveled. Maelich felt the disapproving stares, two dirty children and a beaten scrod. Nobody bothered with them, but they watched. They watched and humphed with their noses in the air. Maelich kept his eyes to the trail and ignored the commentary of the people they passed.

"Well look at there," and old woman's voice crackled, just loud enough to hear. "Where do you suppose them parents be?"

A younger voice answered with a bit more volume, "Who could know."

"Ain't got none by the looks," another answered. "Afraid of water too."

Maelich paid them no mind. He glanced behind at Grinner. Perrin's misty, blue eyes stared back at him, still brimming with innocence. At least the tragic events in her recent history hadn't chased it away completely. That was something. The townsfolk had no idea what they'd been through. They could tell their stories to each other, make up their dramas to add a bit of excitement to their lives. Maelich didn't have anything to prove to any of them. Scuffling with bored folks who had nothing better to do than speculate about a couple of youngsters and a scrod wouldn't solve anything. It certainly wouldn't help Perrin hang on to what innocence she had left after all she'd seen in the few days since their paths crossed. Let them talk.

Validus and Grinner slowed a bit as the road rose up the hill on the other side of the valley and travel became more difficult. Stone towers stood as beacons at the top of the hill far above them. The horses dug in and pushed on as if drawn by these mighty towers scratching at the sky. They were still making good time, and Jom appeared to slowly be regaining his strength. The group rode along in silence. Maelich had nothing he felt like talking about, and Perrin hadn't made a peep. They trudged wearily on, slouching in their saddles. The trail had whipped them.

Once dusk began to settle in, Maelich noticed three shapes that seemed to be floating toward them again some distance back. It appeared the dead-eyed men hadn't given up their pursuit after all.

They had just been more careful not to be spotted in the sunlight. It didn't look as if they were gaining any ground on the group but they certainly hadn't lost any either. Maelich, in his frustration, thought briefly about facing them once more. The idea died a quick death. The trail had taken most of the fight he had in him. Conquering the remainder of the hill would probably earn the rest. Those dead-eyed things would have to be dealt with eventually, but they were a good distance back. Apparently, Jom felt less comfortable about that distance. His hackles went up as he growled a low warning that would have been lost on all but Maelich's small group. Had the scrod not been bound good and tight to Grinner's saddle, he might have tried running those beasts down and having another go at them. As it was, all he could do was lie there and growl.

The path continued to brighten as they approached the kingdom. Torches burned along the road, and light poured out from the huts lining it on either side. The monsters pursuing them were far enough back that Maelich could no longer see them through the torchlight. The fact did little to ease his tension. A bizarre chill lingering about his spine was all the proof he needed that they were still there, and they were coming.

As the group trudged up the hill toward the great city, the buzz they created among the townsfolk seemed to grow into a live and tangible thing. Whispers and grumbles sprang from all sides. Here and there a head would pop out of window and someone would mutter at them. They'd say things about demons wandering around in the darkness or staying off the road or staying away from their home or blah, blah, blah. Maelich ignored it all. His goal was clear to him, and it was all that mattered. The townsfolk knew nothing of him or his small group.

Then, suddenly, as if the massive iron thing had been hiding in the ground and sprung up twenty feet into the air to catch Maelich and is group by surprise, the iron gate loomed before them. As odd as it might sound, the heavy, closed gate—wide enough for two carriages with bars as thick as a big man's thigh—appeared as welcoming as the open arms of an old friend. A great wall of brick and mortar surrounded the oily, wonderful thing, and a mighty iron emblem hung above it etched with the word Havenstahl. The great city Ymitoth had spoken of so fondly finally had a name.

"Havenstahl," Maelich nearly gasped as his eyes moved ever

upward, above that most excellent of words, to a picture of a fallon with a grand rack and a helmet, the symbol of his father's house, the house that finally had a name, Havenstahl.

Relief swept over Maelich like the first bit of warmth off a new fire on a cold night as he marveled at the symbol stretching toward the sky before him. Rapt with delight, he hardly noticed Perrin's sleepy eyes peering over his shoulder.

"Is this being our home now?" Perrin's voice sounded small.

"That's what I be hoping," he replied as he pressed his gaze through the thick, iron bars.

The biggest bridge Maelich had ever seen stretched up against a giant wall on the other side of a wide chasm. How deep he could not tell from his vantage point. It was quite deep, from what Ymitoth had told him, and at the bottom flowed the river they had crossed into the Sobbing Forest. He had told Maelich that to get to the great kingdom of the north you must cross the river twice. This would be the second crossing.

Two guards dressed in full armor—so shiny they seemed to glow in the torch-light—stood posted in front of the gate with spears at the ready.

"State your name and business with the house of Havenstahl, lad," the guard to the left spoke with authority.

Maelich was quite sure of his name but not completely sure of his business. "I be Maelich, this be Perrin, and we be seeking one that we lost," his voice carried as much confidence as he could muster in his tired, road-weary state.

"Maelich, whom do ye seek? What business do children be having traveling alone in the dark? What house ye be riding for?" the guard's tone carried an undeniable note of skepticism.

"If I be riding for a house, it be the house of Ymitoth. As for the business of children, we've not a place to stay nor a parent to care for us. The road has been our home for a time," Maelich had enough of his wits left about him to handle the guard's interrogation quite handily.

"Ymitoth ain't no house," the guard began. "Ymitoth rides for the house of Havenstahl which be standing before ye now. What do ye know of the great and mighty Ymitoth?"

"I be knowing that he's raised me from a babe, trained me as a warrior and been the only father I ever known," his reply was curt.

"Ymitoth ain't no one's father. A warrior be he, with the fury of the mightiest army on Ouloos at his command. Now ye tell me that he be a father? The duty of me post don't allow for laughter, but what ye say be more than ridiculous," a slight chuckle accompanied the guard's words.

"I be speaking what I know," Maelich continued. "The man who raised me was named Ymitoth, and he acted as me father till he abandoned me the last time the moon been at its fullest. I've lost track of the days, as I be weary from the road, but I be guessing it to be weeks by now."

The first guard whispered something to the other and then returned to Maelich. "Water your horses there and then go inside and sit by the fire till I call for ye," he said as he pointed first to a well and then to a hut on Maelich's left side. "I've sent for Ymitoth. Welcome home, Maelich. Forgive the questioning. Ye be quite dirty from the road and I had to be sure that ye are the one Ymitoth be expecting. My Lord would be all full of the rage if I'd be sounding out a false alarm."

Maelich did as he was instructed. First, he watered the horses, and then he took Perrin and Jom inside the hut to wait for Ymitoth. Shadows crept around the stone room as flames danced about in a small fire. The girl and the scrod found sleep quickly while Maelich thought about what he might say to his father. His mind was like a mass of mashed stew. It was certainly nice to be expected, but the road had been an unforgiving witch. Perrin and Jom were evidence of that. Their eyes were nearly closed before he had even gotten them inside the guards' room. Maelich was twisted in a tangle of mixed emotions when the heavy, wooden door burst open.

"Maelich, me son!" Ymitoth boomed.

Maelich hesitated only for a moment before running to his mentor and embracing him. "Father," was all he could muster at first.

"Ye've passed your last test. Ye be ready for the trials," pride dripped from Ymitoth's words as he all but shouted.

"I be having a few words about me test, father. I thought ye abandoned me, that ye left me to die. I did almost die. How could ye do that to me?" Maelich's tone grew almost accusatory as his anger mounted.

"Maelich, me son," Ymitoth began as he pushed Maelich back to arm's length and looked him in the eye. "That be the way it had to be. The road before ye ain't an easy one by no measure, and I be needing to know that ye be prepared for it. Had the road claimed ye, then I'd know ye ain't suited for your purpose and your life would be without meaning anyway. Ye'd have no reason to be, lad."

"So ye'd be chancing the sacrifice of the closest thing to a son ye've ever had to test your ability as a trainer?" Rage bubbled up in him, betrayed by the only parent he had ever known, "Be I but a tool for your ego, father?"

"Stand down, Maelich," Ymitoth commanded with a king's authority in his voice. "I've done nothing without purpose, and the trials ye be facing be much more perilous than anything the road could have offered ye. Ye must be trusting me when I be saying that had ye known I been testing ye, ye'd not have been challenged at all. Ye've a great mind, Maelich. Ye know this to be true."

Maelich's rage yearned to spill out at Ymitoth, to engulf him in a flood of accusations, but he did speak the truth. He had trained Maelich to do exactly what he had done, conquer the road to Havenstahl. Had he known his purpose, it would have been no challenge at all. Now, however, there was this new thing, the trials. Judging from Ymitoth's brief description, they would not be easy tasks. Maelich's ire faded slowly like dyed fabric left out in the bright sun, as his thoughts turned toward his next challenge.

"Son," Ymitoth began again, "I knew ye would conquer the road. Ye be the mightiest warrior I've ever had the pleasure of standing next to in battle, and I be meaning that. Ye'll be passing the trials and continuing on your path. Ye'll be the greatest hero this world has ever known. They'll sing songs about ye, lad. Now, let's get ye cleaned up."

As Ymitoth turned back toward the door, he nearly tripped over Perrin and Jom. "What have we here?" he asked with a raised brow.

Maelich had all but forgotten. "Oh," he began, "I found this little lass in a small village on the banks of the river. Her name be Perrin. Her home had been attacked by amatilazo the night before I arrived. The scrod be Jom. He be the only reason she survived. No one else did. She'd no one to care for her so I took her as me own till I be finding a safe home for her."

Ymitoth frowned a bit and shook his head. "Tis a noble thing ye done, son. Though I be wishing ye were without the baggage, ye did the right thing. We'll be finding a caring family to raise her."

The two men roused Perrin and Jom and headed out of the small hut, chatting as they went. Ymitoth ordered the guards to send for someone to care for the horses, and then he and Maelich's group started across the great, wooden bridge into Havenstahl. They were just inside the gate when a scout who had been watching the perimeter of the outlying town came charging up the road, hailing Ymitoth.

"Sir!" the scout shouted.

Ymitoth stopped and turned, "What be troubling ye, scout?"

"Cloaked men on the road milord, they seem to be floating above the ground!" the scout reported, stopping to salute.

"Floating? That be sounding like the myth. Could it be?" Ymitoth asked, mostly to himself.

"What myth?" Maelich asked.

"There be a myth about men with black, dead eyes and wild, orange hair. They be the high priests of Kallum," Ymitoth answered offhandedly, still trying to reason why they'd be heading up the road to Havenstahl. "They don't be having thoughts of their own. Kallum's thoughts be all they know, but they were all men once. They be the only men to have direct contact with Kallum. They enforce his law. It can't be. Even if they be real, what could they be wanting with Havenstahl?"

"Black, dead eyes?" Maelich asked. "Those be the men who attacked us in the Sobbing Forest. They attacked us both in the forest and in the night while we camped. They've been following us since the forest."

"What?" Ymitoth almost hissed. "Run, Maelich." He pushed his son further across the bridge. Then he turned back to the guards, "Close the gate! Don't be hindering them, they'll have at your hides, but don't be hurrying about nothing either."

Ymitoth scooped Perrin up under his arm and sprinted across the bridge that quickly closed after he, Perrin, Maelich and Jom had crossed it. As they ran he instructed Maelich to tell him exactly what they were doing when first attacked by the priests in the forest. Maelich recounted the whole story as they ran. He told him about the song he was singing the first time they encountered them, how fiercely the trees had defended them. Then he recounted the episode on the dark trail and how they followed the rest of the way to the great, iron gate. Ymitoth listened, shaking his head and cursing under his breath.

Once safely inside the city walls, Ymitoth quickly guided them to an interior guard station, leaving Perrin and Jom with the two stout men on duty there, along with instructions to hide them both until he returned. Then he explained to Maelich the severity of what he had done in the forest.

"Maelich," he began, quite out of breath. "Ye be knowing about Kallum's law. Ye be knowing that ye're to be worshipping none other than he. When ye sang in honor of them trees, well that been a kind of worship. Ye broke the law he gave us, lad. Ye've disrespected Kallum. Ye've disrespected your god, your maker. Do ye understand me, son?"

"I...I...meant no disrespect, father," Maelich stammered.

"This I be knowing. That don't change the fact that ye broke his law, and those priests be wishing to punish ye for your transgression. That means Kallum be wishing to punish ye for your transgression. We must get ye to the temple so ye can beg his forgiveness and, hopefully, lessen your penalty. In the future, son, don't be trusting the trees. They be evil."

"Aye, father," Maelich had no idea how to respond.

Maelich was barely aware of the polished, stone streets his feet hammered against, or the massive walls stretching toward the sky beside him, as he charged along close at Ymitoth's heels. How could singing to trees be an affront to his god? How could sharing a tune be a sin? It made no sense. The trees didn't seem evil at all. Sure they were frightening at the outset, but once they grew comfortable with him and his group, they were downright friendly, even helpful when those vile creatures set upon them. How could those things be priests of Kallum? They seemed evil, like something that crawled out of the deepest, darkest pit to terrorize the world.

The questions fled when Ymitoth reached back, grabbed a firm hold of Maelich's sleeve, and all but dragged him up the steps toward yet another large, brick building. Everything in the city was brick upon brick. Maelich gave half a moment to consider who might have laid all that brick, and how long it must have taken. The thought was there and gone, chased away by the marvel before him—windows of colored glass glowing red with light from within and etched with scenes of stories Maelich had learned reading the book—and the righteous terror on his tail. They pounded through a heavy, wooden door, Ymitoth still dragging Maelich behind him. Inside the temple, rows of wooden benches lined either side of a wide path leading to a shimmering prang altar. An image of a bold and vibrant old man, painted in colors so bright it seemed he might step right off the brick, graced the wall behind it. Above the image was that of the great eagle, Kallum, wings spread and ruling the sky. Ymitoth dragged Maelich all the way up to the altar and then stopped.

"Kneel!" Ymitoth commanded. "Beg Kallum's forgiveness. Pour your heart and soul into the prayer, son. Pray like ye've never prayed before."

Ymitoth's eyes darted about the room while his hands trembled. Maelich had never seen him so aghast. Ymitoth feared nothing, at least, that is what Maelich always believed. Watching his hero shiver and twitch like a coward among corpses chilled Maelich to his bones. He clinched his eyes up tight and feverishly prayed. His lips moving around silent words, apologizing over and over again for his song to the trees and then reciting every prayer he knew. Ymitoth knelt beside him and offered his own prayers begging Kallum's forgiveness for his thick-headed son. Both men had their heads buried in folded hands as their feverish whispers choked out the silence of the temple.

The temple door blasted open again as the priests flooded in. Ymitoth spun and flung himself at their feet, wrapping his arms around the leader's legs.

"Please have mercy, milord. The lad knew not what he did!" Ymitoth nearly sobbed.

Maelich turned in time to see the priest grab a handful of Ymitoth's cloak and toss the great warrior to the side, slamming his helpless body against the wall. Maelich's fear melted against the fire burning in his gut. He was ready to go round with the monsters again. Kallum's priests or not, he was done fleeing. His jaw flexed as he stood tall before them like a stone statue facing off against a furious storm.

Ymitoth gave into the sobbing and begged, "Maelich, please," he cried, "stand down!"

"Shut your dribbling gob, you worthless scrod," the leader hissed at Ymitoth. "The great and mighty Ymitoth blubbering like a damned fool."

His eyes turned back to Maelich who remained unflinching. "Maelich," he began. "Are you afraid, lad? Are you afraid of what I'm going to have these monsters do to you? Are you fighting back tears? Do you want to run from me like some kind of animal?"

Ymitoth cried out to Maelich, "That be the voice of Kallum himself, son. Don't ye be challenging him. Kneel before your god, boy!"

One of the priests stalked over to where Ymitoth lay against the wall and grabbed him up by the throat. He picked him up off the floor like a sack of rags before slamming him into the wall. Maelich scowled as his father lost consciousness at the dead-eyed man's feet.

"Get away from me father!" Maelich commanded, his booming voice filling the temple and echoing back off the polished, stone walls.

"You've yet to answer my queries, lad. Are you afraid?" The priest's voice was powerful and frightening, but Maelich remained unmoved.

"I be full aware of me transgression in honoring the trees with song. I stand before ye now, ready to accept me punishment, truthfully unafraid. Me father, though, he be committing no sin. He be spending his whole life in your faithful service. I be asking that ye be merciful to him." The fire burned hotter in him than it ever had before. His eyes began to glow a dull red.

The priest that had been speaking began to chuckle and then stopped just short of an all-out laugh. "Maelich, the trees are of no consequence. They do serve the dragon and symbolize all that is evil, but your resolve is much too strong for their wiles. I sent my priests to test your might. Trees or no trees, you would have met these beasts one way or another. The forest was simply the perfect, dark, frightening place for you to have your first meeting. You are to be my champion, Maelich, the champion of this world. I need to know you are ready, for the road before you is much more perilous than the road behind. You are ready, my son. You are ready. As for your…father, you have no idea how much courage it took for him to stand before me as he did. As your mind ages you'll begin to understand. For now, don't let his whimpering lessen your image of him. You're different than him. You're different than any of my creations. I still keep Ymitoth in my grace. He is a faithful servant to me and a brave testament to what a man should be. You will continue on your path and he on his. We are finished for now. I am the god of all creation. I am all powerful."

With the last statement the three priests replaced their hoods in unison and floated backward out of the temple. Maelich was ready to explode. His mind was a battlefield of emotion, each fighting to take control of him. Very slowly, he relaxed. Everything that had happened between his hut in the forest and standing before the god of all creation played through his mind like an endless wheel. The one thing he could not come to grips with was Kallum speaking to him. He finally had evidence of his importance in this world. The Lord, Kallum had spoken to him. The book, Kallum's word, only records two other human beings ever having direct contact with Kallum. 'Why me?' he thought. 'What makes me different than any other?' He still didn't have any real answers, but he felt closer than ever. Ymitoth began to stir.

Maelich rushed over and roused him. "Father. Father, are you alright?" he asked as he shook his father a little less than gently.

Ymitoth mumbled a bit, but none of the sounds coming out of him could be considered words. His eyes chased around the room. Then he coughed a bit and rubbed at his throat. The dead-eyed men were strong. Maelich could attest to that, and one of them had given Ymitoth a good squeeze of his throat. Maelich helped the old soldier to sit upright against the wall.

"Maelich!" Ymitoth cried out.

"I'm here, father," Maelich replied softly in Ymitoth's ear.

"Are we dead?" he whispered.

"No, father. The priests have gone. Kallum spoke to me. He said you are a brave man and you stand tall in his sight," Maelich's tone was reassuring. Ymitoth would be crushed at the thought of falling from Kallum's grace. He was a man of strong faith who had devoted his life to the service of his god.

"Aye, lad, I heard him speak." Ymitoth thought for a moment and then continued, "He called me a scrod. I wept before me lord." Tears welled, threatening to pour over his eyelids.

"No, father," Maelich shook his head. "You were merely in the way of his purpose. You distracted him, nothing more, and that brought his angry tongue upon you."

"Maelich, ye be like the lord now. I always been believing the myths and been believing ye to be the one they be speaking of, but now there be proof. Ye be me lord now. I be unfit for your presence." His eyes quickly dropped away from Maelich's.

"No, father…" Maelich began.

"Don't be calling me that no more. Ye be me lord now," Ymitoth's words came amid sobs that had taken him. "Ye be the father now. I be fleeing from your sight. I be unworthy of your company."

"But father…" Maelich stopped. Ymitoth was asleep. The encounter with the priests—and finally being forced to face Maelich's purpose—was too much. Maelich held him close and eventually drifted off to sleep himself amid thoughts of all that had been and all that was yet to come.

CHAPTER 5
A BIT ABOUT DWARVES

Doentaat examined himself in a full-length mirror as he fastened a decorative red bow to the bottom of the last of three perfect braids in his thick, healthy beard. Bindaar, his housemate, would undoubtedly give him grief for getting all gussied up to head off for a long, hard day toiling away deep in the mines below Maomnosett, but Doentaat didn't care. He remained one of very few Dwarves who held tightly to the grandeur of dwarf history. Why strive to be only as good as men or giants expect you to be? After all, dwarves graced the sweet face of Ouloos long before men or giants began haunting her lands, using up her resources, and erecting massive stone towers to ruin her landscape. That should count for something.

After finishing up with the last bow, Doentaat gave his burgundy tunic a quick smoothing with his hands. He paused briefly to fret over a small, gray stain, moistening his finger and rubbing roughly at it. All his effort only managed to lengthen and darken the spot. He wet his finger again and groaned as he worked at the spot more with greater vigor. It didn't help.

"Damn," he sighed and glanced around the tiny room. At roughly ten-feet by ten-feet, it housed and represented all Doentaat had to his name. The small room also represented the extent of the hut he shared with Bindaar at the edge of the city of Maomnosett. Sadly, the mirror before him, which was probably a fake rather than the shiny prang it mimicked, was the nicest item in the lot. A small hearth with a crumbling chimney occupied most of the wall to his right. A heavy, black kettle hung from a hook above the meager fire burning within. Immediately behind him was a small wooden table, faded, chipping, and probably a summer from being good for nothing but cutting up and stacking in the hearth. Immediately behind that, two bunks stacked on top of each other took up most of the back wall. A rusty, old wash basin beneath a small cupboard occupied the final wall. That was it, and he had to share it all with that pathetic, waste of a dwarf, Bindaar.

As if on cue, Bindaar farted, rolled over, and mumbled incoherently.

"Get up, ye thin, stinky dwarf!" Doentaat hollered in a hoarse whisper as he walked around the table and shook his housemate.

Bindaar didn't move. He was a waif of dwarf, much too thin. His hair was light and scraggly, and the scrub brush on his chin could hardly be called a beard. Not one to worry about hygiene, he oftentimes smelled like a lavatrina—a pit in the ground where dwarves relieve themselves. The pathetic waste might just be the laziest dwarf to ever live.

"Come on," Doentaat continued. "They'll string ye up this time for sure, ye lazy oaf!"

Bindaar grumbled, and rolled closer to the wall.

Doentaat didn't give up. Playing wakey, wakey games with Bindaar had been a part of his normal morning routine for better than ten summers. None of his friends could understand why he wasted time on the useless scrub, counseling him regularly on giving up the effort. Truly, he couldn't say why he wasted his time on Bindaar, probably because nobody else would. The scruffy oaf always seemed to be in a scrape. If not for Doentaat's efforts, Bindaar would have been wiped from the face of Ouloos long ago.

Perhaps it was frustration from the stain, but Doentaat's fuse was much shorter than most mornings. He grabbed a pot from the cupboard and went out to the well to draw some water. Then, with a nice big splash in hand, he stormed back into his shack and doused his housemate. Both Bindaar and his cot were drenched and dripping. Doentaat's first smile of the day crawled across his face. The water from the well was downright icy. Watching Bindaar sprawl out of his cot onto the dirt floor of the shack was quite satisfying.

"What in dragon's fire are ye doing, ye stupid bastard?" Bindaar howled as he flopped about on the floor as if he were being burned alive.

"Saving your worthless hide, ye scruffy-faced burden," Doentaat replied with just a hint of a chuckle in his strong, serious voice. "Get your lazy carcass off of that floor."

"Aw piss on ye. Pretty princess, with your fancy braids and your yes sir, yes sir, beat me again sir. Leave me to be. Let those weak bastards who want to be serving that overgrown maggot string me up on that tree. Dying on that tree would be better than breaking our backs to make him richer," Bindaar had all but lost his voice by the end of his rant.

"Where does all this come from?" shock twisted up Doentaat's normally measured tone, causing his voice to crack slightly. Bindaar was a whiny waste most mornings, but he rarely fired such sharp barbs.

"I be tired of doing all of what he wants and none of what I want. I ain't the only one, they all just be scared to say it," Bindaar continued to rant. "Ye'd be singing the same song if ye weren't pressing your lips to his big, giant behind. Have ye forgotten Alhouim? Have ye forgotten what great a city we had before Ahm settled his giant arse on our throne and called us Maomnosett? Has he ever bruised a knuckle hammering away in them mines? Ha! Protecting us from the men of Havenstahl who would take advantage of us dim-witted dwarves, is that what he does? Do ye believe that? Ye're a fool if ye do. Them men may have gotten the better end of many a bargain with us, but they ain't never treated us so cruel as the wicked thing we be calling our king."

Doentaat raised his index finger as his lips sneered to fire off a curse-laden response, but it didn't come. Instead, he paused. Bindaar, though lazy, foul-smelling, and near as irritating as an ant trapped in your trousers, wasn't an idiot. When Ahm came to Alhouim—generations before Doentaat or Bindaar had come into being—he brought promises of protection and fair trade with men. According to stories—none that anyone had written down, that kind of blasphemy against the king would get a dwarf strung up on the Great Pine—Ahm's protection quickly turned into a boot firmly placed on the backs of dwarves, and Alhouim became Maomnosett. Most dwarves weren't so vocal about their discontent. However, it would be a difficult task to find one who didn't feel similarly to Bindaar about the topic.

"What?" Bindaar goaded. "I know ye've got more to say. Ye've always got more to say." He paused briefly before adding, "Could it be, wise Doentaat with his opinion on everything be at a loss for words?"

"Ye know, Bindaar," Doentaat just about growled. Whether he agreed with the scruffy pain or not, his housemate had finally pushed him too far, "For the past ten years I been sticking up for ye and looking out for ye and watching after ye, but no more. I be done with ye. Ye can piss on a dragon's lip and get your wee wanker bit off for all I care, ye ungrateful bastard."

Doentaat was still shaking as he stormed out of the shack, mumbling. He didn't pause to glance back at the hut once as he stalked down the trail toward the entrance to the mine he'd be working that day. Whether or not Bindaar managed to get himself there was no longer his concern. In the mood Doentaat was in, he didn't even care if the oaf got himself strung up on the Great Pine. He was done sticking his neck out for that buffoon. Bindaar could look after himself from now on.

Back in the hut, Bindaar stared at the door, fully expecting it to fly open with Doentaat close behind shouting and pointing and shaking. He never came. Aside from some relatively constant creaking—the old boards of the hut complained loudly about the stiff morning wind— the place was completely silent. After a few minutes, Bindaar finally pulled himself up off of the floor. He made some foul gestures toward the door of the shack. They were meant for Doentaat, but he would never see them. Bindaar stretched, scratched his scruff of a beard, then his behind, and then he dried himself off. Once he was dry and changed into some equally soiled clothes, he ate first his meal and then Doentaat's. No sense in letting it spoil.

Once Bindaar was full and satisfied, he tromped on out of the shack. He paused long enough for a glance down the trail toward the mine. He could go that way. He could show up late and possibly convince the foreman to keep his tardiness a secret, but he had no intention of doing that. Instead, he walked south and continued on out of the city. He strolled right past the sacred pine and down into the fairy weed field.

Fairy weed was one of the few pleasures left to dwarves. The weeds grew wild in the field and, according to dwarf myth, forest fairies fly up the mountain every night and dance among the weeds. The magic dust from their wings falls all about them. That dust has quite an odd effect on the mind of a dwarf, quite odd and quite pleasant. Of course, no dwarf has ever seen a fairy, and no one knows if they really exist. It is a distinct possibility they may have only existed in the imagination of some happy dwarf enjoying some fine fairy weed. That didn't matter a lick to Bindaar. He didn't care why the weeds were enchanted, he was just happy they were.

He flopped himself down in the high weeds and plucked some beautiful buds to pack into his pipe. He had a nice long smoke and then laid back and watched the clouds make fantastical shapes for him in the sky. 'This be what life be about', he thought. As the day drifted slowly away, Bindaar drifted with it, floating like the clouds above him. Doentaat, the mines, Ahm, none of them were among the thoughts he was lost in. There was nothing to worry about except the clouds, the big, fluffy, wonderful clouds. Ahh.

Miles away from the fairy fields, and deep beneath the streets of Maomnosett, Doentaat toiled away with his pick. His thoughts weren't so happy and peaceful. All the things he hadn't said to Bindaar that morning played over and over in his head. He'd love to beat the little runt, whip him like a naughty child. That's basically what he was, an overgrown child. Still, Doentaat loved the oaf like a brother or even a son. Bindaar's words that morning had cut deep. After everything he had done for that ungrateful mouse, Bindaar was constantly spitting on his efforts and stomping all over his good deeds. He couldn't take it anymore. He wouldn't. How could he ever have a life of his own if he were constantly looking after that imbecile? Would he never have a wife and be stuck with an ugly scrap of a dwarf for the rest of his days? No, he was finished with Bindaar for good. If the solidas didn't find Bindaar and string him up, he'd send him away.

Rock and dust flew about as Doentaat's pick hammered the mine wall, freeing precious pord. Lost in his laments, he hadn't noticed what a productive day he was having. The evidence lay strewn about his feet, but he didn't notice. His mind was focused solely on Bindaar and the battle he'd have with the runt when he returned home for the evening.

Back in the fairy weed field, Bindaar was deep in a waking dream, toiling away in his own right. Of course, his toiling didn't require physical effort like Doentaat's. Bindaar's toiling was all about convincing a shy fairy to waste the afternoon away with him.

"Oh go on," Bindaar giggled. It didn't matter that he was alone in the field. He was deep in conversation. "Oh no ye don't…really?…Oh stop it…Well, I try to keep in shape, ye know…Who cares what they be thinking about a fairy and a dwarf…"

"Quit your giggling, ye idiot," a deep voice boomed from further up the hill. "There be nobody here but ye."

Bindaar recognized the voice immediately and decided just as quickly to ignore the command. The burly bellow roaring across the field belonged to Laarvel, one of Maomnosett's solidas. Of course, he wouldn't be alone. There was no doubt that Aarvin would be right there along with him. Bindaar wasn't interested in the lecture they'd have for him, and he wasn't about to abandon the fine, young fairy he was chatting up. She was a joy, giggling and flirting. Why would he trade that for the scowls of two rough dwarves?

"What an imbecile," Aarvin whispered, confirming what Bindaar had suspected. Laarvel and Aarvin were as inseparable as they were insufferable.

The sun had just passed its highest point when Bindaar's attractive, imaginary friend convinced him to accompany her to the fairy forest. A bit impaired from all the fairy weed, Bindaar struggled to get to his feet. He nearly fell on his face on the way up. Barely managing to pull it together, his journey was cut painfully short. Before he could take a step toward the forest, Aarvin's big body dropped him back to the ground.

"What on Ouloos are ye doing, ye big oaf?" Bindaar groaned around a mouthful of dirt with all the wind he had left.

"Relax or I'll snap your neck like a twig, ye scrawny runt," Aarvin growled in his ear.

"What in Kallum's name are ye doing out here in the fields when ye're supposed to be in the mines earning your keep?" Laarvel asked emotionlessly.

"Well I'd been doing quite well with a fine fairy maiden until you oafs showed up and frightened her off. Haven't ye any respect for a dwarf's love life?" despite the mouthful of dirt he was chewing on, Bindaar's reply was quite matter-of-fact.

"Idiot," Aarvin continued in his ear. "There ain't nobody here but yeself. Ye're a sad, sorry excuse for a dwarf, scrawny waste of space."

"Let him up," Laarvel sighed.

Before Bindaar could complain any more, or even blink, Aarvin's weight was off of him and his biggest toe was barely touching the ground as it dangled beneath him. Aarvin was strong, even by dwarf standards. He could lift an ass and carry it around on his shoulders without aid. Bindaar had seen the feet several times. However, what the mountain of a dwarf boasted in muscle, he lacked in wit. Obviously pleased with himself, Aarvin glanced back at Laarvel with a smirk and a shrug. That was just enough time for Bindaar to stomp on his foot and stumble off down the hill.

The solidas were on him immediately. Laarvel almost got a hand on him right out of the gate, but Bindaar stumbled over a rock and managed to trip him on the way down. A quick dash to his left as soon as he regained his feet was just enough to avoid Aarvin's charge. If only he were a hair faster, he might have made the crest of the hill and found a place to hide among the pines. Unfortunately, his sprint toward freedom was painfully short. The slow jog it became was only fast enough to get him caught. He zigged and zagged a few more times, avoiding and embarrassing his pursuers, but it wouldn't last. He managed to avoid one more charge from Aarvin—even got his foot out quick enough to kick the big dwarf in the behind—before Laarvel hammered into his back and drove him into to the ground

A few shots to the back of his head from Laarvel were sufficient to scare him off of trying to escape again. A solid kick the to the head from Aarvin as the big dwarf walked by shook away the cobwebs enough that he began regretting his shenanigans. Solidas were soldiers, warriors, and they were a proud bunch. Most dwarves thought them traitors on account of their loyalty to Ahm, but they weren't a group to be trifled with. Only the strongest of dwarves were invited to serve, and those who did spent their time training, learning to fight and kill rather than wasting away in the mines. As Bindaar began to realize the weight of the situation, he thought it might be even heavier than Aarvin had been while laying across his back.

It wasn't long before Bindaar was shackled and collared. He felt like a leashed scrod with Laarvel dragging him by a chain connected to the thick, leather collar around his neck. Aarvin brought up the rear, occasionally whispering threats and nastiness in his ear.

"Ahm will have your head off for sure this time," Aarvin chuckled quietly. "Ye won't be thinking ye're so funny then. Maybe I'll be asking him if I can keep your ugly mug as a prize for me wall."

Bindaar didn't respond. His balance still wasn't all there, and coming down off the fairy weed had him ready for a long nap. His shackles were heavy too. They seemed to gain weight with every stumbling step he took. Even if he weren't ready to pass out right there on the trail into the city, he'd pass on another go round with Aarvin. He'd had enough brawling for one day and had no intention of causing any more trouble.

The three dwarves walked up the main road through the center of the city, past the shacks that served as the dwarves' homes and then past the shops and pubs. All the while they moved farther up the mountain. The shops were all run by older dwarves who no longer had the back to be working in the mines. There wasn't much business during daylight hours. That's when most of the population was down in the mines or out in the fields and the old folk manning the shops had time to gossip. Bindaar could hear them mumbling all up and down the road. Stories of him being dragged past in shackles would definitely be the talk of the town once the mining folk returned from their toils. Those nosy ninnies would go ahead and gab about him to any who would listen. He ignored them as best he could. There wasn't much else he could do. Even if he wanted to stop and give them a piece of his mind, Laarvel kept a firm grip on his chain and he wasn't leaving much in the way of slack.

As the small group moved toward the center of the city, the land flattened out. Mount Elbahor—the peak mined by the dwarves of Maomnosett since the beginning of time—had been leveled to provide a flat, solid base for Ahm's palace. As much as Bindaar despised everything it stood for, he couldn't help but be overcome with awe every time he beheld it. And there it was, stretching up toward the sky before him. The massive structure was made of brick and mortar reinforced with prang that glowed like the sun during daylight hours. The outside walls measured one thousand feet each making a perfect square, and all four were fifty feet tall except at the points of the compass. At each of the cardinal points, stood a guard tower rising another ten feet toward the sky. Below the guard towers were gates, entryways into the courtyard. Every entrance was twenty-five feet tall and fifteen feet across. At the top of the southern gate was the crest of Maomnosett, an eagle with wings spread carrying a mighty hammer in one talon and a giant spear in the other. Within the outer wall was another wall identical to it, with the exception of being set in fifteen feet. In between the two walls were three floors, each fifteen feet above the prior leaving five feet of wall above the top floor. On the inside of the outer wall were stairwells every fifty feet on each floor for access to the floor above. These walls were meant to give the solidas a safe place from which to defend the palace in case of enemy attack. Up to this point in Maomnosett's history, there had never been cause to use them.

By the time Laarvel, Aarvin and Bindaar arrived at the gates of the courtyard, Bindaar was starting to get his wits back about him. In fact, he was beginning to get nervous. Doentaat had been completely right about his being out of chances. It was quite possible he wouldn't get the chance to hear Doentaat tell him so. A shiver raced through Bindaar, rolling down his spine and shaking through his arms hard enough to get the heavy links of his shackles banging and clanging on one another.

"Ye be thinking about them crows plucking out your eyes while that merciless sun cracks your skin, ain't ye?" Aarvin whispered in his ear, as if the jingling of Bindaar's shackles were some kind of cue.

That didn't help at all. Bindaar was certainly too frightened by this point to offer even a remotely cheeky response, but he hadn't yet considered what might happen after facing the great and terrible Ahm. The thought of standing before the most frightening creature east of the Great Sea was enough to chill him to the bone. The giant's icy stare alone was enough to cause the mightiest of dwarves to soil themselves. The thought that what came after might be even worse was something Bindaar didn't need lumbering about his head.

Two guards manned the front gate. They wore brown, leather tunics over sturdy, leather trousers just like Laarvel and Aarvin. They'd look identical to Bindaar's captors if it weren't for the heavy, prang gauntlets they wore. Those were the mark of Ahm's royal guard, the best of Maomnosett's army. Bindaar knew them all a bit too well. Maartuk was the one on the left. He was a giant, as far as dwarves go, nearly as tall as a man. He'd tapped the back of Bindaar's favorite head against more than a few walls. The ornery cuss got great pleasure out of hurting things smaller than him.

Shigaan stood rigid to the right of the gate. He wasn't the biggest, nor the meanest, but he could wield a dwarf axe with one hand as fluidly and effortlessly as most could with two. Bindaar had watched the artist cleave a grong into three pieces with two graceful blows once; a forehand through the thing's thick neck and a backhand through its waist. Neither the scales nor the spine slowed him in the least. Two slashes in one fluid motion, and there was a pile of three twitching pieces squirming in the dirt.

Maartuk stepped toward Laarvel and glanced disapprovingly at Bindaar. "State your business with the house of Maomnosett," he growled with a bit more throat than was probably necessary.

Bindaar would have rolled his eyes at the formality if he weren't shaking to the core.

"Laarvel reporting, sir. I be accompanied by Aarvin, me partner, and Bindaar, a stray from the mines. We be seeking an audience with the great and mighty Ahm to get his judgment on this disobedient dwarf's fate," the big dwarf saluted as he finished.

Maartuk returned the salute, about-faced, and marched just inside the gate passing the message on to another guard who would take it to Ahm. All the formality was nearly enough to raise Bindaar's level of frustration higher than his level of fear. It was such a pain, not to mention a huge waste of time. Maomnosett hadn't seen war since the great campaign. There hadn't been a threat of dragons in centuries, and men feared giants. What did Ahm have to worry about? Who would dare challenge Maomnosett and her great army of dwarves? Exactly nobody, that's who. Even still, Ahm would march his solidas all over the courtyard and all around the city on a daily basis. A faint sigh slipped past Bindaar's lips, so slight nobody noticed it but him.

Bindaar didn't need to see inside the gate to know what was going on behind the towering walls before him. This was far from his first visit to the courtyard where Ahm passed his laws down to the tribal leaders and sat in judgement of dwarves who didn't follow them. He probably knew the place as well as any solida, maybe as well as the great Ahm himself.

At the back of the courtyard, connected to the northern guard wall, were Ahm's living quarters, the palace of the palace. This building stretched from the eastern wall to the western wall and extended out three hundred feet from the northern wall with tower after tower reaching up to the sky well beyond the reach of the outer walls. Bindaar could only imagine all the rooms inside the place or how immense each must be. At the front of the palace was a grand stairway leading up to a set of thrones in front of two gigantic doors where Ahm, with his wife Loh by his side, decided dwarves' fates.

By the time Maartuk returned—after what seemed like three eternities—Bindaar's clothes were soaking from sweat. The prim, palace guard instructed the group to enter the courtyard. Inside the gates two columns of solidas, standing fifteen feet apart and facing each other, stretched from the gates to the stairway of the palace. Bindaar looked up and saw the giant, Maomnosett Ahm. He was terrifying, fifteen feet tall with daggers for teeth. It wasn't the first time he had stood before Ahm to be judged, and the last time had been quite uncomfortable. Ahm might just pop his head right off. There wasn't anything he could do about it. He had no choice but to follow Laarvel and Aarvin to his doom. The two stopped and bowed ceremoniously about five feet in front of the grand staircase while Bindaar stood behind them shaking like a fairy weed bud in a gale of wind.

"Bow, idiot," Aarvin hissed.

Bindaar stooped awkwardly. It was more like a curtsey than a bow. "Sorry," he whispered.

"Rise," Ahm commanded, his booming voice filling the courtyard like thunder rolling across a low valley. Once the dwarves were standing again, he continued, "What are the charges you bring against this dwarf on this day?"

"Most noble and mighty Ahm," Laarvel began, a hint of fear lurking around in his voice, "the dwarf before ye be Bindaar. We found him in the fairy fields shirking his duty in the mines, all confused from the fairy weed. He'd been having a fanciful chat with a fairy that weren't even there. He be a poor excuse for a dwarf."

"Bindaar," Ahm boomed, his glare nearly boring a hole through Bindaar's middle, "this is not the first time I have sat in judgment against you, not the first time by far. What have you to say for yourself?"

Before Bindaar's feeble mind could stop his stupid mouth from spewing all sorts of nonsense, it did. "I say this. I be tired of breaking me back in them mines so you can wrap your fat arse in the fruits of me toils, ye giant slug!"

Bindaar's hands immediately shot to his mouth as Laarvel and Aarvin both looked back at him, slack-jawed and eyes bulging. It was over. He couldn't help himself. That wouldn't matter to Ahm. The giant would probably eat him right then and there. He'd chew him slow and make him suffer.

Ahm remained surprisingly calm. He raised his eyebrows and smiled with only half of his mouth. He held it together for just a moment before he burst into laughter. Bindaar's hands were still covering his mouth to keep any more nonsense from trickling out. He winced as if he were already being chewed by the giant, but there was no shouting. Ahm's laughter filled the courtyard and echoed off the walls until it sounded like an army laughing. Not Bindaar, nor anyone he knew, had ever heard Ahm laugh. Bindaar was barely aware of the nervous glances being shared by solidas all around him as his wide eyes remained trained on the laughing giant. A smile was all set to replace the shock on his face when the laughter stopped as suddenly as it had begun.

Ahm's stern, sober expression returned as he casually muttered, "Hang the insolent worm from your sacred pine."

CHAPTER 6
THE SACRED PINE

No words were spoken as the three dwarves solemnly marched back through the city. The entire episode from the fairy weed field to the courtyard was almost humorous right up until the cold end. Bindaar glanced over at Laarvel. The way the stout solida met his gaze was at once saddening and uplifting. Most of his kin wouldn't make eye contact with him. As he trudged along shackled and guarded, with moments of his life dancing by like scenes on the stage of his mind, he found it difficult to damn them and blame them the way he normally would. He was a scrubby waste of space. Somewhere deep in the back of his conscience, he had always known that. Somehow, just then, it was brighter and louder, screaming and flashing like a night sky hosting a furious storm. He had spent his life trying to be worse than what they thought of him.

He kept his eyes locked on Laarvel's for a good, long while. They had never been friends, and, truthfully, they probably weren't just then either. Even still, there was warmth, sadness, and honest caring in Laarvel's gaze. Watching a dwarf get hung upon the sacred pine, the symbol of dwarf heritage, was like stabbing your mother. It would be tough to find a solida who didn't hate the practice as much, if not more, than any other dwarf. Bindaar knew the concern on Laarvel's face was probably more for the stain the act of hanging a brother from the great tree to die would have on his soul than any new found love for him, but he'd keep it nonetheless. It would probably be the closest thing to comfort he'd have to take with him to the Lake.

When Bindaar did finally shift his gaze away from Laarvel's, he looked over at Aarvin. Again, the customary scowl that would adorn the face of a fellow dwarf when they cast a brief glance full of judgement at him before looking away in disgust just as quickly was absent. It looked as if he wanted to say something, perhaps offer some words of encouragement. Nothing came, though. Even still, Bindaar found some solace in the concern painted across Aarvin's face.

The pace of the group slowed as they progressed past all the same shops and nosy people they had passed on the way into the city. Bindaar was barely aware that all of the sniggers and quiet, damning comments that greeted him on his way into the city were missing on his slow march to the Sacred Pine. He glanced at some of the faces. There wasn't a scowl or sour look among them. He even found a few eyes failing to keep all of their water in them.

Bindaar's world spun slowly around him, like he'd had a bit too much ale to drink. Death had never seemed like a real thing. Now it did. As he marched slowly toward his doom, death became a thick and heavy burden perching upon his shoulders. No slick comment or adolescent gesture could stop it, and no amount of begging or pleading would change his fate. He was going to die. He would take his last breath while strapped to the Sacred Pine.

Bindaar finally found his voice as the gates of the city came into view, "Ye could just let me go, Laarvel." For the first time in his life, the little bit of sweetness in his voice was sincere.

"I be wishing I could, Bindaar," Laarvel began, "but ye be knowing as well as I, Ahm would be crushing both me and Aarvin's heads if I'd be doing something so foolish."

"Damn it," Aarvin sighed. "Why'd ye have to be pushing him so?"

Bindaar didn't answer. He'd never been very good at holding his tongue. Of course, the stakes had never been quite so high.

The Sacred Pine stretched toward the sky. It was the biggest on the mountain reaching almost four hundred feet into the air. It was sixty feet in diameter at the base. Chains hung from it. Bindaar couldn't bring himself to look at it for more than a few moments. Laarvel and Aarvin would bind him to the tree with those chains and he would hang there until he died. By the time he finally did, it would be a relief.

Bindaar offered no resistance as Laarvel and Aarvin fastened cuffs to his wrists and his ankles. Once the cuffs were secure, Laarvel stayed with Bindaar as Aarvin walked around to the back of the tree. A few moments later, Bindaar's arms began to rise and he was slowly pulled against the tree. The gears of the spindle on the opposite side of the tree clicked loudly. Before long Bindaar was rising off of the ground. He let out a little squeak as the chains pulled his arms and legs apart, as if they would wrap him around the tree. His chest, stomach and groin burned in response to the force cranking at his limbs. All of his joints felt ready to pop.

"That be far enough!" Laarvel yelled to Aarvin, the strength gone from his voice. A tear trickled down his stony face as his eyes met Bindaar's, "That be far enough. Kallum be with ye, Bindaar. May he be speeding ye home."

By this time a large crowd, made up mostly of innkeepers and shop owners, had gathered around the tree. Never in his life had so many shown up to be a part of something that had anything to do with Bindaar. His already wet cheeks received a fresh coating of tears as his emotions poured from them. One of the priests from the temple was among the crowd. Laarvel bowed his head to pray. Aarvin moved back around the tree, stood next to Laarvel and followed suit. The rest of the crowd did the same, and the priest led them in prayer.

"Oh mighty Kallum, maker of all things, oh all powerful god of gods, hear us as we offer up praise in your name. Take our brother, Bindaar, and forgive his foolish ways. Soften your heart to him and bring him home. Oh great and mighty Kallum, let this torture he must endure on the tree serve as his penance, and let him walk through the gates of the house ye provided for us in the life after this. In your name, we pray, Telos," when the priest had finished the prayer he remained with his head bowed.

The crowd mumbled in response, "Telos," which simply meant, end. All prayers to Kallum end in that way.

Most of the crowd began to slip away here and there, back to the shops. There were no stones thrown and no insults either. There were times when the tree was a fitting punishment. Bindaar's shenanigans didn't amount to one of those times. Judging by the looks on the faces in the crowd, it seemed to Bindaar, at least most agreed. Ahm had no patience for dwarves anymore, and there was no distinction about the severity of some crimes over others. Every transgression was treated the same. There were no real fair trials either. Dwarves were oftentimes locked up due to false accusers. It kept most dwarves doing their best to remain on the straight and narrow. Bindaar wished he was more like most dwarves.

By nightfall, Bindaar's head had fallen far enough that his chin rested on his chest. His tongue slipped out of his mouth and dragged across dry lips already cracked from the day's blazing sun. If only he could have a few drops of water, something to sprinkle on the burn. His gut ached from hunger, and his head was beginning to throb. A soft, low moaning slipped by those cracked lips. He was barely aware of the sound and hadn't the energy to try stopping it.

By this time the original crowd was all gone save Laarvel and Aarvin. They had to stay and guard their prisoner. Bindaar knew this, but, based on the gentle way they had dealt with him since Ahm had passed his judgment, he hoped they would have stayed anyway. It seemed likely. Both of them had fallen to quiet mumbling. He couldn't hear most of what they said, but the things that stood out sounded dangerously like damning words against their king.

The sun had just dipped below the horizon when two guards came to relieve Laarvel and Aarvin's post. It was a great effort to raise his head at the commotion, but it was worth it when he saw Laarvel send them away. He even managed a weak smile. There was at least one dwarf who cared enough for him to stay until his journey was completely finished.

Bindaar's chin had nearly fallen back to his chest when an even greater commotion grabbed his attention. Doentaat charged through the gates with a canteen of water. He raced straight past Laarvel and Aarvin and up to the Sacred Pine. Neither of the guards attempted to subdue him. Instead they simply watched him tend to his friend.

It almost felt like a dream as Doentaat dumped water on his hand and splashed it all over Bindaar's face. His tongue darted out of his mouth desperately trying to sop up some of the moisture. Then the mouth of the canteen was at his lips and Doentaat was helping him tilt his head back to drink.

"Stupid oaf," Doentaat scolded as Bindaar drank. "I be so sorry I left ye alone this morning. I be wishing I could be taking it all back."

Bindaar continued to drink as Doentaat rubbed his head with his free hand. As focused as he was at getting the cool water into his belly, Bindaar was acutely aware what a big risk his old friend was taking. If any dwarf had a mind to rat Doentaat out to Ahm, his old house mate would be strung up to it as soon as Bindaar's carcass was taken down.

"Thanks, me friend," Bindaar did his best to smile through the pain as he whispered all rough and gravelly, "but ye shouldn't be risking your own hide for the sake of mine. Me crimes ain't on account of ye, and ye shouldn't be paying for them."

Doentaat's eyes welled up, "Ye can be shutting your gob of that nonsense. This be all my fault, and I ain't leaving your side. Ahm be damned."

Doentaat wrapped his arms around Bindaar, buried his head in his chest and wept. Bindaar leaned his head down until it was resting atop Doentaat's, and he wept too. Before long, Laarvel and Aarvin were wrapped up in the mess, sobbing along with them. Sadly, for Bindaar, it was the most love anyone had ever shown him, and it would be the last thing he would ever know.

CHAPTER 7
THE COURT OF YFREGEOF

Sunlight poured in through the window, less than gently tugging at Maelich's eyelids. He was slightly disoriented as the world came into focus around him. The window letting in all of that light was monstrous, double-pained and lightly etched with two fallon. It looked south down the mountain. The view it offered was like nothing Maelich had ever seen. The world stretched out before him, sprawling out, rolling toward a slight, green smudge on the horizon. That had to be the Sobbing Forest. He suddenly remembered how he had gotten there. Everything flooded in. All of the events at the temple, Ymitoth crumbling before him but not before Kallum, the Lord, had spoken to him. He couldn't try to think of that just yet. Other questions needed his attention. Where was he? Where was Ymitoth, and where were Perrin and Jom? He climbed out of the bed he was in and went to the window. Even those would have to wait a bit. That view simply refused to release his gaze.

Once Maelich was finally able to grab control of himself, he turned to find a door and found something quite a bit more interesting to him, a looking glass. Perched atop a terribly fancy chest of drawers was a giant mirror. He had never seen one before. Ymitoth had described them to him when he had discovered his blurry reflection in Yester's Pond, but he had never actually seen one. Ymitoth said to him at that time, "Don't be looking too long, lad. Ye can't be getting a good look at ye self unless ye see it in a looking glass. That be what ye really look like." He was absolutely right. Maelich had never seen himself before. Now he did, and he was pleased with what he saw.

His hair was long and golden. It draped over his shoulders, framing his face on its way down. His eyes were big and as blue as the sparkling waters of Yester's Pond. As he looked in his own eyes he noticed how deep they were as well. He toyed with the idea that he could see into his own soul through this magic glass. What would he find if he looked hard enough? His skin was smooth and tightly wrapped around high cheek bones and a strong chin. Gazing at himself, he thought he was quite handsome compared to other men he'd seen. Did other people see him in that way, or was he pleasing only to himself? He wrinkled up his nose and raised his eyebrows, then toyed with other faces as he giggled, forgetting about all of the heavy business weighing on him. He stood there making ridiculous faces at himself until the door to the room swung slowly open.

"Sorry to disturb ye, milord," Ymitoth said with a bow as he crossed the threshold into Maelich's room. "Did ye sleep well?"

"I suppose I did," Maelich began. "I guess I'd be none the wiser if I hadn't"

"Maelich, listen to your voice and the way ye be talking. Ye sound different," Ymitoth said with an odd look of surprise.

"I guess I do," Maelich made a face like he had just had a taste of some spoiled tubberslat. "What do you suppose that is all about?"

"I be at a loss milord," Ymitoth shrugged.

"Father, please stop referring to me as your lord. In my heart and in my mind there is nothing different between us," Maelich sighed as he put a hand on Ymitoth's shoulder.

"I be sorry milord, but no matter how hard I be trying, I can't be seeing ye as nothing less now," the humbled father replied.

"Father," Maelich began, "I am not yet ready to be free from your wise tutelage. I still need you to guide me. Everything I've seen since I left our hut has me confused and unsure. I'm starting to understand my importance in our world, but I still haven't an answer as to why I am so important. You know more about me than I do, and I need to draw from your understanding in order to form my own. No matter how you see me now, understand that you raised me and much of what I am, if not all, is directly because of you."

Ymitoth looked to the ground and slowly shook his head with tears threatening. "Milord," he paused and corrected himself, "Son, there be many reasons for me feelings right at this moment. Most, I be guessing, be because of what I seen last night in the temple, but some because I be knowing that ye be leaving me. And I be knowing I ain't your father. I be wishing that I was, son, but I ain't. Ye be a god, Maelich. Your story be written in the book. How can a mere man like me be presuming to teach a god anything?"

"Do you hear the words coming out of your mouth, father?" Maelich's tone was almost pleading. "How can you presume to teach a god? What do I know but what I have learned from you? You taught me all I know, and you raised me to be what I am. If you revere me as a god now, it's because of your teaching that I am. What would I be if left to raise myself but a rotting carcass? Now, if you won't oblige me in my request, then I will command it. Furthermore, if you insist on forcing me to lay commands down to you, I have this one. Don't ever question your importance in my life. You are my teacher, my mentor, my father, and my hero. Nothing, not you, nor my destiny, nor Kallum will ever change that. Do you understand me?"

Ymitoth lost a tear down his cheek that had been teetering at the edge of his lower eyelid, as he smiled and embraced Maelich, "Aye, son, I be understanding ye, even with all your funny talk."

After the embrace, Maelich glanced quickly around the room and asked, "How did I get here, and how did you come to live in such a magnificent palace? We're in a tower, aren't we? How high up are we?" Maelich paused long enough to raise an eyebrow before adding, "This place seems way too fancy to be home to the grizzled warrior who trained me in the ways of the blade."

Ymitoth chuckled as he scanned the room before agreeing, "Aye, these walls always seemed they had a mind to crush me down to nothing, like they might be crushing the wind right out of me chest." The old warrior's smile fled in favor of something a bit more nostalgic, "How'd ye get here, though? That be what ye be wanting to know. A couple of guards came round and roused me. Ye were sleeping so sound, I ordered them not to wake ye. They be the ones what brung ye here."

Maelich beamed, as he looked around the room again, "That explains that, but it doesn't explain how the mightiest swordsman in all the land grew out of this opulence. I mean, you were made for the trail. You could track a fallon with nothing more than a nicked leg for miles through heavy brush. How does that come from this?"

Ymitoth shrugged, "I be the eldest son of a second son. Me father,

Ymantl, was brother to the king. Being the second son, he didn't earn the same attention from his father that his brother, the future king, received. Being left to his own devices, he found he was quite a bit fonder of the knights, hunters, smiths, and stable boys than any of them powdered and pampered types what liked to hang around the courtyards. Ye think I be handy with a blade, lad? I'll tell ye, me father had no equal, trained by the finest of Havenstahl's guards. I ain't had no chance of ever warming the throne with me own rump, so he trained me in all of the same."

"So, you're a prince?" Maelich asked before confirming his own question, "You're a prince of Havenstahl, the greatest city of men. You are royalty."

"Bah," Ymitoth scoffed, "I be a soldier and I ain't never been nothing more. Yfregeof, he'd been the prince. His father, me uncle Yfrahnu, was king until he and me father were betrayed. Now, Yfregeof be the king, and I still ain't nothing but a soldier. That's all I be wanting to be. I be seeing what that throne will do to a man. There be coward's blood flowing through the veins of me cousin, the king."

"The king of the greatest city of men is a coward? How can that be?"

"It ain't nothing but who ye be born to what makes ye a king. It ain't no feat of greatness, just blood. Whose blood ye got in your veins, that be what make ye a king."

Maelich's eyes squinted slightly, "I am truly unable to imagine a man who deserves your jealousy."

"I ain't jealous of the man," Ymitoth rolled his eyes, "but I ain't carrying no love around for him either. He's lucky me blade never made its way into his chest. I told ye that his and me father had been betrayed. Them two had gone to negotiate new trade with that bastard, Ahm. Well, it weren't no negotiation, it weren't nothing more than an ambush. He ate them, alive if ye believe the stories. All of Havenstahl, me more than any, wished our new king to be mounting an assault on Maomnosett. What that giant did been an act of war. Yfregeof, the great king," Ymitoth spat on the ground, "cowered on his new throne. Well, the people were having none of it. They formed up a council to dethrone the gutless waste and put me at the head of it."

"How is it that he still breathes and still wears the crown?"

"The lord, Kallum, called me to a greater purpose, raising the savior of Ouloos and teaching him to be a warrior and a man."

Maelich sat down on the bed and scanned the room again, his head slightly shaking back and forth as it moved from wall to ceiling to wall and then back to Ymitoth, "So, that's how it ends. You left to raise me, and the effort perished?"

"Perished?" Ymitoth's left eye squinted a bit as he shrugged, "No. Ain't nothing perished. All them same ones what thought my rump right for that throne still be wanting to see me upon it. Soldiers ain't leaders, though. Me cousin did a right fine job of keeping all the swords what mattered fat and happy. He's always done right by his generals. The ones what followed me, they still be wanting to see a crown sitting on this old head of mine."

"And you don't want that?" Maelich hardly paused before adding, "No. The greatest sword in all the land would lose his mind trapped in a throne room."

"Aye," Ymitoth chuckled, "your words be true. Still, Yfregeof be a weary, distrustful man. He be seeing all men as a threat to his throne. That be making him dangerous."

"Well, I'm not afraid."

"And ye shouldn't be," Ymitoth replied quickly. "Ain't a man alive I'd rather have at me back in battle. Ye should be wary, though. Even the frailest of creatures can be fierce when backed against the wall. He'll be complaining ye be too young to take the trials. I be fearing what fate he might be having in store for ye."

Maelich stood and lifted his chin, "I'm ready for whatever task he has in store. Nothing will stop me."

"Ye're a brave lad, Maelich, but ye ain't seen much of the world yet. And ye ain't faced one so wily and cunning as the king. I ain't a lick of trust in me for the man," Ymitoth paused for a moment, a faraway look settling into his eyes. He shook it off and continued, "Ain't nothing can be done about that. Ye be needing to take the trial, and the king be the one handing them out."

The old soldier turned toward a wardrobe against the wall opposite the window. The wood was stained a rich mahogany. A black pattern adorned the edges, curving tightly and coming to points before forming the rack of a fallon at the top. Both doors had large diamond shapes carved in their middles with smaller diamond shapes surrounding them. The door pulls were stretched diamonds, like pointy tear drops of polished prang. Ymitoth opened both doors wide and rummaged around a bit. When he returned to Maelich, his arms were full of fine fabric, all bright colors like the fancy folk wear.

"Ye can put these on," Ymitoth instructed as he laid the pile of clothing on the bed next to Maelich.

Maelich's mind turned circles trying to keep up with all of what Ymitoth had to say. He barely noticed how nervous the old man seemed. Now that was a switch. Ymitoth had nerves of steel. He would face down a pack of Amatilazo alone with nothing but his two fists and a scowl to defend himself, and there would be no evidence of nerves on his face. Yet, the great warrior certainly appeared out of sorts.

"Is the mightiest man I have ever known nervous?" Maelich mused.

Ymitoth rolled his eyes and waved the idea off, "I might be trying that if we had time for it, but we ain't. Now, hush up with them jibes and put your focus to these words what about to come out of me mouth. First, I'll be presenting ye to Yfregeof as me student and a pledge to ride for the mighty house of Havenstahl. The king will be complaining that ye be too young and not of this house. Pay that no mind. It don't matter a lick. There be a greater power at work here, and Yfregeof won't dare be thinking about disobeying the word of Kallum. Even still, he'll be doing his best to be coming up with a task he ain't thinking ye can accomplish." Ymitoth paused and looked deeply into Maelich's eyes before adding, "Ye can't be failing, lad, no matter what task that vile coward be laying before ye."

Maelich dressed as the time to address Yfregeof drew near, and Ymitoth moved onto lighter topics. The room they occupied was part of his quarters. Being an heir to the throne, he made his home within the castle walls. Oftentimes, however, he found himself staying with friends in the city. These quarters were a bit too lavish for his liking. He continued by telling Maelich that Perrin and Jom were being cared for by the family of one of the most trusted warriors in his command, and they would remain there until a proper home could be found for them.

By the time Ymitoth had finished explaining everything to him as best he could, Maelich was dressed. His garb was quite a bit fancier than anything he had ever worn before. Fine, shiny boots hugged his ankles tightly all the way up to his knees where they gave way to pale blue trousers that were soft and snug. They were so light, it felt as if he wore nothing at all. His shirt was pure white, loose fitting with ruffles at the chest and cuff. His jacket was a darker blue, made of a stiffer, more durable fabric. Decorative gold stitching adorned the lapels and cuffs. He looked like a prince, and Ymitoth, looking quite proud, told him so.

As Maelich stood admiring himself, Ymitoth went to the wardrobe and fished something out of the bottom. He emerged carrying a long, rolled up cloth. He gently laid the bundle on the bed and unrolled it. When he finally turned back toward Maelich, his face beamed just as bright as the sunlight glinting off the curvy, prang handle of the sword he held up with both hands.

Maelich failed to suppress a gasp.

Ymitoth's smile widened as he approached Maelich and bent to one knee, "Son," he began, holding the shimmering thing up toward Maelich, "I had this sword made for ye by the finest swordsmith in all of Havenstahl. Don't be letting her shimmering beauty fool ye. She ain't just a shiny decoration. This dame's been folded two-hundred-and-fifty times and sharpened 'til she could split a blade of grass. This blade will never be letting ye down."

Maelich's breath caught in his throat as he took the sword and unsheathed it. He had never seen its equal. Not even Ymitoth's mighty blade stood as great. The light pouring in through the windows radiated off of it as if it were a burning, white-hot blade of fire. He went through a couple of his sword motions as a smile quickly surfaced on his lips. It was perfectly balanced. It felt good in his hands, like it belonged there. He fastened it to his belt and embraced Ymitoth.

"Thank you, father. I will make you proud."

Then the two men headed down to the throne room where the king held court. Maelich counted the floors as they walked down a grand, spiral staircase. By the time they reached the bottom, he had achieved a count of ten. The stairway let out into a great hallway with paintings of men adorned in garb similar to the fancy clothes Ymitoth had given him. He felt like royalty, and according to Ymitoth, he was. The great hallway seemed to stretch forever before finally cutting to the right and spilling into a gigantic hall. Havenstahl had no shortage of amazing sights, and the king's throne room was no exception.

The room was one hundred feet deep by seventy-five feet wide. Two thrones sat against the wall opposite the entrance beneath a great emblem that matched the one at the gates of the city exactly. The only difference between the two was the fact that this one was etched in prang rather than iron. A man bearing an uncanny resemblance to Ymitoth sat in the throne toward Maelich's left. He wore an immense, elaborate crown made of prang and encrusted with all forms of jewels. Maelich reckoned this was Yfregeof. He held a scepter in his hand, as one might expect a king would, and a melancholy look upon his face. In the lesser throne on the right sat an historic beauty. Despite her obvious sadness—she wore a look nothing short of despair—the years had failed to mask the delicate elegance of her features.

From the sadness on one throne and the melancholy on the other to the doorway of the great room ran a velvety, red carpet flanked on either side by warriors. Hard looking men, they were dressed for battle with swords drawn and resting against their shoulders.

With Ymitoth at his side, Maelich approached the thrones while trying to appear as regal as possible. Embarrassing his father was the last thing he wanted to do. Despite the guards scrutinizing him with scowls and sneers as he and Ymitoth passed them by, he didn't miss a step. Keeping a tight hold on his excitement, he remained expressionless.

The two men stopped roughly ten feet before the thrones. As they did, three other guards appeared from behind the king. These appeared ready to fight. Maelich only gave them a moment before directing his attention back to the king. If need be, he was ready to trade steel.

Ymitoth stopped about ten feet before the throne and bowed, Maelich followed suit. "Your highness," Ymitoth offered as a greeting.

"Ymitoth," Yfregeof replied, seemingly bored by their presence. "Would this," he paused, looking Maelich up and down before continuing, "waif of a lad be the one ye presume to offer up for the trials?"

"Aye, your highness. This be Maelich, the chosen. Chosen by Kallum himself to ride against the dragon, he must bear the crest of Havenstahl. He must be taking the trials."

The king forced an unnatural laugh. "This lad won't be passing no trials, just have a look at him, ridiculous."

"Test him first then," Ymitoth's response was quick and soaked in anger. "I've trained this boy since he's been big enough to raise a sword. I put him up against your best warrior."

Yfregeof looked up at the soldier to his right and motioned his head toward Maelich. The warrior responded by charging headlong and drawing his sword as he came. Maelich pushed Ymitoth to the side and then dove over the man's head, smacking him in the backside as he passed. He hit the grounded lightly on his hands and then smoothly rolled back up to his feet. After tossing a quick wink to the king, he spun to face his attacker who had landed in a heap on the ground. The warrior's cheeks were a deep shade of red by the time he made it back to his feet.

The soldier charged again, this time stopping short and slashing with his sword. Maelich easily dodged the assaults, gaining more confidence with every slash. The blade flashed, catching sunlight from the window and splashing on the walls. The angles seemed impossible, but Maelich slipped around the shimmering thing as it split the air yearning to taste his flesh. The fury of the assault slowly faded as the muscles behind the blade began to fail. Finally, the thing slammed against the floor. Maelich never paused. He stepped on the blade, pinning it to the floor, and drove his right fist into the big man's nose. He earned a bit of gore on his face as the bulbous thing shattered along with the soldier's cheekbones. He followed his right hand with a left that connected squarely with the man's jaw and sent the dazed warrior stumbling to the floor in a pile. The blade Maelich had been dodging clanged to the floor. He gave it a little kick to put it out of his adversary's reach.

By the time Maelich turned back to the face the throne, two more of the king's guard were charging. He stepped to his left and kicked the first one in the ankles sending the brute sprawling to the floor. Then he jumped up and kicked the second soldier in the chest. Arms flailing, the thickly-muscled man stumbled backward several steps before Maelich's foot pounded into his jaw. The latter kick deposited the warrior in Yfregeof's lap. With that the king jumped up off his throne toppling his soldier to the ground at his feet.

"Enough, ye fools!" He shouted. "Me best warriors and ye can't even strike down a wee lad?"

Maelich wore a cocky smirk as his gaze met Yfregeof's head on. He meant no disrespect, the man was the king after all, but wanted to send a clear message he was not afraid.

"So Yfregeof, about Maelich's trials, would ye like for him to lay your entire army to waste without drawing his sword? Or would ye rather lay the test before him?" Ymitoth beamed as his words strolled slowly from his mouth.

Yfregeof sighed and looked up at the ceiling as his expression became resolute. He remained like that for a moment, frozen, like he thought they might leave if he ignored them. After what seemed an eternity to Maelich, the king lowered he head and smiled. "So it be a test ye want then, lad? Well then, it be a test ye shall get. Bring me the head of Ahm."

Maelich's smile pushed his cheeks nearly to his forehead. He had no idea who, or what, Ahm was, but was eager to test his might against a worthy opponent. His jaw went slack when he heard his mentor's protest.

"What?" Ymitoth hissed. "The trials normally be consisting of the head of an amatilazo or a grong. Now ye be requesting the head of a giant, the same giant who killed both our fathers? This be no test. Ye be sending him off to the slaughter," spit flew from his lips as his cheeks shook like trembling mountains roiling above an active fault.

"I accept your challenge!" Maelich triumphantly announced before Yfregeof could respond to Ymitoth's protest.

"Ah, of course ye do, lad," Yfregeof chuckled. "Ye be too dumb to be feeling a lick of fear of any man or beast."

"This be wrong, Yfregeof, and ye know it. Despite the lad's skill and confidence, this test be wholly unfair."

"Me lips have spoken me final words on the subject," Yfregeof's nonchalant reply nearly smacked of boredom. "Accept the challenge or don't. I ain't a care to waste on it. The journey be two days on foot across Galgooth's Pass to the city of Maomnosett. If ye be accepting me challenge, ye'll be leaving just as the day be fading to night. Ye'll be going alone. Ye won't be entering the gates of me city again without Ahm's head on a spike. That be all, ye best go make your preparations."

Ymitoth's tightly set jaw with cheeks all pulsing and flexing knocked a bit of the wind out of Maelich's sails, dulled his bravado. Why the scowl? The challenge was his to accept, and he did. The same man who had spent the best part of Maelich's life blabbing about how he would grow to be the greatest hero Ouloos had ever known suddenly seemed full of doubt in his star pupil. Maelich chewed on the doubt oozing off Ymitoth's face as they walked back toward the throne room's entrance. It didn't make any sense. If he were to be the savior of Ouloos, how could Ymitoth doubt his chances against any foe? What was a giant anyway, besides a very large man? All of it was too much to keep in his head, that had already grown a few sizes after besting the king's guard.

"Why would you presume to keep me from my destiny?" he erupted as soon as the two men had made it back to the great hall. "Have you no faith in your pupil? Have I not shown you time after time I can bear the burden of my destiny? Also, tell me this, what have I if not the confidence and support of my mentor?" Rage at Ymitoth's lack of faith churned in his guts.

"Ye don't understand…" Ymitoth's expression softened as he tried to explain, but Maelich cut him off.

"Oh no, I understand completely," he fumed as the two men stormed down the hallway matching each other's stride perfectly. "I am hardly more than a parlor trick to you. Some fancy moves to topple a few guards and showcase the fantastic tutelage of the mighty Ymitoth are fine. It is just fine when they are all marveling at this thing you have molded with your own two hands. But a real test of your star pupil's ability? No, a real test is something I can't handle. I cannot believe you do not trust me to conquer this challenge."

Ymitoth stopped and sighed. His gaze dropped away from Maelich's to the floor as he slowly ran a hand through his hair. "Maelich," he began softly, a bit of gruffness in his voice, "it ain't a lack of faith be sparking me concerns. Yfregeof has beaten these people of Havenstahl down. They be living in fear of that monster, Ahm, and in this," he paused and rubbed his neck, "in this he be winning no matter the outcome. If ye be killing that giant, he be looking like the hero what saved Havenstahl from the shadow of Maomnosett. And if Ahm be killing ye, then Yfregeof be justifying his lack of response to the murder of me father and his, and the people of Havenstahl be living in even deeper fear of that monster."

Maelich stopped, took a deep breath and continued calmly, "Do you think I can defeat Ahm?"

"If there be any soul in this land what be having a chance, it be ye," Ymitoth replied in a somber tone. "If ye be taking this challenge son, ye can't be failing."

"I won't," Maelich said, sober and confident. Then a bit more quietly, "I won't."

The two men walked back to Ymitoth's quarters in silence. Maelich would need clothes suitable for travel and conquest. He'd need food as well. Ymitoth brought up the idea of sneaking away and meeting him on the other side of Galgooth's Pass to assist him. Maelich quickly shot the idea down. It was his test and his test alone.

Pass or fail, he would take the challenge unassisted. Ymitoth agreed and helped him only to pack for his short journey.

CHAPTER 8
MAELICH'S TRIAL

Blazing orange on the eastern horizon licked up into the sky before melting into fiery reds and finally giving way to purples and pinks as Maelich and Ymitoth made their way down to the north gate of Havenstahl. The north gate of the great city was a near mirror image of the south gate, minus the grand bridge over the River Galgooth. Rather than pouring out onto a gentle slope into a wide valley, like its southern counterpart, the north gate led out to a narrow path on ground that remained level for about one hundred yards before plummeting down the side of the mountain. Maelich squinted slightly with his left eye as the sun defiantly blazed against dark skies eating at the edges of its light and bathed his destination in rusty orange. From where he stood, Mount Elbahor seemed to be glowing rather than reflecting the rays of the dying sun. Maomnosett, formerly Alhouim, was built on the peak of the mountain, twin to the peak Havenstahl rose from, and Maelich could faintly make out the shapes of the grand towers of Ahm's palace. Two day's journey indeed. There wasn't much rest factored into that estimate. That was fine with Maelich. He was ready to finish his trial and move on to the next thing, whatever that may be.

Ymitoth explained the best path for Maelich to take and warned him not to camp on the river. Grongs sometimes come out at night to water themselves by the river and Maelich would want to be fresh for his meeting with Ahm. Brawling with brutes would do nothing to help his campaign. There was one good thing about the grongs. They had a taste for amatilazo and hunted them frequently.

"If ye be staying true to the course I be laying out for ye and not dawdling, ye should be reaching an old oak what's had its insides hollowed out. It ain't a dead thing though, like ye might be thinking, but she be alive and enchanted, if ye be believing any of them stories what be told about the ancient thing. Ye can be camping there, sleeping right inside that magical thing. Travelers of old been having stories about how that old tree kept them safe in their slumbers. I ain't heard nothing would make me believe them stories not to be true." Ymitoth seemed a bundle of nerves as he rattled off instructions to Maelich.

Maelich replied with a wide grin, amused at his mentor's concern, "I have been trained by the greatest swordsman in all the land. I expect to be exceptionally hard to kill."

"Aye, have a laugh at the bumbling old oaf if it suits ye, but pay heed to me words, lad. Only be traveling by the light of the moon. Catch your sleep in the early hours of the sun, that be the best way if ye be hoping to conquer Galgooth's Pass alone. Keep a steady pace, and ye'll be hitting that tree by sunrise. Rest your bones until midday, and ye'll be reaching Maomnosett by the wee darkest hours of night. That'll be your best time to strike."

Maelich's expression sobered as he embraced Ymitoth. He squeezed him tight once and whispered, "Thank you, father. I will not fail you."

Descending Mount Elzkahon was more than a chore. The moon was far too low in sky to offer much assistance. On top of that, the path was steep, covered in loose dirt and gravel. Luckily, Maelich was traveling light and, despite slipping and earning a good scare a handful of times, had a relatively easy go of it.

As Maelich made his way down the path, sliding more often than walking down the exceptionally steep spots, he tried to imagine how the path could ever have been used as a trade route. Even in the brightest hours of daylight, there was no way any man or dwarf could tackle the precarious trail loaded down with goods and supplies. The longer road around the east edge of Mount Elzkahon must be the route they used. It was a significantly longer distance, but Maelich knew of no horse that could easily make this climb with a rider much less hauling a full carriage. The only souls who could possibly find a use for this trail would be hunters or travelers, and those couldn't be hunting anything very large or traveling very far.

Maelich heard the river before he could see it, a heavy current coursing through light rapids, fast moving water slapping against rock. After snaking its way down the side of the mountain, his trail flattened out and wound around trees and heavy underbrush. By this point, the moon had risen high enough in the dark sky to aid him slightly, if only just enough to keep him from tripping over gnarly roots jutting here and there out of the ground. His trip thus far had been surprisingly uneventful. Prior to reaching the river, the most exciting thing that happened was a trip and near fall over a large rock in the middle of his path. That was it. As he crossed the river he did notice a small mob of shapes moving along the banks. Probably grongs, he thought. They would be a good test, but he decided to take Ymitoth's advice and hurry along rather than have a go at them. They obviously hadn't seen him or they'd be moving on him quickly, roaring and growling and gnashing their teeth, scaly bastards. He'd save them for another time.

Ymitoth had been right about the tree, a mighty oak a few miles up the hill from the river with the trunk hollowed out. The sun was just beginning to peak over the horizon and Maelich was ready for a bit of sleep. He couldn't tell if it was the lack of sleep or just the odd lighting right at sunrise, but the tree seemed to be glowing or sparkling. It was difficult to say which. Perhaps it was just his mind playing tricks because Ymitoth had suggested the tree was enchanted, but it did seem to have its own life force. There was also the fact that the trunk was completely hollow. The tree should have been quite dead, yet it wasn't. In fact, it was quite the opposite, lush and green and full of life. Whatever the case might have been, it was a fine place to get some much-needed rest.

Inside the great oak was a vast room much bigger than seemed possible when examining the tree from the outside. The oddity of the thing barely troubled Maelich at all as he found a nice cozy spot at the back of the room. Sleep came easily. He was quite weary from traveling all night without any rest. Even the excitement of his challenge was no match for his heavy eyelids. His slumber was disturbed by nothing, not even dreams.

He awoke a bit before midday, perfect timing. He hit the trail again. The way up Mount Elbahor was much easier than the way down Mount Elzkahon had been. That was good. He made good time and, judging from the distance ahead of him, would arrive right on schedule. He noticed that trees had starting popping up here and there as soon as he had passed the river. They grew thicker as he gained altitude. In fact, by the time he made half the distance from base to peak, a full-fledged forest of pine surrounded him. His thoughts drifted back to the Sobbing Forest. How could those trees that had seemed so fond of him be evil. Why would they help him? Had it all been a trick, and why? He couldn't spare too much thought on it. There was more pressing business at hand. His pace quickened as he continued into the thickening pines.

Night had completely fallen when Maelich began to see lights from the city of Maomnosett up ahead. He looked to the sky and reckoned himself to be just a few hours earlier than planned. It wasn't quite midnight yet. That was okay. He would wait. He stepped off the path, sat against a sturdy pine, and snacked on some dried tubberslat Ymitoth had packed for him. He would need all his energy in case his plan didn't go as smoothly as he wished. Ahm would be his greatest challenge yet. Ymitoth had suggested Ahm stood at least fifteen feet tall. Maelich glanced up at a towering tree across the path trying to gauge how high up the thing the giant's head would reach. Fifteen feet was more than double Maelich's height plus half again. He could scarcely imagine how the beast must look.

Roughly two hours had passed when Maelich decided he had waited long enough. The torchlights of the city had dimmed, and it looked as if Maomnosett's population of dwarves was fast asleep. Even still, he stuck close to the edge of the path, clinging to the shadows. As he approached the gates of the city, he could barely make out two shapes that appeared to be standing guard before the tallest pine he had ever seen in his entire life. There may have been another shape against the tree but he couldn't be sure. As he neared the spot, he realized there were two shapes against the tree. One was chained to it and the other hugging it. The air suddenly seemed heavy, saturated with despair. He could cling to the shadows and slip around the group completely unnoticed, but something deep in his gut wouldn't let him. After a brief struggle with his logical side, emotion won the day. Whatever calamity had dumped the sad group into their current state, he aimed to fix it for them.

Outside of the warm, orange glow of the torches that remained lit, the darkness was a black void. Maelich used that to his advantage. The dwarves neither saw nor heard him until he was upon them. Before he spoke to them he noted that all four of them were sniffling, the ghost of a good cry lingering among them. The sadness of the two against the tree seemed quite reasonable, but the other two were obviously guards. It seemed odd that two warriors, especially gruff dwarves, would shed tears for the sake of a prisoner. Perhaps an alliance with some unhappy dwarves would prove more useful than the element of surprise he would most certainly not get with this unhappy party going on right at the gates of the keep he intended to storm.

"Why so glum, my friends?" Maelich inquired with a soft, caring quality in his voice.

Aarvin spun, brandishing his axe. "Who goes there?" he demanded.

"Easy now, easy," Maelich continued with his soft tone as he stepped into the warm glow of the torches, "I am a friend. I wish only to help. It seems as though you have yourselves in a predicament none of you are happy with."

"That be our business," Laarvel answered as he turned to face the intruder. "Why not go ahead and state your business."

Maelich advanced with his arms outstretched, showing no signs of aggression. He could slaughter all of them in an instant if he saw fit, but he had no quarrel with them. Still, he hadn't much experience with dwarves, and the one with the axe looked as if he were ready for war.

"My name is Maelich," he began, "and I've come to relieve your king of his head." His smile beamed wide and friendly. He was ready to dodge that big axe if its blade sliced toward him, but something in his gut had him near certain these guards were at least slightly less than happy servants of Ahm.

Aarvin laughed out loud. "Aw piss off! Ye're nothing but a wee lad. Aye, ye might'n be taller than me, but ye're no man. That's for sure."

As Maelich's eyes became accustomed to the glow of the torches, he noticed what poor shape Bindaar was in. Pushing past Laarvel and Aarvin, he ran to the broken dwarf. Lips cracked to the point of bleeding served as the focal point of a face dry and pale from dehydration. Eyes wildly rolling about in their sockets assured Maelich the poor bloke was firmly planted on death's doorstep. The heat radiating off Bindaar's forehead nearly burned Maelich's lips as he gently pressed them against it. Time was no friend to either of them. Maelich quickly fumbled around in his cloak until he found his canteen. First, he splashed some water on Bindaar's face. Then he put the canteen to the poor dwarf's lips and coaxed him to drink slowly.

"That's it," Maelich coached, "nice and easy. You're going to be just fine." Then he turned to Doentaat, "Go. Fetch your friend more water. Hurry."

Confused apprehension settled into Doentaat's twisted expression, but he did as Maelich commanded. Maelich barely noticed Laarvel and Aarvin as they stood watching him work. He was too busy gathering a clear assessment of how much time he had left to keep the dwarf's soul from making its final journey to the Lake. As his eyes quickly scanned over Bindaar's beaten form, he noticed blood trickling from both the prisoner's wrists where the cuffs that bound him mercilessly cut into his flesh. He must have been bleeding for a good long while as his sleeves were soaked up to his elbows in what looked to Maelich like thick, black tar in the torchlight.

Maelich had nearly finished his assessment by the time Doentaat had returned with more water, two big jugs this time. Maelich motioned to him, "Come. See to your friend while I free him from these chains."

Doentaat didn't respond but again did as Maelich commanded.

Maelich glanced back at Laarvel and Aarvin as he circled the tree. They both seemed a bit apprehensive, but neither moved to stop him. Hopefully, that meant he could count on them to help him steal into Ahm's keep unscathed rather than attempt to stifle his efforts. He couldn't worry about it just then. A dwarf's life depended on him. Once he finally made it round to the opposite side of the tree, he released the brake on the spindle holding the chains, grabbed hold of the handles, and slowly lowered Bindaar into Doentaat's waiting arms.

Maelich charged back around the tree and hurriedly removed the cuffs first from Bindaar's wrists and then his ankles, which were in as bad of shape as his wrists. Then he tore off his cloak and quickly ripped it into strips.

He started firing off orders, first to Doentaat, "You. Run to your hut and fetch some food, bread if you have any," then to Laarvel, "You. Head into the field and bring me some fairy weed," and finally to Aarvin, "You. Just beyond the edge of the trees is some wild dragon blossom. Bring as much as you can carry."

The three dwarves paused briefly, sharing confused glances. Finally, Doentaat shrugged his shoulders and darted off for his hut.

Laarvel and Aarvin followed suit and got to their respective tasks as well. Once the dwarves left, Maelich began soaking some of the strips of his cloak and cleaning Bindaar's wounds. The wounded dwarf's condition finally seemed to be improving. At least his eyes weren't so crazy anymore. His lips began moving as if he were trying to speak.

After some effort, soft and raspy sounds accompanied all the movement. "Thanks," he began, barely a whisper.

Maelich cut him off, "Don't speak. Save your energy. There is no need to thank me now. If you really want to thank me, save it for when your strength has returned."

Aarvin was the first to return from his task, his arms full of dragon blossom. He dumped the flowers into a pile next to Maelich. Maelich smiled and nodded a thank you. Then he grabbed a handful of dragon blossom and began grinding it up on some of the soaked cloth strips he had made. Once he had a handful of the cloth strips saturated in dragon blossom, he used them as bandages to mend the wounds the cuffs had inflicted on Bindaar's wrists and ankles.

He looked up at Aarvin, "The dragon blossom will help the wounds to heal and ease the burning."

Aarvin nodded, "Aye. Do ye practice medicine, lad?"

"No," Maelich shook his head and smiled, "but I was trained to survive in the wild by a great warrior. Your friend is in good hands."

"Aye, I be seeing that. I be wishing I could be calling Bindaar friend. Alas I be one of the reasons he'd been hanging on that tree." A tear trickled down his cheek as his head shook slowly back and forth.

"Don't blame yourself," Maelich reassured him. "Ahm is your king correct? Fear is a great motivator. It will make a man, or a dwarf for that matter, do things he wouldn't normally do."

Just then Laarvel came running up with a handful of fairy weed buds. Maelich took one bud, rolled it up and stuck it between Bindaar's lower lip and his teeth. Then he gave him a bit more water. Bindaar looked as if he might try to get up off the ground, but Maelich put a hand out onto his chest. He looked in his eyes and shook his head.

Maelich kept his eyes focused on Bindaar's as he continued speaking to the other two, "The fairy weed will ease his mind, relax him. We need him to be relaxed."

It wasn't long before Doentaat returned with a great horse sack full of food. There was much more than even all five of them could eat. Maelich stood to greet him, giving him a smirk and slight chuckle for all his extra effort. Doentaat returned Maelich's smirk with a look of true concern. The poor fellow was really taking the blame squarely on his own shoulders. Maelich gave the dwarf's shoulder a light pat as he took the horse sack from him.

"Now is time for healing, not regret," he said.

Maelich sat Bindaar up against the sacred pine and began feeding him little bits at a time. It would be some time before the dwarf was back on his feet. Sadly, Maelich had already wasted too much. Judging by the stars, it had to have been close to midnight. He'd have to leave Bindaar with his friend and hope the other two would help him.

"You," Maelich pointed at Doentaat, "what do they call you?"

"I be Doentaat, of the line of Alhouim," Doentaat's distraction was apparent in his tone.

"Ah, royal blood, splendid," Maelich felt genuinely honored to be in the presence of one who might be king of Alhouim under different circumstances. "Do you suppose you can carry your friend on your own. I fear I'm running out of time, and I must tend to the business of lopping off your king's head."

"Aye. I can carry him," Doentaat nodded. "Do ye suppose ye can really be killing that bastard Ahm?"

Maelich gave Doentaat a wide, confident smile, "There is no doubt in my mind. His mother will cry if she sees him when I'm through with him."

"Good go ye then, lad!" Doentaat gave Maelich a stiff palm to the shoulder, "Bloody his arse!"

With that Doentaat gathered up Bindaar, the horse sack, and what was left of the "medicines" and headed on back to his hut. The slightest glint of hope fraternized with the despair weighing down the dwarf's brow. That little glimmer, that brief speck, moved Maelich more than anything he could remember, even more than the sight of Bindaar nearly dead and chained to that giant pine. Ahm's head was more than just a prize. That monster's head on a spike represented freedom for an entire city who had been oppressed by the giant for generations. Maelich's desire to earn the coveted crest of Havenstahl suddenly paled against his desire to see true justice for these poor, beaten dwarves.

Once Doentaat had left with Bindaar, Maelich turned to Laarvel and Aarvin. "Well gentlemen, sorry, gentle-dwarves," he began as he raised his eyebrows and put a mock look of royalty on his face, "will you be helping me find my way to Ahm? Or will I be on my own in my quest?"

Laarvel spoke first, "Aye, lad, I be terrified of that monster, but if ye think ye'll be defeating him, I be showing ye the way. Don't be taking no offense to this, but I won't be taking ye all the way in. Just in case, ye know."

Aarvin piped up in the same chord, "I be with ye too. I hope ye be killing that bastard. We been living in fear long enough."

"Good then," Maelich beamed, "take me as close as you are comfortable. I'll see my way in from there."

The streets of the city were dark and empty. Nevertheless, the group stuck to the shadows to avoid any peeping eyes that might have been aroused by Doentaat. He hadn't been terribly quiet with the load he bore. Luckily, the trip was uneventful. Not a soul stirred on the dark streets of Alhouim.

Laarvel quietly stopped the group behind an empty barrel that sat in front of "Boonda's Pub". It was too dark to make out the wooden sign on the front of the building. That was a shame because it was a lovely sign. Boonda's was painted in a fancy font above a humorous picture of a happy dwarf toting a pint of ale and clicking his heels. The word Pub was painted below the picture. It was fine work and considered one of the best signs in Maomnosett. It hearkened back to happier, carefree times.

Laarvel spoke quietly, "There it be, the south gate to the courtyard. We can't be taking ye any further than this."

Maelich nodded and whispered back, "What do they call you two fine, sturdy dwarves?"

"I be Laarvel," Laarvel replied in the same quiet tone. "This fellow be Aarvin."

Maelich gave them both another wide smile, "Well, Laarvel and Aarvin, I've a giant to slay and a head to collect. I expect to share a pint with you after my trial is complete."

"Aye, lad," Aarvin whispered, "a few pints we be sharing then."

Maelich continued alone, remaining in shadows until he reached a spot just east of the south tower. The gate yawned, a deep blackness within. No guards were posted there. That was a bit unsettling. Bare streets could easily be justified given the late hour and early start necessary for every dwarf. A lack of guards at an open gate was not. Was it hubris on the part of their giant king or a trap? There was no way to be sure. At that moment, Maelich was only certain of one thing, it was too late to turn back. His path led into the ominous darkness of that massive, unguarded gate. He quietly drew in a deep breath, gathered himself, and stepped as confidently as he could into the orange light. Nothing.

Unsettling quiet surrounded him as he remained completely still holding his breath and listening until his lungs burned. All he could hear was the faint squeaking from the chains of shop signs hanging in front of their respective shops and motivated by the lightest of breezes gently pushing them about as they gave sway to the soft caresses. He lost himself in their rhythm for a moment. Then he shook his head. Forward or back, he decided, but he couldn't stand there all night.

Adrenaline raced through his body as the hair on his arms and the nape of his neck raised up in anticipation of whatever might be lurking around the next corner. A desire to charge headlong through the gate died a quick death at the hands of a need for caution. He slipped quietly up to the edge of the gate, gathered himself, and then spun quickly around the corner. Nothing still. He found himself in the hall between the inner and outer walls of the courtyard. He stood for a few moments again, listening. Moving toward the inner wall and pressing closely to it, he peered into the courtyard. There was nothing but more darkness. He stared into it for a moment, long enough to give his eyes a chance to adjust. They quickly became accustomed to the dark, but he still saw nothing. 'Now or never,' he thought.

Fighting back the fear causing him second thoughts, Maelich sucked in another deep breath and strolled nonchalantly into the empty courtyard. Fifty steps in, the world around him blazed to life. The gates crashed down behind him as hundreds of torches lining the walls of the courtyard instantly blazed to life. It was like midday. Apparently, his visit was no surprise to the king. He spun in a circle, quickly surveying his surroundings. The courtyard was wide and open, no cover whatsoever. Hundreds of dwarves dressed in full battle armor charged from every direction. Their axes were sharp and ready. Maelich's fingers brushed the leather grip of his sword handle before quickly retreating. He decided to let his attackers make the first move. There was still no sign of his giant, and he was still holding onto the hope that dwarves would rally behind him when he attacked. A few moments passed, and he was surrounded. The dwarves advanced no further.

Maelich's voice was smooth and friendly as he played as calmly as he could, "Hello, my friends. I fear I'm a bit lost. I'm looking for a large fellow who goes by the name of Maomnosett Ahm."

No dwarf spoke, but Maelich did get a response. "You are lost like a lourng among amatilazo, my miniscule friend," Ahm's voice boomed, disturbing the silence and sending a chill down Maelich's spine.

Maelich wasn't completely sure of the reference, but he believed the lourng to be an animal of the pasture bred for food and clothing. On the other hand, he was quite certain what amatilazo were and more certain he wasn't at all fond of the reference, "This lourng is unimpressed by a hunter who hides behind dwarves. If you fancy yourself the amatilazo who would feast upon this lourng, come claim your prize. That is…unless you're a coward and would have your army attack me in your stead."

Ahm grunted something that might have been a chuckle, before replying with a deep growl, "Perhaps I'll feast upon your loose tongue first. I have never entertained disrespect in my court and don't intend to accept it from an unseasoned, false warrior such as you. When Yfregeof told of the sacrifice he would be sending, he never mentioned the extra spice that would be included in my meal."

Maelich's jaw fell slack as his attempt to suppress the surprise on his face miserably failed. Yfregeof had warned Ahm of his coming. He had no intention of letting Maelich take the trials. He had merely intended him as a sacrifice to Ahm. Why? The question burned in him. Why would the king of the mightiest clan of men offer sacrifice to the likes of Maomnosett Ahm?

Despite his shock at the betrayal, he did his best to sound undaunted, "Then you know why I have come."

"I know why you are here, and I know why you think you are here," Ahm continued, adding a note of condescension to his voice. "You believe you have snuck into my city and breached my stronghold in order to slay me and have my head as your prize. This in an effort to obtain the mark of a warrior from the…" he paused and chuckled slightly, "great city of Havenstahl. The true reason you have been guided into my presence is to serve as a sacrifice from my loyal servant, Yfregeof. You see, Maelich…" the giant paused, "What's that? I sense surprise in you. Of course, I know your name. I know all about you, hero. As I was saying, Yfregeof became my servant when he decided he was ready to take the throne of Havenstahl away from his father. I was quite displeased with Yfrahnu anyway. He was always trying to renegotiate new trade agreements and other such nonsense, terribly boring. When Yfregeof came before me and laid out his plan, I was intrigued. It was delightfully wicked. I raised the price of prang for Havenstahl twice what it had been. This sent Yfrahnu into a wild rage. He came unannounced, just as I expected him to, and demanded I submit to negotiations or face a war with Havenstahl. He brought with him his only brother, Ymantyl, which perfectly completed my plan because he would be Yfregeof's only challenger to the throne of Havenstahl. I feasted on them both."

Ahm made a slurping sound and some other grunts, feigning pleasure, and continued, "Have you ever had occasion to try the flesh of men? Of course not, my young slayer of giants. I assure you it is quite succulent. In any event, I now had control of the throne of Havenstahl, and it's been that way ever since."

Maelich stood dumbfounded as he absorbed Ahm's words. This treachery would enrage Ymitoth. As he digested Ahm's pompous proclamation, his own rage grew. Perhaps the story was some kind of trickery to dissuade him or take him off his guard, but it all fit too perfectly. A sudden sense of urgency manifested deep in his gut. Ymitoth was the only heir to the throne, and the only man alive who knew of his cousin's treachery was safely out of the way, a gift for a giant. If Yfregeof would send his own father to be slaughtered, he wouldn't have a second thought about having his cousin slain. As thoughts raced through Maelich's head, his control slowly began slipping away. He had to hold on. Rage alone would not be enough to defeat Ahm.

He did his best to match Ahm's condescending tone, "I see you're as boring and long-winded as you are tall and worthless. Enough of your venom, viper, kneel before me and I'll make this as quick and painless as possible."

Maelich's words drew a great bit of laughter from the solida's surrounding him. Ahm appeared less amused. As Maelich hoped, the proud giant wouldn't stand for too many pokes at his ego, especially jabs fired by a mere boy.

"Enough," Ahm shouted. "Damn fools, make way!"

The solida's who had been surrounding Maelich backed quickly away, loosening their formation and spreading out behind him. Their laughter ended instantly. Maelich strained his eyes in the direction of the palace but he still could not see where the giant was hiding. He gasped when he finally spied the massive creature. Like a living mountain wielding a mighty spear, the beast leapt high into the dark sky, covering roughly half the distance between the throne and Maelich, before landing surprisingly lightly and pounding his spear into the dirt. The mass of hard flesh quickly produced a bow, pulled an arrow from the quiver on his back, and took aim at Maelich.

Ahm was even larger than Maelich imagined. He wore a long nap of thick, black hair and a bush of a beard. His features were like that of a man, but he was nearly three times the size. The monster's scowl revealed teeth sharp as daggers.

Doubt threatened to humble Maelich before the greatest battle of his life even began. Luckily, he had precious few moments to admire his opponent before it did. An arrow the size of a spear raced from Ahm's bow. The world slowed around Maelich as he became acutely aware of every sound, sight, and smell right at that moment. Ahm's bow vibrated from the shot, humming lightly beneath the whistle of the arrow slicing through the calmly swirling air of the courtyard. The stench of an army of dwarves sweating under the weight of full palace armor danced around among the currents. Light from the torches around the courtyard glinted off the razor edges of the arrowhead. Maelich stepped left and leaned away from the attack. Reaching out with both hands, he caught the arrow about halfway down its shaft. The great size of the thing coupled with its momentum carried him about ten feet before he fell to the ground with it. He quickly regained his feet and fired it back at Ahm with all his might.

The arrow raced toward Ahm's face. The giant was readying another arrow and didn't see the one heading for him until it was too close to completely avoid. Though he saved his face by dodging, he earned a deep gash in his left shoulder. In his failed effort to avoid the arrow, he pulled his next shot to the right completely missing Maelich and impaling a dwarf against the hard stone of the courtyard wall instead. The arrow's shaft cracked in half on impact and twisted the poor soul apart in a bloody explosion of meat and entrails.

Ahm dropped his bow as his hand instinctively shot up to the wound on his shoulder. The low groan slipping past his lips seemed to vibrate the air.

Taking advantage of Ahm's momentary incapacitation, Maelich

drew his sword as he charged. He covered the distance quickly, but the giant was just as quick to get his head back into the battle. Maelich barely brought his blade up in time to parry Ahm's spear. The blow carried so much force, it sent him flailing to the ground.

Once Maelich managed to regain his feet, he opted for dodging the blows rather than trying to match strength with the giant whose spear seemed to attack from every direction. He flipped, slipped, and weaved around thrusts and swings, finally sidestepping as the massive thing crashed to the ground barely missing his head. There was his opening.

As Ahm raised the spear back up, Maelich jumped up onto the shaft of it. It was thick as a small tree's truck. He used the momentum to help carry him over the giant's head, flipping over the mountain of flesh and landing softly behind him. Crouching low into his landing, he spun around and slashed the back of Ahm's legs. The cut was deep, almost to the bone. It tore muscles and tendons as it gashed into the giant's flesh, wrecking the monster's hamstrings. The walls of the courtyard shook with Ahm's cry, as both he and his spear crashed to the ground.

Maelich was in the air before Ahm's big body hit the ground. He leapt onto the giant's chest with his sword raised high. Just as he was about to bury his sword deep into Ahm's black heart, the beast swatted at him. The massive arm slammed into the full length of his body, knocking the wind from his lungs and tossing him to the side. At least fifteen feet of earth passed beneath him before he hammered into the dirt.

"Solida's," Ahm yelled, "seize him!"

No dwarf moved.

Ahm shouted again, "Shackle this runt or I'll crush every last one of you!" His tone was near frantic, but every dwarf remained still.

Maelich shook his head and slowly rose to his feet. It took him a moment to get his wind back. The giant was strong. Once his lungs stopped burning, he sucked in a deep breath and stalked back over to where Ahm lay. By this time the giant had rolled onto his stomach and was trying to crawl back to his palace. Without the use of his legs, he was having a rather difficult time of it. Maelich stood over his left shoulder as Ahm looked up at him and roared. The wind from the giant's lungs was so furious it blew Maelich's hair all about. Maelich raised his sword and slammed it through Ahm's neck. The stroke was clean, removing the beast's head amid a crimson gush.

Though brief, the battle had taken a toll on Maelich. He kept his feet only long enough to catch a glimpse of Ahm's eyes as they lolled wildly about in their sockets and marvel at the rage in his expression as his tongue and lips convulsed. Maelich fell exhausted to the ground next to his victim wondering if thoughts still ran through the disembodied head.

Silence filled the courtyard. Maelich lay flat for a few moments, just long enough to regain his composure. Then he sat up and examined the mighty Maomnosett Ahm for a moment. 'I have proven my worth as a warrior,' he thought. The moment of peaceful clarity was far too brief as he remembered the army of dwarves surrounding he and his victim. The battle was not finished. There was no time for rest or quiet contemplation. He quickly scrambled to his feet and spun to face the solidas.

The expressions on the faces staring back at Maelich from the crowd of solidas surrounding him appeared shocked rather than angry or vengeful. In fact, many of them even appeared relieved. The attack he expected never came. Instead, the entire crowd erupted in a cheer so throaty it shook the walls of the courtyard even more than Ahm's roar had. It took him a moment to process what was happening, but it finally occurred to him that the eyes staring back at him weren't looking upon an adversary who had just killed their king. Instead, they were gazing in amazement at the young hero who had freed them from the weight of a cruel tyrant.

Axes fell to the ground and fists pumped into the air in victory. Dwarves rushed to Maelich from all sides, raised him up on their shoulders, and chanted his name. Laarvel and Aarvin were among the throng. They laughed and patted Maelich on the back. Other dwarves danced while still others leapt and flipped and rolled. The mighty Ahm had been killed at the hand of a hero who had strolled into their midst a mere boy. From that day on, they would know him as the man who saved them.

It wasn't long before ale flowed and music played. The air around the courtyard seemed lighter. Here and there among the crowd there were even dwarves singing. The dwarves of Alhouim were famous for the songs they would belt out while tromping off to the mines in days all but forgotten. According to what Maelich had learned of the dwarves before starting his quest, no dwarf had sung a note since shortly after Ahm took the throne.

It was all nearly too much for Maelich to digest. He had expected to at least have a need to flee with Ahm's head if not spill many a dwarf's blood. Instead he found himself as the guest of honor in a celebration pulsing with the energy of centuries of frustration. The party lasted until the sun threatened to rise. Alhouim was alive again like it hadn't been in hundreds of summers.

CHAPTER 9
TWO KINGS

The morning had come and gone before Maelich woke to the tantalizing aroma of some form of meat. He couldn't quite place it, but it smacked of something that needed investigating. Or so he thought. His head spun like the wheels of a horse carriage moving at a gallop when he tried to sit up. It didn't seem possible, but the pounding engulfing his entire head was even worse. He had never been stabbed in the head before, but he imagined the pain must be similar to what he was feeling just then. That pounding must be exactly what it feels like to have your head mercilessly impaled repeatedly. He quickly laid his head back onto his rough pillow. Nausea swept over him, quickly bringing the contents of his belly and the acid taste of bile to the back of his throat. His entire body convulsed and then locked as he leaned over the side of the cot and vomited a thick, rancid fluid onto the dusty wooden plats of the floor. It burned as it went and left a foul, sour taste in its wake. Once his belly had nothing left to say, he lifted his pillow and rested his head back on the cot.

"A bit too much of the ale," Doentaat said with a chuckle as he came with a mop to clean up Maelich's foul-smelling mess.

Maelich rubbed his head and mumbled, "Where am I?"

Doentaat continued to work diligently as he replied, "Ye be at the humble abode of Bindaar and Doentaat. Don't ye remember being dropped here last night," he paused and then corrected himself, "or rather, early on this morn by Laarvel and Aarvin?"

"No, but that answers my second question. How did I get here?"

He still couldn't manage more than a mumble.

"Ah lad," Doentaat spoke soothingly, "just ye relax. Sleep off that hangover ye got yourself into, and we can worry about getting ye home later. Just look at me luck," he continued mostly to himself, "two cots full of sickies for me to look after."

Maelich did sleep a bit longer as Doentaat concocted some brew on the fire that filled the small hut with steam. The steam was said to cure the effects of too much ale. It wouldn't hurt Bindaar's condition either. He was slowly regaining his strength and even speaking a bit. Doentaat told him all about the events of the prior evening. Maelich had guaranteed that no dwarf would ever again be hung from the sacred pine, and the city of Maomnosett was no more. The city of Alhouim had been reborn in one mighty slash of a young lad's powerful sword.

When Maelich finally woke, the sun was already beginning to set. His head still felt a bit thick and his belly a bit squishy, but he was a world apart from his condition that morning. Doentaat had a pail of warm water he had heated on the fire ready for Maelich to wash himself up. He did just that and his condition improved further. There was a city of dwarves out in the streets waiting to cheer their hero one more time and send him on his way with his prize. When Maelich appeared in the doorway of Doentaat's hut, the crowd outside erupted. They had impaled Ahm's head on his own spear to present to Maelich. They did this quite ceremoniously among shouts of, "Hooray for Maelich, conquering king of Alhouim!"

Maelich accepted the prize and spoke in as strong a voice as his groggy condition would allow, "Now is not the time to accept the rule of another from outside of your ranks. Dwarves have served the purpose of others long enough. Now is the time for dwarves to control their own destiny. There is one among you who displays dwarf perfection and falls in the bloodline of Alhouim, father of all dwarves. This dwarf will serve as a gracious and powerful king." Maelich reached back, put an arm around Doentaat's shoulder and continued, "Give your allegiance to Doentaat of Alhouim!"

The crowd erupted again. This time with chants of both Maelich and Doentaat's names. The dwarves of Alhouim would require a good deal of assistance to establish their own rule and draft their own laws, Maelich knew this. However, he also realized they were a hard-working race that was up to the task of rebuilding the grandeur of their history.

It was a task that should belong to them.

Maelich thanked the crowd and said his good-byes as dwarf after dwarf begged him to stay just a while longer. He would have liked nothing more. Unfortunately, it was time to go. He was already well behind schedule. The longest good-byes were saved for Doentaat, Bindaar, Laarvel, and Aarvin. They all took their turns telling him what an impressive lad he was, and they all invited him to come back and visit often. Then they packed him up and sent him on his way, watching him bound down the trail as he headed south toward Havenstahl.

Maelich moved quickly down the path, ignoring the fatigue that gripped him. He would nap a bit at sunrise, but he couldn't afford to lose much time. He would more than likely be presumed dead. That would be fine, for his return would be the first news anyone in Havenstahl would have of his success, including that vile bastard, Yfregeof. He didn't want the king to have any warning. There would probably be a battle when he finally arrived, and the only ally he was certain of was Ymitoth.

Maelich made much better time returning to Havenstahl than he had on his way to Maomnosett, or rather, Alhouim. It was about midday when he finally arrived at the north gate where Ymitoth waited for him, pacing nervously back and forth. Ymitoth saw Ahm's head first as it poked up over the hilltop before Maelich could be seen. He drew his sword and charged at the giant, hoping to slay him before he hit level ground. His heart sunk into his boots as the realization that Maelich had failed and was probably being digested sunk in. Sadness quickly gave way to rage as he raised his sword. Suddenly, Maelich's head appeared. Ymitoth dropped his sword and ran to his son, embracing him and marveling at Ahm's giant head perched atop the mighty spear Maelich now bore.

He opened his mouth to speak, but Maelich beat him to the punch. "Stop them!" he shouted. The two guards at the gate quickly retreated toward the palace.

"Guards," Ymitoth hollered, "halt!"

The guards looked as if they might disobey their commander, but they reluctantly heeded his word. Ymitoth squinted his eyes and looked first to Maelich, then to his guards, and asked, "What?"

"I have much to tell you, but first, Yfregeof cannot know of my return before I see him," Maelich spoke quickly and quietly as the guards nervously considered his presence there.

"So, tell me then," Ymitoth replied, raising his palms as if to ask, 'what?' again.

Maelich continued, "The murder of your father and Yfregeof's father was not due to the heat of failed negotiations. It was planned by Yfregeof and Ahm. Yfregeof was so desirous of the throne he struck a deal with Ahm to eliminate the king and the only other immediate claim to the throne. In exchange, Yfregeof would send him sacrifices and submit to the unfair agreements Ahm was attempting to force on Yfrahnu. That is why he would not send the warriors of Havenstahl to slay the wicked king."

Ymitoth shook with rage as he picked his sword up off the ground. His teeth clenched tightly as his lips moved around silent curses. He looked back to the guards and then charged them. He kicked one to the ground before grabbing the other by the hair and yanking him to his knees.

"Are ye under orders from that coward Yfregeof?" he growled through clenched teeth.

The petrified guard could manage only a whimper as he put his hands up and quivered. This enraged Ymitoth even further, "What be your orders, scrod?"

"M...M...Milord, Yfregeof be having us inform him if the lad be making it back. He did, so that's what we mean to do." The guard's fear sickened Ymitoth.

"Ye'll be informing no one of nothing," he hissed as he brought the handle of his sword down against the side of the guard's head.

Then he kicked the guard on the ground in the head and looked back at Maelich, "We go. Ye will be storming into that throne room with that spear held high, as if ye know nothing about his treachery. I be waiting in the hall."

Maelich charged on up the steps and made his way toward the palace and on to Yfregeof's throne room. He received many an odd look charging through the streets of the city with an impaled head perched upon a giant spear. Under different circumstances he may have given some thought to how comically grisly he must have looked lugging around a spear the size of a tree with a giant's twisted head upon it. There wasn't any time for that.

The short jaunt from the north gate to the door of Yfregeof's throne room seemed a lifetime. The shock squatting on the faces of the guards posted there assured Maelich they couldn't be counted as allies. They both looked like they had seen a ghost. That meant they expected Maelich to be one at that point. That also meant they knew of their king's plan. He was right on their heels as they fled into the throne room.

A look of confident pleasure fought past Maelich's rage and rested upon his face as he marched triumphantly into the hall with his prize held high. Yfregeof jumped up from his chair and appeared as if he might flee. Instead, the king sat back down and dropped his gaze to the floor. Maelich almost felt sorry for the king. The poor sod looked like he was trying to solve a dandy of a riddle. If only Maelich could be in the king's head just then.

"Maelich," Yfregeof attempted to boom, poorly feigning joy as he stood with his arms outstretched. "Welcome home, lad!"

Maelich remained cool. The entire room stunk of Yfregeof's fear. This fact could have only one of two possible outcomes. Either Yfregeof would crumble and beg for mercy, or he would feel backed into a corner like a scrod who's been whipped too many times and lash out with all his fury. Maelich couldn't decide which he'd prefer. He'd love to look deep into Yfregeof's empty eyes as his blade slipped into his heart. However, depending on how much support Ymitoth had left in the city, Yfregeof may still be well protected. Maelich continued to play the part.

"If his majesty finds it pleasing," he began, bowing ceremoniously and raising Ahm's head high above his own, "I offer the head of Maomnosett Ahm. His terror will haunt Havenstahl no more."

Forcing a painfully fake smile to his lips, Yfregeof stammered, "Ye have passed your trial, Maelich. I must say, I be quite impressed with ye, lad. Ye have earned the crest of Havenstahl."

Yfregeof clapped his hands. The loud smack echoed through the quiet chamber. The master of his guard moved quickly to a spot directly before the throne and bowed while crouching to one knee. "Step forward," Yfregeof commanded. Then he whispered something into the guard's ear. The guard nodded and then disappeared behind the king's throne. Yfregeof squinted and unconsciously sneered as his eyes followed the man until he was out of sight. The fake smile quickly returned to his lips as he rose and approached Maelich, arms outstretched as if to embrace the lad.

Maelich thought about drawing his sword as Yfregeof neared, but it was too early to show his hand. Instead his eyes scanned the king intensely like a loquoi gliding along the river searching for fish among the currents. When the king was within five feet of him, he noticed that his right hand was moving to a slight bulge in his robe under his left arm. Maelich threw down Ahm's spear and jumped backward pulling his head farther away as he went. Yfregeof's dagger whistled mere inches in front of Maelich's nose. He gathered himself and leapt further backward still as the king slashed again and again at him. Pure unfaltering hatred gleamed in the king's eyes as he advanced.

Maelich timed the attacks as he retreated, finally stopping short and throwing his left arm out to meet the blow. He pounded Yfregeof's forearm with his own, aiming for the nerve running down it. Apparently, he hadn't hit it squarely. The king's grip loosened, but he didn't drop the dagger. Maelich didn't bother dwelling on the failure. He balled his right hand up in a fist and fired it at Yfregeof's jaw sending phlegmy spit and blood all over a guard's helmet and the king reeling. Immediately after his punch landed, he snapped a kick to Yfregeof's ribs and dropped him to the floor.

Maelich drew his sword as Yfregeof's head pounded against polished marble. He would have preferred to save the vile waste for Ymitoth, but the king forced his hand. He would act as executioner and avenge the death of his mentor's father. However, Yfregeof proved far wilier than Maelich had given him credit. He didn't see the king's dagger flying toward him until it was too late. Despite dodging the assault, he was much too close to get away clean. His heart remained unscathed, but Yfregeof's dagger sliced deep into his shoulder.

A wild howl tore through the room. Maelich's chest and arm burned as if a flaming torch were pressed against them. The blade of his sword dropped to the ground as he stumbled backward, away from Yfregeof. Blood soaked his sleeve as his shoulder pulsed with pain. He maintained his grip on the sword but the pain in his arm kept him from raising it up off the ground. His other hand shot up to the dagger. He had never felt a pain like this before. There was something else he was unfamiliar with, fear. It gripped him as his eyes darted about the room. What would he do next?

Before Maelich could put together a cognizant thought, Yfregeof's voice boomed, "Seize him!"

The guards appeared apprehensive as they approached, but they advanced toward Maelich nevertheless. His head whipped back and forth as he contemplated his new opponents. Doubt filled him. With his own blood freely flowing, he felt none of the invincibility he had felt when facing Ahm. He gave Yfregeof's blade a yank and pulled it out amidst a sloppy, slurping pop followed by an even stronger stream of blood than had been flowing. The room seemed to tilt slightly as he stumbled while attempting to raise his sword high enough to defend himself against Yfregeof's guards. He sluggishly moved through his sword techniques, but they were sloppy. They wouldn't have intimidated a child, much less seasoned warriors. The guards continued to advance. Maelich looked back to Yfregeof who mocked with a sickening grin.

"Halt!" Ymitoth's voice filled the throne room with all the strength and authority Maelich remembered from his training. "Place the king under arrest for plotting the murder of his father and mine!"

Maelich followed Ymitoth's fiery gaze to Yfregeof's shocked expression. The king's guards stopped their advance. Ymitoth was the commander of all the warriors of Havenstahl. They had to obey him. Yfregeof looked to his guards pleadingly while more and more soldiers poured into the room, swords drawn. Even if the king's guards had wanted to protect their king, they were horribly outnumbered and would surely be slain. Relief swept over Maelich as he slumped to his knees.

Ymitoth ordered two guards to bandage up Maelich's wound and then fixed his gaze back on the viper who shared his bloodline. "Treacherous bastard!" he shouted at Yfregeof.

"No, no, there be no truth to it. The lad lies," Yfregeof whimpered as he put his hands out before him and shook his head, cowering before Ymitoth.

The king's eyes moved from door to door. All of them were blocked. There would be no escape. "Please," he pleaded. "Ye be me blood. Don't I be deserving a trial?"

"Aye," Ymitoth scowled, "this be your trial. The evidence has been heard and now I be giving your sentence, worm!" His cold stare pierced into Yfregeof's soul, "String him up."

Yfregeof struggled as hands grabbed at him and a noose was fashioned around his neck. He kicked and screamed and cried out, but his efforts were unsuccessful. Within moments his limbs were all tied fast and he was perched on a chair wearing a noose at the end of a thick rope that had been flung over the rafters. He wept as he begged for Ymitoth's forgiveness and admitted his guilt and sorrow for all he had done before all who watched. The court was unimpressed. The faces echoed their feelings of betrayal at having supported him in the loss of his father. There had been genuine pity for him throughout the kingdom, and it had all been a lie. There was neither love nor sympathy for the great king Yfregeof in that room. None.

"I won't be asking if ye'd be liking a blindfold," Ymitoth's teeth were clenched tight, "as I be intended to watch your eyes as ye die, vermin."

Ymitoth's foot shot out like a snake as he kicked the chair out from under Yfregeof. The king fell to a spot just inches above the floor. His neck didn't snap. Ymitoth watched intently as Yfregeof's eyes rolled wildly around in his head, and his body flopped about on the end of the rope. Torment twisted his face up around a silent scream. The struggle lasted a matter of a few minutes until there wasn't a twitch left in him. Ymitoth carefully examined the hanging carcass. Then he quickly pulled out his sword and plunged it into Yfregeof's chest, through his heart, and out the other side. The dead king's blood spattered his face as he howled and fell to his knees. His roar filled with anger, hatred, loss, and agony. He stayed there for a moment speaking to his father in prayer, asking for his blessing on the vengeance of his name. He took a deep breath, rose, and collected his sword, wiping Yfregeof's blood off his blade quickly like it were some form of poison. Finally, he felt closure.

After a time, he ordered the removal of Yfregeof's carcass. It would be tossed over the side of the mountain, as was the customary way to deal with treason. There would be no honorable funeral. Then he quickly addressed those in the court. He explained the depth of Yfregeof's treachery, and he accepted the throne amidst the cheers of those who had thought for years that it should be his. Their allegiance to him had been earned long before his father had even been slain.

Before the day was over, Ymitoth had already begun work on his first order of business as king. He established a delegation to march to Alhouim and repair Havenstahl's relationship with the great dwarf city. Yfregeof had done much to damage that friendship, but both cities were led by new kings. Things were changing, and he would make sure they changed for the better. He would follow his delegation a few days later. He still had to see Maelich off to start the next part of his journey.

That would be a sad good-bye.

CHAPTER 10
HUMILITY

Maelich lay asleep upon a bed, soaked in the sweat of two days of fever. Hagen, the greatest healer in Havenstahl, arguably the greatest healer in all of Ouloos, watched over him. Yfregeof's dagger had infected Maelich, and he had been in the grips of a relentless fever for the better part of two days. Hagen had finally managed to break the fever, but the lad was still under the attack of infection. Ymitoth had been in to visit quite often, pacing and worrying over him. However, there was much to do, and there were many seeking an audience with him. Therefore, though the visits were quite frequent, they were brief.

Maelich began to stir and babble. He tossed and turned, apparently battling some foe in a dream. Hagen looked on with little concern at this point. The lad was healing nicely. It wouldn't be long before he woke. Then some fresh sheets, water, and perhaps a bit of a meal would have him on his feet again in no time. Still, his obviously violent dream did appear to be taking a toll on him.

The battle, or whatever was going on in Maelich's dream, lasted for about a quarter of an hour. When it finally finished, he sat straight up in his bed and howled like he had been stabbed through the heart. His head turned this way and that, as his eyes moved all about the room. His breaths were short and heavy, nearly gasps. Hagen ran to him, held him and wiped his forehead with a wet cloth, reassuring him that he was safe and everything was right in his world.

After a short time Maelich relaxed. His heartbeat slowed to a more normal pace, and he gained some control of his breathing. Though he had slept for almost two days straight, he felt exhausted. As he calmed he realized he was in the same room where he had spent his first night in Havenstahl. His encounter with the king in throne room rushed back, but the end was missing. What of Ymitoth? What of Yfregeof? His head throbbed. He needed water and answers.

As Maelich gained a bit of control over his breathing, he considered the fellow caring for him. He had no idea who the man was. Should he feel safe or prepare to defend himself? He had no idea. Equally vexing was the fact he had woken twice in this room with no knowledge of how he'd arrived. It was a lovely room, but he had no idea what it was like to enter it. The simple oddness of that thought kept his mind for a moment.

When Maelich finally spoke, what he had of a voice came out hoarse and rough. "Who are you?" was the most immediate question on his mind.

"They call me Hagen. Lay back. Save your strength. I'll fetch you some water," Hagen's replies were short and carried little emotion.

"Hagen," Maelich began, still with the gravel in his throat, "how did I come to be in your care?"

"Ymitoth summoned me to heal you," he replied as he drew water from a jug on a table across the room from Maelich's bed.

If Ymitoth summoned this fellow, then he must still be alive at least. "Where is Ymitoth, and what of the king?" A little excitement had crept into Maelich's voice.

"Relax, lad. The two you speak of are one and the same, and that one is tending to matters quite pressing. He has been in and out, but there are many grabbing his ear right now," the healer's reply remained monotone.

Maelich considered Hagen's statement for a moment and then continued, "So what then of Yfregeof?"

"Yfregeof is no more," Hagen had returned to Maelich's bedside offering water and a fine chalice containing a rancid smelling liquid. "Drink this, then the water. This elixir has a foul smell and an equally awful taste, but it will help you to gain your strength back. Then we'll see if we can't get some food in you."

Maelich sniffed lightly at the purple liquid. The pungent odor twisted his face up and had him on the verge of gagging. He looked pleadingly at Hagen. All the old healer offered in return was a raised eyebrow and a slight nod of his head. Oh well, Maelich drank. He took it all in one big gulp not wanting to prolong his torture any more than necessary. Oddly, the flavor didn't match the smell. The taste certainly wasn't pleasing, but it wasn't nearly as awful as he expected. Still, he chased it with water as soon as the chalice was empty.

Whatever was in the drink he had just gulped must have been some pretty strong medicine. He could feel heat radiating out from his chest to the rest of his body. An odd numbness took hold of him. It seemed out of place with the heat, but it brought a dopey grin to his face. It was probably his imagination, but he almost thought he could feel himself growing stronger as the heat and numbness danced their strangely pleasing dance through his body. After a few moments, he decided it had to be more than his imagination. He suddenly had an appetite.

"What was that?" He beamed.

Hagen humphed, "Now lad, if I gave away all my secrets of healing, who then would have a use for me? I'd become a door without a handle, completely useless."

Maelich quickly forgot he had cared at all about the wonderful elixir as his stomach growled loudly. Quickly shifting to more pressing matters, he said, "Well, how about a meal then? You aren't protecting any secrets about food I hope." His smile widened as his aches noticeably diminished.

"I've already sent for a meal. I…" Hagen was interrupted by a knock at the door. "Perhaps it has arrived."

Maelich sat up a bit in his bed as the heavy door slowly creaked open. He didn't see anything that might have been food. Instead, a happy bark rang out a moment before Jom bounded right up next to him. Maelich's face reddened slightly as he failed to suppress an excited squeal. He thought it something more fitting to spill from the mouth of a little girl than a battle-hardened warrior who had faced down a giant and lived. His embarrassment was short-lived. He threw his arms around Jom who, with tail quickly wagging back and forth, licked his face as if it were a sweet cake.

"No, no, no, a sick lad's room is no place for a mangy scrod!" Hagen scolded, but it was too late. There was no way Jom was leaving Maelich's side.

"Maelich!" Perrin squealed. The shrill tone sounding much more customary coming from her lips than it had from Maelich's. "I missed ye!"

Maelich hardly recognized the angelic girl who skipped into the room. He had never seen her without a good bit of dirt in her hair and on her face. She was a vision with soft, pale skin wrapped around her deep blue eyes. Her golden hair glowing as it draped down around her cheeks and all about her shoulders. He didn't speak. He just looked upon her for a moment as a parent might look upon a newborn babe.

Perrin giggled and folded her hands behind her back as she bounced and swayed like someone excitedly waiting for a surprise. "Do ye like me new dress? How be I looking?"

Maelich thought for a moment, searching for the perfect word. "Breathtaking," he said and then fell back onto the bed as if he truly had run out of breath.

Perrin ran to him and hugged him as if she'd been missing him for years. She buried her head in his chest and he wrapped an arm around her, wincing as pain shot out from his wound. He did his best to hide it, and no one seemed to notice. Then Jom nuzzled up under his chin on the other side and he wrapped his other arm around him. He glanced over at Hagen, waiting to be scolded. The old healer just frowned and shook his head.

"Stolen from death's grip," Ymitoth's voice filled the room with all its deep authority, "here be lying the hero. Maelich, your stubborn refusal to perish be a blessing to us all."

"Father," Maelich did his best to sit up against the weight of Perrin and Jom on his chest, barely noticing the pain in his left shoulder. His eyes widened when he caught sight of Ymitoth adorned in a crown and robe. "You have taken the throne?"

"Aye, thanks to ye, lad. Havenstahl shall be living in fear no more. I'll be seeing to that," he replied with a wink and a broad smile.

Maelich chuckled, "How many men did it take to wrestle you down and plant that hunk of metal on your head?"

"Aye, it weren't no easy thing to be accepting. This damned crown be far heavier than how it be looking. It's me duty, lad," Ymitoth replied. The laugh following his statement was less than convincing. He looked at the ground and chewed his lip for a moment before changing the subject, "Now, ye need to be telling me about that giant. I ain't had no time to get all them details. Let's be having it then."

Hagen watched closely as the group hung on Maelich's words. The lad recounted his meeting with the mighty Ahm. Perrin jumped when Maelich described the giant's spear. Ymitoth wore the proud smile of a father reveling in his son's success. The old healer's desire to have his patient rest and see his visitors out slowly dissipated. The visit seemed to be helping. The color slowly returned to Maelich's cheeks as his voice grew stronger. Another soul stolen from the Lake. A few instructions about changing bandages and applying ointments, and Hagen's work was done.

As Ymitoth saw Hagen out of the room, Maelich's meal finally arrived. He tore into it like a starving man. It occurred to him, as he was working over too large a mouthful of tubber, he was a starving man. He grinned around the mouthful.

"Have you eaten?" he asked Perrin as he held a forkful of tubber and potatoes out toward her.

She shook her head, "No, ye be needed all that to be getting your strength back and all. Ymitoth says ye've a great journey ahead of ye. He's been saying ye'll be leaving me soon." Her soft, blue eyes misted as she added, "Everybody leaves."

Maelich pulled her close as he swallowed hard on the mouthful of meat. Then, in as gentle a tone as he could muster, said, "What did I tell you when we first met?"

"Ye promised me ye'd be taking me wherever your path might be leading ye," she replied quietly as she lost a tear down her cheek. Her voice grew even quieter as she added, "Ye be leaving, and I be staying. Was all what ye told me a lie then?"

Maelich deflated as his own eyes misted, "It wasn't a lie. You won't be alone, and I will return. This journey is something I must do." He squeezed her tighter and continued, "Ymitoth is stern, but he'll watch over you. You will be safe."

Perrin didn't answer. She just curled closer into Maelich's chest. He thought of more words he could say, but none of them would ease her disappointment. No matter how he shined it up, he was still leaving. Like she said, everybody leaves.

***

Once in the hall, Ymitoth said, "Thanks for all what ye did with Maelich. I ain't be needing to tell ye how important he be."

Hagen turned and smiled, "You certainly do not. It was an honor for me. I know the lad doesn't yet fully realize it himself, but Ouloos depends on him."

Ymitoth scratched his head, "So then," he began, "how long until the lad be getting back to the trail?"

Hagen looked toward the ceiling, shrugged, and said, "He's a strong young man and seems to be perking up nicely. In a week or two, he should be sore but fully functional. By that point, he should be ready to handle anything you might throw his way."

"No, no, that won't do. The lad be needing to get back to his journey," Ymitoth shook his head as he spoke. "He already be spending too much time in Havenstahl. Them caves of Alharin ain't waiting. Ye know the importance of this."

Hagen considered Ymitoth's words for a moment as he nodded and stroked his chin beneath a frown, "Yes, he does need to be on his way, doesn't he?" His eyebrows raised slightly as he shrugged and added, "Knowing you, I must assume he's resourceful."

"Aye, I trained the lad myself," Ymitoth quickly replied. "Ain't seen the likes of him. That lad truly be special. The trail won't be giving him no challenge."

Hagen scratched his head as his frown deepened once more, "He'll have to change his bandages. What about fresh, clean water? Will he have access?"

Ymitoth smirked, "Now ye be sounding like a mother. It be a great shame ye ain't had no sons of your own to be raising. Ye be treating all your patients as if they be your own." His expression settled into something more serious as he finished, "Tell Maelich what he be needing to do, and the lad will be getting it done."

The old healer didn't like the idea one bit, but Ymitoth was correct. The great power awaiting Maelich in the caves at Alharin was many things, but patient wasn't among them. The lad had already lost too many precious days on a lengthy trial and sweating out a fever. Hagen bowed slightly as he patted Ymitoth on the shoulder and started down the hallway.

After a few steps, Hagen turned and said, "Get the crest on the lad's chest, and send him on his way. For his sake and ours, I hope he's as ready as you say."

***

When Ymitoth returned to Maelich's room he found him

speaking to Perrin about the dwarves and something about the sacred pine while he stroked Jom's fur. The thought of interrupting the lad's story with instructions and news died a quick death. Instead, he pulled up a chair and listened intently, losing himself in Maelich's words. Pride swelled in his chest as his boy told a story of a dwarf snatched away from the jaws of death. His pride grew as Maelich told the lass about Ahm and the journey home. Maelich's story reminded him of some of his old adventures. No, the trail wouldn't be claiming Maelich's life. Even with a healing gash in his shoulder, the boy was ready.

"…and then the world went black. The next thing I remember is waking up in this room," Maelich finished the story with a shrug.

Perrin's eyes were round and big, "Ye be so brave. That giant be sounding scary."

"What about you?" Maelich asked. "Tell me about your adventures since last we spoke."

Perrin beamed, "Me and Jom was stuck in that shack with them guards for so long. That be a boring place, and them guards ain't no fun. They don't be talking or laughing or nothing. They always just be looking out them windows and scrunching up their faces around frowns."

Maelich chuckled as Perrin mocked the angry faces guards make.

Realizing she had Maelich amused, Perrin grew more animated as she continued, "Then, them same grumpy guards took me and Jom to this fancy room full of all these fancy ladies." She hopped off the bed and strolled around it dramatically swaying her hips back and forth while pretending to fix her hair.

Maelich's chuckle grew into a proper laugh. It didn't help the pain in his shoulder, but it was worth it. After all he'd been through, he needed a good laugh.

Perrin grabbed a brush from the dresser and began brushing her hair while still swaying her hips back and forth, "Them fancy ladies be telling me I be a vision sent from Kallum himself, all while they be giving me baths with bubbles and fussing over me hair and telling me I be just like a doll. Them nice ladies even be putting Jom in the bubbles. He ain't been liking it so much. He liked that they ain't made him sleep outside, been by me side all the time. Ain't ye thinking that's odd?"

"What's odd, that they brushed your hair and called you a doll?" Maelich grinned.

"No," she rolled her eyes, "ain't ye thinking it's odd they ain't had Jom outside? They'd been letting him sleep right in the bed with me. Even Mama never been doing that."

"I don't think it's odd at all," he replied. "Then again, after the past few days, I imagine it will be quite a time before I find anything odd again."

Perrin squinted and looked as if she might have something to add. When she didn't, Ymitoth took advantage of the brief lull in the conversation, "Perrin."

She glanced over at him, her pale blue eyes as big as ever. Maelich glanced his way as well.

"Do ye be remembering them two nice folks ye met over at that pub where we'd been eating them eggs the other morning?" Ymitoth continued.

Perrin nearly jumped on Maelich as she grabbed his shirt and pulled him close. "Oh, Maelich," she began, "I nearly been forgetting all about them nice people, what with being so happy to see ye."

"What people," Maelich looked back toward Ymitoth.

"Master Ken…" Ymitoth began but Perrin cut him off.

She grabbed Maelich's chin and turned his face back toward her as she said, "I be telling ye about it right now."

Maelich put his hands up as he gave her his full attention. "Okay, okay, tell me all about it."

Perrin relaxed her grip on Maelich's chin and continued, "Master Kendal be owning this pub, or whatever ye be calling it, and he be knowing old man Kelsho! Can ye even be believing it? He be old man Kelsho's brother."

Maelich looked over at Ymitoth who nodded, confirming Perrin's statement.

"And his misses be called Haleen," Perrin pressed on. "She might be the sweetest lady I ever been meeting," she paused a moment before finishing, "except for me mama."

"Wow," Maelich exaggerated his enthusiasm for Perrin's sake, "you met old man Kelsho's brother? That is exciting!" Then he glanced over at Ymitoth and asked, "Why is this such big news?"

"How would ye like to be staying with them two nice people while Maelich be off to his adventures?" Ymitoth asked Perrin.

Perrin seemed less excited than Ymitoth had hoped she'd be as she nodded and asked, "Will they be letting Jom stay too?"

Ymitoth gave her a wide, reassuring smile and said, "Aye, they be looking forward to having a sturdy scrod around to be helping them look after that pub."

"Aye," Perrin brightened, "then I be liking that very much." She turned her attention back to Maelich and said, "The misses was all tears when she be holding me. I wiped them off her cheeks and asked her what she be crying for. She said she ain't never had no daughter and thought I'd be a nice one for some lucky lady, what with Mama being gone and all. She said I could be calling her that if I be wanting."

"And what did you decide," Maelich asked.

"Aye," Perrin smiled, "I be calling her that."

"Master Kendal said ye can be calling him father, or papa, or Master Kendal, whatever ye be liking," Ymitoth interjected into a conversation of which he started but didn't feel a part.

Perrin's eyes remained on Maelich as she said, "Papa Kendal, that's what I be calling him."

Before Ymitoth could tell her what a good idea he thought that was, Perrin had laid her head down on Maelich's chest and fallen fast asleep. All the excitement of seeing Maelich and sharing stories must have been too much. Within moments she was snoring loudly enough to scare Jom right off the bed. The scrod walked a few circles, flopped down onto the floor, and chased right after her into dreamland.

Ymitoth took a chair across the room from Maelich's bed. His smile remained shallow as he thought of Maelich's impending departure. At times, he forgot the lad had only seen twelve summers. He began his training so young, he never really had a chance to be a boy. The road wouldn't get any easier for him either.

As Ymitoth's mind wandered, Maelich managed to slip out from beneath Perrin and take the chair next to him. Ymitoth had become so wrapped up that he didn't even notice Maelich sit down.

"Finally," Maelich began, "they have both found sleep. We can have a relaxing chat."

Ymitoth's mind had wandered rather far, and he jumped a bit, "For the love of Kallum, lad, ye nearly scared the boots right off of me feet. I ain't even heard ye walk over here."

Maelich held his wounded shoulder as a giggle shook through him. "Forgive me, father. I didn't mean to startle you. Where were you off to just then?"

Ymitoth's eyes were still far away as he replied, "There just be many things what be weighing on me right now. The greatest of which being watching as ye be leaving the safety of me city. I be wishing to Kallum I could be at your side as ye make the next part of your journey."

"I would welcome the company," Maelich replied, "but you needn't worry about me. I am ready, father. You have given me everything I need to survive my journey."

"Aye, ye be ready," Ymitoth conceded, before adding, "but that ain't making it any easier to be watching ye go."

"Thank you," Maelich said quietly.

Ymitoth's eyes lost their faraway look, "What in the name of Kallum be ye thanking me for?"

Maelich smiled, "Just for letting me know you care. Sentimental is something you've never been, but you're the only family I have. I mean, Perrin has depended on me, but you're the only one who's been with me my entire life. It is nice to know I won't be forgotten when I leave."

Ymitoth stopped just short of getting misty as he replied, "Aye, ye have been the only son I ever had. Ye'll be missed, lad." After composing himself, he added, "So, how be that nasty gash in your shoulder feeling?"

"What gash?" Maelich countered with just a hint of a chuckle. "It stills stings a bit when I move wrong, but Hagen's elixir has me feeling quite strong."

"Son, all what ye said to me that morning after the shrine. Ye be right, and I be proud of what ye've become. No longer will I be feeling that I should be shamed in your presence. Kallum his self be setting us on our paths, so he must have been choosing mine when I got picked to rear ye as me own. Ye won't be hearing me deny ye anymore," an earnest expression spread across Ymitoth's face as he spoke.

Maelich simply replied, "Thank you, father."

The two men looked at each other for a moment and then both burst into laughter for no good reason at all. They laughed heartily for a good bit until they remembered the sleeping lass that they shouldn't be disturbing in her slumber. Their laughter slowly turned to chuckling and then finally ceased as a troubled look crept onto Maelich's face.

"Father," he began, "I may not be feeling as confident in my abilities as I'd like you to believe. I was almost killed by the likes of that serpent, Yfregeof. That weakling of a worm bested me. I still don't recall how I managed to escape with my life. I know my journey is just yet beginning, and the rest of it shall be on my own. If I could be bested by the likes of Yfregeof, how will I conquer whatever other challenges I might encounter?"

Ymitoth grinned, "Ah, humility. Aye ye're a mighty powerful warrior, yet ye lack experience. Not every foe ye meet will be wanting a fair fight with ye. Ahm, in all his conceit, could never be fathoming the idea a wee lad such as yourself might be besting him. Amatilazo be too stupid to fear ye, and Kallum's messengers...well, Kallum's messengers be fearing no man. Ye nearly scared Yfregeof right out of his crown when ye stormed into his throne room with Ahm's head. He'd been knowing that in a fair fight ye'd have his head without any effort at all. Ye'd never be getting a fair fight out of the likes of him. Ye learned a lesson, Maelich, be keeping it with ye."

"Are you saying I shouldn't be confident in my abilities?" Maelich was perplexed.

"No, no, son," Ymitoth shook his head. "Ye must be confident in yourself but that ain't no cause for being careless. Ye are like a god, aye, but ye are also of flesh and blood. Never be forgetting that death can be finding ye. The serpent be wanting ye to believe ye can't be killed, for when your guard be down be when he strikes."

Maelich looked at the ceiling, "You always offer wise counsel, father." He grimaced slightly as he grabbed his injured shoulder and added, "It is a painful lesson I won't soon forget."

Ymitoth smiled, "Aye, lad. Of that, I be certain."

Both the new king and the wounded warrior stared out the window across the room. The sky grew dark as the sun made way for a full moon. Each had a fresh set of challenges to contemplate. They remained like that until the sky outside the window had completely darkened.

Ymitoth finally broke the silence, "That vile snake found his way over the side of the mountain after a thick rope choked all the life out of him."

"A fitting end," Maelich replied.

"History will be remembering an execution as me first act as king," Ymitoth said, soberly. Then he added, "I ain't even really been the king yet, but that's what they'll be saying."

"I suppose they will," Maelich nodded.

Ymitoth turned toward Maelich, "While I been watching ye on

the brink of death, all tossing and turning and shouting out from the fever, I be wishing I could be killing that snake over and over again. One death just ain't be seeming enough for that treacherous bastard."

Maelich shrugged, "One death is all any of us get, one last journey to the Lake."

"Aye," Ymitoth agreed as both men turned their gazes back toward the darkness.

After a brief silence, Ymitoth said, "Though ye been mostly asleep for the better part of the past few days, ye should be getting some rest. Ye've a big day tomorrow. The ceremony of the crest be something all the city be coming out for. Ye won't be wanting to fall down them steps or some other fool thing what being in front of all them folks."

Maelich grinned, nodded, and said, "I'm actually pretty tired. This visit has taken more out of me than I would have thought."

Ymitoth placed a hand on Maelich's good shoulder and smiled. Then he gathered Perrin up from the bed. She mumbled some gibberish but didn't wake. Jom did, however, just long enough to hop back up onto Maelich's bed and curl up right in the middle of it. Ymitoth chuckled. winked his goodnight to Maelich and carried Perrin out of the room.

CHAPTER 11
THE CEREMONY OF THE CREST

Even in the dim light of the early dawn, the room seemed far too bright. Maelich stretched and blinked several times, finally clamping them tightly together and turning his head away from the open window when his eyes refused to adjust. He nearly jumped out of his bed when he opened them again. Ymitoth's face was barely an inch from his own. He barely had time to notice the odd mix of pride and nervous excitement on his stern mentor's face as he slid away and brought his fists up.

"What in Kallum's name are doing?" he shouted hoarsely, sounding more like an old man who had spent his life smoking too much fairy weed than a brawny, young lad.

Ymitoth stood up straight and planted his fists at his hips. His eyebrows raised as he looked down on Maelich and said, "I be trying to get your lazy bum out of this bed. The rest of us all be ready. Ye be the guest of honor, and here ye lay sleeping."

Maelich sat and stretched. His eyes finally grew accustomed to the light and he began to get his wits. When he finally looked back at Ymitoth, what he saw surprised him. As far as he could remember, he had never seen the man without a good bit of dirt on his clothing. Ymitoth was a warrior, an adventurer, and far more comfortable on the trail than in a castle or even a hut. Today was different. He wore a heavy, velvet robe, deep red with a collar of white fur. His crown was shiny prang with jewels that snatched every bit of light, bent it, and splashed rainbows of colors all about the walls. Similar, though smaller, jewels adorned his cuffs and lapels and played the same games with the light. Maelich could barely find his tongue.

Once Maelich overcame his shock and could find his voice, he said, "You look like a king, father."

Ymitoth's cheeks reddened around a sheepish grin, "Yeah, well I be feeling like a damn fool, all dolled up like a princess."

Maelich chuckled at the old soldier's embarrassment. Then he said, "Well, you don't look like a fool. You wear the king's robe well."

"Thanks, lad, but I be sweating up a storm already," Ymitoth replied as he tugged at his collar. "I ain't certain these fancy clothes will be making it through the end of the day."

Maelich shook with laughter until he caught sight of Perrin standing quietly in the corner. She looked like a princess in her long, formal white gown. Lacy gloves reached all the way up to her elbows. Her hair was pulled back from her face save a few well-placed ringlets dangling next to her plump cheeks on either side. Those plump cheeks reddened at least as much as Ymitoth's had when her bright eyes met Maelich's. They quickly shot to the floor as she moved her hands behind her back and nervously rocked back and forth on jewel encrusted shoes with the slightest heel.

"No craftsman in all of Ouloos could ever make a doll so beautiful," Maelich remarked.

Perrin shyly looked back up and replied, "Do ye think I be looking silly?"

"Silly?" Maelich feigned shock, "You are a vision, like a perfect sunrise over a vast sea."

Perrin smiled and rubbed the back of one of her gloves against her cheek, "I be liking these gloves them nice ladies gave me. They be so pretty and they be tickling me cheeks. Have ye ever been feeling anything like this before?"

Perrin went to Maelich and gently rubbed the back of her glove on his cheek. He exaggerated his giggle. The thing felt kind of rough, but he played it off as if nothing had ever tickled him so mightily in all his days. "Wow, that does tickle!" he lied.

As Maelich and Perrin giggled over the glove, Jom finally joined the land of the living. He nearly kicked Maelich off the bed when he stretched his legs out and planted all four paws into Maelich's back. Maelich moved his face close to the scrod and gave him a sour look that earned him a long lick, chin to temple up the side of his face, from

Jom's sloppy tongue. Then they both hopped off the bed almost in unison. Jom found a fresh bowl full of water in the corner while Maelich rubbed the sleep from his eyes.

"This be about all ye'll be having time for," Ymitoth said as he offered Maelich some fruit and bread along with a cup of water.

Ymitoth had laid out the same princely garments Maelich had worn when he addressed the former king. Maelich rather liked the outfit. Scraping off the dirt and getting a little shined up didn't trouble him as much as it did his father. Sadly, the garments would not be accompanying him on his journey. As he dressed, Ymitoth prattled on nervously, like any father would, about what the ceremony would entail. Maelich could barely keep up with him as he rapidly fired off instructions about everything from what Maelich should say to how he should carry himself.

Maelich finally interrupted his concerned father's rant, "Father, please, slow down. I have never seen you so nervous. It's as if you're the one earning a crest today."

A brief look of frustration twisted up the corners of Ymitoth's mouth before fleeing to make way for a proud smile. Then he crossed the room, grabbed Maelich by the shoulders, held him at arm's length, and said, "Aye, I be nervous as a mouse tiptoeing beneath a sleeping horny witch. Ye ain't born of me seed, but ye be me son. I ain't never been prouder of nothing in me whole life." He took a long step back and added, "Look at ye. Today I be hanging that crest about your neck and calling ye a man."

Maelich's eyes grew warm as he lost a brief battle with a tear. It quickly raced down his cheek. He didn't bother to wipe it away. He wanted it there. It was all too overwhelming. The words wouldn't come. That tear was the only response he could muster for his proud father, and he wanted to him to have it. For Maelich, it represented his appreciation for all Ymitoth had done. As stern and serious as the man had been throughout his training, everything Maelich had become was because of him.

Once Maelich was dressed and had eaten, the entire group strolled out into the hall to make their way down to the courtyard. Maelich remained cool. Ymitoth had taught him to keep a level head no matter the situation. As Ymitoth nervously twitched and bantered, Maelich couldn't help but feel his instructor hadn't paid enough attention to his own teaching.

"Maelich, I ain't the words to be telling ye how important this day be," Ymitoth gushed. "All the greatest warriors since the beginning of days been wearing that crest ye'll be getting on this day." He held up his own crest and added, "Ye'll be hard pressed to be finding any man who'll be wanting a duel with ye when ye be wearing this symbol."

As desperately as Maelich wanted to laugh at his unshakeable mentor's blatant loss of control, he held it in. This day was as much for Ymitoth as it was for him. He wanted him to revel in it, and remember it fondly for all his days. Instead of poking fun, he said, "I will wear my crest with pride, and it will remind me that I would never be the man I am if not for all you have taught me whenever I look upon it."

Now Ymitoth lost a tear. Then he gave Maelich a shove and said, "Ye should be saving that drivel for after the ceremony. Them folks what be wanting to see their king pin the great city of Havenstahl's crest on their newest hero ain't wanting to see that king blubbering like a damn fool."

Maelich nodded and kept his mouth shut for the rest of the walk. It wasn't long before Ymitoth got back to gushing about the importance of the day. Even Perrin and Jom, following closely behind, seemed giddy with excitement.

Just before the group reached the trellis, they were met by Perrin's new family. She ran to Haleen and nearly shouted, "Mama!"

Wearing a smile Maelich assumed only a mother could muster, Haleen embraced the girl. Then she looked up at Maelich and asked, "Well, would this be the Maelich what we been hearing so much about?"

Perrin's excitement, and the ease with which Haleen held the girl, like they had been mother and daughter for Perrin's entire life seemed so natural. The small gesture, which no one else probably noticed, almost completely erased all Maelich's concerns about how Perrin would handle him leaving her behind. Genuine happiness settled on his face in the form of probably the most honest smile he had ever worn. As was customary, Maelich offered his hand to Kendal when he replied, "That would be me."

"We must be thanking ye for bringing this beauty safely to us from the peril what befell her village," Kendal said with a nod. "Aye lad, ye be a true hero and well deserving of that crest they be pinning to ye today."

"Thank you, sir," Maelich smiled. "I trust you'll be taking good care of this beautiful lass then? We've been through quite a bit in the short time we've had together and I fancy her to be one of my own."

"Aye," Haleen piped up. "Kallum ain't seen fit to be blessing us with no child of our own. We been begging him for one since the day Kendal stole away me heart. This little ray of light be filling that empty space. Ye can count on her being more than well cared for."

Haleen took Perrin's hand and Perrin took Maelich's as Kendal put an arm around his shoulder. Maelich decided he liked these people. Perrin seemed pleased with them, and Ymitoth felt they would make suitable parents for her. Ymitoth had always seemed an excellent judge of situations. He had to assume his mentor was at least as good a judge of character. As difficult as it would be to leave the youngster—aside from Ymitoth, she was the closest thing he had to a family member—at least he wouldn't have to worry over her care.

Maelich glanced around at the faces surrounding him before settling on Perrin's. Her eyes had changed. The fear he remembered from their first encounter had been replaced by something resembling hope. She had a new family to love and protect her, and she seemed to finally be at peace with her world. He couldn't tell if she hadn't dealt with his departure yet or if the comfort of her new family was softening the blow. Either way, she no longer seemed concerned he was leaving. That was okay. A little bit of sadness about being so easily replaced was worth the knowledge she'd be able to enjoy a more normal life than what a hungry pack of amatilazo had left her with.

Maelich had become so distracted with thoughts of Perrin's future and fretting over whether she would miss him that he nearly walked right into Ymitoth when the new king stopped the group in between two matching sets of giant wooden doors. Each of the four doors sported a detailed carving of Havenstahl's grand emblem, the same emblem depicted on the crest Maelich would receive momentarily. Before he could comment, everything flooded in. Two sets of doors on either side of him led to different futures for everyone who meant anything to him. The doors to his right opened to Havenstahl's, now Ymitoth's, throne room. He could scarcely imagine the gritty warrior who taught him to hunt, swing steel, and be a man feeling comfortable trapped in any room, much less one filled with lines of people hoping to bend his ear. How would he manage?

The doors to Maelich's left stood open as well, but these poured out onto the courtyard and new beginnings for the rest of his group. Perrin had her new parents, and they—beaming like young parents catching their first glimpse of their newborn—finally had an answer to their lifetimes of prayer. Maelich's journey led through that same set of heavy wooden doors, but his path continued far past them, the courtyard, well beyond the gates of Havenstahl, even further still beyond the villages dotting the rolling prairies gently sloping away from Mount Elzkahon. He suddenly felt homesick. The journey before him was a lonely one, and he didn't even know how long it would take. When would he return? Would anybody even remember him?

Perrin's arms squeezing tightly around his waist kept Maelich from traipsing too far down the path to hopelessness. Maelich knelt beside her and gave her a squeeze, "I expect I'll miss you most of all."

"Aye," she agreed, her voice muffled into his shoulder, "ye'll be missing me, and I'll be missing ye. And ye'll be coming back to me with more stories about all your adventures."

Maelich chuckled, "Hopefully, you'll have some adventures to share with me then too."

Ymitoth patted Maelich on the back. "Time to be getting to it, lad," he said.

Maelich stood and faced the king as Kendal gathered up Perrin and strolled out of the palace with her and Haleen. Loneliness crept back in as one member of his family left with her new family and the other looked on with proud, if just a little bit sad, eyes. Maelich's lips began moving before he could properly arrange his thoughts. "I killed a giant," was all he could come up with.

Ymitoth smiled, grabbed hold of his arms, and said, "Aye, ye did. Ain't no other man in the history of men can be making that boast," after a brief pause, he cocked his head slightly and asked, "So, why on Ouloos be this hero among men looking at me with something akin to fear in his eyes?"

"What if I'm not as great as you think I am?" Maelich's eyes shot to the ground as he shrugged. "What if I was lucky? You said yourself, Ahm's downfall was his pride. What if I was just the lucky recipient of a gift from a boastful giant?"

Ymitoth sighed deeply as a tear worked its way to the edge of his eyelid, "Well, there ye be going, ain't ye? Ye ain't to be finding happiness until ye have me blubbering like a damn fool. Forget that giant for just a moment and be listening to these words of mine good.

I ain't no poet, so don't expect nothing pretty, but ye know I be honest as they come. I'll tell ye lad, all the pride what be swelling up me chest today been there long before ye'd been trading blows with that monster up in Alhouim. I know we ain't sharing no blood, but ye be the only son I've ever known. And I be proud to be calling ye that to any who be asking. Ye ain't never let fear be stopping ye from doing what be right. Ain't another sword in all the land, any land I've ever been, I'd rather be marching off to battle with." The tear perched on the king's eyelid finally spilled over and ran down his cheek, as he pointed at Maelich's heart and added, "What I truly be proud of though, is what be in here. All of what ye do, all them things ye done what made me so proud, ain't even what I truly be proud of when I look at ye. What ye got in there, in that heart, is what I truly be proud of. Ye ain't done it for spite or revenge, maybe glory a time or two, but all what ye do be in the service of others. Ye be the kind of man I be wanting to be. Ye ain't lucky, son. Ye worked hard, and ye be doing what's right. Ye be a true hero."

Maelich lost a tear of his own as he embraced his father. As good as it felt to hear those words come from Ymitoth's lips, it didn't make the prospect of leaving any easier. Things had been different. In the brief time they'd had together since he arrived in Havenstahl, the stern mentor who had raised him was finally opening up to him. At least he could carry it with him on the trail.

Maelich wasn't quite ready for the embrace to end. It seemed he had a lifetime to make up for with his father. However, when Ymitoth pushed him back to arm's-length and looked on him with the eyes of a proud father once again, he knew it had to be. His journey was just beginning, and there were throngs of people waiting in the hot sun to watch him receive his crest. It was time for duty. It was time to be a man.

By the time Ymitoth asked, "Be ye ready to have that crest pinned on your chest and become a true warrior of the greatest city of men?" Maelich was ready.

The two men stepped through the doorway onto an open veranda that spread forth in a half circle from the palace. Its floor consisted of alternating tiles of fine polished stone and precious prang surrounded on the edges by a carefully carved, decorative border. An ornamental, prang fence surrounding the veranda glistened in the sun, glowing like a rich sunset over a dark forest. The fence stopped short of the wall on either side to make way for twin stairways curving fifteen feet a piece down to another half-circle platform made of the same stuff as the veranda above. From there, steps forming concentric half circles poured down another fifteen feet into a courtyard full of people eager to lay eyes on the killer of giants. At the center of the group was a fountain boasting a massive polished-stone statue of Eringaal, the first king and founder of the house of Havenstahl.

Maelich's chest swelled as he and Ymitoth made it to the center of the veranda. The crowd in the courtyard below erupted in a cheer like nothing he'd ever heard before. He glanced up at Ymitoth and asked, "Is that all for me?"

"Aye, lad," Ymitoth chuckled, "What did ye think I'd been meaning when I said, 'Hero'? Ye be that to these people, and to me."

Both men waved to the crowd whose cheering, as impossible as it seemed, increased in volume. After a few moments, both men turned and took one step away from each other, paused, and then turned a half-circle so they were facing each other once again. A few more moments passed before they drew their swords in unison, touching them first to the ground, then to their shoulders, and then to each other's blades. Again, they turned away from each other, this time making their way down separate stairways to the landing below. Once they met again, they went through the same motions they had on the veranda.

Standing in the hot sun with sword aloft, the slight breeze that picked up and gently tugged Maelich's golden hair away from his face was a blessing. It cooled the bit of sweat beading up on his forehead. He sighed with relief when he counted off the final beat in his head and sheathed his sword as Ymitoth did the same. Maelich dropped to one knee and looked up at Ymitoth who reached into his robe and produced a shimmering prang medallion, the sacred crest of Havenstahl. Another cheer blasted from the crowd. Then the newest hero of Havenstahl had that crest pinned to the breast of his robe by the new king of the greatest city of men.

Ymitoth pulled Maelich back to his feet, turned him toward the crowd, and shouted, "I give ye, Maelich, warrior, protector, and keeper of Havenstahl. He will bear this crest as a champion of the people!"

The crowd erupted and poured up the steps to the landing, gathering Maelich up as they sung praises to his name. Perrin and the rest from up on the veranda came down and did the same. It was difficult for Maelich to not feel at least as great as Ymitoth said he was. He was hugged, he was kissed, and he was patted on the back. The latter of the three sent little shocks of pain through his shoulder. He didn't think anyone noticed and figured it wouldn't matter to them if they did.

After a time, Ymitoth made his way back up to the veranda and called the crowd to attention. "People of Havenstahl," he began, "ye be welcome to join us for a feast to honor our new soldier. Please convene to the throne room."

With that several guards moved into the crowd and began directed people up the steps to the veranda and into the palace. In the throne room table after table had been set and a feast like Havenstahl hadn't hosted in ten summers had been spread. Savory scents saturated the air, mingling with laughter, shouting, and praises in Maelich's name from the crowd.

Maelich found himself off to the side, a bystander half in the moment and half somewhere far away on a journey yet unseen. Everything was so much different than it had been barely more than a week prior. He'd hardly time to process anything.

"What ye be thinking about?" Perrin pulled him from his trance.

"Oh, nothing," he replied with a forced laugh that was painfully fake.

Perrin's big eyes stared back at him, all bright and blue and full of questions. She obviously wasn't going to let him off the hook without having an answer. Despite having only five summers under her belt, recent events in her life had seemed to wisen her well beyond her years.

"Oh, alright," he grudgingly gave in, "it's just that sometimes this feels like someone else's life. I feel like all my decisions have been made for me, and this is all just a game for me to play through. Though I don't know the outcome, it has already been decided."

Perrin seemed thoughtful for a moment and asked, "What if ye don't be doing what ye're supposed to?"

Maelich rolled his eyes and began to retort, but paused, "I ca…" He had never really thought about it. "I don't know. What if I didn't?" he asked instead.

Throughout his entire life, he had always done what he was told. Through his training and his challenges, it never occurred to him he had a choice. Life had always been just what it was. It was precisely how it was supposed to be. Fate is fate. You can't change fate. He was destined to be the hero. What if one day he decided not to be that?

As Maelich worked through this new, deep thought Perrin had given him to ponder, a heavy hand fell onto his shoulder. Ymitoth's voice followed it, "Maelich, have a bit of tubberslat. Ye can't be challenging no trail on a great quest without first filling your belly."

Ymitoth's proud eyes chased all Maelich's questions away. "Yes," Maelich replied, "I suppose my belly should be full."

Maelich followed Ymitoth to a gaudily-decorated table at the front of the throne room. He managed to quiet his questioning mind long enough to enjoy some food and light conversation with his tablemates. Besides Ymitoth, Perrin, her new family, and four of Ymitoth's most trusted guards shared the table of honor with him.

The celebration was a wonderful, however brief, distraction for Maelich. As fate would have it, there was enough light for him to get a few hours of travel in before he would have to make camp for his first night on the trail. Since a few of Ymitoth's servants had forgone the feast to pack for their new hero, Maelich was trail-ready as soon as he finished eating. He counted this a blessing. It helped foster the illusion of a great need for haste. A long good-bye would only make leaving all the more difficult.

By the time Maelich made it back out to the courtyard, Validus was packed up and ready for travel. After a quick check of his horse sacks, he figured both he and Jom would remain fed for two to three weeks. The give or take would depend entirely on their appetites and his own self-discipline. Even if they gorged themselves at half their meals, by the time they worked through their supplies they would be well into territory that boasted ample game for hunting. From that point on, he would have to keep them fed.

Growing up with Ymitoth, Maelich shouldn't have been surprised at the amount of preparation his mentor had put into a trip the man wasn't even taking, but he still was. Ymitoth had thought of everything. Maelich looked on as Ymitoth quickly went over last-minute instructions and pointed out a couple of dangerous spots on a map he had prepared. Not only were the dangerous spots marked, but the safe ones too. If Maelich and Jom kept a steady but comfortable pace, they'd earn a perfect spot for camp each night. Ymitoth had even considered the wee bit Jom would slow the journey. Based on Ymitoth's calculations, if they stayed the course and didn't dawdle, the entire journey should take about a month and a half.

"Ye'll be following Galgooth, that river what ye crossed on your way from the hut. There be a road what runs right alongside it. She be crossing it a few times back and forth, but ye'll be right next to it until ye hit The Bloody Mountains. Ye'll be takin' care through them mountains. They earned that name from belching liquid fire up into the sky from deep under the ground. Ye mind that fire, lad. It be raining back down on ye and ain't caring one way or another what your mission might be. It be a dangerous place. Ain't no spot for dawdling. Beyond them mountains be a lone peak all by itself. This be Alharin. Ye'll be finding a cave up around its peak, Brerto's cave. Brerto be powerful and enlightened beyond all men. He be having control of the elements. He'll be the one to complete your training, son."

Maelich recognized the name and asked, "Brerto, the great wizard from your stories is to be my mentor? I thought he was a character you had made up, a myth. If he's a real man, he must have been around for ages."

"Aye, but I don't know that ye can be calling him a man really," Ymitoth wore the expression of one trying to explain something he himself didn't completely understand. "He be like a man, but he be immortal, been around longer even than the language we be speaking. I ain't never seen him, and most nobody does. All them stories what I already told ye be all I ever known about him."

Maelich gazed down into the valley as his mind tumbled over this new info, "This is exciting to me, an honor. I can't believe I'm to be trained by the great Brerto. Do you think I'm worthy?"

"Aye," was all Ymitoth said.

"How long will I train?"

"That I ain't be knowing," Ymitoth shrugged. "until ye be done, I guess. I do be knowing that when our paths be crossing again, I'll be an old man, and ye'll be a grown man."

Ymitoth spared only one last tear as he pulled Maelich in close again, "Till our path's be crossing again, son."

"Yes, father," Maelich replied quietly, "until then."

Maelich then moved on to Perrin. He scooped her up and hugged her tight. "I'll miss you, little lady!"

Perrin giggled through the tears that had already started welling up in her eyes. "Aye, I'll be missing ye too. Come back to me when ye can."

"Of course, I will," he kissed her cheek and gently set her down.

He then looked to Kendal, "Look after her. She's like blood to me."

Kendal nodded, "Aye, she's like me own now."

Maelich leapt onto Validus's saddle and waved. Most of the crowd from the ceremony had followed him down to the gate to see him off. They followed him as he trotted down the stone street toward the south gate with Jom at his side. Horn blowers stationed along the road on either side blasted as he rode by.

Hidden among the euphoric crowd, happily cheering their new hero on to great glory, a stranger peered at Havenstahl's newest warrior from the darkness of his heavy hood. While he watched the hero trot by amid booming cheers, his fingers traced the lines of the crest hiding beneath his cloak. The prang thing was identical in every way to Maelich's save one detail, instead of an image of a fallon with a grand rack, this man's crest sported an image of a mighty dragon belching fire.

CHAPTER 12
WATCHERS

Moshat watched intently as Kaldumahn sat shaking and mumbling in a trance-like state upon his throne. Moshat's curiosity grew as the hours slipped past. He thought about rousing his brother at one point when he shouted something inaudible, but he thought better of it. The last time he had interrupted one of Kaldumahn's vision it began an argument that lasted the better part of ten summers. On top of that, he knew how jarring it was to be woken from a trance, especially one that includes a deep connection with someone else's mind. Despite being somewhat miffed the spell Kaldumahn had cast on Daritus—the object of his brother's vision—didn't include him, he decided to wait it out without intruding.

Finally, Kaldumahn woke. After sucking in the kind of bottomless breath a drowning man takes when finally reaching the surface of the water, he shouted, "Maelich has earned the Crest of Havenstahl! He has left the city."

Moshat thought for a moment, "Should we move on him?"

"Not yet," Kaldumahn's reply was quick. "He is not yet ready."

Moshat continued diplomatically, "I know we disagree on this, but don't you think the longer we wait the more solid his beliefs will become?"

"Perhaps, but he is of no use to us right now," Kaldumahn shrugged.

"We could finish his training," Moshat's retort was matter of fact. "We could help him tap into his power and teach him truth."

"If we move now, we will bring Kallum's fury down upon us. In Maelich's current state he would be of no use as an ally, and we would have no time to convince him of our cause even if he were. No, he must complete his course," Kaldumahn finished with a shake of his head.

"You fear Kallum?" Moshat goaded his brother, a hint of disgust dancing among the notes of his voice.

"Kallum? No," he scoffed. "Kallum, Brerto and Maelich together, absolutely. If Maelich's power were unleashed before he has learned to contain it, all could be lost. We have no idea how he would react in a battle such as that. Furthermore, we do not know where Ijilv's allegiance lies. He, as yet, is undecided. He could tip the scales for us or against us."

"So, we wait?" Moshat's tone now completely saturated in disgust.

"Yes, we wait. The lad has a logical mind. In the end, the choice must be his. Hopefully, he makes the correct choice," Kaldumahn's tone hinted at optimism.

"A gamble on hope is not a safe bet in my eyes. I prefer action to idealistic banter. I must walk in the garden and contemplate," Moshat spat before he first dimmed, then faded, and finally disappeared completely. His voice remained, however, for one last jibe, "The complexity of your nonsense frustrates me to my core, Kaldumahn."

Kaldumahn humphed at the empty throne Moshat had occupied only a moment prior. It was just like him to leave mid-debate after a juvenile statement. Moshat was frustrated by his complexity? Well, he was equally frustrated, no disgusted, by Moshat's simplicity. This plan had been laid out eons ago. There was no sense in rushing when the end was so near. Besides, the plan was a recipe of one far greater and more enlightened than they. Who was Moshat to question? He was so utterly impatient. Twelve years would be but a blink, a whisper.

Kaldumahn laid his head back against his throne and closed his eyes. There was much to see. Moshat could wander and contemplate all he wanted. Kaldumahn opened his conscience and let it stretch out across space. At first the sensation was like flying, tossing on a high wind. As it slowly mellowed, flying and tumbling became more like floating on calm waters. Then the visions came. He watched Maelich, head held high, trot down the road out of Havenstahl. The time would come, but it wasn't now.

CHAPTER 13
THE ROAD TO ALHARIN

The River Galgooth, the great river of the north Maelich now had a name for, came into Havenstahl from the east. It wrapped around Mount Elzkahon and then doubled back, forming the valley between Elzkahon and Elbahor. From there it headed in an easterly direction. Maelich traveled back into the valley between Havenstahl and The Sobbing Forest and took the main road east from there. That road took him straight east, crossing Galgooth once before angling northeast. Another two days beyond the crossing, he met back up with the river. His progress slowed a bit beyond the river as the valley gave way to hills that proved demanding for Jom. The scrod was setting the pace.

As the days on the trail melted away, Maelich grew more and more impressed by Ymitoth's planning of his trip. The spots he had mapped out for sites to make camp never came more than half of an hour before or after Maelich was ready to quit for the day. The fact he had factored in the limitations of a scrod made the feat nothing short of amazing.

The road dragged on as days became more and more difficult to differentiate from each other. For the most part, the journey proved uneventful. Following alongside the river, each curve of the trail seemed nearly identical to the prior. They passed through a handful of small settlements along the way. That broke up the monotony a bit. Maelich was even invited to share a meal once or twice. His newly-earned crest garnered much respect among the townsfolk and wound up sparking more than one conversation. More often than not, his young age became a dominant theme. However, once his hosts heard of his trials, those questions were quickly forgotten. His mastery of language didn't hurt either. Of course, he told the story of the young boy taking the giant's head so many times, he had nearly grown tired of it. It was worth the full horse sacks. It seemed he couldn't leave a village without having his supplies replenished.

Before long, the hills gave way to flatlands, speckled with small outcroppings of trees. Every now and then the road would cross the river. It seemed a bit odd to Maelich to be flitting back and forth from one side of the river to the other while remaining on the same road. Perhaps someone needed a good reason to build bridges, too much wood hanging about. In actuality, the cause always seemed to be another road coming to the river from another direction. No matter the cause, Maelich was growing bored and lonely on the trail.

Those roads coming from who knows where, crossing the river, and then heading off to another who knows where began earning more of Maelich's attention. Where could all those roads possibly lead, and would he ever have cause to explore them? Up until a few weeks ago, his world had been so much smaller, not much more than a hut, a hill with a massive tree, and a big pond. Sure, Ymitoth had taken him into a small town a time or two, mostly for supplies and whatnot, but they never travelled more than a few hours across the prairie. In the past few weeks, he had done more traveling than the twelve summers prior, and this current jaunt represented the farthest he had ever been.

Maelich glanced down at Jom, as if the scrod might somehow validate his amazement at how very big was the world he lived in. The scrod didn't seem to care. He just trotted along, sniffing this and poking at that. A few times, he chased off after some critter making too much ruckus along the side of the trail. On these occasions, Maelich gave him a break from the trail and brought him up onto Validus's back with him. These were intended as punishments, but Maelich was beginning to believe the scrod was earning them intentionally.

As the land remained flat for a time, Maelich marveled at how vast a distance he could see. Of course, aside from the river he traveled alongside, there wasn't much to see. He seemed to be sailing through a sea of gently-rolling, green waves interrupted painfully infrequently by random clumps of trees.

On one occasion, when Maelich stopped to snack on some dried tubber and water the animals, he found something else interrupting the great, green sea. A dark shape far off in the distance seemed to be traveling along the same trail. Maelich stared for a long moment, finally deciding that, though it was much too far off to distinguish what it was, it was not his imagination. Something was following. The day had far too much light left to offer to backtrack and investigate. Not to mention, as much as he could see that something was following, whatever that something was would see him heading back the way he had come.

Shortly after the western sky completely lost the last glow from the setting sun, and both Jom and Validus had bedded down for the night, Maelich started back down the trail on foot. The moon was bright and full that night. He didn't even have to strain his eyes to see the trail. The light was so good in fact, he started out the journey at a run. The fresh prairie air whipping about on a brisk, northerly wind had him feeling alive. Hair blowing about behind him, he devoured the trail. He was one with the night. The soft taps of his feet lightly gliding across the packed dirt of the path spun round with the whoosh of tall grass bent over by the strong winds. Randomly among the light beat of Maelich's feet and the rhythm of the wind, animals chirped, croaked, rustled, or howled their melodic solos completing the symphony.

Suddenly, a horse grunted loudly from a dark patch of trees just north of the trail. Though Maelich had spent most of his life in and around the hut he shared with Ymitoth, he was well versed in what should and should not be lurking about the darkness of the great prairie east of Havenstahl. Books were wonderful things. There hadn't been wild horses in these lands for probably one-hundred summers. If there were a horse lurking about in the trees, its rider couldn't be far away.

Maelich slowed and crouched as he moved off the trail and into the tall grass. He crept quietly toward the shadows of the trees. His breaths remained as tight, short, and calculated as his movements. A blind man standing beside him would have been completely ignorant to his presence.

Once in shadow, he caught the dim, orange flicker of a dying fire. Though he couldn't see the flames, he imagined their wild dance as they leapt from glowing coals gobbling up all the air they could grab and casting shadows random and grotesque to mar the clean stability of those born of the moonlight. Within moments, Maelich had found a dark spot from which to spy.

The horse Maelich had heard from the trail stamped and whinnied, fighting against a thick rope binding him fast to a tree. The beast's eyes were wild with agitation. Maelich remained completely still as he watched the animal work itself into frenzy. There is no way the horse could have heard Maelich's approach. Perhaps it had gotten a hold of his scent.

Movement next to the embers of the dying fire lighting up the clearing dragged his attention from the frightened horse. A man jumped up from behind the fire. The fellow appeared confused, disoriented, and at least as startled as the horse. The same something that had startled the beast must have startled this man as well.

Maelich focused on the symphony of sounds filling the nighttime air, seeking an out of place footstep or heavy breath. Nothing reached his ears over the sounds of the heavy horse's hooves pounding the earth along with its frantic snorting and whinnying. Even the man's shuffling footsteps were drowned out by the animal's panic.

Though much quieter than his horse, the man seemed equally agitated. He drew his sword as his head darted around at the trees. Perhaps Ymitoth had sent one of Havenstahl's finest to ensure Maelich's safe passage. The man was obviously a warrior. Though startled, he held his sword with confidence and moved as if he knew how to use it. The medallion hanging from his neck caught hold of the flickering firelight as he turned toward Maelich and confirmed it.

Maelich's eyes locked on the medallion as it bounced in the fire's orange glow. The shimmering, prang thing resembled his own in every way except for one important detail. The image etched upon it wasn't the mighty fallon of Havenstahl, far from it. A dragon in flight with fire bursting forth from its lips met his gaze. Maelich set his jaw tight as he reached down and gripped the handle of his sword. Though he had never seen the image before, Ymitoth had told him everything he needed to know about it early on in his training. The breast it danced upon belonged to a blasphemer, a vile scrod who worshipped the ultimate evil as a god. The simple act of allowing the evil image to touch your skin was breaking Kallum's first law, "You shall serve none other than I."

Heat formed in Maelich's belly and raced out to the rest of his body as adrenalin coursed through his veins. Seeing the evil image Ymitoth had warned him about sparked a rage in him and brought a deep scowl to his face. This man was no escort sent by Ymitoth to guard Maelich's back. He was a villain in service of the most horrible evil on Ouloos; sneaking and hiding in the dark, waiting for the perfect moment to strike. Maelich wouldn't give him the chance. He leapt to his feet, drawing his sword as he rose. However, just as he prepared to charge, he paused. There were others hiding about in the darkness.

In a flash, the horse Maelich believed his scent had disturbed was flailing. Blood gushed from a wound on the animal's head. The frantic thing moaned and kicked, violently trying to free itself from the rope binding it to the trunk of a formidable, old oak. As the poor animal struggled helplessly against its bonds, four large, greenish-brown creatures rushed into the center of the clearing. Each of the beasts brandished heavy, wooden clubs. One of them—obviously the cause of the giant gash on the horse's head—dripped fresh blood from a slick of red that glistened in the firelight.

Shock, surprise, or a morbid desire to see the evil dragon warrior's skull cracked open by the club of a savage beast, Maelich couldn't be certain, but something stayed his feet and kept him from charging into the melee. The beasts were grongs. Though he had never seen one up close, there could be no mistake. They fit the description perfectly. Covered in scales, their squat, massive bodies gave way to thick necks and oblong heads. From the tops of their heads to the tips of their short, thick tails, small armor like plates jutted out of their skin. Long, slithery tongues slipped quickly in and out between thin, dry lips that barely concealed sharp, needle-like teeth.

As Maelich examined the nasty grongs, the dragon warrior sprung to action, dodging clubs and parrying blows from the crude, heavy weapons. The four beasts attacking the man fought with savage urgency, but he was wily and quick. Their weapons tasted no flesh, just dirt and bark.

There wasn't anything in the clearing Maelich considered friend. As far as he was concerned, all five combatants brawling in the fire's glow were adversaries. The grongs would have to be dealt with first. They were slow and somewhat clumsy in their movements, but they were big and swung their clubs with great force. The dragon warrior looked like he may prove more challenging. Hopefully, he would survive long enough to be questioned before Maelich gave him a traitor's death.

Maelich sucked in a deep breath and charged into the clearing. His sudden presence startled every soul on the small battlefield save one disemboweled grong frantically trying to shove his guts back into his gullet while falling toward the dying fire. That made one less soul for Maelich to send to the Lake. He owed the dragon warrior a debt for that, a debt he would repay with his sword.

One of the grongs took advantage of the brief distraction Maelich had provided and brained the dragon warrior. It was a glancing blow, but it sent the man careening into the trees and left Maelich with three beasts with which to contend. They charged all growls, snarls, and slithery tongues.

The clubs came faster than Maelich expected. They weren't nearly as sluggish and slow as they had appeared from the safety of shadows. Still, Maelich danced and weaved around the attacks leaving them nothing to taste but empty air. After a few graceful steps, he had their timing down. The first slash of his blade cut one of the clubs in half. The second relieved the owner of that club of his right leg and sent the brute rolling across the fire picking up sizzling embers as he went. That made two, one for Maelich and one for the traitor he hoped still lived.

Maelich didn't pause. As his blade reached the apex of its slash, he lunged and stabbed it into the heart of another grong. A thick ooze of foamy blood gurgled forth from the beast's mouth. The thing gazed wide-eyed and confused at Maelich who had precious few moments to consider the life he had just taken. He dodged just in time to avoid another club sailing at his head. Instead of cracking open his skull, it smashed into the face of the grong whose chest still held his sword fast.

Maelich yanked hard at his blade as the beast fell. It came free amid the sounds of cracking bones and sloppy meat. He barely had time to bring it above his head and block another shot from the club he had just dodged. It was a heavy blow, nearly powerful enough to plant his own blade into his skull. After halting the club's momentum, Maelich jumped back to regroup and go on the offensive. Before he could swing his sword again, another blade punched through the grong's neck. The creature looked pleadingly at Maelich, gurgled something throaty and inaudible, and fell to the ground. The dragon warrior stood in the thing's place wiping grong blood from his blade with his cloak.

The man looked Maelich up and down before saying, "You're quite handy with that blade," then smirked before adding, "for a lad."

Maelich raised his sword, leveling its blade at the man, "And you're wearing the crest of the dragon. That is beyond bold standing in the presence of the crest of Havenstahl."

The man laughed, full and hearty. He could barely speak, "Bold?" He laughed a moment longer before managing to compose himself and then continued, "You're a special one, yes, but make no mistake about that crest you bear. That's a coward's mark. Bold, you say? Yes, I am that, but this crest is not intended to strike fear in the hearts of my enemies. Oh no, I wear this crest with pride to honor the bravery of those who went before me defending the sweet name of the Dragon. My crest is not like yours. It is no boast of my greatness. We who bear this crest choose to remain humble in our works."

The man's insolence was confounding. "Yes, I say bold," Maelich spat, "as that crest you hold so dear and wear with such pride will be the reason I have your head!"

"Ah," the man chuckled again, "so it is as it always is with the unenlightened of Havenstahl. Fear fuels the men of your city. Your worship of that fiend, Kallum, stinks of it. Tell me this. Do you worship him because of his greatness, or do you worship him because you fear his greatness? Answer what you will. I tell you it truly makes no difference. I know the answer in your heart. The venom that spews forth from your lips can never change what your heart knows."

Maelich paused. He really wasn't sure why he revered Kallum. Ymitoth's fear of his maker was obvious when they faced the three in the cathedral at Havenstahl. However, he didn't think he shared his mentor's fear. It would be hard to know with certainty, given all the anger and adrenaline he had coursing through his veins as those three creatures assaulted the man he revered as trainer, mentor, and father. Truthfully, he had never given it much thought. Kallum was the creator of all things. That alone earned the worship of men. He was the father. Before him was no other.

After a few moments of wrestling with questions which required much more thought than he could give just then, Maelich decided he'd had enough of the debate. "You worship a demon, and I worship the one true god of Ouloos. That act breaks Kallum's first law, and your sentence is death. Though I realize you would not grant me the same courtesy, I will treat your corpse with respect and pray for your soul. What do they call you? I would beg forgiveness in your stead and ask Kallum to show you mercy."

"Mercy?" the man scoffed. "Your god knows nothing of mercy. Just look at his flock. Look at you. You would spill my blood because I think differently than you. What difference will my name make to you or your god? Do you request the names of all you slaughter in his name? Surely, you've slain many. Can you repeat all those names? Do you chant them to yourself to help you find slumber when the dark things in your mind keep you from it? Does the knowledge of your power to indiscriminately take life in the name of some violent infant of a god help you feel safe? I bet it does. I'd wager you charge across this land comforted in the fact that average men quake at the sight of your crest," the man circled Maelich as he fired off question after question.

A deep scowl cut its way across Maelich's face. The more the man spoke, the more he wanted his head. However, something about the vermin intrigued him at the same time, presenting questions and ideas that had never occurred to him before. Maelich checked his rage and pressed on, "You wear the crest of a warrior. A dark warrior, most certainly, but a warrior nonetheless. You handle your blade expertly. There must be years of training behind you. So then, tell me, what is it that separates you and I, aside from the fact I fight for the truth and the light and you fight for darkness and deceit? Is your rank not accompanied by some form of honor?"

"Ah," the man nodded, "so there it is. We fight for honor, do we? What honor is there in spilling blood? Your god—the one true god, as you so eloquently phrased it—relies on blood, fear, and death to ensure the obedience of his minions. It is the only way your kind knows. You kill what you don't understand, and you destroy that which does not share your opinion or fit your plan. You question my blade? My people must learn to wield these weapons of destruction to defend the innocents against killers like you. Never compare the likes of you to the likes of me. I won't have it. You're on a path to kill the last Dragon. Isn't that what your book says? Isn't that what your precious pack of lies tells you of your role, your destiny? I tell you now, I stand in the way of your destiny." The man then cocked his head to one side and smiled, "You asked who I am? I will give you that. I am Daritus of Druindahl. Have my head if you can, but know this. There were many hands at work in the creation of this world, and your precious god's do not bear the soil of the effort." With that, Daritus raised his sword and struck a defensive pose.

Maelich's chin dipped a bit. Of course, the man was evil. Everything Maelich knew about the crest he bore made it obvious. No man in the service of Kallum, the truth, would dream of letting that vile, evil image touch their flesh. However, Daritus had raised some good questions for which Maelich truly had no answer. On top of that, the man was making too much sense. It's typically rather easy to make your argument when you know what you're saying is true. The challenge for Maelich, just then, was the fact that the words hitting his ears were making more sense than those leaving his mouth. What did he really know about his creator other than what the book recorded? His only first-hand knowledge was that of a frightening, violent, childish god.

Maelich faced off against the swordsman in the flickering glow of the dying fire, working through everything the liar had said, for what seemed an eternity. Doubt was relatively unfamiliar, but standing in that clearing ready to cut evil down in the glow of smoldering embers, it was coursing through Maelich's mind like the currents of a fast-rushing river. Finally, Ymitoth's sure and soothing voice popped into his head, 'Son, the dragon be deceitful and so be his minions. He'll be telling ye lies and trying to make ye question your heart. Don't ye be falling victim to his wiles, lad. Remain steadfast and headstrong."

That was all Maelich needed. A warrior's life is duty, and duty doesn't doubt or question. Regardless what treachery pours from vile lips, truth is truth. Maelich's eyes squinted as the sneer returned to his face. Through clenched teeth he growled, "Daritus of Druindahl, in the name of Kallum, the one true god and creator of all things, I sentence you to die."

Maelich's blade sliced the damp, forest air. It arced toward the dragon warrior's neck, but his opponent was quick. By the time Maelich's blade reached its mark, the target had moved. Maelich slashed again and again, and again and again, he missed. Doubt returned. This time, it didn't race into his mind to challenge truth. Instead, it was subtle, slowly chipping away at his confidence in his blade and his ability. The man effortlessly slipping his attacks had yet to raise his blade, and Maelich couldn't get the edge of his sword anywhere near the man.

Before doubt could completely conquer him, Maelich wrestled it not quite into submission. It remained, but rather than numbing his limbs and making them heavy, it smoldered in the back of his mind, adding clarity to each input he received from his senses. He paid attention to Daritus's movements. A slash toward the throat resulted in a duck, while slashes toward the man's legs earned a flip. With each flip came a grunt, and with each duck a short, sharp exhale. The cool breeze on his skin helped him focus. A slight taste of blood in his mouth alerted him to stop biting his lip with each slash. The smell of glowing embers was pleasant, calming. Relax.

Maelich remained relentless with his blade. However, instead of randomly slashing and thrusting, using every sword stroke Ymitoth had ever taught him, his attacks were calculated. The result of each attack was logged in his brain. All the while, a plan developed in his head. Once it had finally matured into something he could act on, he did. He feined a high forehand slash and earned the duck he expected. Doubt fled.

Daritus's neck looked soft and exposed in the soft, orange glow of the fire. Maelich thrusted his blade at a spot just below the Adam's apple. He finally gained a response. The clash of the two blades echoed back off the trees of the clearing as they finally connected. One corner of Maelich's mouth raised up just shy of a smirk as he watched the corners of Daritus's mouth dip nearly to a frown. The battle began in earnest.

The blades flashed in the firelight, ringing out loudly as they crashed against each other. Moments melted into minutes before Maelich realized a broad smile had found its way onto his face. This man, Daritus of Druindahl, dragon warrior, was his equal in every way, if not even a wee more experienced with his blade. As Maelich marveled over his opponent's technique, he hoped the smile gracing Daritus's face was born of similar admiration. Regardless of whether it was mutual or one-sided, Maelich was quickly gaining a great deal of respect for Daritus. He was also growing concerned he wouldn't be able to finish the man. Respect or not, this wasn't training with Ymitoth. The blades crashing against each other had edges meant for slicing flesh, and the man trading those blades with him was better than any he had faced before. One of them wasn't leaving the clearing.

The battle raged on long enough for Maelich's limbs to tire. Each deep crouch brought a burning in his quads, while each slash of his blade left his triceps screaming. Failing to overcome Daritus with his mastery of his blade, Maelich dug deep into his training. Ymitoth had taught him much more than simply how to swing a sword. The greatest swordsman in all Ouloos had taught Maelich how to incorporate his body into his attacks, how to use his opponent's force against him, and how the body clinging to a sword is merely a collection of auxiliary weapons to be used in concert with the blade.

Using a technique Ymitoth had spent long hours teaching him, he shifted his sword to his left hand and slashed down at Daritus's head. As his sword sailed toward the man's face, he slid his left foot in between his opponent's feet. Daritus had raised his sword up to protect the top of his head. This left his jaw open, and Maelich hammered it with his right elbow. At the same moment, Maelich lifted his foot just enough to catch Daritus's foot as the dragon warrior stumbled toward the fire. Maelich didn't give Daritus a chance to right himself. He followed him toward the fire, slamming the pommel of his sword against the dragon warrior's temple and depositing him roughly to the ground.

The battle could only end in death. Maelich knew if he didn't finish Daritus, the vile wretch would finish him. He quickly flipped his sword over, held it tightly in both hands, and drove down into Daritus's chest. At least, that was his intention. By the time Maelich's sword was close enough to cut, Daritus's dragon medallion had slid directly into its path. Maelich had a new reason to despise the vile symbol of the greatest evil on Ouloos.

The great clang of metal on metal was nothing compared to flash of light that burst forth from it. It was like looking at the sun without shading your eyes. Maelich was instantly blinded. He barely had time to notice the sensation, as the concussion of the blast flung him through the air. Consciousness fled so quickly, he had a mere moment to consider the evil force contained in the wicked symbol.

When Maelich finally woke, he felt sore but refreshed. How long had he slept? Based on the light in the sky, though the sun threatened, it had yet to break the horizon. Unless a full day had passed along while he slumbered, he had only slept a few hours. After a long day on the trail, a few hours of sleep shouldn't be enough to feel as good as he did.

After a good, long stretch, Maelich's wits slowly returned. The events of the prior evening trickled in. He suddenly felt exposed, vulnerable. His sword wasn't in his hand. He quickly scooted back against a tree and scanned the clearing. It was still very dark. Though the sky above was brightening with the promise of a new day, the great trees surrounding Maelich kept any light from reaching him. On top of that, the fire had completely burned out at some point while he slumbered. It wouldn't be any help either.

Maelich relaxed and let his breathing grow steady. No matter what may have been sharing the clearing with him, panic would not help him survive it. Pushing back his fear, he listened. A herald of the morning crooned somewhere nearby. Maelich lost himself in the melody. It was a pretty tune for one already awake. It was less enjoyable for one still clinging to sleep. Maelich thought for a moment. He couldn't remember the last time he heard a herald's song that didn't annoy him for that very reason. On this particular morning, it was quite pleasant and helped him relax even further.

After a time, the clearing began to brighten. Maelich couldn't tell whether his eyes had grown accustomed to the dim light or if the earliest rays of the morning sun were penetrating the darkness of the forest. It didn't matter much. The important thing was, all evidence of the scuffle had vanished. Everything in the clearing should have been coated in blood and dead meat, but nothing. No dead grongs, no smoldering fire, and no dragon warrior, the ground was clean and the forest empty. It couldn't have been a dream. Everything was too real.

Doubt had nearly taken hold when Maelich noticed a bit of blood and twine on the tree to which Daritus's horse had been tied. It wasn't a dream. However, someone had obviously taken great care in wiping away any evidence.

Maelich searched the trees around the clearing in vain. His opponent was nowhere to be found. Why hadn't the man killed him when he had the chance? He'd been helpless for who knows how long, at least long enough for the dragon warrior to kill him while he slumbered. If the man had enough time to wipe away nearly all traces of the battle, he certainly would have had enough time to kill an unconscious fool. Perhaps it was a warrior's honor that saved him. Perhaps even warriors in service of the dragon respected some code of ethics in battle.

Mulling over potential reasons he yet lived and breathed proved a futile effort. He'd probably never know why a vile servant of the dragon would spare him. Perhaps if he ran into Daritus again, he would ask him. If that day ever came, it wouldn't be the only thing he would ask. The crazy ideas the man had about the dragon and Kallum were so backward. Yet, the way he presented them somehow made them seem less so. It just didn't make any sense. If only he could simply discount the man as a brute or an oaf, but he couldn't. He spoke well, and the things he said made sense.

Doubt was one of the dragon's greatest tools. That had to be it. Working through an honorable warrior, the dragon was able to trick Maelich into doubting both his quest and his purpose. Perhaps Daritus's medallion was the key. Maybe it was some kind of tool for control. When Maelich's blade slammed into Daritus's crest, the control was broken. The idea seemed a bit far-fetched, but better than anything else he could come up with.

There was nothing left to be learned in the clearing, so Maelich offered praise to Kallum for his good fortune and moved on. Daritus's questions continued to gnaw at him. He shoved them aside and focused on Alharin. The little adventure had cost him some time. He'd have to hit the trail hard to get back on schedule.

Maelich made it back to his camp quicker than expected. Validus and Jom were just waking as he arrived. The resourceful animals had found a small brook from which to water, so Maelich only had to worry over feeding them. They were back to the trail and charging along at a good clip before the dragon warrior entered Maelich's thoughts again.

Daritus must have taken a different path out of that clearing. The ground wasn't muddy, but it was soft enough from recent rains to leave evidence of travel. His horse had been clubbed to death by a grong, so he would have been on foot. There wasn't so much as one lone footprint younger than three days old.

Finally satisfied he wouldn't stumble upon Daritus again, at least along the path his group traveled, his mind drifted back to the mysteries of the prior night. Where were the carcasses? Four grongs and a solid steed had met violent ends, and there was hardly a sign of struggle. No fire with smoldering carcasses, no burial pit, there was just a bit of blood on a tree. He rifled through his memories from the night before repeatedly until he finally decided it just didn't make sense, and it wouldn't. With nothing but his memories for evidence, the mystery would remain unsolved. At least he was sure he wasn't being followed. The flat land behind him offered few hiding spots. If anyone were following him, he'd know.

Days passed, then weeks, and Maelich's battle with Daritus slowly drifted from his mind. Questions raised during his scuffle with the dragon warrior faded like old paintings left too long in the sun, hints of color without form or shape. Those in service of the dragon were a godless bunch, full of deceit with nothing but lies to dribble from their filthy gobs. None of their vile blabbering could be trusted. Still, Maelich couldn't help but be intrigued by some of the foul deceiver's questions. Ymitoth had been terrified by the presence of Kallum's priests and with good cause. The group of three was far more frightening than the entire pack of amatilazo Maelich had faced down at his mentor's side. They had no mercy and seemed to scorn all life. How could they represent the creator of all things?

After a time, Maelich decided he had wasted too much time on fruitless questions. Who was he to question Kallum's way or the manner with which he enforced his laws? The minds of men were much too feeble to comprehend Kallum. He was the creator of all things. How do you question that which created all? He finally decided you don't.

Before long, the flatland gave way once again to rolling hills. Rocky peaks jutted up from the ground as more and more trees speckled the landscape. The path still followed the river, at times high above making the act of gathering water a proper chore. Still, he was right on course. According to his calculations, the Bloody Mountains were but a week's journey. As far as he'd already come, that would go quickly.

Jom was handling the task of his travel famously. The sturdy scrod attacked the trail. He had even taken to chasing and toying with all forms of wild vermin residing in the hills, small animals that became increasingly easy for him to catch. The animal never seemed to tire. He was the perfect companion. He kept himself fed—like any good hunter, he ate what he killed—and he was never ready to quit before Maelich.

Maelich reached the base of the Bloody Mountains right on schedule, and they were at least as ominous as Ymitoth had described. Charred peaks stretched up so high, Maelich had to strain his neck to see the tops of the tallest ones. Smoke billowed from some of them, making it impossible to tell if they were fraternizing with clouds or their own gasses. Rivers of liquid fire oozed all about them. Some formed pools while others made their way down into the River Galgooth. Hissing clouds of steam rose up from these spots as the water cooled the fire and hardened it into charred, bulbous rock. The rivers of fire were fed by gurgling, spitting geysers which, at times, shot high up into the air.

Maelich stared in awe at the spitting, gurgling, burning thing long enough he almost thought of seeking a way around the mountains rather than over them. That would never do. They stretched for miles in either direction. How many, he couldn't tell. At least enough that his keen eyes couldn't make out either end of the range. No, he'd have to take the narrow path winding up into the peaks, dangerously close to those smoking rivers of fire.

He watched the living thing breathe and belch and burn long enough that he began to get comfortable with its movements. It seemed to have a rhythm, a pattern. If they stuck to the trail, and didn't dawdle, they should conquer the Bloody Mountains unscathed. Hopefully, Jom wouldn't see anything tasty creeping along the trail and forget himself.

According to Maelich's map, there was a cave near the spot where that treacherous looking path crested the mountains. They would have to camp one night there. That would put them on the other side of the mountain range within two days. With his plan all worked out in his head, Maelich made camp. They would slumber at the river's edge and attack the Bloody Mountains after a good night's rest.

The way up the mountain was less treacherous than Maelich had expected. It wasn't without incident, however. There were a few scares as fire spewed forth from the roaring mountain. Validus had all he could handle to keep he and his riders from getting scorched. Though Maelich had the utmost confidence in Jom, he felt it a much safer idea to strap him onto Validus. Jom wasn't a fan of the plan. A couple hours passed before the energetic scrod gave up the fight and finally lay still. They made the cave by nightfall and had cleared the path down the other side by nightfall on the following day. In the darkening sky, Maelich could faintly see the outline of one lone peak.

Mount Alharin truly was a sight to behold. Maelich's first good look came when there were clouds in the sky and he couldn't see the peak. Still, it was amazing. Taller than anything he had ever seen. It was just as Ymitoth had described, a lone peak jutting up out of nothing. Once the sky cleared and he could see the top, he noticed it was covered in snow. The air around him was quite warm, so he reckoned the snow must be there all the time. Ymitoth hadn't mentioned that.

The distance between The Bloody Mountains and Mount Alharin was short, two days journey at best. Then about one week up the mountain. Validus would never make it with a rider. The climb was much too steep. The horse would need to be led. The path up Alharin also wound around a bit curving back and forth. The going would be slow.

The way up the mountain was at least as challenging as Maelich had expected, but the air was crisp and fresh. At first, it was invigorating. By the third day, the thin sheen of sweat never came. By the fourth day, it had become noticeably cool.

The farther up the massive peak they climbed, the more breathtaking it became. Not just for the visions it presented, but also in the sense that the air grew thinner as they gained altitude. The lack of oxygen, coupled with the fact that the path was steep and physically demanding, added up to short days of travel. Despite the strenuous and slow climb, Maelich remained in awe of his surroundings. He could scarcely comprehend the distance he could see in any direction. That is, except in the direction from which they came. The thick smoke billowing off the Bloody Mountains damaged the view.

As his group continued up the mountain, the steadily dropping temperature slowly chipped away at Maelich's awe. By the time they hit snow, he was ready to quit. Half a day into that snow, it was waist deep. Jom could barely keep his head above it. Validus led the way, his broad chest clearing a path. Even with the sturdy horse churning his massive hooves through the powder, the going was slow, and the group needed frequent breaks.

The air grew colder and colder, like nothing Maelich had ever felt. There was no wood for burning, so they had to rely on each other's body heat to stay warm. Each time they paused, they dug into the snow and huddled together to keep from dying in the cold. In the few days they spent traveling up Mount Alharin they were caught in many snowstorms. Still they trudged along always moving up. At times they hoped rather than knew they were on the path, as it was well out of sight.

The snowflakes grew steadily fatter as the wind swirled and howled, pelting Maelich's face. Both animals whined. It hurt to move, each step so painful Maelich didn't notice his constant shivering. He had finally had enough. His knee dipped to the ground a moment before his hand touched something unexpected. It felt like grass. He crawled forward a few feet, and the snow was gone. Jom and Validus pushed through the snow alongside him.

Maelich rolled onto his back and sucked in as much air as his lungs could hold. It didn't burn. The biting chill he fully expected wasn't there. Warmth surrounded him. He lay there for a few moments, afraid to move or look around and realize it was a vision or mirage. Finally, he decided he'd waited long enough. Whether he was dead or imagining things, it was time to move on.

Maelich rose and nothing changed. The air remained warm and comfortable. He glanced around, half expecting snow to begin pelting his face again, but it didn't come. Instead, lush grass so green it looked painted filled his vision. Tall trees full of leaves just as green as the grass and flowers of every color Maelich had ever seen dotted the scenery. Around all of it was deep blue sky. There was no snow, no sleet or rain, not even a cloud. It was perfect.

Maelich still wasn't completely convinced what his senses were showing him was reality. Maybe he was dead or dreaming. At that point, he didn't really care. The only thing that mattered just then was he no longer felt cold. Suddenly, Jom charged into the grass and rolled about on it, panting and barking. Then Validus snorted and lay down in the grass letting the sun warm his frozen body. Maelich shrugged and followed suit. If he were trapped in some vision moments from death, at least he would die warm and comfortable. All three of them slowly drifted off to sleep.

A full night and half of a day had passed before Maelich woke to Jom's sloppy kisses. Thank Kallum, they were still alive. An excited giggle slipped away from him as he tackled the scrod and wrestled around with him a bit. Validus continued to slumber, and Maelich decided not to wake him. The journey had been hardest on the sturdy horse. Instead, he and Jom explored their new surroundings, quickly discovering a pond beyond a slight hill. Maybe they had died. The place certainly resembled stories of the place souls go upon leaving their bodies, stories Maelich had learned as early as he could remember.

The water was cool and fresh. They were both totally revived, feeling none of the weariness a traveler often pays a long road. The air in this place didn't have the lightness of the air up the mountain. After a nice long drink from the pond both Maelich and Jom felt as if they hadn't journeyed at all. The place seemed to have some sort of healing quality about it, a paradise surrounded by desolation.

Maelich pulled out his map. They had arrived. Amazing. Even with all the confusion the snow had provided, they had managed to stay on course. Brerto's cave wasn't more than a mile from where he lounged with his scrod. It suddenly occurred to him that none of them had eaten in days. He should have been starving, but he wasn't. He had no desire to eat. He had a satisfied, full feeling. Jom appeared to be feeling the same way, perfectly content. They sat for a bit at the edge of the pond, Jom's head in Maelich's lap as the content scrod enjoyed some wonderful scratching behind his ear. They could have remained in that spot forever.

After a time, Validus strolled up and took a good, long drink from the pond. The horse seemed to be feeling as fresh as Maelich and Jom. Maelich wasn't sure if it was the air or the water or something else entirely, but the place certainly had a revitalizing quality about it. Whatever the cause, it was a welcome mystery after such a long journey. Once Validus had taken his fill from the pond, Maelich decided it was time to take the last leg of their adventure.

Maelich had no desire to ride, so he strolled alongside Validus as Jom chased this and that through the grass. The urgency he had felt for the entire journey up to that point had melted away. A comforting peace washed over him, as if his small group was merely enjoying a relaxing stroll through the mountains with no destination, no purpose. They were just enjoying a nice walk. All of them deeply inhaled the sweet air as if it were feeding them, each breath more refreshing than the last. Maelich wore a dopey grin which perfectly matched what was on his mind, absolutely nothing. His thoughts were totally of the moment, no troubles, no cares at all.

The last bit of the journey bore a stark contrast to the arduous task that had been the rest of it. It was painfully brief. The mouth of Brerto's cave yawned before Maelich far too quickly. He decided to enter alone and seek the great Brerto. Jom and Validus could remain outside and enjoy the perfection of their surroundings. Before Maelich had a chance to take one more step toward the cave's mouth, a man emerged from it.

The man wore long, straight, silver hair that was pulled back from his face and draped down behind his shoulders. His beard appeared just as his hair, silver, straight and perfect. It came to a point around the middle of his chest. His skin was fair and did not reflect the age one might expect to accompany hair so silver. Quite the contrary, it appeared youthful and taut. He wore a pure, white gown etched with the color of prang. The gown itself seemed to glow from within, as if it had its own source of light and didn't require the rays of the sun to shine. The man held a scepter in his hand, crafted of a substance foreign to Maelich. Typically, a staff of such intricate design would be made from prang, it being the most precious substance on Ouloos. However, this scepter was made from something else, something that appeared to be even more precious than prang. Its shape seemed rather simple at first. After deeper inspection, it wasn't. The thing was a long rod with what appeared to be a tangle of thin barbs entwined at the top. However, this was no random tangle, but a delicate, intricate design thoughtfully crafted by an obvious master. Maelich didn't have to ask the man's name. He matched Ymitoth's description of Brerto perfectly.

Brerto's voice was as deep and powerful as Maelich expected, "Maelich, though it may feel as if your journey is complete, I assure you it has yet to begin. Your travels and your training, your conquests and your honors are nothing compared to the road lying before you. You must temper your feeling of accomplishment with the humble knowledge that at this point you know nothing. You have been trained as a warrior and taught to survive, at that you are expert. But know this, you are an empty vessel which it is my duty to fill. That is why you have come to me."

Maelich bowed, "I am honored to be in the presence of one so magnificent and revered. Moreover, I am humbled to be trained by your greatness."

Just then, Brerto opened his eyes. They were without color. At least, they were without a color Maelich could explain. They weren't black. They weren't anything. Yet, they were everything, at once both empty and full. For a moment, Maelich thought the great and mighty Brerto might be without sight. The idea quickly proved false.

Brerto's voice first raised and then roared, "What is this vile creature you bring before the great Brerto? A scrod? The steed I can forgive as the manner with which a warrior must travel, but a scrod? You presume to bring filthy, worthless animals in my presence? This disrespect will not be tolerated! You have desecrated the perfection of my garden. For this you must be punished!"

"But," Maelich began, bewildered by Brerto's sudden rage, "I…I didn't know. Jom has been by my side for my entire journey. He is my companion. He has…"

"Silence!" Brerto boomed, the ground quaking under the might of his voice.

Jom whined and hid behind Maelich. The bold scrod had never shown fear like that. Maelich's awe of Brerto quickly turned to vehemence. Jom was much more than a filthy animal to Maelich. He had even saved his life. Furthermore, no matter what anyone else thought of it, he happened to be Maelich's best friend, his only friend on the most challenging journey he had ever taken. He was not about to let anyone, not even the great and mighty Brerto threaten and terrify him.

Maelich pushed back his fear and stood tall, defying Brerto, "That's enough." Filling his voice with all the strength he could muster, he continued, "This scrod is my companion. He has saved my life and never left my side. I don't intend to have him terrorized by an angry old man who sits alone for eternity atop a mountain letting his hatred fester like a disease. If he is not welcome in this place, I am not welcome in this place, and I'll find my destiny without your help or training."

Brerto did not respond. His face became graven, and his eyes suddenly had color. Not just one color but many colors. It seemed they were all colors all at once. A strong wind picked up on the mountain as he raised his hand and clenched his fingers into a fist. In the same instant, Jom's whining became stronger, quickly growing to a howl.

Maelich slowly turned toward Jom who writhed in pain on the ground, eyes wild with fear. The young warrior bent down to console his friend, but the scrod snapped at him. He watched helplessly as blood began to ooze from Jom's nostrils. At first a slow drip, it quickly became a steady flow. Before long, the poor animal was choking and coughing as blood began oozing also from his mouth. Jom's howls grew stronger and louder until they eventually ceased, and all that was left was a dull moan. Then nothing.

"Jom?" Maelich knelt beside the scrod and shook him. "Jom?" he said it again. It was no use. Jom's face twisted in an expression of unimaginable pain, and the poor animal was quite dead.

Maelich's eyes welled up as he fought back tears. His eyes squinted up tightly as his mouth formed soundless words. Rage filled him while his head shook slowly back and forth. Brerto waved his hand, and Validus charged off back the way he had come, back into the snow. Maelich's eyes remained squinted up tight as he stood to face the menace who had just taken the life of his dearest friend. The muscles in his face bulged as he clenched his teeth. His entire body tightened, all his muscles flexing in unison beneath quickly reddening skin. As his skin grew redder, so did his eyes. Brerto would die. Maelich didn't care how long this bastard had been alive. The murdering worm would never see the sun rise on Mount Alharin again.

Maelich remained tense. His fists clenched so tightly that his nails dug into his hands leaving thin cuts in them. Before long, thin trickles of blood oozed past his knuckles and dripped to the ground. His skin had continued to redden and began growing quite hot. A burning smell filled the air as something crackled close by. In his rage, Maelich barely realized his cloak burned around him. He didn't care. His gaze remained locked on the cowardly bastard who would use his great power to kill a defenseless animal. Anger and loathing coursed through him. He curled up and brought his fists next to his head. He was all a blaze, flames licking up to the sky from his body. All at once he stretched his limbs out in unison, and fire exploded from him in all directions. It burned everything around him. A giant ball of flames, a perfect sphere of fire at least five miles in diameter engulfed the entire mountaintop. Then darkness.

CHAPTER 14
THE JOURNEY OF DARITUS

Bright white stole Daritus' vision a moment before he felt the pain. He had caught the pommel of Maelich's sword in his periphery only a moment before it blasted the left side of his jaw. The lad hit like a charging horse. By the time the blinding, white flash faded in favor of dark trees bathed in the flickering orange glow of a dying fire, the horizon had shifted. Unable to gain his balance, Daritus stumbled. The forest floor was unforgiving when his shoulders pounded into it hard enough to knock the sword from his hand. It had seemed nearly soft as he lounged upon earlier in the evening, before the lad of the Lake had come calling. Now it felt like unforgiving stone, ancient and unmoving.

Daritus couldn't decide which part of his body hurt the worst. Was any part of him not throbbing or aching in that moment? The cobwebs slowly dissipated. The sound of Maelich's footsteps seemed incredibly loud as they echoed in Daritus' throbbing head. He couldn't just lay there. He was in a fight. He was on his back. He needed to get back to his feet and find his sword.

By the time Daritus regained enough control of his body to turn his head and locate his sword, Maelich was kicking it further out of reach. It glinted in the fire's orange glow as it skittered away. His heart sank into his gut as Maelich's boot slammed his chest and pinned his shoulders back against the ground. He struggled against the weight, but his muscles still weren't responding with any urgency. The look on Maelich's face, along with the lad's sword bearing down on him, assured him there was great need for urgency. Unfortunately, despite his desire to live, despite his mind shouting at his muscles to move, shift, do something, he couldn't. This was his end. The Lake would have him.

Time is such a strange thing, never seeming to move at the same rate from one moment to the next. What is a moment? Daritus wondered at that. He expected he should be quite dead with Maelich's beautiful sword punching through his chest and out his back. There it was though, hanging above him, slowly falling toward his chest. He'd rather it be quick. He failed. He lost. The lad had bested him. Get it over with already.

Finally, it came, the pressure in his chest would mount until the pop. He'd been stabbed before. Obviously, it had never been a fatal cut, but he knew how it felt, the pressure. Those were moments when time didn't make sense, when things slowed and allowed the briefest moment of panic before the inevitable. Then the pop would come. The pressure was always worse than the pop. Pain came later. That was a different thing. Daritus had become so absorbed in the pressure, the panic in waiting for that pop, he hadn't noticed Maelich's expression change. Once he did, he hadn't long to muse over what it might mean. Suddenly, the world was again bathed in bright, white light.

The ground was gone. In fact, so was the pain. Daritus felt nothing. Perhaps he had left his body laying skewered on that forest floor and his energy was returning home, returning to the Lake. Perhaps you don't feel the pop when it ends you. Death is another of those things like time, things that don't make sense. It's different, of course, time is something you gain experience with as you age. Death only happens once. It can be contemplated and studied, great minds can theorize, but until it happens, you don't know.

As the white light faded, death seemed less and less likely. Daritus floated above the clearing, the apparent scene of his demise. Scanning it, he failed to find his body. Had he been carried away body and soul? Perhaps he wasn't dead.

Suddenly, a swirling wind picked up in the clearing below him. It swept everything away. The carcasses of the grongs, his horse, packs, food, gear, they all spun higher and higher. Except Maelich, his body remained. It lay upon the ground, untouched.

Nothing made sense. Was it real, or was it his mind showing him visions as his essence sped toward the Lake? Had the lad really killed him? Was his body clinging to life with Maelich's sword sticking out of its chest? Did he need to do something to survive?

Suddenly, the world went dark. Daritus' mind grew quiet as he raced toward what he did not know. The motion was apparent. However, there was no light, nor was there any sound. Neither was there a taste or smell, only the feeling of flying through…something. Then he was falling, faster and faster. He screamed. At least, he tried. There was still no sound. How long? How far? He couldn't tell. As perplexing as time could be with all one's senses, it was even worse without them. Finally, he stopped.

For a moment, there was complete stillness, nothing. Then there was light. That was something. It didn't seem natural though. It was thick and red. It made his skin appear as blood. There was water below him. At least, he hoped it was water. Bathed in that same red light, it looked more like blood. However, it couldn't be that. It was a large body, the size of a lake and surrounded by cliffs which extended as far up as he could see. That would be quite a bit of blood. Perhaps the lad had slain him in the forest. This was death. What a mockery of his life that would be. The great warrior Daritus felled by a mere lad, a lad who bore the mark of Havenstahl. He shook his head slowly and closed his eyes.

Then he fell again. He plummeted into the blood water. Again, he tried to scream but still couldn't find his voice. His heart pounded against his chest as he thrashed about, wildly fighting to keep his head above the water. Something pulled at him, some force. It sucked him down, deeper and deeper. His limbs worked against it, thrashing and swimming and pulling. It was too strong. He plunged deeper and deeper into the water and into the darkness. His lungs burned. He needed air. Breathe. Water rushed into him as his lungs yearned for air. His body convulsed as he swallowed gulp after gulp.

Daritus struggled as long as he could, finally giving in. Once his fighting ceased, he slammed onto dry, rocky ground. The water was gone, but his lungs were still full. He rolled about the ground fighting to get air into his lungs. Finally, he coughed, gurgled, and then vomited. Buckets of water and bile passed by his lips. His body heaved again and again. He thought the gush would never end and then, air.

He lay there gasping. Moments passed, or eternity. What did it matter? He was breathing and there was solid ground beneath him. He slowly fought to his feet and tested that ground. It was good and solid.

Darkness had returned. He squinted, searching, but there was no light, not even the blood light from above the water.

"Where am I?" he asked, finally able to hear himself again.

He sat upon the hard stone. Though reasoning through recent events didn't seem an effort which would bear any fruit, he needed to get his wits back, and he desperately needed to catch his breath. Death still seemed the most likely explanation for the events following his battle with the lad, but he didn't feel dead. Of course, how would he know if he did? Now what? That was the question. Whether he was dead or yet lived, he couldn't just sit there for eternity. At least, he didn't want to. If he was dead, his desire didn't die with his body. He had want.

Enveloped in darkness, the prospect of attempting travel seemed ludicrous. His surroundings were a mystery, as were any potential destinations. He could crawl upon the ground, but to where?

Then there was light, dim, merely a glow. He thought it might be his imagination at first, but it continued to grow. It took him a moment to discover the source, but it was coming from him. His crest, the Dragon, was glowing. It was dull at first, almost imperceptible, but it grew quickly. Before long it was bright enough he had to squint to protect his eyes. With his hand beneath his chin to shade his eyes, he took in his surroundings.

Rocky walls sprung up around him. They had obviously been there all along, but he was just now seeing them. He scanned every inch of his surroundings. It appeared as if he had been sucked into a cavern, the ceiling of which was well beyond his sight. Straight ahead was another light. It seemed to shine in response to his crest. He wanted the light with every shred of his being, wanted to go to it, explore it. Consciously, he knew this. However, at the same time, it felt as if he had no choice, like this new light controlled his decision. Either way, the two lights would meet.

When he arrived at the source of the light—the seeming answer or counterpart to his crest—he realized it was a perfect match, only opposite. The peaks in his crest were valleys in the other. It was almost as if... He quickly grabbed for his crest and placed it into the match oddly floating before him. The fit was perfect. With a metallic click the two pieces snapped together and the light from both melded into one. Daritus had to shade his eyes and look away as the combined light of the two grew increasingly brighter.

The ground trembled beneath Daritus and knocked his equilibrium slightly off kilter. A couple of deep, steadying breaths and the act of focusing his eyes on a single point kept him from vomiting out whatever might be left in his gut. The feeling of control didn't last long as the rocky ground shook more violently, bucking and swaying like a chunk of it was trying to tear loose from the rest. When it finally did and began to lower, Daritus fell in heap on the bucking stone beneath his feet.

As the ground slowly lowered, the violent shaking ceased. The idea of standing back up died a quick death in Daritus' head. Banging it when he fell had left a dull ache, and the only consistent thing about his journey from that clearing in the forest—which seemed an eternity ago—was violence. After flying, falling, drowning, and being tossed about like a pebble in an avalanche, he decided lying against the cold stone was the least stressful part of his journey up to that point.

Daritus' eyes slowly grew accustomed to the bright light gleaming from the two emblems. He couldn't look directly at them. However, squinting his eyes up tight, he was able to take in his surroundings through the slits which remained open. The glimmering emblems floating above him were at the center of a perfect circle of stone. At least, he assumed it to be stone based on the rusty, reddish-brown color of the substance. The walls stretching up above him as the rocky ground he lay upon sunk deeper were perfectly smooth. The engineering that must have gone into making a platform sink into a shaft triggered by a hovering key which didn't appear attached to anything was beyond the ability of any architect Daritus had ever met. It seemed impossible. Then again, nothing he experienced since facing the lad of the Lake in the forest really made any sense. If a giant fairy sprinkled dust on him and ate him, it wouldn't seem odd at all.

Eventually, the platform reached the bottom of the shaft and a circular room spread out around it. A few moments later, it ceased its descent and fit the rest of the floor perfectly without so much as a seam between them. The wall of the room was just as smooth as the shaft had been. Blazing torches adorned it at intervals of roughly fifteen feet. Bathed in the impossible light of the interlocked emblems, they looked more like shadows or voids, like some weird negative light.

Suddenly, a light matching that which emanated from the two interlocked crests shined directly in front of Daritus. His key, along with the lock he had placed it in, first dimmed in response, then brightened to match the new light. Once both sources of light shined in equal brilliance to each other, they grew brighter still. As impossible as this seemed to Daritus, he quickly realized it no longer hurt his eyes to behold. He could stare directly at this new light source through wide eyes rather than the slits he'd been looking through since the earth moved beneath him.

At first, it looked the same as the rest of circular wall surrounding him, an impossibly bright spot on an otherwise identical section of wall. Looking more closely, he realized that wasn't the case at all. Hanging from—or perhaps floating in front of—the wall was a much larger version of the crest Daritus had worn around his neck since he faced his trial and became a servant of the Dragon. Immediately in front of it sat two thrones, both occupied by men wearing perfect, white robes decoratively stitched with the color of prang.

Both men seemed ancient, but the one on the right appeared elder to the other. His shimmering silver hair was straight and perfect, as was his perfectly groomed beard. The staff he held seemed to glow with its own life force. The image of a Dragon with wings spread in a victorious pose perched at the top of it. The material with which the staff was crafted was foreign to Daritus, but it appeared even more precious than prang.

The man on the left appeared just as dignified as the other, but somehow seemed lesser. Daritus couldn't tell if it was because this man's hair and beard had color, dark and streaked with silver, that made him appear younger or if it were something else. Perhaps it was the Dragon riding the top of this man's staff. Both were identical in every way save the image of the Dragon they bore. This man's dragon looked fierce and ready for battle.

Daritus carefully considered both men as he approached. Both wore closed eyelids, and neither sported any kind of expression. They could have been sleeping if not for how straight and tall they sat. On top of that, even though their eyes were closed, they both seemed to be looking at him.

The simple queerness of being scrutinized through closed eyelids was unsettling enough that Daritus didn't immediately notice all the sources of light surrounding him growing brighter as he approached the two men. It seemed impossible to him. Even though all the lights in that room had been brighter than any light he had ever seen—or could even imagine—they all did grow brighter and brighter. His crest coupled with the crest floating above the platform, the crest hanging from the wall behind the two thrones, and the Dragon statues riding the staffs of the two men in those thrones, all of them increased in brilliance with every step Daritus took. His amazement and confusion grew as quickly as the light increased. He had become so engrossed that when the man to his right spoke it nearly startled him out of his boots.

"Daritus," the man's voice was deep and commanding, somehow equal parts menace and comfort, "you follow the way of the Dragon. You are a brave defender of your people. Your mind has been greatly enlightened through the teachings of the Dragon. Knowing this, my question to you is thus. What imbecilic, miniscule portion of your thoughtless brain spawned the idea you should battle with the lad of the Lake? Have you not been taught he is the prophetic son? Did you not learn the fate of our world rests in his hands? He is the tool for our success. He needs guidance not interference. You know this."

As the man spoke, Daritus remembered the dream which had sent him on his journey to Havenstahl. He lay in hot sand without the energy to rise. The sun baked his skin as he looked out on a horizon fuzzy from heat rising off the ground. Nothing but sand upon sand surrounded him in every direction, and it remained completely flat for as far as his eyes could see. He should have been burning and dying from thirst, but he felt nothing. Then, as he lay not dying in blistering sun which should have been killing him, a shape approached in the distance.

Giant, leathery wings stretched out from it flapping up and down with impossible grace. They made a thunderous whoosh as they thrust slowly and powerfully up and down and propelled a massive red body through the smoldering air. Twenty men would easily fit atop the beast, along with all the necessary equipment to safely keep them there. However, there were no men riding the monster.

Perched atop the flying thing was a beast like nothing Daritus had ever seen. It was giant and completely covered in silver fur reflecting the brilliance of the blistering sun in such a way it seemed to magnify it. The hair around its face and on its neck was much longer than the stuff covering the rest of its body. It looked like a crown, a great silver crown of fur. Beneath that crown was a wide, flat snout above jaws which hung open to expose glistening, white fangs. They looked like they were meant for tearing up flesh. The body carrying the terrifying head around was equally menacing. At least the size of six large men, it sat on top of four muscular legs ending in humongous paws. They looked like there was a great deal of strength behind their swat. However, none of those were the most frightening things about the monster. Its eyes were. They had no color at all. They weren't black. They were nothing.

Daritus remembered the terror in that moment, trying to gain his feet and flee. He knew now that it had been a dream, but at the time it was more real than anything he had ever experienced. Lying there in blistering sun that refused to give him the peace of death, the only part of his body he could move were his eyes. As much as he wanted to, he couldn't stop them from moving down from the silver beast to behold the Dragon bearing down him.

He had been raised to revere and protect the Dragon. That didn't make it any less terrifying. The massive body that could easily crush a man beneath its weight wasn't the red of blood but more like fire. Almost orange, it seemed to glow as if it were a source of light rather than a reflection of the sweltering sun. The thing's face consisted mostly of jaws extending roughly six feet from the rest of its head and ending in somewhat of a beak. Those jaws hung slightly open exposing hundreds of razor-sharp teeth. From behind them a forked tongue protruded, slithering all about as if it had a mind of its own. The Dragon's eyes glowed with the same red fire as its body. That body was gigantic, much larger than any animal Daritus had ever seen. It was easily the size of three huts, but these huts had a long, thin powerful tail hanging from them. Between the body and the head was an equally powerful neck. It was roughly half the length of the tail. It had its legs curled up into itself. The back one's looked thicker and more powerful, while the front ones looked as if they would function much like arms. All four ended in claws attached to appendages that looked quite human. The front looking like hands and the back looking more like feet.

The dragon was all but on top of Daritus, when the terror tormenting his mind became too great. He slammed his eyes shut, but the horrifying image remained. The wind pounding down on him from those powerful, leathery wings offered no reprieve. He lay helpless beneath them, ready to die. A deafening roar raised up above the thunderous flapping. It left his ears sore and ringing. He wasn't sure if it had come from the Dragon or the beast upon its back, but it didn't really matter. Either way, it was menacing.

Of course, he hadn't died, not in that moment or any time since. Instead, just as he reached the most hopeless point he could remember in his entire life, everything stopped. He suddenly felt as if he were floating, gently swaying on a relaxing current. He opened his eyes to find himself in a boat surrounded by water. There was no land as far as he could see in any direction. The light rocking of the boat soothed him, slowly calming his nerves. Then he noticed he wasn't alone. The great, silver beast was with him, but without the blinding quality about its fur. It looked at him with eyes that were the absence of color.

"You will go to Havenstahl," the beast spoke like a man. "You will find the lad who seeks the crest, and you will follow him. Do not disturb him. Do not reveal yourself to him. Watch him, and your master will be well served."

Daritus found his voice, "Who are you?"

"I am your Lord, Kaldumahn!" the beast boomed. "I am the lion! I am the sun! I govern the skies of day. See to your task, and I shall shine on you with glory!"

The dream ended there. Daritus had all but forgotten the details until this man in the cave spoke to him. His voice was the same as the beast in his dream. With the revelation came the realization that the man addressing him was none other than Kaldumahn himself. Daritus quickly cowered to his knees, bowing before his Lord.

"Forgive me, my Lord," he sniveled, "Maelich in his ability is much more than a lad. I sought only to protect myself from the fury of his blade. He does not worship you. He worships Kallum and wished to kill me for my service to you."

Kaldumahn still bore no expression, "Why didn't you flee? When that grong struck you and threw you into the trees you could have escaped while Maelich was busy dispatching those grongs. Furthermore, you were instructed not to be seen by him. How is it he managed to come upon you as you slumbered? Then, instead of fleeing when he did find you, you engaged him in a discussion of your theological differences. Do you know of the brain?"

Daritus remained silent, not realizing Kaldumahn expected an answer.

Kaldumahn asked again, "Well, do you?"

Stuttering a bit, he answered, "Yes…yes I do."

"Good," Kaldumahn boomed. "Then you understand its purpose

is not strictly to keep your skull from collapsing on itself. You have failed me. Still, you have served me well in the past. When you wake, you will find yourself in a dark forest far from Druindahl. You will be quite lost. If you survive and find your way home, you will have paid your penance to me. Now sleep."

Daritus lost consciousness with Kaldumahn's last words echoing in his ears.

CHAPTER 15
REBELLIOUS PUPIL

The world blazed in brilliant glory as Maelich's eyelids first fluttered then snapped open. It couldn't have been much before or after midday. He blinked a few times before scrunching his whole face up, as if the added weight of his cheeks or brow would help to protect his sleepy eyes from the glaring sunlight. When he opened them again, they were no more than slits, barely wide enough to let even the essence of light in. It was enough. Mere moments passed before he could open them wide to let the light in.

His head wasn't nearly as bright as the sky just then. The sun did wonders to chase away the fog, that slow grogginess typically saved for early mornings. It lingered like the last lonely bloke left at the pub, dreading his return to real life, clinging to the security of his near-empty pint the barkeep refused to refill. A few deep breaths fully chased the sleep hangover away, and Maelich's senses finally began registering reality.

Even with his senses functioning at full capacity, it still felt he was trapped in a dream. The sun blazed mercilessly above him, cooking him like a thick slab of meat over a fire. Though he felt the intense heat burning his exposed skin, it wasn't uncomfortable. Not a drip of sweat clung to him. A light breeze, barely notable, blew about the heat. As faint as it was, he could feel every hair on his arm moving. Each individual hair gently danced in the light breeze, and he felt every movement. More than that, the glory of the bright sun, which had nearly blinded him moments prior, faded to something more akin to the smoldering remains of a dead torch. Everything was just as bright as it had been, but it no longer hurt his eyes. All his senses seemed to be in overdrive, yet something was protecting them from extremes.

Once Maelich accepted that the sun wasn't burning him—even though it should have been—he realized in what an awkward position he had woke. He was curled nearly in half with his right shoulder twisted up so it rested on his left knee. He prepared to move his head. The thought seemed a bit silly. However, the way his body was twisted, he knew it was going to hurt. Bracing himself, he turned his face toward the sun. It didn't hurt at all. No lightning flashes of pain raced through his shoulders or down his spine. A grin slipped onto his lips. He wasn't stiff at all. In fact, he felt completely refreshed.

A quick glance around chased away his joy as quickly as it had come. The altar beneath him was unfamiliar, but the rest was as fresh as the cool, mountain air. Brerto, Jom, everything flooded back in. Alharin spread out around him. However, the beautiful garden he remembered was now scorched and dead. His eyes quickly scanned the area, searching for Jom's carcass. It was gone, but the memories of what that old bastard had done to him remained. Validus had run off and was nowhere to be found. Maelich suddenly felt very alone.

The fact that the paradise he had found with Jom and Validus was now a barren waste didn't matter. It was just scenery. He had no one. It was difficult to determine if rage or hopelessness were the greater of his emotions. If he could get his fingers around Brerto's throat just then, he would squeeze and squeeze until one of them died. As powerful as the old wizard was, Maelich knew he probably couldn't kill him. At the same time, he wanted nothing more than to lie down on the charred ground beneath him and cry. He would have done that too, if he thought it would solve anything. It wouldn't, and he couldn't stay there. Jom's face lingered in every burnt thing on the mountain top. He had to get away from that place. He would have to trudge back down the mountain through the deep snow.

Suddenly, the blackness of the ground began to give way. The greenery he remembered before the...event was returning. He remembered the burning. There had been so much smoke as his clothes smoldered around him, but he hadn't burned. His hands quickly shot to his cheeks, rubbed them, examined the skin there. His flesh remained perfect, unscathed. Yet, he clearly remembered the flames licking past his face, burning as hot as his rage for Brerto.

Perhaps the old wizard was dead, a victim of his fire. That was the last thing he remembered, his anger finally growing to a point where he could no longer contain it. The flash had been so bright and hot. Could anything have survived? How had he survived?

Before long, the mountaintop looked just as it had when Maelich first arrived. The charred remains of his rage had fully given way to the lush, green paradise he remembered. The fire was still confusing, but it was a riddle which would remain unsolved. He didn't have any answers for it. The only thing he was certain about was it came from him, or his rage. Either way, he had something in him which could make fire from nothing. Ymitoth had never prepared him for anything like this. Had he known?

"That was quite a mess you left for me to clean up, Maelich," Brerto interrupted, his voice just as powerful as the first time Maelich had heard it.

Maelich scanned the mountaintop. The old wizard was nowhere to be seen. "Show yourself, coward!" Maelich growled. "I had hoped you were dead, burned in the flames of my fury!"

Brerto laughed full and hearty, "Foolish child, you are powerful but rough and unrefined. Your little tantrum was a magnificent display of raw power, but quite expected. In fact, unlocking that little burst is exactly the reason behind the death of your scrod. Honestly, I'm quite fond of scrods. Unfortunately for you, when you challenged me on behalf of that scrod, you unwittingly accomplished two tasks. First, you sparked my ire. That is something no man, even one as special as you, should ever endeavor to do. Second, you exposed your deep emotional attachment to him. That weakness is a trait you get from the blood of men which courses through your veins. The attachment to worthless animals, other members of mankind, and silly trinkets are all are very human weaknesses. These weaknesses make the race of men an easy exploit. I used the attachment you felt for the animal to fuel your rage. That rage is what allowed the fire which burns inside you to escape. In time, I will teach you to summon and control it. Before I could do that, it first had to be released. Now that it has, your training can begin."

Unable to mask his bewilderment, Maelich fired back, "Do you honestly believe I would stay here on this mountain and train with you after everything you've taken from me? You are a heartless monster. I shall find my own way, but only after I send you to your grave."

The rage returned, that burning. It started in his gut, nothing more than a small flame. Rather than try to control it, Maelich let it come. It grew quickly, fueled by images of Jom tromping through tall grass juxtaposed against images of Jom struggling as that bastard squeezed the life out of him. Flames quickly began burning all over Maelich's flesh. The hotter his rage burned, the hotter his skin became. His fists clenched tightly as he curled himself up and prepared to release his flame and burn Brerto, burn the mountain, burn everything.

Suddenly, Maelich was on his back, tossed to the ground like a child's toy during a violent tantrum. Pain radiated out from his sternum like he'd been clubbed across the ribs, but there was no one around. He quickly rolled and regained his feet. The flames had subsided when he hit the ground, fleeing with his focus. Scanning his surroundings for Brerto's vile smirk, he couldn't regain the fire. Smack, he was blasted in the jaw. Something more powerful than anything he'd ever felt had hit him harder than he'd ever been hit, yet there was nothing near him capable of doing it. He swung wildly at nothing just before being hammered in the gut by that same invisible thing. He stumbled and swung again, but there was nothing to fight.

Finally accepting he couldn't hit something that wasn't there, Maelich stopped swinging. He calmed his mind and circled slowly, trying to anticipate from where the next attack may come. The answer came quickly enough when a strike to the back of his head sent him sprawling to the ground. The world spun before him while little white dots danced in front of everything else. Bile raced up the back of his throat in response to the dizziness. Years of training with Ymitoth helped him navigate the pain and maintain control of himself. His breathing grew steady and the urge to vomit passed.

He had almost made it back to his feet when pain gripped his chest and held him fast in place. This pain was different than the strike he had felt earlier. That was a blow like someone had hit him. This felt like something had reached into his chest, grabbed hold of his heart, and squeezed. Both his hands clutched at his chest as he choked and gurgled on saliva, which quickly began to taste like blood. It suddenly occurred to him that this must have been what Jom was feeling as he died.

"Exactly, Maelich," Brerto's voice was calm and sure, "what you are feeling is exactly what Jom felt when I killed him. You will learn to obey! I have much to teach you. Whether you want to learn it does not concern me. You will train, or you will die."

The pain suddenly fled, and Maelich fell in a heap. Struggling to catch his breath, he began crawling. He didn't know to where, but he needed to get away. Blood filled his nostrils and throat before trickling down his chin. He coughed and snorted, trying to clear the thick congestion clogging his sinuses.

Brerto continued, "Feel free to take your time in deciding. I am eternal. You will find you can travel to the edge of the snow but no further. Your path was laid long before you came to be, Maelich, and I will not attempt to trivialize your importance. You must complete your journey. However, you must first learn to obey."

Maelich continued to lie on the ground, even after he sensed Brerto's presence leave the mountaintop. There didn't seem to be a compelling reason to do anything. If the old bastard could be trusted, he didn't have a choice but to submit.

Ymitoth had been hard, stern. Of the all the words Maelich could think of to describe his training under Havenstahl's greatest swordsman, cruel wasn't one of them. Everything that man did had a purpose. Brerto was an entirely different story. Killing a defenseless animal isn't a lesson. It's violent and hateful and, above all else, unnecessarily cruel.

Maelich lay there for a long while lamenting, debating with himself whether he should submit to the monster on the mountaintop. Luckily, the pain the old brute had caused faded quickly. The healing quality of the mountaintop was uncanny. Perhaps it affected his mind as well as his body. Despite all the rage he felt for Brerto, an odd sense of understanding slowly crept into his awareness. It wasn't blatant or obvious, but it was there lying somewhere deep beneath the hatred and fury.

Everything that had happened to him since he left the hut he had shared with Ymitoth was proof he was who Ymitoth said he was. Surely, his role in Ouloos' future was more important than his relationship with Jom. Brerto was ancient and enlightened, and apparently not bound by the same attachments which shackle men to this cause or that. Perhaps cruelty was not the fuel for Brerto's rage. Maybe it was purpose. Like most beings Maelich had encountered on his journey, Brerto knew more of him than he himself did. Jom's loss hurt, and it probably would for a long time, maybe eternity. It didn't, however, change Maelich's purpose or his fate.

It wasn't long before Maelich's strength completely returned. He couldn't just lay there forever, so he wandered the mountaintop instead. He explored every area except Brerto's cave. Maybe he'd be able to face the old wizard again someday, but he wasn't ready yet. Though a part of him had begun to justify Jom's loss somewhat, he wasn't quite ready to accept it yet. Nor was he ready to submit. Instead he ventured to the edge of the green space, the garden, as Brerto called it. Apparently, the old wizard thought of the entire mountaintop as the garden. Maelich decided to explore it all.

The entire mountaintop, or garden, wasn't more than a few acres which consisted mostly of grass. At its center was a slight hill marking the entrance to Brerto's cave. Directly to the West was a pond and just South of that a stone path led under a vine-covered archway into what Maelich would consider a proper garden. More than proper, it was amazing. The place boasted a bounty and variety like nothing he had ever seen. All forms of fruit grew in abundance on vines and trees. Things he had never seen or tasted. There were big round, red ones and orange ones, long, curved yellow things, purple things and green things. There were even small, brown furry things. None of them looked to belong together, but they all grew in and around each other, exploding in a juicy, ripe spectacle. Beneath all of this, more varieties of vegetables than he had ever seen sprang right out of the ground. Foods he never knew existed seemed to burst forth from everywhere. Surrounding all of it, fragrant flowers filled the air with the sweetest perfume.

Maelich suddenly found it difficult to fuel his anger for what Brerto had done to poor Jom. He reached up and grabbed a juicy, orange orb from one of the trees. Its skin was thick, so he stuck his thumb in and peeled it away. Juice ran down his arm as he bit into soft sweetness. It was impossible, like eating a dream. Food just didn't taste like that. He bit into the thing again and laughed as juice ran down his chin. The pure serenity of the place was easing his pain and filling his mind with reminders of more pleasant memories.

Despite the assault the place had on Maelich's senses—the colors, the sweet and foreign tastes, and all the wonderful scents dancing among the gentle breeze—a part of him remained skeptical. The voice grew smaller and quieter with each passing moment, a hushed scream begging him to turn and flee the enchanted place before losing himself completely. He finally decided to listen to that voice before the place eroded away his good sense completely.

Maelich held up what was left of the delicious orange orb in his hand and threw it to the ground. Then he spit the mouthful he'd been savoring out onto the ground. It seemed a shame to waste it, but that voice—as small as it was—would not relent. It quietly shouted that none of it was real, not the green paradise at the peak of a snow-capped mountain, not the smells, not the delicious fruit bursting in perfectly ripe sweetness from the trees. It was all an illusion meant to trap him without realizing he was in a prison. A man can break free from strong arms holding him in place. However, a man who wants to be somewhere has no reason to attempt escape. This magical place was nothing more than a very attractive cell concocted to erase his desire to leave.

Brerto was widely known as the greatest wizard in the history of Ouloos, more of a force of nature than a man. Bending nature to his will didn't seem outside the realm of possibility. Neither did the possibility that the top of the mountain was covered with as much snow as the rest of it, and he had merely convinced Maelich otherwise. The result was the same either way. It was all a grand fakery.

There was only one real answer. It was obvious Maelich couldn't get his hands on the wizard. His might, his sword, and his lifetime of training to use them both in battle wouldn't do him any good. All he could really do was walk away.

By the time Maelich made it back to the place where he had entered the garden, the small voice had grown as much as the enchantment of Brerto's garden had diminished, and Jom's face had returned to the front of his mind. All the rage and sadness he felt looking down at his best friend's pleading eyes and knowing there was nothing he could do to help gained a sharper edge since Maelich had a taste of what the poor scrod felt in that moment. If he ever returned to this place, it wouldn't be to train. It would be to destroy.

Something was different about the trail. At least, it didn't appear as Maelich remembered it. There was no gradual transformation from the pleasant atmosphere of the garden to the foreboding snow of the trail. In fact, there was no noticeable trail at all beyond the stark transition from green to white. It seemed some invisible barrier separated the two climates, both pushing against each other but neither willing to give any ground.

Maelich tried to step into the snow, but his foot would not pass the barrier. There was no wall to stop him, no visible obstruction, he simply could move his foot no further. He repeated this exercise all around the edge of the garden and earned the same result each time. There were the strong arms to hold him. Only these weren't physical things he could fight through. This was something he didn't even know how to fight.

Sitting at the edge of the garden lamenting his inability to pass seemed a useless endeavor, so he didn't do it for very long. If he were going to solve the riddle of the place, he'd need to learn its secrets. He wandered around the mountaintop for seven days and nights looking for answers, something tangible which might give some clue as to how the place could be defeated. Occasionally, he'd stop to drink from the pond or venture into the garden to snack on fruit he had never tasted. Hunger didn't drive these visits to the garden. He couldn't even remember the last time he'd felt hungry. The tastes of those foreign flavors were so enticing, he couldn't help himself.

By the time Maelich had explored the expanse of the mountaintop, he couldn't recall why he wanted to leave in the first place. Everything he'd ever need was in reach. All he needed to do was reach out and grab anything he wanted. A nagging notion he was leaving something undone remained, but he couldn't put his finger on it. All he really remembered was why he had come. He was to train with the great and mighty Brerto. It was time for that training to begin.

CHAPTER 16
DARITUS' FLIGHT

Total darkness on its own is enough to scare most right out of their wits. Add to it the feeling of waking someplace completely unfamiliar with no idea how you arrived, tears just might be shed. Daritus wasn't much for tears, nor did he scare very easily. However, in that unfamiliar darkness he could at least admit to himself he was a bit on edge. After blinking several times to confirm his eyes weren't merely closed, he gave up on them as a tool. Apparently, Kaldumahn had made good on his promise.

Thinking about how angry his god had been at him for engaging Maelich reminded Daritus of his journey from the forest to wherever that queer place had been. He wondered if the ground might give way at any moment and plunge him once again into deep, unforgiving waters. No, this place felt different. Despite not being able to see anything, he knew the place was real, tangible. At least he was in his own body. On that horrible jaunt from the forest to Kaldumahn's feet, he had felt he was outside of himself watching things happen to him rather than experiencing them. There was something solid behind him, and cool air clung to his cheeks. Wherever this dark place was, it was real. That was something.

A slow grope about the ground and the solid things behind him convinced Daritus he was deep in a forest. One tree doesn't make a forest, but night on its own could never be so dark. Deep in a cave could be so dark, but trees typically don't grow deep in the darkness of caves. Considering there was at least one tree, and absolutely no light, deep in a forest seemed the only logical answer. That riddle was easy. The next would be a bit more difficult. How would he get anywhere that wasn't right where he was?

The darkness on its own didn't offer any real peril. He could sit against that tree behind him, remain completely still, and more than likely not risk a thing. However, things lurk in the darkness, hungry things. He needed a plan and sitting in the darkness for the rest of his days wasn't a good one. He recalled something his father had told him when teaching him to keep his belly full on the trail.

"Many trails run through these woods," his father's voice echoed in his head. "They zig and they zag. They double back, and they do it again. If you ever find yourself lost among that maze, don't just go racing along them without a plan. You will only become more lost than you had been. Instead, you ignore that trail. You pick a direction, and you stick to it. Eventually, you'll come across something you recognize, or at least something useful."

Daritus shook his head at the thought. It was good, sound advice for someone who could see. However, keeping a straight line was a trick in a well-lit forest. It would be impossible in total darkness. Walking out of the forest wasn't the answer, but maybe he could find something useful.

Daritus slowly moved his hands across the ground, feeling every inch as he crawled around the tree he'd been leaning against. He didn't find anything but a bunch of dirt and twigs. There may have been an acorn in there too, but he couldn't be sure. The twigs would be useful if he had anything he could use to start a fire. Unfortunately, his gear was back in the clearing where he faced down the lad of the Lake. There would be no fire. There would be no light.

Daritus increased the circumference of his circle. Aside from more dirt and more twigs, all he found were more trees. They were about as helpful as the dirt and twigs. As he crept along the dirt feeling about with his hands, he became acutely aware of every sound around him. The dark forest was alive. All the nocturnal critters hunting and feeding on each other scurried and grunted, a macabre orchestra, a melody dancing over the rhythm of swaying trees and rustling leaves. Then, like a solo, an eerie moaning rang out in the distance. It was a sound of deep sadness, the kind of sadness not even a mother's love can conquer. It almost sounded like wailing. He shivered at the thought of what sadness might cause a sound so desperate, so distraught.

Perhaps if he remained too long in the place, it would bring the same sadness upon him.

The pain of the cries quickly grew more immediate. They surrounded him, nearly choking out every other sound. They were getting louder or closer. He couldn't be sure. His thoughts turned back to his meeting with Kaldumahn. This place would be his penance. Kaldumahn's words had been very clear. Whatever thing was making that awful noise couldn't be anything Daritus wanted to meet. Sight would be a dream. However, punishments weren't meant to be easy.

Suddenly, another sound snapped him away from his thoughts. There was something rustling around in the trees, something big and close. Daritus spun his head in the direction of the sound. It didn't do any good. His eyes hadn't adjusted to the darkness one bit, and at some point, the wind must have picked up. He hadn't noticed while he'd been mesmerized by the moaning or wailing or whatever that awful sound had been, but it had definitely picked up. It lashed at him with icy fingers and raised bumps on his flesh. Then the rustling came again, loud and near. It was out of sync with the rustling of the leaves and too close to the ground. It was near and quickly approaching.

Daritus slid back against a tree. It may have been the same tree he'd been leaning against when he woke, but he couldn't be sure. The darkness mingling with all the terrifying sounds dancing around in it had him completely disoriented. Being able to see probably wouldn't have made a damn bit of difference at this point. Well, if he could see he might just run.

Pressing his back hard against the thick trunk behind him, Daritus remained completely still and waited for the sound to repeat itself. Moments passed, or minutes. He couldn't be certain, but it felt like a lifetime. His heart slammed against his chest. Each beat echoed like thunder in his ears, sounding like the thing was beating inside his ear canal rather than his ribcage. All the while it's rate steadily increased.

The sound finally repeated, closer now. He tensed, fear flooding his mind like water overflowing a basin. Despite the chill air swirling around him, a bead of sweat ran from his temple to his chin. He knew he wouldn't see anything, but he was unable, or unwilling, to give up on the idea of sight. The sound grew closer. It was big. Bigger than a scrod, maybe even a full-grown fallon. His legs may as well have been planted in the mud. They just lay shaking, ignoring his pleas to flee, to charge off into the darkness. That was probably for the best. He'd be a far easier target unconscious from braining himself on a tree.

This was unfamiliar territory. He couldn't remember the last time he'd been truly afraid for his own life. Sure, he feared for the lives of those he'd sworn to protect, his family, his people, but he couldn't recall ever fearing for his own skin. He tried to reason his way out of it, the heavy thing perched on his brow, the sinking feeling in his gut that he'd not see another day. If he couldn't see anything, then nothing could see him. It wasn't working. Fear was an enemy he just didn't know enough about. He had no experience dealing with it. How do you stop your mind from envisioning bloody, horrible ends, and how do you stop from trembling? He was quick, logical, and always in control. He could talk his way out of most situations without even drawing his sword, but this was different. Would his voice even work if he tried it?

It didn't matter. A low growl began behind him just before a hellish screech rang out in front of him. Hot breath blasted his neck. It smelled like a spent battlefield, stale blood and rotten flesh. Something splashed his face. Blood? Saliva? Then something warm and wet dripped on him. Now he could see, but not with eyes. Visions of fangs stretching out from a bloody muzzle, dripping with anticipation of the next bit of soft flesh they'd punch into.

Daritus finally found his voice and cried out, instinctively throwing his elbow back at whatever was sniffing about his throat. It landed with a crunch on whatever was creeping around the tree. He had hit something. That something howled like the souls of the Lost Wood. Whatever the thing was, it was now in a bit of pain.

Daritus' legs finally agreed it was time to move, and he quickly scrambled off the ground. He barely made his feet before he was slammed back into the tree. Something strong and fast had blasted him across the face and left his jaw throbbing. Blood ran down his cheek, four thin trickles streamed freely from fresh cuts. He fired his fist at the darkness. It connected solidly with a crunch. A slick ooze covered his knuckles. The thing bled. Instinct suggested he follow up the shot with another, but logic prevailed. Instead of trading blows with some beast he couldn't see, he slid around the tree and began to run—or as close as he could come to it while feeling his way through the darkness.

The trees and brush were a thick tangle. As Daritus navigated through the mess as quickly as he could, he realized the moaning had returned. It grew louder with each tree he leaned against or rounded.

He cleared a half-dozen of them before realizing the trees themselves were moaning, rather than some creature lurking among them. The volume of their cries steadily increased. Did they cry for him or his attackers? They offered no resistance. Perhaps he could count them as friend. If only they could fight.

The bodies crashing among the brush behind him grew closer. He had hit two of them. Based on the ruckus quickly gaining on him, there were at least five times that many. Branches cracked, and leaves rustled all around him. He reckoned they were trying to surround him, circle him up, and cut off his escape. He would have cried out again, but his voice had left him.

Then the fire came, running from his shoulder blades down to his waist. It felt like four blades slashed him in unison, tearing open his cloak and cutting deep, bloody ravines down his back. This wasn't a trickle. Blood gushed from the cuts, quickly saturating his tattered cloak and down to his trousers. His arms flew out to his sides as his chest shot forward reflexively trying to flee the pain. He lost his footing, stumbled into a tree, and fell around it. His back slammed into the forest floor, and his new wounds erupted, agony radiating out from them to the rest of his body. He moaned something pitiable. His voice had returned.

The sword slipped from its scabbard, the only friend Daritus could count on in the fight. The trees cared enough to cry for him, but they didn't raise a branch to help. Just him and his sword then. It wasn't the first time. If he survived, it probably wouldn't be the last. Instinct, more than anything else, sent the blade in a wide arc above his head. There was a moment of brief resistance. It was quickly followed by sloppy gore and cracking bones, and then the sound of something heavy hitting the ground beside him in more pieces than it had been. He slashed again. This cut didn't feel as deep, but it bought him enough time to regain his feet.

Once his boots were beneath him, Daritus was once again pushing through the brush and around the trees. He stumbled along, fighting against pain that pulsed through his back with each step. As he worked his way through the darkness far too slowly, he paused occasionally to slash behind him. His blade tasted flesh a couple times. Others earned it nothing but air. The beasts hunting him down didn't seem discouraged by his efforts. They just kept coming.

It seemed impossible, but the brush grew thicker. Apparently, he had picked the wrong direction in which to flee. Branches scraped his face as his pace slowed, groping and feeling his way through brambles. They were gaining, slashing at him. Nothing had touched him since his back had been torn open, but they were close enough he could feel wind on his back with every swipe.

Then something got him. This time it was shallow and on his arm. The next caught his calf as he came as close to running as the thick brush would allow. They moved better than he did, faster. It was only a matter of time before they overtook him.

Dizziness crept into his head. It became more and more difficult to keep his feet. The cuts on his back were deep. How much blood had he lost? It still gushed. He must have dumped a good bit of what he had in him onto the forest floor and splashed more onto the trees. He stumbled, and then fell. It wasn't the wooziness of blood loss that got him. It was a hill, high and steep. He rolled end over end. It didn't help his head at all. However, it did put a bit of distance between him and the horde chasing him down. They weren't all over his back anymore. Perhaps he'd get a moment of relief before bleeding out completely.

The bottom of the hill finally came, and Daritus stopped rolling. Scrambling to his feet seemed the logical thing to do, until the effort was abruptly stopped by something unmovable. He felt around it enough to determine he'd come to rest under a fallen tree. Perhaps Kaldumahn had taken pity on him.

Daritus lay completely still beneath the tree. It was all could do. His fight was gone. He heard the throng of beasts make the hill. A couple of them must have fell, crashing through the brush like he had a moment prior. He gripped his sword tighter. He wouldn't be able to slash anything from his position, but he could stab and poke, and give them something to remember him by. His breath grew steady as he lay waiting to take as many of the bastards with him as he could.

They grew closer and closer, grunting and snarling as they came. A howl ripped through the darkness. Daritus tensed. In moments they'd be on him. Just as he was about to stab his blade into anything that got close, they charged right by. He could here claws cutting into the tree above him as they raced past him and continued deeper into the forest. Apparently, in all the excitement of their hunt for him they had given up on their sense of smell. Before long, he heard them no more. They were gone.

Time hadn't made any sense since Daritus had woke lost and confused in total darkness. An eternity or a few moments, he couldn't say. It felt safe under that tree. He didn't want to move. It didn't seem the beasts who had attacked him were coming back, but he needed time to regain his strength. On top of that, there wasn't any point in attempting travel in the darkness. Besides, his eyelids were so heavy, it took all his strength just to hold them up. He couldn't do it for very long.

By the time Daritus' eyes opened again, there was light. It wasn't much. However, it was enough to tell the sun was high in the sky, and the forest was at least as dense as he'd imagined. It was also enough to make an honest attempt at finding a way out of the forest. Hopefully, he wouldn't run into anymore nightmares in the deep wood. At least now, he could see them if they came.

Regaining his feet proved an even greater task than he'd expected. Everything ached, and his limbs weren't responding like they should. Eventually, he did make it out from under the fallen tree and onto his feet. It immediately seemed a folly. The trees swirled around him, spinning faster and faster. He quickly picked a spot on the ground and focused on it. The trees spun on while a thick puddle of his own blood stared back at him. His knees buckled. Moments later he was staring up at the thick canopy, green upon green with filtered sunshine sneaking through. Then darkness again.

Reality was a tricky thing. Was he awake or dreaming? The forest was dark, just enough light to see horses approaching. Did he imagine them? Did it matter? Was he alive or dead? The next time he woke, the ground raced by beneath him. His body swayed as the horse beneath him galloped along. The wetness on his back was gone, and the sting of wounds had diminished. Many men on horseback surrounded him. He dozed again.

He sunk into the mattress, plushness cradling him like a lover's embrace. Had it really been a dream, a nightmare? The thought of rising fled quickly, chased away by memories of his dizziness in the forest. His surroundings were completely foreign. Just then, he didn't care. He dozed again.

Daritus slipped in and out of reality. For how long? He didn't know. Finally, he woke, and everything felt real. This time he was sure it wasn't a dream. The room he occupied was the size of a small hall. The place seemed a king's quarters, far nicer than his own. Sun poured in through a massive window, glinting off ornate, prang frames of mirrors and fine works of art. He considered each piece separately. All depicted battles and all were scenes of men triumphantly toppling a Dragon or many Dragons. The Dragons looked fierce and menacing, while the men seemed heroic and righteous. 'What a pack of gat,' he thought. Still, they were beautiful, if ill informed. He noted they were also meticulously placed, each in the perfect spot to give them the exact amount of light that would present them in their most exquisite appearance.

As he continued to scan the room it occurred to him that the men and the horses had been no dream. Who did they serve? For what house did they ride? Questions swirled about his clouded mind. He needed answers he couldn't get while lying on his back. As he began to rise out of the bed, he realized his crest was gone. Before his anger had time to rise, his thoughts were interrupted.

"Not just yet," a voice from the shadows began, low and monotone. "You were cut deep by amatilazo and you've lost much blood. The strength you feel now will quickly fade as soon as your feet hit the floor."

Daritus was startled. While he was scanning the room, he completely missed the man who now stepped out from the shadows. "Who are you?" was the first question to pop from his mouth. It just beat out, "Where am I?" as the most important question on his mind just then.

The old man smiled. He looked old and haggard behind his long stringy tangle of gray hair. Yet his eyes were keen, sparkling with a lifetime of unlocking the mysteries of life. They told a much different story of the old man than the rest of his appearance. "I might ask you the same question, but first I'll give you an answer. I am Hagen. I'm a healer and have been given the almost detestable task of nursing you back to health. You are in Havenstahl in the guest quarters of King Ymitoth the fury. He has many questions for you, as you have much for which to answer."

"Havenstahl?" he all but shouted, "How did I come to be in Havenstahl?"

"Ah, not yet. I gave you an answer. Now I get to ask a question of you," Hagen smiled again.

As far as Daritus was concerned, all in the service of Havenstahl were vermin. However, there was something comforting in Hagan's tone and manner. Daritus wanted to answer, even felt compelled to. "I am Daritus of the Dragon," he proudly said, "I serve in her army, charged with the task of her protection. I serve with my life, if necessary." It was partly truth. He was in the service of the Dragon, but he withheld the part about being the king of the city which worships her.

"Daritus," Hagen repeated, "that is a powerful name. It's amazing you survived The Sobbing Forest. The fact you did tells me you are as powerful a warrior as your name suggests. Those cuts should have killed you. How does a warrior with such might come to serve the dragon?"

"She is truth. She is peace. She is enlightenment," Daritus fired back quickly, then paused before adding, "It's my turn again. How did I come to be here?"

Hagen answered offhandedly, "Havenstahl received reports from the valley that amatilazo were attacking the villages there. The beasts were hiding in The Sobbing Forest by day and terrorizing the villagers by night. The soldiers drove the forest on a hunt. They found a pack of forty and slaughtered them. Five men were lost in the hunt and many wounded. They happened across your near-dead carcass while they were sweeping the forest for injured soldiers. You were almost left because of your crest. However, it ended up being your salvation when a wise general realized that a live soldier in service of the dragon may prove useful to our cause."

"So, I'm a prisoner then?" Daritus' response was quick and curt.

The old healer looked thoughtful for a moment, "Somewhat, I suppose. For now, however, you are my patient. Once you are healed, you will be a prisoner. Keeping prisoners isn't my lot. Mine is to heal. Once you are healed, I will be removed from your service." He then became more serious and added, "Know this. I know of your cause and your beliefs, and I do not refute them outright. I myself am struggling with my own beliefs. While you are in my care, you will remain safe. I cannot aid you in any way other than healing. I will not hinder you either, but for now you need rest."

With that, Hagen offered a rancid smelling purple liquid in a fine chalice and some water. Daritus nearly gagged at the smell. Luckily, the taste of the foul brew didn't quite match the odor. It wasn't something he would seek out, but a mild fruitiness dampened an odd combination of metal and sea. Daritus eyed Hagen as he drank down the old healer's concoction. The old man had honest eyes. Perhaps he could trust him for the time being.

A warmness radiated out from Daritus' chest, stretching slowly toward his extremities. It wasn't uncomfortable. On the contrary, it was like soaking up glorious sun on a lazy afternoon. It may have been his mind playing tricks, but it seemed his strength was returning with the warmth. The sensation was enough to turn up at least one of the corners of his mouth.

"That's nearly a smile," Hagen suggested before offering a wet cloth.

Daritus graciously accepted the gift, quickly mopping at his hot face. It had grown warm while he drank. It seemed Hagen's wonderful elixir was locked in battle with whatever infections were rampaging through his body. He barely noticed the old man leave the room just before the world once again went dark.

Hagen kept the door cracked slightly open and watched until he felt confident Daritus had found slumber. The sleep would do the battered soldier nearly as much good as all the medicine he had just pumped into him.

Purposeful footsteps echoed through the hall before the door had finished closing. Hagen had been exploring the halls of the castle long enough to identify just about every soul who haunted them. These belonged to a king who desperately wanted to interrogate a prisoner. That would have to wait.

Hagen turned and bowed, greeting his stern-faced king, "Your highness."

Ymitoth's expression softened slightly as he replied in kind, "Hagen."

"You look troubled, my king," Hagen continued.

"Aye, I be troubled," the king began. "For a week that vermin's been holed up in me palace and I ain't had even one word with him yet. Has he woke?"

"Yes, he has, but he is still too weak for questioning. Any technique you may use to try and get information out of him could very well kill him, your highness."

"When?" Ymitoth remained cool.

Hagen thought for a moment as he stroked his chin, "One week. He'll be strong again…strong enough, I should say, in one week."

"Fine," Ymitoth looked away, failing to mask his disappointment, "but now that he's woke, I'll be posting guards by the door."

"Wise choice," Hagen replied as he bowed again. "I leave you to your task, highness."

With that, Hagen retreated down the steps of the tower and continued out of the palace. He'd done all he could. Hopefully, Ymitoth could hold off on harassing the prisoner too soon. Killing the man before any information could be attained wouldn't help anyone.

CHAPTER 17
CIALIA'S QUEST

Cialia strolled through the darkness among trees which stretched toward the sky to heights that seemed impossible. Though she clipped along at a steady pace, her legs didn't seem to be moving. On top of that, she couldn't feel the packed dirt of the trail beneath her feet. It seemed she wasn't walking along the trail at all, instead floating just a hair's width above it. There was no way to confirm it. Thick fog surrounded her up to her waist. It poured onto her path from a source unknown. Her skin appeared ghostly in the darkness, as did the thin, white gown draped loosely about her. It was quite sheer and quite unfamiliar. She was too fond of bright colors to wear anything so boring as white.

The thin, foreign white gown suddenly gained all her attention. It was so sheer and left her arms completely bare. The damp forest air grew quite cool in the evening. She should have been freezing, especially with a stiff breeze blowing her blonde hair all about behind her like it was. Instead, she was quite comfortable.

The gown kept Cialia's attention until she realized she had no idea where she was going. Nor did she have any idea why she may want to visit the unknown destination. She tried to stop but failed. Something other than her own will drove her on.

Suddenly, she stopped. The fog quickly fled away, and she was standing in a perfect circle of moonlight. There didn't seem to be a moon at all that night. However, there she stood, bathed in its eerie glow. A looking glass materialized before her. At least, it hadn't been there a moment prior. It must have come from somewhere. Her face stared back at her from the glass. She had never found it very appealing, but the boys seemed to, even most of the men. They doted over her. The attention always made her uncomfortable. They would always use the same words to describe her, striking beauty, and bottomless, blue eyes. They saw her as a thing not a person, and certainly not an equal. Boys were so immature and unoriginal. Striking beauty, what does that even mean? They could barely put together a cognizant thought.

As creepy as boys could be, the men were worse. At least the boys carried a bit of innocence about them. She was barely two moons into her thirteenth year, and the men would still gobble her up with their eyes. They probably didn't even notice hers were any kind of blue, much less bottomless. Whatever that meant. Of course, they had a bottom. Everything ended somewhere. They'd never see it, just look at her bosom and mention the pretty ringlets of her golden hair resting there. Gazing into the glass, she didn't see what they saw. If only they didn't.

Then the face staring back at her changed. It was still her, kind of, but somehow not. It made about as much sense as the fog coming from nowhere and then racing away, or the vast pool of moonlight with no apparent source. She could still see herself in the reflection, but it was no longer a perfect depiction.

The strange face quickly faded along with the light. Only darkness remained. Then she was moving again. This time, the pace wasn't easy like a slow stroll as it had been earlier. This time, she was now being thrust into the darkness, into nothing. It surrounded her.

Again, there was light. As quickly as it had blinked out, it returned. However, this light wasn't cool and eerie like moonlight. This light burned bright like staring wide-eyed at something even brighter than the sun. Squinting didn't help, neither did closing her eyes completely. It only made the bright glow red instead of white. Thankfully, it dimmed quickly.

A few moments passed before she felt comfortable to open her eyes again. By the time she did, the light was no longer unbearable. However, it was all around her. The darkness had fled, as did the trees. It was daylight, and a flat, barren land surrounded her. A massive shape quickly materialized before her. It was massive and silver, a beast like none she'd ever seen. It roared, blowing all about her with its breath as she cowered before it.

The thing's voice boomed like thunder, "Cialia, princess of Druindahl, you will travel to Havenstahl. There your father is being held. Your task is to free him. Make haste. His time is short. Though it is not our way, you will find cause to spill blood on your journey. Do not hesitate. Your purpose is great, and those whose blood you must spill will have yours on their hands if they can. Now go!"

Her inquisitive mind wouldn't let her obey immediately. Needing answers tended to make her forget her fears at times. She asked, "Who are you? Where is Havenstahl? Why is my father their prisoner?"

The beast's eyes closed, "I am your lord! I am the sun! I am Kaldumahn, the great lion who stalks across the skies! You will know the way. Now go. Travel hard and rest infrequently. Go!"

Before Cialia could ask any more questions, she woke back in her room. Everything was in its place. There were no great beasts assaulting her with hot breath or mighty roars. It was just her, safe and alone in the dark. It had been a dream. Kaldumahn had come to visit her in a dream. Father had been captured on his journey, and she had to rescue him. He was the mentor. If they were able to capture him, how would she stand a chance? He had told her she was ready when he had presented her with the crest of Druindahl, the mark of the Dragon. However, the trial he had given her seemed unusually easy. He had denied it, but she'd always felt he was protecting her. Despite being the best man she'd ever known, he was still a man. There was no way he'd give her a fair trial she might potentially fail and face some sort of peril.

Doubt is far from a warrior's best friend, but she'd never been tested, not for real. Still, Kaldumahn himself had given her this task. Perhaps this would be her test. Druindahl boasted some of the fiercest warriors in all the land, and the mighty Kaldumahn had chosen her. Nervous excitement rose in her belly, chasing away all the fear and doubt.

The excitement brewing in Cialia's belly slowly began to feel like confidence. After all, she had been trained by her father, the greatest swordsman in all the land. At least, she'd yet to meet anyone who didn't revere him as such. He had been a harsh teacher. By her twelfth summer, she could trade blades with any man, or sneak about the trees without making a sound. She was ready.

She gathered her armor together on her bed. It wasn't big and clunky like the armor worn by some soldiers she'd seen. It was light but effective, part of the gift her father had given her at the end of her twelfth year. Gauntlets, greaves, and a light chest plate accompanied two swords, two daggers, and a short bow. At the time, her father had explained he designed them to perfectly match her style and movements. Except the swords. Those had been a gift forged by Agrimon the Fierce and passed down by her grandmother. She had never met the woman, but the blades—vengeance and mercy—fit her perfectly. Some warriors must rely on bulk and power. Not her. She was quick and moved like a viper, slithering around attacks and striking quickly. Her armor needed to be light to avoid restricting her movements. The two blades allowed her to attack from any angle, and she could wield them both with deadly precision. All the pieces were meticulously etched with designs inspired by Dragon's fire.

As Cialia dressed, it suddenly occurred to her this mission was her first. Her trial had been a mission of sorts, but it was controlled and planned. She knew what she would face and what to expect. This would be different. This mission would take her to a foreign land to face foreign soldiers, and she had no knowledge of either. On top of that, the mission was to save the man who served the role of her mentor, teacher, and father. Of course, she knew Daritus wasn't her natural father. He acted as such, but they shared no blood. She was just beginning her fifth year when he had married her mother, Druindahl's queen. Though they both knew they shared no genetic bond, it never felt that way. She became his daughter that day, and that was it.

"Today, I am the luckiest man in all the land," he had said as he knelt and looked earnestly into her eyes, "Some folks get whatever the great Kaldumahn decides to give them for a family, but today I am fortunate to choose my own. I choose you to be my daughter, Cialia. If you'll have me."

What could she say? He'd brought a smile back to her mother's face, and he offered something she'd never known, a father. She agreed, and he became that. He raised her as his own, and she never felt like less. Now he needed her. She finished dressing and slipped out of her room, past the guards, and down to the forest floor.

The city of Druindahl had been built among the trees in the Forgotten Forest centuries prior, when men hunted Dragons in a great campaign that nearly ended all life on Ouloos. It wasn't called that then, but Kaldumahn realized all would be lost if the last Dragon fell.

Ouloos would be completely cut off. He made a covenant with the people of Druindahl. He would protect them, and they would protect the last Dragon from any who would do her harm. The people built the great city in the canopy high above the forest floor, and Kaldumahn cast a spell on the place to hide it from sight. That's when the place came to be known as the Forgotten Forest. The place would live on in the myths of the cities of men who would do the Dragon harm, but they could never remember where it was. At least, that's what the stories she'd learned would suggest.

Cialia stuck to the shadows. The guards wouldn't hinder her, but they would try to drag her back to her mother to explain why she was wandering about in the darkness dressed in armor. Mother would try to talk her out of it. There wasn't time for that. It would be much easier to simply avoid detection.

Despite all Cialia's ability with blades, stealth was still her greatest weapon. Like all the warriors of Druindahl, she'd been trained to move through the forest without a sound. A warrior who can master that can travel anywhere undetected. She whistled sharp and short. That would get some attention. Luckily, Purity was the fastest horse in Druindahl. A short few moments passed before the mighty, white mare charged out from deep in the trees. They were gone in a whisper. Even if they'd been spotted, they'd be far out of reach before anyone could even attempt to give chase.

The horses of Druindahl were trained in much the same way as their masters. Even during the darkest hours of night, buried in the deepest depths of the forest, Purity could travel at a full gallop. The horse knew the trails. Cialia gave her a little bump with both heels, and they charged into the darkness.

By the time the two made the edge of the forest, they were halfway up a mountain range, and the sun was on the rise. The Edge Mountains got their name from their location. They stretched toward the sky at the very edge of all the maps of men. Some maps did not even depict them, as men really had no reason to ever travel that far east. There simply wasn't anything out there. At least, nothing anyone remembered. Nothing but an old road out of Druindahl and out of the Forgotten Forest.

The sun rising behind Cialia bathed the mountains in orange and gold. She loved the sunrise. Some mornings she and Boringas, her best friend in the world, would sit on the highest branches of the trees at the very edge of the forest and watch the mountains glow in the rising sun. Boringas would always try to hold her hand, even tried to kiss her a few times. She wouldn't have it. She was training to be a warrior, an adventurer. The only husband she'd ever take would be the trail, and this mission would be her first romance.

The journey from Druindahl to Havenstahl would take more than two months at a normal pace with proper stops. She had no idea how or why she knew that. Kaldumahn had told her she would know the way. Perhaps he was guiding her. Regardless why she knew, she figured it could be cut down to a little better than a week. She and Purity had been trained to be rugged travelers, conditioned to travel light on minimal food and function quite effectively on little sleep. They would rest infrequently and own this trail.

The time raced by with the changing scenery. Hills gave way to flat, grassy prairies which gave way to dry, arid lands. Those, in turn, gave way to hills once again. Purity attacked the trail, devouring it like a starving man setting upon the first meal he's had in a week.

The two would bed down when the moon was at its highest point and would rise before the sun. They built no fires. They ate dry food, and they ate very little, rationing what they had. Purity had an affinity for finding water, so their canteens were always full. Water was something they didn't ration.

Just after midday on the eighth day of their journey, the towers of Havenstahl came into view. They scratched at the sky from a mountaintop, stretching higher than anything Cialia had ever seen. Though she'd never seen the place, or even heard a description of it, she knew it was her destination. That's where her father was being held. She knew the river they'd been following since the prior day was the River Galgooth, and she knew it would lead them around the north side of Mount Elzkahon in the valley between it and its twin peak, Mount Elbahor. All of it must have come from Kaldumahn. None of those were words she'd even known prior to seeing the place. As she looked up at the mighty castle perched high in the clouds, she also knew how she'd get in. They stopped on the riverbank to wait for nightfall.

Once the sun had fallen for the day, Cialia mounted Purity and got back to the trail. The pace was slower now, cautious. They passed several abandoned encampments along the way. Grongs, she'd never seen one, but they fit descriptions father had given her far too closely to be anything but. Considering the beasts were nomadic, the presence of camps didn't necessarily mean any were in the area. Still, she remained acutely aware of every sound and smell around her. Purity seemed equally wary as they moved slowly along the riverbank.

The bright moon had reached its apex by the time they reached the base of Mount Elbahor. They crossed the river and Cialia dismounted Purity. She didn't bother tying the horse. Purity was a faithful steed who would only run off to protect herself. If need arose for the horse to flee, Cialia certainly didn't want to hinder the effort. Purity found a spot in a thicket to bed down, and Cialia started up the steep path up the side of the mountain to the city.

She moved silently up the trail until the gates were in sight. Then she left it, scaling the rest of Mount Elzkahon to the wall of the city. Remaining close to the wall, she reached the gate without making a sound. Once she reached the gate, she held her breath and listened. Two distinct breathing patterns reached her ears from the other side. Scaling the wall, she perched atop it and beheld her prey.

Two guards stood silently at ease, both casually scanning the area. Neither looked ready for much more than a nap. There was never much action by the north gate. Even if Cialia wasn't somehow aware of it, the fact was easily enough deduced. She had just climbed the only route to the north entrance to the city, and it wasn't an easy one. Sneaking into the city unnoticed would be the only good reason to use the north gate during the dark hours of night. Based on the casual boredom of the two guards, there hadn't been many attempts.

Cialia scanned the area searching for a path which might allow her to avoid the guards. Spilling blood was something she hoped to avoid. Unfortunately, it wasn't meant to be. The area inside the gate had been designed quite well. The wall she perched upon, along with the one on the other side of the gate, both ended after ten feet and merged with the walls of the palace. Though they were made of brick, there were no obvious hand or footholds. As good a climber as she was, she'd never be able to scale them.

The thought of what she had to do had barely formed by the time the dagger was out of its small scabbard and effortlessly slicing through the air. A moment later, the handle of it was jutting from one of the guard's throats. Cilia wasn't sure how she felt about it as she watched the man tug at the thing, gurgling and kicking his legs in panic. The other guard moved quickly to assist. He scanned around as he tried to help his comrade pull the blade out.

As the two guards struggled, one bleeding to death while the other failed to help, Cialia leapt from her perch. By the time the second guard had managed to free the blade from his friend's neck, Cialia's legs wrapped tightly around his waist. Her left hand pressed against his forehead and pulled it back, while her right hand dragged her other dagger across his throat. She released her grip, and both guards fell.

Two sets of eyes stared up at her from expressions frozen in terror and confusion. They accused her, and she was guilty. The dead guards represented the first lives she had taken. At least, they were the first men she had ever killed. Father had taken her on many hunts. However, killing a man is different than taking down a fallon, a rabbit, or a dove for food. A dark and heavy weight rested on her soul. There wasn't much in her gut after her journey, but, for just a moment, she thought she might spill its meager contents all over the stone beneath her feet. If only there were someone to tell her she was justified in what she had done. Of course, there wasn't. She was alone staring down at her first kills.

She stood there staring at death far too long. She kept everything in her belly where it belonged, but it wasn't easy. Though she failed to completely justify her own actions to herself, she at least achieved some acceptance of it. Given the opportunity, they would have done the same to her, maybe worse. They may have killed her slowly and painfully. At least she had blessed them with quick deaths. If stories of the folk who inhabited the greatest cities of men were true, they would have seen her crest and punished her for serving the Dragon. It would not have been quick nor painless. Finally, she drew in a deep, slow breath, calmed herself, retrieved her daggers, and slipped silently into the palace.

Like a ghost in the shadows, Cialia crept along the halls of the palace. There were guards about. Occasionally, she'd hear their voices and pause to let them pass, but she never paused long. There was no time to dawdle. Before long, the dead guards at the north gate would be discovered, and the rest of Havenstahl's army would be looking for her. By the time that happened, she and her father needed to be far from the castle and the great peak it crowned.

She came to a circular stairway leading up. It was the way. Just as it had been for the rest of her journey, she didn't know how she knew it. She just did. Up and up into darkness, she passed nine floors before hearing more voices.

"So, what do ye make of this dragon warrior they got in there?" a gruff, whisper of a voice asked.

"I don't be knowing," another equally gruff whisper answered. "All I be knowing is this. If the worm be trying to escape, I'll be having his head."

The brief conversation was followed with a bit of low, muffled laughter. Cialia heard enough to know she'd found her destination. Slipping both daggers out of their scabbards, she charged the rest of the way up the stairs to the next floor.

Both guards nearly jumped out of their skins when Cialia rounded the corner. They clumsily fumbled for their swords. She didn't give them a chance to draw. Flicking both of her wrists at once, she fired her daggers. A moment later, the guards were falling, both sporting daggers in the centers of their foreheads. Their armor clanged as it hit the hard stone. That would attract attention. More guards would be coming. She couldn't worry about that. She grabbed her daggers as she slipped past them and into the room they'd been guarding.

The room was dark, but enough moonlight filtered through a small crack in the draperies covering the window at the other side of the room to allow Cialia to see a shape lying on the bed. Though she couldn't tell much more than it was a person lying there, based on what she could see, she knew it was father. She rushed over and shook him gently.

"Father," she whispered quietly in his ear, "you must wake, quickly. We must leave this place. More guards will be coming."

When Daritus' eyes finally opened, they were full of confusion. He must have been deep in slumber. After blinking several times at her, he finally replied, "Cialia, is that you? What are you doing here? This is no place for you."

She whispered quietly but quickly, "Kaldumahn came to me in a dream. He came as a silver beast. He said he was…" she paused, "Never mind that right now. I'll explain later. We need to leave this place."

"And who might ye be?" a voice asked from the darkness, bold and deep. "Perhaps ye be a ghost or a demon, slipping into me palace to be stealing me prisoner away."

Suddenly a torch blazed, and the room filled with light. Cialia spun to see a massive man bearing an ornate crown. The prang shimmered in the torchlight as the jewels encrusted on it twisted the light and splashed rainbows of color all about the walls. Cialia had never seen the man before, but she knew him immediately.

"Ymitoth," she shouted, her voice much louder than intended.

Ymitoth looked dumbfounded, like she had hit him with a club. He replied, "Maelich?"

"Who is Maelich?" the name was familiar, but she didn't know why. It was something, but...

Confusion spread across Ymitoth's face as he stammered before her. His mouth moved as if more words would come, but nothing did. Then he squinted, as if pleading with her, and finally gasped, "Maelich?" before falling in a heap on the floor.

A small part of her thought to rouse him and ask him all the questions swimming around her head. Why did he call her that name? Why did she know that name? How did she recognize him when there was no way she possibly could?

Luckily, Daritus whispered, "Go!" into her ear before she could act on the idea and risk both their skins.

Instead of acting on the impulse and rousing the great warrior to get answers, she did as her father commanded. Looking back several times along the way to ensure Daritus was close on her heels, she retraced her steps until they reached the bottom of the great, circular stairway.

"We can't use the north gate," she stammered, out of breath, "You'll need a horse, and a horse will never make it down the northern trail."

"I kept slipping in and out of consciousness when they brought me in, but I think I can find my way back to the stables," he replied, equally out of breath, then added, "Where should we meet? I am unfamiliar with the area, just bits and pieces."

Cialia's head was shaking before he finished, "There is no way I'm leaving your side, father. You're unarmed and weak from your incarceration."

"It was hardly an incarceration," he rolled his eyes. "They actually treated me quite well. It was Kaldumahn who misused me. I managed to rouse his ire. The folks of Havenstahl actually saved my life."

He wasn't making any sense. Cialia decided he was probably delirious from a lack of nutrition. She put her finger to her lips and said, "Later. We can talk later. For now, we need to get out of this place."

"I don't remember which way to go," Daritus replied. "If we can't go the way you came in, how will we find our way out?"

Cialia smiled, "I know the way. Don't ask me how right now. There isn't time. Somehow, I just know."

As they snuck around the courtyard sticking to the shadows, troops were forming up at its center. The bodies of the dead guards at the north gate must have been discovered. That would help. The stables were closer to the south gate than the courtyard. Cialia couldn't have planned it better, had she planned it. By the time she and Daritus reached the stables, there wasn't a soul in sight. They snatched two horses and were off, charging toward the massive southern gate.

Daritus looked over at her and shouted above the sound of hooves pounding against stone, "The bridge is up. We aren't making it out of here. I'll need a sword."

Cialia ignored him. She was already working on the solution, scanning the wall that encased the drawbridge. There it was, a large spindle with handles and a brake. She grabbed her bow and nocked an arrow. The rest of the world slipped away as her focus intensified on her mark. A deep breath filled her lungs. She first released the breath slowly and then loosed the arrow.

Cialia's aim proved true. Her arrow struck the brake and sent the gear spinning like mad. The bridge crashed down with a thunderous boom. Cracks formed all about it as it nearly collapsed under the pressure of itself. It creaked and groaned under the weight of the horses as they charged across. Chunks of the heavy thing began to fall away, careening into the deep abyss below them. The entire construct moaned as if in agony, desperately trying to hold on.

As the bridge fell apart beneath them, instincts took over. Cialia kicked her heels into her horse's sides. At the precise moment she'd done it, she caught her father do the same thing. Even with all the excitement and adrenaline pumping through her veins, she managed to grin at it. Even though they shared no blood, he could never deny her. She was just like him.

Both horses jumped off the bridge immediately when they'd been kicked. A second later and all four of them, Cialia, Daritus, and both horses, would have plummeted to the rocky river far below. Instead, they reached the other side, hooves tearing into the hard-packed dirt of the trail. Charging past the handful of guards posted on that side of the chasm, they galloped off into the night.

The night ride didn't let up until they were safe into the valley and had made it back round the River Galgooth. At that point, Cialia drew back hard on her horse's reins and called out to Daritus, "Hold, father."

Daritus smiled back at her as he obeyed the command.

Cialia, jumped off her horse, turned it back toward the city, and gave it a firm slap on the backside. As the horse charged back toward the city, she turned and gave a short, sharp whistle across the river. Moments later, Purity trotted out from the darkness.

"I'm proud of you, Cialia," Daritus finally broke the silence.

Cialia feigned coolness but felt her cheeks redden as she asked, "For what?"

"You never broke, never wavered. You are a true warrior, and I am proud of you," even if he hadn't said all those things, she would have known how he felt. His expression echoed his words and even more.

"Just putting my training to good work, father," she smiled.

Daritus rolled his eyes, "And she's humble to boot."

Cialia finally let her expression melt. She was proud too, "Let's go home, father."

CHAPTER 18
THE BEGINNING

The cave yawned foreboding darkness, as if it were the very mouth of Ouloos waiting to swallow Maelich whole. It almost seemed to be quivering, yearning to slam shut on some tasty morsel. Of course, it wasn't really yawning or desiring anything. It wasn't more than a big hole in big chunk of rock leading down into the belly of the mountain. Perhaps the thing only seemed so ominous because of the vile thing who lived inside all that darkness.

After wandering about the gardens for who knows how long—time didn't matter much on the mountaintop—Maelich's ire at the old wizard had faded. Initially, he wanted nothing more than to reduce Brerto to ash for what the old bastard had done to Jom, and for nothing more than sport. Jom had died that most horrible of deaths simply so some curmudgeonly, old man could prove a point. Even that fact failed to raise Maelich's hackles. It all seemed so long ago, like it happened in a different lifetime. Perhaps he had given up, or maybe the garden had enchanted him sufficiently to remove all his cares. Whatever the case may have been, he couldn't find the rage. The only way out was into that gaping darkness, so that's where he went.

The thing didn't slam shut when he stepped into it. It was just a cave after all. However, right at that moment, he realized his clothes were gone. He was quite naked. Had he been naked the entire time he wandered the mountaintop? He must have been. His cloak must have been burned off when he found his flame. Naked was such a vulnerable state. He paused, maybe it wasn't the right time. Of course, it was. What could he do, cover himself with leaves? The idea was silly. He was naked, and that was that. The great and mighty Brerto would just have to deal with it.

As impossible as it seemed, the darkness of the cave seemed to become more and more pitch as Maelich progressed into its depths. He hadn't been able to see anything since rounding a bend roughly twenty-five feet inside, but the darkness seemed darker somehow. It made about as much sense as an oasis surrounded in snow and biting cold.

The ground was damp, even slick beneath Maelich's feet. On top of that, the path was steep. However, the idea he might lose his footing never occurred to him. He hadn't slipped at all as he strolled deeper into the darkness. At least his nakedness no longer seemed to matter. Aside from bare feet touching wet stone, he couldn't even tell he was naked. The air probably should have felt increasingly cool on his skin, but it didn't. He remained quite comfortable.

Hours passed, or maybe not. He couldn't really tell anymore. Time wasn't making any more sense in the cavernous depths of Brerto's cave than it had in his garden. Distance didn't seem to matter much either. He had no idea how far he'd come and didn't really care much. What did it matter? He had yet to arrive at his destination, and he wouldn't until he did.

The darkness wasn't offering anything in the way of company. Darkness rarely did. Maelich figured the darkness cared about as much about him as he cared about it, hardly. It wasn't hindering him at all, and he wasn't hindering it. Unfortunately, since it couldn't keep him company, he was stuck with own thoughts, trapped in his own head. Sadly, that place was unusually empty just then. It seemed the garden had stolen most of his thoughts and cares, and the cave was doing its best to finish erasing them completely. All he really had left were tidbits about Jom, and those were hard fought to retain. It would probably be easier just to let them go. He wasn't quite ready to do that.

The path suddenly ended. It was no turn or bend in the path. It was an end. Though he could see nothing in the darkness, a quick examination of the walls surrounding him confirmed it. There were no alternate paths and no small crevices to squeeze through. It just ended.

A moment of hopelessness fled as quickly as it came. He leaned up against the wall. How long should he wait? Perhaps Brerto had given up on him. The idea seemed rather odd, given how important

Ymitoth claimed this training to be. However, the old wizard was nowhere to be found. He could journey back to the cave's mouth and search for some alternate paths or turns he may have missed, but why bother. It hardly seemed worth the effort. He had been very careful during his journey into the cave to look for alternate paths but hadn't found any. Besides, he didn't know where he would go from there. He slid down the wall until his rump found the rocks beneath it. It wasn't long before his eyes grew heavy. He didn't fight it. Sleep seemed as good an idea as any.

The world in which Maelich awoke was far different than that which he had left when he drifted off to sleep. The darkness had fled, chased away by pure, white light. He could still feel the ground against his back and bottom, but he could see neither wall nor ceiling. His eyes couldn't be trusted. They would have him believe he was floating, adrift in endless light. There was no beginning or end to it and no discernable source. It was everywhere and everything.

Brerto's voice, strong, emotionless, and equally without source, surrounded him, "You have found your way. This pleases me. You are ready to begin your training?"

Maelich searched for the source of the voice but his eyes were equally useless in the blazing light as they had been in the darkness. Tentatively, he answered, "Yes...I think so." Realizing how his indecision might anger Brerto, he quickly added, "I mean...yes, I am ready, master."

"You must always be sure of yourself, Maelich. There can be no question in your heart. Hesitation is your enemy. What is right, is right. Your heart knows this, and you must always trust it." Brerto's tone wasn't scolding. Rather, it was instructional, as if training had already begun.

Maelich didn't respond. He simply nodded and waited for more. The silence had him instantly on edge. As the moments bled into minutes, he thought perhaps Brerto was testing his patience. Struggling against impatience, he waited. What if that was wrong? Perhaps Brerto wanted him to be aggressive and seek answers. No, the master had just instructed him to trust his heart. Ymitoth would have instructed him to trust his gut. The initial reaction of both his heart and gut had been to wait. He did.

After a time, Brerto spoke again, "What do you know of Kallum's Word?"

"The Book?" Maelich's response was quick and eager.

"Yes," Brerto continued, "The Book."

Maelich continued with confidence, "I am well versed in 'The Beginning', 'The Rise and Fall of Dwarves', 'The Rise and Fall of Man', 'The Coming of Giants', and 'The Law'. I have no knowledge of 'The Prophecies' or 'The Great Gathering', as my mentor reserved those for another. I imagine that to be you."

"Yes, that would be me," Brerto confirmed. Then, still with no emotion in his voice, he continued, "So, you say you are well versed in the books of old. Recite for me then the first two chapters of 'The Beginning'."

A smile spread across Maelich's face. He knew them by heart. He spoke as if he were reading, "In the beginning, there was nothing but Kallum, and before Kallum there was nothing. He came upon a place of great sadness and sensed evil within it. Being perfection, he abhorred evil. So, he said, 'Because I despise evil, I will make this a place of happiness. I will make it a place perfect like myself.'

In this evil place was a great gathering of water, and Kallum made himself to float above it, and from beneath the water he gathered up the dry land. This land he did bring to the surface, and with it, he did split the great gathering of water. Now this land was quite flat and unspectacular, so he did make many peaks to rise up from the flat land until he found it to be pleasing."

"Exquisite," Brerto now had tone in his voice. He sounded pleased, "Continue, the third chapter."

"When he had finished, he saw that the land was barren. With this, he was displeased. He cut ravines across the dry land in and around the peaks. Then he called water from the great gathering of water and did make it to flow through the ravines. He called these rivers, and they did bring water to the land. In spots the water pooled up, and he called these places lakes. He looked upon all that he had done and was quite pleased."

"Go on, chapter four."

"He looked upon one lake that had been there before he cut ravines through the dry land. This lake was in the center of the land, and it did hold onto the evil that had been held by the great gathering of water that the land split. Here the evil endured. Here the evil remained. Kallum commanded the evil to leave, because he despised it. It would not go. He cursed the lake saying that none shall look upon its evil or bathe in its waters. He would hide it from sight."

Brerto's response almost sounded like excitement, "Excellent! I am quite pleased with your command of The Book, Maelich. Do you know what lake is being described?"

Maelich's reply was quick and sure, "The Lake of Dragons, the origin of evil."

"Precisely. Do you know what significance that lake has for you?"

He thought for a moment, "No, I'm afraid I don't."

"I didn't expect you would. Would you like to know? You've always had questions about your origin. Where did you come from? Who is your father? Ymitoth served that role, but you know it wasn't he who planted the seed that spawned you. So, who then? Would you like to know?"

"Of course," there was no hesitation in his voice. "My whole life I've asked those questions and received no answer. Is it you who will tell me?"

"Yes," Brerto replied. "The lake is your father."

"What?"

"The lake is your father. Your father is not a man."

"How is that possible? I am the son of evil?"

"It would appear so. Wouldn't it? It is true, the blood of the dragon courses through your veins, but your mother was pure. She was a true child of Kallum. You are a god, Maelich, both man and dragon. That is what the books which have been hidden from you say. That is the truth you've been seeking. The fire of the last dragon cannot be extinguished but from the fury of his own fire. That fire exists in you. You are the key to unlocking peaceful bliss on Ouloos. You are the gateway to paradise."

Maelich shook his head. It swam with bits and pieces of memories. Filled with things Ymitoth had told him and things he had seen. Finally, he asked, "How could the lake be my father? Many things have been hidden from me, but I know how men are made."

Brerto humphed, "Perhaps you're not ready. You've seen that the rules which bind men do not pertain to you. Still, you view yourself as only a man. Did you not bring forth a fire that burned everything on my mountain? Did you not unleash a fury that would decimate anything made by man? Then how do you justify the belief that you are the product of a man? Kallum made himself to appear to your mother in a dream. He came astride the wind as a giant bird, an eagle, and he did speak to her. He told her to journey to the lake, a place where she had never been, and bathe in it. Though she knew not the location of her destination, she did find it. And she did bathe in the lake, and, from the lake, she did become pregnant. You are the fruit of that union. That is what The Book says. That is the truth."

Maelich knew Brerto was right. Though he tried to deny it, the evidence was obvious. That was what Ymitoth couldn't tell him. That was what his mentor couldn't understand. The confusion which had always strained his voice as he tried to explain it finally made sense. He knew but didn't understand. Maelich was torn. A part of him felt regal and powerful, but part of him felt loneliness. He didn't have a father. He had a lake, a lake that was the origin of all evil. And his mother...

"What of my mother? The lake impregnated her. She gave birth to me, and then what? What became of her?" This was the real question.

After a long pause, Brerto replied, "Sadly, the weight of your mother's role in this world was too much for her to bear. She loved you, just as was written, but she knew she would be a hindrance to you on your quest. She journeyed to the temple at Havenstahl and left you on the steps in a basket. Then she flung herself off Mount Elzkahon never to be seen again. The priests of the temple knew the prophecy well and immediately knew you would be the one to fulfill it. Ymitoth was a young warrior with royal blood, the greatest warrior in Havenstahl, even in all of Ouloos. That is why he was chosen to raise you and teach you the ways of the warrior. He has done well. Now, it is my task to complete your training. There is nothing beyond your ability, Maelich. I have been charged with loosing the reigns on your spirit."

In that moment, loneliness was far greater than any feeling of purpose could hope to be. Maelich was truly alone. Sure, Ymitoth had been there to raise him, and now Brerto would accompany him through the rest of his training, but he didn't belong to either of them. His father was a thing, and his mother had taken her own life because of him. He shared blood with no living soul. Tears wanted to flow over his eyes and down his cheeks, but they wouldn't come. The emptiness in his soul was dry. His heart was barren. He felt like stone, like a statue of a young lad. The light surrounding him faded, and sleep swept in to rescue him from conscious thought.

CHAPTER 19
THE HERO RETURNS

Twelve summers passed since Maelich had left Keller's Hill. Now he was complete, and his task had been laid before him. His entire life had been training for the journey ahead. He walked the garden with Brerto as they discussed how he would complete his quest.

"You will head west the way you came," Brerto began, "until you reach a bridge that crosses the river Galgooth. There are many bridges, but you will know this one when you come to it. On your journey to me you looked upon the road it leads to and wondered if you'd ever have cause to travel it. You do. That road will take you South and East. No roads cross it. It leads to where the maps don't go, The Lost Forest. You must go through the forest to reach the dragon. You will be drawn to him. He will try to deceive you. Remain steadfast and sure. Do not let his tongue sway you from your purpose. He must be slain. This is why you have trained, and well trained you are. He will be no match for you."

Maelich looked to the west, "I will fulfill my duty in due time. First, I have a promise to keep, a promise I made to a young girl who quite looked up to me. To her heart I must be true."

A hint of anger slipped into Brerto's tone, "Don't be ridiculous. You sound like a man, holding on to petty, human emotions. You must let those go. For twelve summers I've trained you for this task, a task you must undertake now. Not after you go off to have a teary reunion with some waste of a girl. You must let nothing sway you from your duty. The prophecy is written. It is yours to fulfill."

Maelich held his ground, "Whether you like it or not, part of me is man. That part of me will not allow me to undertake this chapter in my life until I have fulfilled promises made in prior chapters. In The Book, my story ends when I slay the dragon. There is peace and harmony on Ouloos, but there is no word about what happens to me after the dragon is slain. I know what it feels like to find out you've lost someone without ever having said good-bye. I won't put Perrin through that kind of distress."

Brerto glowed as if lightning were flowing through his body, "How dare you? You presume to tell me how it will be or what you will do? Make no mistake about your role, you are a tool. You are a divine tool Kallum intends to use to complete his task. It is his will you seek to fulfill not your own." The mountain rumbled as his crescendo was a full shout.

Maelich smiled, "We both know I have nothing to fear from you. I may be burdened with the mind and emotions of a man, but I'm wise enough to realize I have been picked for my task based on my power. I am complete, and your strength does not rival mine. I can sense this in you. There is fear. You stink of it. You've taught me to fully realize my potential and now can't control what you've created. Stomp about and have your tantrum, but do not threaten me. I won't have it."

Brerto shook with rage, but Maelich was quite correct in his assessment. The great wizard had nothing to fear from Maelich but hadn't control of him either. The bright and shining hero would have his little distraction. All Brerto could do was watch. With teeth clenched behind his sneer, the old wizard vanished in a brilliant flash.

Maelich chuckled at his mentor's little fit and then looked around, taking in the beauty of the garden one last time. He breathed deeply through his nose, inhaling sweet perfume. He gave a sharp whistle and, in a few moments, Validus charged up from out of the snow. Brerto had said the steed would be sleeping until training was complete. Validus, of course, was quite unaware of his slumber and completely untouched by age. Maelich felt a charge of emotion like nothing he had felt since submitting to Brerto's training. There were so many memories but no time to give them any thought. There was too much to do.

The road back to Havenstahl was much easier than the road out had been. Neither Maelich nor Validus ever seemed to tire. They moved across the trail almost as a dream. The Blood Mountains, the flatlands, the river and the hills all floated past effortlessly. Time seemed to have no meaning for them. When Mount Elzkahon and the mighty towers of Havenstahl came into sight it felt as if their journey had yet to begin. The fact seemed less amazing to Maelich than he thought it should. Strangely, he was quite prepared for it. Brerto had taught him how to tap into his great power. Why should this apparent ability to skip across time come as a surprise? The laws of men, the laws of flesh, no longer pertained to him.

As Maelich neared Havenstahl's South gate, he noticed not much had changed since he last left the city. Two guards manned the gate as people bustled about in and out of their huts finishing their chores before the sun set. For the first time in years—maybe the first time since he left the hut he had shared with Ymitoth so many years prior—he felt like he was home.

One of the guards spoke, "State your name and business, traveler."

Maelich brought Validus to a halt and slowly removed his hood. Aside from the beginnings of a beard clinging to his chin, he hadn't changed much. He opened his cloak exposing the crest he earned for slaying Ahm and replied, "I am Maelich of Havenstahl. I seek an audience with my father, the king."

"Highness, please forgive me," the guard replied, the stern tone of his voice melting into something closer to fear.

Both guards dipped to one knee and bowed. Then, in unison, they chanted, "The prince has returned! Hail Maelich, son of Ymitoth, savior of Ouloos!"

Being worshipped still didn't seem to fit, "Rise," he said, slightly embarrassed. "Why seek forgiveness for rightly performing your duties? Is it not your task to protect Havenstahl from any who would do her harm? You are right to question me, a hooded rider who comes calling as the sun fades. You do right by your post."

Moved by the compliment and awed by Maelich's presence, both guards reached up to touch him. He repaid the gesture by placing a hand on each of their shoulders. After a few moments, they parted and let him pass.

Maelich crossed the bridge into Havenstahl, the hero was home. Something about the bridge was different. It almost looked as if it had been replaced. Twelve summers is a long time. He must have missed quite a bit. As he neared the inner gate, one of the guards there recognized him immediately.

"The prince returns!" the guard shouted.

Then more voices in the crowd echoed the same line. Before long the streets inside Havenstahl buzzed with excitement. Maelich was overwhelmed by a mob of anxious people desperately trying to place their hands on him. Many asked for blessings, pushing and shoving each other to get closer to him. It was the type of reception normally saved for kings. Simply laying hands on him seemed to bring those lucky enough to succeed in the effort a sublime sense of joy. It was as if the simple act of touching him, their savior, completely changed their perception of the world and their roles in it.

Of course, it shouldn't seem all that strange. After all, he was preparing for a journey to kill the last dragon, to free Ouloos from the weight of all the evil the beast represented. Everyone in Havenstahl knew the dragon was responsible for all the pain, suffering, and hardship on Ouloos. To them, his journey represented relief. He was fulfilling the prophecy, their champion. He knew that. Even still, it would take some time to get used to all the attention and adoration.

The throng of worshippers continued to grow. They closed in tighter. Validus quickly became nervous and jittery as the mob surrounded them. The horse twitched, stomped, and neighed.

Maelich placed his hand on Validus' head and filled the animal with sweet, relaxing thoughts. Once the horse had calmed, Maelich turned his attention to the crowd. He touched and spoke to as many as he could. Those he did shined with hope. Their energy was palpable, like he could see and touch it. He could almost smell the joy oozing off them. Still, his own joy depended on a few people he desperately wanted to see. The crowd continued to grow.

Before long, Maelich found a familiar face. An old friend had tunneled his way through the mountain of blessing seekers. The king, his father strode up wearing a smile befitting a proud, adoring parent. Maelich leapt from Validus and raced into Ymitoth's outstretched arms. The two men embraced. This swelled a cheer up in the crowd. After the embrace they held each other at arm's length and looked each other up and down, as if refilling memories that had long begun to fade.

"Ye haven't changed a bit," Ymitoth beamed, "except maybe for that weak excuse of a beard ye be wearing on your chin."

Maelich chuckled, "Well neither have you, except for a few more wrinkles and all the gray streaks in your hair. What is it they call that? Oh yes, dignified. I couldn't remember if that was the word they used or if they just called it old."

Ymitoth laughed out loud, "Aye, ye keep me humble, son. Still, the years haven't been too cruel to me. Have they?"

"Not at all. You look good, father. I should say you're a feast for my weary eyes. It's good to be home," his words were earnest and true.

"Come, son, we've precious little time to be reminiscing. I be knowing your presence here must be short. I also be knowing there be another ye'll be wanting to see," Ymitoth finished with a devious grin and a raised eyebrow.

"What's with the funny look?" Maelich smiled, knowing full well of whom Ymitoth spoke, "Why should my desire to see Perrin raise such silliness on your face?"

Ymitoth raised his hands up, shrugged and gave an exaggerated look of confusion, "Oh, there be no good reason for me jest. Except maybe for the fact the young lass ye be speaking of has blossomed into quite a beautiful flower. All the bachelors in Havenstahl be having an eye for that one. She be entertaining no suitors, though. She says she be waiting for one she knows will be coming back to her. Maybe ye be that one."

Maelich's cheeks reddened. "Hmm," was all he could muster.

Ymitoth's report got Maelich's mind wandering. Perrin would be in her eighteenth year. When he had accepted her as his responsibility, and vowed to see her through to safety, he saw her as something of a sister. Judging from what Ymitoth had said, she didn't view him the same way. He was eager to see her, to speak with her, to tell her about his travels. They had missed much. Besides Ymitoth, she was the only thing he had resembling family.

Maelich turned back to the crowd and held out his hands. He gave them a blessing, letting a feeling of easiness and comfort flow from himself into them. Soon the murmurs of the crowd ceased, and people began to leave feeling a relaxing sense of peace.

Once the crowd had departed, Ymitoth had a guard take Validus to the stables. Then he led Maelich back toward the palace, down the stone streets Maelich missed so. It was funny, he had only spent but a few days in Havenstahl, yet he felt such a strong connection to her. It was as if that were his home from childhood rather than the hut at the foot of Keller's hill. No matter what the reason, a fullness nourished him. He felt grounded, finally enjoying a bit of peace for himself.

"It's been a long time, father," Maelich sighed as he strolled along at Ymitoth's side.

"Aye, lad," Ymitoth agreed, "twelve summers be a long time indeed. Ye've missed much, and ye'll be missing more. I be knowing your time here be short. Still, we be having a few moments. Tell me about your training with the great and mighty."

Maelich grinned, "It didn't start out so well. He killed Jom during our first meeting. I haven't forgiven him for that, don't expect I will."

"Why, in the name of Kallum, would he be doing something like that?" shock dripped from Ymitoth's tone.

"Partly to show me his strength, I suppose," Maelich shrugged, "but mostly to raise my ire enough to loose my flame. He certainly succeeded in that. I burned the whole mountaintop."

"I can imagine ye did," the king replied somberly.

A faraway look crept onto Maelich's face, "The pain of that didn't last long. Enchantment hangs about the place. It makes it hard to hold onto to anything."

"Brerto be a powerful creature," Ymitoth noted.

"He is," Maelich reflected. After a brief pause, he added, "The rest of it wasn't very noteworthy. I did a lot of reading, even more meditating. I learned how to reach down to the core of Ouloos and all the way out to the stars. I'm still learning, but I can touch everything. No, that's not quite right. I'm connected to everything, like part of it. It's hard to explain."

Maelich kicked a pebble. As it skittered across the smooth stone, he changed the subject, "What happened to the bridge. It's different."

"Ah, the dragon," Ymitoth began, "It was in the days shortly after ye left Havenstahl for Alharin that the dragon came calling. I had sent a force to hunt down a pack of Amatilazo that were making their home in The Sobbing Forest. After the hunt, while the men were sweeping the forest for injured soldiers, they came across a wounded man. He bore the crest of the dragon so they thought of putting him out of his misery. However, he had the look of a warrior, and they got to thinking he may be having some value for our cause."

Maelich interrupted, "He bore the crest of the dragon? I faced a man who bore the crest on the road to Alharin." He searched his memory and added, "He called himself Daritus."

Ymitoth stopped, "That be the one! That be the man they

captured. His hair being all black and wavy like his beard."

Maelich thought some more, "I didn't kill him then."

"What's that ye say?"

"I toppled him in battle and thrust my sword into his chest. There was a bright flash. When I woke, he was gone. I had all but forgotten about that."

"Nay, ye didn't kill him. A pack of amatilazo almost did. The soldiers brought him back here and Hagen healed him. The first day I could be questioning him, I was. I questioned him until he passed out from exhaustion. Then I watched him slumber. He went on and on about how Kallum be a violent and fearsome god, and all other kind of nonsense like that. He didn't tell me nothing, though. Then, in the darkness, another warrior come to save him. I went to attack, but it was a lass. When I looked in her eyes, it be…it be…well, it be like looking in yours. I lost me bearings and they escaped. The bridge be closed then, and they toppled it. I sent out troops to track them down, but they came up with nothing. I never seen them again," Ymitoth looked thoughtful for a moment.

A confused look slowly spread across Maelich's face, "She looked like me?"

Before Ymitoth could answer, they were interrupted. "Maelich!" Perrin shouted as she ran up the street to greet him.

At first, Maelich didn't recognize her. Ymitoth had not exaggerated. The blue-eyed little girl he remembered had grown into a beautiful young woman. Something swept over him just then, a strange, foreign feeling. He couldn't put his finger on it, but an odd desire swelled in him. It was almost like hunger. Her arms wrapped tightly around his neck as she slammed into him. He pulled her close as she buried her face deep in his chest. They both held on tight as if letting go would cause them to fall. The feeling in Maelich's chest became warmth, then heat. Not like the heat on the mountain with Brerto. No, there were no flames this time. This was something entirely different.

Ymitoth flushed with embarrassment as he said, "I'll be letting ye catch up. We'll be meeting inside."

Ymitoth's words were mostly lost on Maelich. He and Perrin were in a world of their own just then. They had developed a special bond, the kind of bond that's only created under the most extreme conditions. They both had great, empty spaces to fill when they first met. Filling those for each other, they formed a bond none could break.

"I wasn't knowing if ye'd ever be coming back to me," Perrin said, her voice slightly muffled in Maelich's chest.

Maelich's eyes were closed as he embraced her, "I promised you I'd return, didn't I?"

She looked up at him, "Aye, ye did. Truly, I knew ye'd be coming back. It was…it was just so long."

"I know," he replied softly, almost a whisper, as he gently caressed her cheek, "too long."

Suddenly, and quite unexpectedly, she kissed him. At first, he was nervous, stopping just short of pulling away from her. Instead, he kissed her back. He ran his fingers up into her hair as they kissed long and deep. The heat grew between them, their passion blazing, as if they were making up for years of lost memories.

Maelich's thoughts were scattered all about. Perrin suddenly seemed less like a sister and more like something else. Her lips on his felt wrong at first. The sensation didn't last. It was quickly replaced by desire, that odd hunger he'd felt at first seeing her after all the time that had passed. He let it consume him, submitting to feelings he couldn't control. There was a strange sense of freedom in completely letting go, giving up all control to this alien desire. Their passion mounted until they were soaring. Her body slumped against his, as his strong arms held her tight.

Perrin's thoughts were quite focused. She had dreamt of this day since Maelich left her so many years ago. However, her decision to give herself to him came just in the last few years. As she grew, her feelings for him changed. When boys started noticing her, she always found herself comparing them to him, the one who saved her and saw her through the darkness. In her mind, he had always been by her side, ruling her dreams and dominating her thoughts. She had begun to fantasize about spending all her days with him. In his absence, she fell in love with him. Right at that moment, wrapped in arms she'd so longed for, she knew he felt the same for her. Falling deeper into his kiss, her dreams were coming true.

As her lips lingered long on his, the heat between them continued to rise. Pressed tightly against each other, they both felt as if they might erupt at any moment. Suddenly, Maelich pulled away. An embarrassed smile washed over his face, as he gently kissed her cheek.

"What…" Perrin began, her expression echoed her confusion.

"Shh," he whispered, as he put a finger to her lips and pulled her close to him again, "There'll be plenty of time for us to catch up. Before all that, I should probably speak to your father."

Perrin's look of confusion faded into a wide smile, "What could ye be needing to talk with him about?"

"Well," he began, trying his best to look serious, "if it's your hand I wish to hold for the rest of my days, then I'll need to ask for it."

Perrin squealed and jumped up on him, wrapping her arms tighter around his neck, "Do ye mean it?"

Maelich gave a surprised chuckle to her excitement, "I can't think of anyone else I'd rather spend my days with."

She jumped down, grabbed his hand and pulled him toward the tavern, "Hurry up then! Let's ask him."

They pounded through the door at the back of Perrin's Place—the tavern owned by Kendal and Haleen—deep in a mad fit of giggles. They nearly fell to the floor of the roomy hut that connected to the rear of the tavern. Kendal made a good living running the place and the décor in his hut reflected that. The great room occupied most of the space. Haleen sat at a fancy, hand-carved table at its center. Off to the left were a large stove and a counter for preparing meals. To the right, parked in front of a fireplace, Kendal and Ymitoth sat on a pair of finely crafted chairs. A small table between them supported the weight of two pints and a thick book. The table and chairs all rested on a luxurious fur carpet. Next to the fireplace was a doorway that led into another room. Above the doorway was a loft. Maelich tried to collect himself as the group inside the hut all jumped at the commotion he and Perrin made

Kendal rose to greet them, "Well look at ye, lad. Ye be all grown up. Oh…and what be this? Ye even be having the beginnings of a beard."

"The years have been kind to you, sir," Maelich replied, still trying to compose himself as he crossed the room and offered his hand.

Kendal eyed Maelich suspiciously as they grasped forearms. However, before he could inquire about the odd behavior, Perrin interrupted him.

Pushing past Maelich, Perrin hugged her father, kissed his cheek, and chimed, "Hello, Papa," before skipping over to take a spot next to Haleen at the table.

Finally, Haleen piped up, "Well, ye both look like ye be carrying around the biggest secret in the history of Havenstahl. Come on, let's have it then."

Perrin put a hand on each of Haleen's cheeks and kissed her lips, smacking her own lips and making a big mwah sound as she did. Then she giggled, "Mama, Papa, Maelich be having something to ask of ye."

Kendal wrinkled up his brow as he looked back at Maelich, whose face had begun to redden as he grinned like a happy idiot. "Well, lad," he asked, "what is it ye be needing to ask of us?"

Maelich looked over at Perrin and raised his eyebrows. He hadn't intended on opening the conversation in quite this fashion. Unfortunately, his intentions no longer mattered. Perrin had left him in a spot. Oh well, why wait?

"Kendal, sir," Maelich began, "it is my intention to spend the rest of my days with Perrin at my side. She is in agreement…"

"'Tis true, 'tis true, I be in agreement with all of that!" Perrin interrupted.

Maelich looked at her and bugged his eyes out, as if to quiet her. Then he continued, "As I was saying, she is in agreement, and I'd like to ask you to bless our union. As her father, I cannot rightly take her to be my own without your approval."

Kendal looked a bit shocked, as did the rest of the room besides Perrin and Maelich. He scratched his head and stared at Maelich for what seemed an eternity. The room fell silent. Even Perrin's giggling had stopped, as a nervous expression took the place of her wide smile and laughing eyes. Ymitoth rose from his chair stroking his beard. Haleen looked to the ceiling, her left hand resting just below her neck. Kendal looked to Ymitoth as if to ask, "What shall I say?" A dusty piece of wood gave a loud crack in the fireplace and broke the silence. Everyone jumped.

Haleen spoke first, "Whatever made the two of ye think of something like this? Ye ain't seen each other for twelve summers. Ye don't hardly be knowing each other anymore."

Perrin grabbed her mother's arm and pleaded, "But we do, mama. He's been in me thoughts ever since he left me. He haunts me dreams, and I can't think of life without him. Ye must be giving us your blessing."

Kendal looked in Maelich's eyes, "Your journey ain't yet finished, lad. What time ye be having for me daughter?"

Maelich put a hand on Kendal's shoulder, "It's true, my task is not yet complete, and I will have to leave again before we can begin our life together. I can promise you this, though. My heart belongs to Perrin. It always has in one form or another. I will come back for her, no matter where my path leads me."

Kendal let out a long, low sigh, "Maelich, we all know ye be the lad of the Lake. We all know where your path be leading. What nobody be knowing, is where it be ending. What if ye don't come back? What then for me little girl?" He reached his hand out toward Perrin, "Look at her eyes. Do ye want to be breaking that heart?"

Perrin's crystal blue eyes swelled with tears as she pounded her hand on the table, "Me heart will break if ye don't be giving us your blessing, Papa. This man be the only one I would ever be giving me heart to. If ye don't let us marry, I'll be dying a lonely, old woman without a soul to call me own."

"The book may not spell out my end, but my heart will bring me home. I have never broken a promise to her, and I never will. I will come back for her hand."

"Then be waiting till ye come back!" Haleen piped in. "Don't be taking her away from us just to be leaving her a widow."

Then Ymitoth finally spoke, "Though this decision does seem rash, I know me son. He carries a strong love for Perrin. If he be promising to return, there be nothing that be stopping him. If ye're just worried for the loss of your daughter, ye can come share me palace with me. It be a lonely place for me now. He be me only family and he be not with me. We shall all be waiting for his return together."

Maelich swelled as he looked to his father, carrying a thank you in his eyes. Ymitoth nodded his response. Kendal looked to Perrin, her pleading eyes now running over with tears. Then he looked to Haleen, who had lost a few tears of her own. She looked at her daughter and then back to her husband. Her nod was nearly imperceptible.

Kendal looked back to Ymitoth, "What of the tavern? If we come to live with you in the palace, who will be caring for the tavern."

Ymitoth smiled, "How many offers do ye get a day for this place? Ye do a good bit of business here. Ye find yourself someone ye trust, and ye give it to them. Ye won't be wanting for nothing ever again. Ye can come whenever ye be ready."

Kendal again looked back to Haleen and then to Maelich, "Alright then, Maelich, ye can have me blessing."

Maelich hugged the man as Perrin hugged Haleen. Then Perrin ran to her Papa and leapt to him, nearly choking him with the weight of her hug. Maelich went to Haleen, took her hand and kissed it. Ymitoth did the same. Then after all the pleasantries, the new couple hugged again.

The mood quickly lightened as Haleen laid out a light meal for everyone. Kendal had decided to have his good friend Bowley run business for the night. He was loyal and would make a great bar keep. He would be Kendal's first choice to succeed him as the owner of Perrin's Place. The only condition being he never change the name.

As the night wore on, Maelich found himself telling all the stories of his adventures. Time and again, he tried to take the focus off himself and let other people share their stories. However, the group wouldn't let him. The questions kept coming back to him. They all wanted to know about the road. The only one of them that had ever ventured more than a few miles out of Havenstahl was Ymitoth, and he had reasons of pride for wanting to hear Maelich's stories. The hero continued.

The mood quickly turned somber as Maelich recounted the demise of Jom. Everyone's eyes dampened as he described the poor scrod's suffering. None so much as Perrin's, though. Jom had been her scrod, her last link to her earliest memories, and he was gone. She never would get to say good-bye. Maelich caressed her shoulders as she wept and buried her head in his chest. Everyone else sat in silence, respecting her grief. By the time her weeping had subsided, the hour had grown quite late. Kendal suggested they turn in and continue their visit when the sun was again in the sky. Ymitoth agreed and stood to leave. Maelich kissed Perrin on the cheek and stood as well, but she grabbed his arm.

Her eyes red and puffy from tears, she said, "Stay with me."

Maelich looked at Kendal, and he at Haleen. She shrugged.

"Ye don't be having much time with each other," Kendal began. "Ye might as well be spending the time ye do have together."

Ymitoth went to Maelich and hugged his son, "I'll be seeing ye in the morning, son. We'll be finishing our talk then."

"Good night, father," Maelich replied.

Ymitoth left the hut and went back to the palace alone, as he had been doing for years. Perhaps it was selfish, but he truly wanted to take all his son's time for himself. He could never do that, of course. Perrin needed Maelich, and Maelich needed her.

Back in the hut, Perrin and Maelich said their good-nights to Kendal and Haleen. Then Perrin led Maelich through the doorway next to the fireplace. That was her room. Kendal and Haleen climbed a ladder up to the loft above Perrin's room and turned in as well. The hut was silent. Perrin's dreams were in her arms.

CHAPTER 20
DRAWN

The first rays of the morning sun filtered in through cracks around the shutters covering the windows of Perrin's room. They tugged at Maelich's eyelids gently at first. As they gained in power their efforts became more forceful. He blinked and then squinted, giving just a moment to the dust lightly dancing about in them. He was a bit disoriented until he felt the warmth of Perrin snuggled tightly around him. He ran his hand through her hair and silently slipped out of her cot. He kissed her cheek and went to the great room.

Haleen was already up. She sat at the table enjoying a hot cup of dragon tea. It was a favorite of hers. Making the morning tea was easily the highlight of her day, more so than even drinking it. She would boil a big pot of water with a tightly wound ball of freshly picked dragon blossom resting on the bottom. They say a watched pot never boils, but she didn't care. She'd stare until the first bubbles began breaking the surface. Then she'd watch as the blossom rolled and bounced about. She called it the dance of the dragon. The ball would sway and dance, and the water would darken. Once it achieved a deep, greenish hue, it was ready. Sometimes she'd let it go longer than others. The longer it boiled, the deeper, darker, and stronger the tea would be. On this day, the tea was quite strong, filling the hut with a rich, earthly scent.

Maelich looked upon her. Long, dark hair with just a hint of gray waved and curled down past her face and didn't cease until reaching her waist. It was like perfectly-planned chaos. Though she wore every year she'd lived, there was a loveliness about her. Something in the shape of her face and the grace of her form harkened to a youthful beauty that still lingered.

Haleen had become so wrapped in her morning tea, she hadn't noticed Maelich staring at her. Her cheeks reddened with embarrassment when she finally did notice him there in the doorway, gazing on her like a lover might.

"I didn't see ye standing there," she said with a nervous smile.

"I'm sorry," Maelich began, slightly embarrassed himself, "I was trying to picture you at a younger age. Though your face carries the wise lines of a woman who knows and has seen much, there is a youthful softness about your face. I never knew my mother. Sadly, she took her own life. Worse, it was because of me that she did this. If ever I looked upon her face, I would have been much too young to recall. I have heard descriptions of her, and all say she was of unrivaled beauty. My awkward stare is to try and imagine what she might look like if she had not ended herself."

Haleen smiled, flattered more than embarrassed now. She reached for Maelich and pulled him down next to her, resting his head on her bosom and hugging him as a mother might, "Ye've a good heart, Maelich. There's a pure honesty about ye that is much less than common in men your age. Thank ye for those flattering words. Ye make an old woman feel like a young lass. I am sorry ye can never feel the warmth of your mother's touch. I also know that no one can ever take the place of a young man's mother, but ye can always count on me if ye need the soft touch of a motherly type."

Maelich refused to cry. Instead, he heaved a deep sigh and, with misty eyes, fought those tears with all his might. He remained there in Haleen's embrace for a long while. She gently stroked his head while she sang to him. Her soft voice was clear and soothing in his ear like the echo of a bell on the wind.

My lad, sweet lad, lay down your heavy head
My lad, sweet lad, forget the path ye've tread
Relax in mother's arms, let her soft caresses heal ye
Relax in mother's arms, let her soft caresses heal ye
Though the road behind be dark and the road ahead be hard
Never fear, for mother's love will be there to keep guard
When your journey be complete, and your task has been fulfilled

Mother's arms they will be waiting to keep your heart stilled.

She finished her lullaby by gently kissing Maelich on the head. Still, he refused to cry. One tear managed to get past his defenses. That one tear quickly trickled down his cheek. Haleen's song filled him with love, hope, joy, and sadness all at the same time. He couldn't remember the last time he'd felt so content. If his own mother still graced the sweet face of Ouloos, she'd probably behave the exact same way. She didn't, though, and, of course, she couldn't. He would never hear his mother's song, the sweet beauty of her voice. Thankfully, Haleen didn't mind trying to fill that role for him. He remained there, wrapped in her motherly embrace until Kendal returned from his morning run.

Kendal shot a confused look at Haleen, "Ye must really be fond of me wife's tea, Maelich."

Maelich didn't reply. He had fallen asleep. Haleen waved Kendal off, "The lad's been without a mother his whole life. No one has ever held him or sang him to sleep. Can ye imagine what that must be like? I can't. A father's love is fine, but it be hard and strict. A young lad need be much more careful with his emotion around his father. A mother's love be soft and comforting. He wasn't trying to steal me heart, love. He was just wanting to feel that what everyone else takes for granted."

Kendal felt like an oaf, "Sorry, love. It is wrong for me to question your judgement. Ymitoth be about this morning. He be looking for the lad." Then he looked on Maelich with a caring eye, "Funny, Haleen, he don't look much like a savior cradled in your arms like that. He be looking more like a lost child, all scared and alone."

"He is," she whispered as she continued to stroke Maelich's head, "he is."

Just then, Perrin stumbled out of her room absently rubbing the sleep from her eyes. The sight of her mother embracing Maelich brought her quickly too attention. "What are ye doing with me love?" she asked, her voice almost a whine.

"He's to be part of our family, ain't he?" Kendal began. "Your mother be mothering him."

"There's a part of everyone that ever longs for the embrace of their mama," Haleen spoke softly, her gaze fixed lovingly on Maelich, "Ye know this, Perrin. Maelich has never felt the warmth of a mother's caress. His whole life he been caring for others. He been needing someone to care for him. Don't fret, me sweet daughter. I don't be meaning to steal him away." She finished with a raised brow and an odd smirk.

Perrin shrugged. The explanation made sense, but she wanted to be the one saving him. She poured herself some tea and sat down on the other side of him. She gently caressed his back as he slept. Haleen gave her a smile, then sang her lullaby again.

Kendal let it go on as long as he could stand. It seemed cute, at first, but it quickly began turning his stomach. "Okay, okay," he finally broke up the love fest. "His father be looking for him. They need some time to catch up before he be leaving again."

Haleen shot Kendal a frown as she gently nudged Maelich who woke with a start. In his disoriented and confused state, he looked more like a lad than a brawny, young man. Perrin couldn't help but giggle at him as he nearly fell from the bench they all shared.

Once Maelich regained his wits, his cheeks grew pink with embarrassment. He looked to Haleen, "Thank you," he said, as he kissed her cheek. Then he turned and kissed Perrin, "And I've missed you since I woke this morning."

"Alright, Maelich," Kendal broke in, "your father be looking for ye on this morn'. Ye've much to discuss before ye leave again. Ye'll be needing some time alone."

Maelich said his good-byes and left to find Ymitoth. As he made his way down the street, people stopped to greet and touch him. They asked for blessings. They kissed his hands and face. Some knelt and bowed before him. They adored him. Hopefully, he would prove worthy of all their worship. His training had him feeling more confident than he ever had before, but his mind remained riddled with self-doubt. He knew the prophecy inside and out, but it didn't say anything about what happened after his task was complete. He knew he would succeed. Of that there was no doubt. What would victory cost him? That was the question. The sight of Ymitoth on the trellis was a vision.

Ymitoth called out, "Please be letting the prince make his way to the palace. He'll be having blessings for ye all, but first I be needing an audience with me son."

The people made way at the king's command. They threw blessings and well wishes on him as he passed. The faith they had in him was humbling. Even during his absence, while he trained all those years with Brerto, their adoration for him grew. They wanted to be near him, to touch him, to bask in his radiance. He wasn't sure how to feel about it. On one hand, he was proud. He felt honored to be held in such high esteem by so many. On the other hand, their gushing behavior toward him had him more than just a little embarrassed and unnerved. The pressure was massive. Sometimes, when he was all alone, that pressure felt like a weight teetering on his head threatening to topple and crush him at any moment. A sigh of relief slipped past his lips when he finally reached the steps up to the trellis.

Ymitoth led Maelich to a small sitting room he hadn't seen before. Given the brief periods of time he had spent in the castle at Havenstahl, finding a spot he'd never seen wasn't at all surprising. This spot was one that might easily become his favorite. It was cozy and simple. The most notable feature was a fur rug in front of a fireplace. Aside from that, there wasn't much of note. The only window sat opposite the fireplace. Between them, two simple wooden chairs faced the fireplace with a table between them.

As if he were reading Maelich's mind, Ymitoth commented with similar sentiment, "This has always been me favorite room in all of Havenstahl. Every other place in this palace be far too lavish for the likes of me. Most of it has me yearning for the hut where I raised ye during your early years. This place be reminding me of that place, cozy and simple. It makes for a good spot to hide out from all them who be wanting to tug on me ears."

Maelich began first, "When last we spoke, father, you told me of a warrior maiden who had eyes like mine. What of her?"

"No, Maelich," Ymitoth began shaking his head, "not just the eyes, the whole face. She looked identical to ye, just softer and feminine. She be deadly, though. She killed four of me royal guards without a struggle. She slipped in silently, like a snake."

"Who was she?"

"Daritus called her Cialia. I ain't be knowing any more than that."

"What do you know of Druindahl?"

Ymitoth thought for a moment as he stroked his beard, "That name sounds oddly familiar, Druindahl. I think that might be the lost city of the dragon. The myths talk about a city of men who be worshipping the dragon, vile wretches. After the great campaign, they fled into hiding. I always believed the city to be destroyed and abandoned. Those bearing the crest of the dragon are said to be nomads now. Lost tribes who be constantly wandering for fear of being found by men of truth. That's what this Daritus be."

"I've dreamt of a place, father," Maelich looked distant. "This place is deep in a forest at the edge of Ouloos, right at the border of where the maps don't go. A forest lost to the race of men. At least, lost to men who fear and worship Kallum. In this forest is a great city suspended in the trees, hidden from those who don't know of it."

Ymitoth scoffed, "Tis a myth, Maelich. If that place existed, we'd have stormed it and burnt it down by now."

"Ages have passed since the great campaign. How far east do adventurers travel anymore? Certainly not even past the Blood Mountains. That's not even close to far enough to find a lost forest, The Lost Forest."

Ymitoth shook his head, "No."

Maelich pressed on, "In my dreams, a silver lion comes to me. His fur shines like the sun, brilliant. It is even too brilliant to look upon without shading your eyes. He speaks to me and tells me to follow him. He leads me to a forest. I've seen this city in the trees. I've seen this girl who has my face. She beckons me. I know not who she is or what fate she would have for me, but she does call. I'm drawn to this city. There are answers for me there. I fight it, but my instincts tell me to follow the call and find the city before I face the dragon."

"Maelich, the prophecy be clear. Ye are to face the dragon. Though I be greatly pleased at your presence in Havenstahl, even this little distraction has led ye off your course. Forget this imaginary lost city. Ye must face the dragon before all else."

Maelich gazed into the fire, "That is my plan, father, but it will be hard to convince myself to stay on course when the road forks before me. I know the book from front to back and back to front. I could recite it to you from memory. Yet I still have unanswered questions. I feel this place has answers, and the call is loud."

"Stay strong, son. I've always told ye this, don't ever be wavering from your path."

The conversation lightened after that. Ymitoth did some story telling. The first was an account of the battle with Ahm's sons. Loh left quietly after Ahm fell, grateful to be out from under his rule. His sons were not so grateful. They had been off to adventure, as young giants do. When word of their father's demise reached them, they were infuriated, drunk with rage. Luckily for the house of Alhouim, the twin horns of Galgooth had been reinstalled shortly after Doentaat had taken the throne. During the great campaign the horns had been constructed to act as a beacon, a warning either from Alhouim to Havenstahl or from Havenstahl to Alhouim that dragons were attacking. When the horns blared, they could be heard for miles around. Each rested high atop a tower in their respective city.

A group of scouts from Havenstahl spotted Aht and Ahn on their approach to Alhouim. They quickly warned Ymitoth and he ordered the horn of Havenstahl be blown for the first time in centuries. The sweet sound peeled through the air like thunder, and it wasn't long before the horn of Alhouim answered the call. It was magnificent. Two armies, one of men and one of dwarves descended on the giants as one force approaching from two directions. They caught them in the great clearing between Havenstahl and Biggon's Bay. A few lost their lives, but in the end the coalition of men and dwarves prevailed. It was a great day for both cities and further solidified the renewed relationship between them. It was also the last they heard of any giants.

The two men talked the morning away. By midday they had mostly caught up with each other. The light conversation was a wonderful distraction, a brief respite from responsibility for them both. Unfortunately, duty called, as it often does. Ymitoth had the greatest city of men to lead, and Maelich had to head off to face the dragon and fulfill a prophecy written centuries before he was born. They decided to meet up with Perrin and her family for the midday, and Maelich's last home-cooked meal before hitting the trail.

By the time Maelich and Ymitoth made it back to Perrin's Place, the sweet smell of roast tubberslat wafting out the windows was nearly strong and sumptuous enough to drag both men along by their nostrils. No words were necessary between them. Their dopey grins said it all. The royal cooks were okay. However, in Havenstahl, Haleen's tubberslat had no rival. The two men jogged the last few feet to the hut.

Ymitoth hadn't even finished knocking when the door swung open. A smirking Kendal stood where it had been. "Well, look who be showing up right at mealtime," he chuckled while waving them in.

Once inside, Ymitoth asked in the humblest tone he could muster, "Would ye be having any room for two weary travelers?"

Haleen laughed, "Two lazy oafs with weary tongues maybe. Of course, highness, ye always be welcome at our table. And this one," she gazed lovingly at Maelich, "this one be promising to return as our son. Certainly, we can't be turning him away."

Perrin rose and greeted them properly, planting a soft kiss on both, one cheek each. Then they took places at the table and enjoyed the best meal either of them had eaten in as long as they could remember. The mood was pleasant and the chatter lively. None of them seemed surprised after all the talking they had done in the past day and a half, they still had much to say.

As the meal finally wound down, and all had stuffed as much into their mugs as they could without bursting, Ymitoth stood to make a proclamation. "Maelich should be getting to that trail with all haste, but none of us be knowing when that trail will be giving him back to us. Being that as it is, he'll be staying on with us a week more. I be certain the great and mighty Kallum won't be holding these few precious days we have left against us."

None at the table was more surprised by the king's words than Maelich. Ymitoth had always put duty before all else. Perhaps he was softening in his old age. Either that, or he would miss his son as much as the rest of the makeshift family sitting around the table. Maelich didn't care either way. He'd take that week and squeeze as much into it as he could.

CHAPTER 21
THE ROAD TO TRUTH

The faces and voices all melted together into one waving blur as Maelich made his way out of Havenstahl on the main road. Both sides of the great, stone road were lined with people. It seemed at any moment a parade might come drumming and marching out the front gate. Of course, there was no parade. All the people were there for him, there to bid their savior good fortune on his journey to face the dragon. Unfortunately, even as he looked at those faces, he knew he'd never remember one of them. The only faces he cared about in that moment were the ones he had just waved good-bye. He could still taste the salt of Perrin's tears on his lip. If only he were riding back into the city instead of out. Alas, there was work to do, and he was the only one who could do it.

It seemed Validus could sense the homesick feeling already coiling itself up in Maelich's gut. The journey past the gates, past the village, and down into the valley was probably the slowest leg of any journey the horse had ever taken. Maelich waited until they had made the valley before urging the horse to a trot. One last glance over his shoulder, a short wave to the crowds still gathered, and they were on their way.

After his time with Brerto on Mount Alharin, Maelich didn't need maps or directions. He had developed a connection to the things around him. It was subtle, something he couldn't explain. More like a feeling or a hunch than anything tangible or definable. When he thought about it, the best way he could describe it was a knowing. That knowing guided him along his path. The path he knew he should take.

However, there was something else lurking in his consciousness. It was another, different idea or hunch. Something he just couldn't ignore. He tried. He did. During his time with Ymitoth, the grizzled, old warrior had drilled a sense of duty in him that was nearly strong enough to keep him on his path. Nearly. Despite his best efforts to ignore this other thing, this yearning, the calling was too strong. There were answers far to the north and east. He had no idea what the questions were, but he knew there were answers, answers he couldn't rest until he learned.

Maelich followed the path he was supposed to take all the way until his first crossing of the river Galgooth. Then he left that path. Straight north into loose groupings of trees. It wasn't long until he was crossing the river again, this time after it rounded Mount Elzkahon and doubled back. There was another path beyond the second crossing of Galgooth, a path he'd never traveled, a path which led to answers. He couldn't explain how he knew. He just knew. The path before him was his path.

Just as his journey back to Havenstahl from Alharin, time meant nothing. He and Validus charged on untouched by the weariness of travel. This was another gift Brerto had seemingly unlocked in him but not explained. Something within him seemed to constantly recharge both him and Validus. It wasn't something he could will or control, but he was aware of it. The road continued and so did they.

Maelich had no idea how long or how far they had traveled, but as they crested the Edge Mountains, it felt like only moments had passed since departing the gates of Havenstahl. The Forgotten Forest expanded for miles from the base of the mountain below. It stretched so far, he couldn't see its end in any direction. Somehow, he knew the place. Despite never having been there, and having no knowledge of the place, he knew he was looking at the Forgotten Forest, and he knew that within its trees there were answers waiting for him.

The sun was setting as they breached the forest. Though it was quite dark, Maelich's vision was unaffected. Another of his gifts, the forest appeared as bright as an open field at midday. He allowed Validus to see through his eyes and the steed made his way through the darkness without incident. Maelich could feel they were close to the city. Myth indeed, Druindahl was real, and he was upon it.

The air changed suddenly. A light whisper sliced through it, and an arrow bore down on him. He prepared to dodge the brand slicing the air toward him, but its trajectory was all wrong. It would pierce the ground harmlessly, three feet to his left. Either someone was a very poor shot, or it was intended only as a warning. It was probably the latter. In a whisper he was off Validus' back and standing sword-drawn on the forest floor.

A shape fell from the trees, landing softly on the forest floor. No other eyes on Ouloos would have noticed it, but Maelich could see everything. The hooded warrior was no doubt the owner of the errant arrow. The warrior quickly drew his sword and leveled it at Maelich. No tricks. One should fight a warrior as a warrior. That's what Ymitoth would say were he standing there. Though he could suck the air from the hooded swordsman's lungs and leave him helpless and twitching on the ground, there would be no honor in it. It would be sword against sword. The only edge he would allow himself was his superior skill with a blade.

Maelich circled to his opponent's left, inviting an attack. His adversary took the bait. The blade whistled toward his throat. It was almost too easy to parry the assault. The condescending stance he attempted in mockery of his assailant was not. The next attack came immediately. Maelich would have to take him seriously. This time he attacked, flicking his wrist to make an opening and thrusting toward his opponent's heart. The warrior's defense was superb. Maelich was impressed. The hooded swordsman from the trees had an answer to every one of his attacks. The battle raged on.

The warrior was relentless, as was Maelich. Neither one could gain an upper hand. For every slash there was a parry. For every thrust there was a dodge. This hooded man was a student of the blade. Maelich was well matched. It was time to change tactics. He thrust and slashed his way close enough to strike with his elbow. His opponent blocked the blow, but it threw him off balance. He charged to take advantage of the effects his elbow had. Suddenly, he was on the ground. The man had dipped and swept Maelich's feet. He rolled to his left just in time to miss being run through by his attacker's blade. He kicked the man in the face and leapt back to his feet.

The man stumbled backward and Maelich followed up with a kick to the midsection that sent him sailing. He pounded into a tree, smacking his head and falling to the ground. As the hooded swordsman slowly regained his feet, he lost his hood. Maelich dropped his sword and gaped, dumbfounded. He was looking at himself, only softer, feminine. Suddenly, he knew her. He knew everything about her. It all came flooding into his mind at once. She was Daritus' daughter, but not really and...

"Cialia!" Maelich yelled, confused surprise dripping from his words.

She bore the same expression, "Maelich?"

They circled each other, each filling with the other's memories and emotions. Both completely confused and in dire need of answers. Many they got from each other. Many went unanswered. Then a vision.

Maelich spoke again, "Your mother...she...she looks like you?"

"Yes," she answered in the same confused tone. "You haven't a memory of a mother."

"She flung herself off a cliff in despair of what I meant to her. Your father is not your birth father. You know not of your birth father."

"Your father is the king of Havenstahl. He trained you as a warrior as mine did for me. He is not your birth father either. Your father is...your father is a lake?"

"The Lake of Dragons, my mother bathed in it and became pregnant. It is my fate...well, you know all of this, don't you?"

Cialia looked away briefly, "Yes. But how?"

Maelich looked away as well, "I don't know. I know all your thoughts. You look like me."

"And you me."

Their conversation was interrupted by another. "Well, well, well, if it isn't the lad of the Lake all grown up. Off to slay the Dragon I presume." It was Daritus, the same condescending tone he had when last they met.

"I killed you once, vermin," Maelich growled. "This time my blade will be true."

Daritus looked at his daughter and then back to Maelich. A shocking realization hit him. Something he hadn't noticed when they fought. Perhaps he was too disoriented when they had met on the trail. It was right before his eyes now, staring at him. The lad of the Lake was Cialia's twin. He tried to shake off the vision, but it wouldn't leave. They were mirror images of each other. His eyes widened in disbelief as he ran his hands through his hair.

"You're twins!" Baffled, he continued, "That means...come with me, both of you."

Maelich sheathed his sword, as did Cialia. They followed Daritus to a cart, out of place on the forest floor. This was no crude thing. Carved with elegant patterns and richly-stained, it belonged in a palace. Impressive as was the design, the real marvel was the smooth movement of the thing. This wasn't some rough contraption consisting of ropes and pulleys, as one might expect. If Maelich closed his eyes, he wouldn't even realize he was moving.

The moment the cart reached the end of its journey, the door slid open on its own. The fabled city of Druindahl spread out before Maelich's eyes. He gasped. It was twice again as magnificent as the stories he'd been told. The way the builders had incorporated the trees into the construction of the round huts among the canopy spoke to the skill of the planners and builders. Connecting all of this was a series of wooden walkways exhibiting equal craftsmanship. Nothing about the design was simple. Posts and rails were more than just functional, they'd been carved with reliefs, intricate, artistic expressions, each telling a piece of the story of Ouloos. Of course, the story depicted wasn't the one Maelich knew. This was some alternate, false history told from the perspective of wicked men in service of the dragon.

Travelling among this false history, the small group eventually reached the center of the city and a building larger than the rest, higher among the canopy too. Another cart pulled them up to a balcony populated by a couple of guards who were obviously for more than just show. They both carried the marks of real soldiers with hard eyes and scars a plenty. The rough looking men bowed in unison to Daritus who responded by absently waving them off as he guided the twins past them.

A hall stretched out from them in either direction rounding the circumference of the building. From what Maelich could see, it was lined with many doors. Apparently, he wouldn't get to explore them just yet, as Daritus led he and Cialia through the one directly in front of them.

The walls inside the room were polished prang, shimmering in the torchlight and resembling the sky at sunset. A narrow, burgundy carpet ran from the doorway up to two thrones It was flanked on both sides by heavily armed guards. One of the seats was empty. The other was occupied by an enchanting beauty. Her golden hair flowed all about her, while deep brown eyes—which seemed to carry a lifetime's worth of knowledge—peered out from soft, flawless skin. As perfect full lips parted into a welcoming smile, Maelich instantly knew her face. He tried to run to her, but his legs went slack beneath him. He fell.

The guards helped him to his feet as the queen ran to him. He lost his feet again as she wrapped her arms around his head and pulled him to her bosom. He felt helpless as a babe. She rocked back and forth as she cradled him. He tried to speak but no words would come.

Then she spoke, "My sweet boy, I've been calling to you. I was beginning to think you wouldn't hear my voice." She stroked his hair.

Maelich tried again to speak. The words were in his mouth but wouldn't come. His eyes were pleading as he gazed up at her. She just smiled and pulled him closer, surrounding him. Her scent was sweet, like wild flowers of the field. Daritus, Cialia and the guards looked on in shock as the queen cradled him, all of them knowing but none believing.

"Yes," she whispered softly to him, "I am your mother."

He shivered in her arms. His heritage had always been a mystery to him. Accepting that his father was a lake rather than a man was hard enough to deal with. Learning of his mother's demise was worse still. All he knew were lies. She didn't take her own life. She wasn't dead at all.

His mind was a swirling pool of questions and doubts. How could Ymitoth have lied to him all those years? How could this woman, his mother, so perfect in every way live in the service of such evil? Maybe it wasn't true. Maybe this was the lie, a vile witch promising a mother's love but hiding a black, villainous heart. No. Despite his best efforts to convince his mind otherwise, his heart knew she spoke only truth.

It suddenly occurred to Maelich that on this day he had gained more than just a mother. Cialia was his sister, his twin. He'd spent his life believing he shared blood with no one alive, and now he had a family. The room began to spin, the walls, the people, the faces. They all circled round him as if held aloft in a whirlwind. It was all too much. Their faces faded as consciousness fled, and the world went black.

Maelich woke a few hours later–saved from dreams filled with confused images and contradictions—in a plush bed surrounded by four large, decoratively-carved wooden posts at its corners. What the room lacked in size, it made up for in lavish decorations. Moonlight poured into the room from its only window, slicing through the darkness and giving everything inside a ghostly glow.

Maelich glanced around at his surroundings. The grandeur of the place lost on him as he desperately tried to get his bearings and make sense of everything. He didn't know what to think or what to believe. His mother, who he thought had taken her own life, was in fact the ruler of a people fighting to protect the very evil he sought to destroy. He had quite literally spent his entire life training for a task to which she led the opposition. A shape stirred in the corner and pulled Maelich away from his fruitless effort.

"Who's there?" he whispered, scrambling to his knees as he prepared to defend himself.

Cialia spoke softly as she moved into the light, "Maelich, my brother, is it true what father has said?" The moon's rays glowing on the soft curves of her face gave her a dream-like appearance.

Tension gave way to confusion as Maelich scratched his head and asked, "Who is your father? You mean the Lake has spoken to you?"

"What lake?" she shook her head. "Daritus is my father. Well, he's not really my father, but he acts as such. He married our mother in my fifth year. Ever since then, he's raised me as his own." A slight grin crept onto her lips as she continued, "Apparently, he's done rather well in training me. You're lucky I only used one of my blades."

He grinned through the anguish, "Yes, indeed. You are quite handy with a blade. Ymitoth spoke of your abilities to me as well. It seems you're quite the assassin."

She looked defiant, defensive, "We take life only when we must to protect our own. The demon king of Havenstahl would have killed my father had I not done what I did. And those guards would have killed me if given the opportunity. Besides, I was called to the task by my god, Kaldumahn."

"What? Demon king?" Maelich was shocked. "Ymitoth raised me in much the same fashion Daritus raised you. Stern? Yes. Loving father? Also, yes. And he fights to protect Havenstahl and all Ouloos from the horror you protect. I know nothing of this Kaldumahn of whom you speak, but your faith is false. Is he the dragon?"

"Kaldumahn is no Dragon, but, like me, he protects her from those who would do her harm."

"Her? The dragon is a her?" the idea seemed ridiculous to him.

Cialia's anger rose, "You think that strange? Women can't be powerful? Does not your own mother govern the great city Druindahl? Daritus is king only through marriage to our mother. She governs the people of this great city. She makes and enforces the laws for these people. Helias, the Dragon is the Great Mother. She guides and nurtures us all."

"Helias? So, the beast has a name. Well if she is a she, then she is the evil of this world, and I intend to extinguish her flame."

Cialia stood and stormed to the door, "There are many who will lay down their lives in her defense, including myself. Your quarry will be no easy prize!"

A wide confident smile spread across Maelich's lips, "I respect your passion, but there are things about me you don't know and couldn't possibly understand. If your people wish to lay down their lives to me, I will have no choice but oblige them. However, my quarrel is only with the dragon. I truly hope I have no cause to spill any blood but his. Excuse me, hers."

Cialia slammed the door, and Maelich was alone once again. It wasn't a condition he liked all that much, but it was better than fruitless debate with one who obviously knew very little about the world and how things are. None of it made any sense. How could such an evil being earn such passion and respect from these people? How could his own mother serve the beast? How could anyone see something caring and maternal about a winged monster who belched fire and sought to destroy the race of men? Yet, they did.

His thoughts were disturbed when the door of his room began slowly creaking open. Great, Cialia returning for a second round of debates? However, once the door swung wide, it wasn't his twin's face scowling at him. Instead, Maelich's gaze was met by the friendly smile of his old friend, Hagen.

"What on Ouloos are you doing here?" Maelich blurted while wondering if his feet would ever again find solid ground.

Hagen's smile widened, "I was searching for truth, and, at the end of my journey, I wound up here." He continued into the room and sat next to Maelich on the bed.

"Truth?" Maelich shrugged, "What is truth? I have been told so many things by so many people I don't even know what that is anymore. My eyes have seen things I can't believe. Everything I know contradicts everything I'm hearing. The only thing I can have faith in is The Book. Right at this moment Kallum's words are the only thing keeping me centered."

"You sound just as I did," Hagen said quietly as his smile gave way to something more like sadness. "Maelich, I have been around for quite some time, quite a bit longer than any man should. These old eyes have seen their fair share. However, I was raised much like you were, much like all the men from Havenstahl, much like all the men from all the great cities, for that matter. Even dwarves are taught the same things. From the time we are old enough to understand, they begin teaching us the words of Kallum. They tell us his laws. They scare us with the violent repercussions which will surely befall us if we don't submit and grovel before him like scrods. They make us afraid of things we've never experienced by calling them evil. Have you ever met a Dragon? Of course not. Have you met anyone who has faced a Dragon? No one alive in the cities of men has. Still, you like everyone else, believes she is evil. Well, you believe he is evil. In Kallum's book, men rule. Women serve only to give them sons and clean up their messes. The power to give life is credited to the staffs of men not the wombs of women."

The old man paused, but Maelich couldn't fashion a response. Trying to comprehend the filth being vomited to his ears by one he respected so greatly took every ounce of cognizant effort he could muster.

Hagen continued, "Failure to follow the laws or even questioning them with a logical mind is met with violence and destruction. I decided to get up off my knees and walk like a man. I questioned, not publicly mind you, but in silence, in secrecy. Because I sought to discover truth for myself and not have it fed to me, I was forced to go into hiding. I was afraid my questions would cause men to bring violence on me, and they would. What have I learned in all this time? There are many books, Maelich. Not all of them are saturated in violence. Many of them share similar sentiments to those found in Kallum's book, but many of them also express stark differences. None of that really answers your question though, does it? What is truth? That is what you asked. I don't know what it is for me. I'm still looking. Your truth is something you must find for yourself."

Maelich was still trying in vain to wrap his mind around one singular thought as he replied, "I too have questioned in my mind. But what can I know which I haven't been taught?"

"Ah, that question surprises me from you. Your mind is like none other in this world, save maybe your sister's. Do you just open it up like an empty chalice and allow anyone to pour ideas into it? Do you let folks tell you how you feel about things? Do you enjoy the violence your path presents you?"

"No. I never wish to spill blood, but I have to. That is my purpose. That is my role. It was written by Kallum himself," Maelich's tone was matter of fact.

"You learned that from the book. You learned that because that's what you were told. You didn't come to that conclusion after analyzing facts. You were told it and now you refuse to entertain any contradictory idea. Additionally, Kallum's word was written by a man. The message came to him in a dream as images, pictures. The man's name was Eringaal…"

"Eringaal," Maelich interrupted, "the first king of Havenstahl?"

"Well, not in the fashion you might be thinking. The city of Havenstahl wasn't completed until long after Eringaal died. The people did follow him, and the city adopted his surname. He never actually ruled the city though. After writing Kallum's law, he began teaching it. He spread word of it to all who would listen. Most who listened became followers for fear of the fate promised by the book if they refused. After a time, his tribe became quite powerful and the fate of those who refused was accelerated. Many people were tortured and killed for clinging to beliefs which didn't match Kallum's law."

"They killed people for not agreeing to follow them?" Maelich asked, distraught by the idea.

"Why does that seem odd to you?" Hagen challenged, "Did you not mean to kill Daritus on the path to Mount Alharin, simply because he bore the crest of the Dragon?"

He thought for a moment, "I suppose I did."

"Of course, you did," the old man shrugged. "And his only crime? Not sharing your belief."

Maelich's tone gained a bit of force as he replied, "No. His crime was worshipping the dragon. His crime was worshipping evil!"

Hagen offered a sad chuckle as he slowly shook his head, "And who says Helias is evil? Your book. Your book says everything worshipped other than Kallum is evil. Therefore, anyone who doesn't share your belief is evil. And what is the penalty for breaking Kallum's first law?" He paused for effect, "Death. Just as it was over a thousand years ago when the savage tribe of Havenstahl was purging Ouloos of nonbelievers, so it still is today. You are now Kallum's right hand of vengeance."

Maelich sat silently, stunned. The idea sickened him, but the old man was right. Brerto had basically told him as much. He was nothing more than a tool. He was a tool of vengeance. He was the tool Kallum would use to eradicate the last dragon. But if the dragon is evil, why is that wrong? If he can bring peace to Ouloos by destroying her, is it not worth violent measures? What if Kallum were evil? The idea was ridiculous. Kallum created all things. He abhorred evil. The book said so.

Hagen could see the battle going on in Maelich's head expressed on the lad's face. Unfortunately, it was a problem he couldn't solve for him. He could only show him a path.

After a few moments, Hagen offered one last challenge, "Grant an old man one request. I realize years of having an idea battered into your head will be difficult to overcome. However, when you do face the Dragon, look in Her eyes. You have the power. Look into Her soul. Search it for the evil you're convinced exists there before you end Her life. I think you'll be surprised by what you find."

"But she will try to deceive me. She is treacherous, a liar. How can I believe what I find in her mind, in her heart, if she has one?" he shrugged.

The lines of sadness deepened on Hagen's face, "If you believe She can deceive you, then I guess you can't be sure. You can see past lies and deceit. Know this, the only limits you have are self-imposed. Nothing is out of your reach. Once you truly understand this, you can do anything. You can kill the Dragon, extinguish Helias' flame, or you could choose not to. I must tell you that killing Her will destroy our world. Kallum's hunger for power has made him conceited and blind. If he succeeds in having you kill Her, we all will be destroyed. Even the great Kallum will meet his end."

"More words," Maelich muttered.

"Yes," Hagen agreed, "Someone else telling you how things are and what you should believe. I know. Please, do not take my word for it. Use that brilliant mind of yours. Come up with your own answer."

The old man rose and left the room. Again, Maelich was alone with a mind full of thoughts to sort through. He remained in the bed; his mind full of things to contemplate, ideas to chew on, and contradictions to sort out. He didn't want to do any of it. Swords are so much easier than words. It wasn't long before sleep took him again. Sadly, all the things in his head he was avoiding weren't going anywhere. They would wait.

CHAPTER 22
BLACK DEAD EYES

The entire morning had been a blur. Maelich had woken to his mother's kiss on his cheek. After he dressed, she led him to a room where they could relax, talk, and share a meal. Details were scarce for him. He couldn't stop staring at her, scrutinizing. The idea she was alive was still something he couldn't quite digest. On top of that, he wasn't quite sure how he felt about her. The idea he had held his entire life about who she was seemed a distant memory, trampled to death by the real thing. She was nothing like that dead idea.

The room they ended up in was very small, quaint. The only furniture in the room was a fancy table, etched with hand-carved decorations, and big enough to seat only two chairs. There were two doors but no windows. Across from the door through which they entered was a fireplace. An intricate sculpture of a dragon sat upon the mantel below a large dramatic painting of a dragon at rest. Maelich's gaze fell on the painting and remained there for a good long while. This dragon didn't look like other images he had seen. This dragon looked calm, serene. In fact, it almost looked magnificent, god-like. He shook the idea from his mind.

As they chatted, a young man entered carrying two plates. The food on them didn't look like anything Maelich had ever eaten, but it smelled divine. It was similar to roast tubberslat, but there was something more, something sweet. The young man set the plates down and left without a word. The queen smiled at Maelich, nodded at his plate and then began to eat. He did the same. His mouth was dazzled.

It was some form of meat, but it was saturated in all kinds of different flavors. It wasn't long before he had cleaned his plate.

Then the queen spoke, "Well, I guess you were hungry. Did you enjoy it?"

Maelich sighed and stretched, feeling satisfied, "It was fantastic, like nothing I've ever tasted. What was it?"

"Tubberslat," she responded in a tone suggesting he should have known that.

"Hmm," he looked as if he didn't believe her, "I've never tasted tubberslat like that before."

She smiled and raised her brow, "That's because you've never had tubberslat prepared by Dalwin. He has spent his life perfecting the art of preparing food. Doesn't that sound ridiculous?" She giggled. "Still, there is no one on Ouloos who can compare with him. He studies food like you've studied swordplay. He uses some form of a glaze on this dish. He calls it morning dew. He's explained to me how he does it, but it makes no sense to me at all. I don't care how he does it. I just love to eat it."

Maelich began to feel a bit more comfortable as his mystery of a mother spoke to him. She seemed quite normal, speaking to him as if it were just another day. Perhaps she did that for his benefit. Maybe she wanted him to feel comfortable, realizing that meeting her would be quite a shock to him. He wondered if she was as confused about him as he was of her. It suddenly occurred to him he didn't know her name.

He asked, "What's your name? In all the stories I've been told of you, no one has ever said your name."

"You don't know my name?" she seemed quite surprised. "I can't believe they didn't even tell you my name. They completely eliminated me from your life. My name is Leisha."

"Leisha," he said her name. Then he said it again, "Leisha, that's pretty."

"So, what have they told you of me?" she sat back in her chair and folded her hands on the table.

He looked in her eyes, "They told me you bathed in the Lake of Dragons and were impregnated by it. Then you carried me in your womb but when you gave birth to me, I was too much for you to bear. Well, not me myself, but your role as my mother. They said you took me to Havenstahl and left me on the steps of the temple. Then they said…" he paused. "Then they said you flung yourself off a cliff."

"Hmm," a forceful chuckle, "Apparently, I survived my fall. That is ridiculous. Do you want to know how the story really went? I can't believe they told you I was dead. What am I saying? Yes, I can. They would say anything to twist your mind. Do you want to know? Or have they bred hatred in your heart for me?" her lip quivered slightly as moisture filled her eyes.

He did want to know, "Yes, please tell me. All my life I've been asking about you, and all I know is what they've told me. Now that I see you before me, I know their stories were lies. I don't understand why they would lie to me, but apparently, they have. Please tell me how we came to be apart."

"I did bathe in the Lake," she began. "We lived in a hut near a river at the edge of a forest. It was a dark scary place, The Lost Forest. They say that's where the lost souls go who have forgotten their way back home, but they aren't lost. They are trapped. My father had always told me never to go in those woods. No one has ever gone in and come back out. Lost souls become jealous when live people walk about their wood. They torment them and drive them insane. On the eve of the sixteenth anniversary of my birth, a silver lion came to me in a dream. He said Coeptus had picked me to fulfill their prophecy. I would travel to the Lake and bathe in its waters. So, the next morning, I ignored my father's warnings and tromped on through the forest.

"The Lost Forest was dark, and it was scary. I could feel those poor, imprisoned souls brushing up against me. I could hear them whispering my name. With every touch my flesh prickled up into bumps. I ran blindly through the forest, falling and falling again." Her gaze was distant, "I can still remember how terrified I was, how I wished I had listened to my father. I finally gave up. I curled up in a ball against a tree as the whispers of those lost souls turned to screeching howls in my ears. I sobbed. They were relentless. I don't remember how long I sat in that spot and cried, but it seemed like forever. Then high among the treetops, there was light."

The young man who had served them their meal had returned with two fine chalices of wine. Leisha sipped from hers and then continued, "The light descended upon me and the screeching ceased. I followed that light the rest of the way through the forest and was troubled no more by spirits."

She sipped from her glass again, "Once I reached the edge of the forest, the light was gone. I can't describe the beauty of the place which bordered the forest. The colors were so vibrant. The air was warm. There were mountains off in the distance and there were trees like none I had ever seen popping up from the field here and there. It was enchanting. There was a path, and I followed it. It led me to a lake. It was strange, like no lake I had ever seen. It was a perfect circle, maybe two miles in diameter. The water was a deep blue, like the blue of your eyes. I slipped into the water. Instantly, there was warmth in my belly and a tingling down below my waist. I remained only a few moments, but right then I knew I was pregnant.

"I left the Lake and went home. The souls of the forest didn't bother me. It was as if some strange force protected me. Perhaps they knew I carried their savior in my womb. Whatever the reason, I made it home. My belly grew. My mother and father called me all kinds of names being I was without a husband. They said I would have to leave them in shame as soon as you were born. Of course, their minds changed when you arrived," she smiled at her son as she sipped from her chalice again.

"Well, I suppose you've already figured out you came as part of a set. You came first, then your sister. Your grandmother named you. She picked you up, looked at me and spoke your name. Then your sister came, and your grandfather did the same for her. Oh, how they loved you." Her eyes drifted toward the ceiling as she continued, "I cared for you but a week when they came, the men with the black, dead eyes." She shuddered at the memory of them.

Maelich interrupted, "Black, dead eyes, those were Kallum's priests!"

"Yes, and they killed my mother and father when they tried to stop them. Your grandmother was a warrior, even better with swords than your sister, and your grandfather was somewhat of a magician. They didn't stand a chance against those soulless monsters. I slipped out the back of our hut and fled into the night with you and your sister. They followed not far behind. I'm not sure how far we got before the warriors came. Men on horseback surrounded us. You and Cialia had been screaming while we ran from the priests. I couldn't stop to feed you. We had no supplies. I couldn't even comfort you as those damned demons kept gaining on us. They seemed to float through the air. Anyway, the riders were there to help us. There were about fifty of them, all bearing the crest of the Dragon. They battled with the three men, but they were terribly outmatched," she shook her head, her gaze still far off.

"I witnessed many terribly deaths that night, images which are difficult to think about. About twenty of those brave men had fallen when one of the monsters reached us. He slapped me with the back of his hand and flung me through the air. I was unconscious. When I woke, I was tied to a horse with your cradle, but only Cialia remained." A tear fell down her cheek, "There were two men with Cialia and I. They told me the dead-eyed men had taken you. The remaining men stayed to fight off the beasts, and these two fled with us to protect what they could. I wept for you for many nights, Maelich. I still do. I've missed so much of your life, and I know you have been trained to hate what I stand for. It sorrows my heart. I wanted to come to you, to find where they had taken you, but I couldn't. They would have killed you. I hoped and prayed to Kaldumahn that one day you would return to me, and you have."

There was just so much Maelich could barely process. He whispered, "How is it you came to be queen of this place? If you lived in a hut, your parents could not have been royalty."

Leisha composed herself, "I fulfilled the prophecy. I had given birth to the one who would ride the last Dragon against Kallum. Upon his destruction, the lost souls will be released, and balance restored on Ouloos. They made me their queen. A few years later, I met a man, Daritus. He was quite dashing, strong and smart. He had a wonderful mind and was not the least bit intimidated by a powerful woman. I married him, and he became the king."

Maelich shook his head, "What? Did you just say I've come to ride the last dragon against Kallum? I've come to slay that dragon. That is what the prophecy says. That is my task. Peace will only come after he is destroyed."

She sighed, "Kallum twisted the prophecy to suit his ambitions. The prophet's name was Maaltuk. He was adventuring, and he napped upon a rock. He didn't know this when he first lay his head down, but Kaldumahn had taken the form of this rock before Maaltuk had arrived. When he woke from his slumber, the rock spoke to him. Kaldumahn spoke to him. He told him this world would become an evil place in the absence of Dragons. He told him that a young girl who had never been touched by a man would bathe in the lake from whence the Dragons came and she would become impregnated by it. He said she would bear twins, and they would ride the last Dragon against Kallum. Upon his destruction, the lost souls would be free to go home, and balance would be restored on Ouloos. Maaltuk wrote all he had heard down. However, when Kallum spoke to Eringaal, he twisted the prophecy. Just as he had twisted the minds of men against Dragons in the great campaign."

Her words stung Maelich, "I can't believe that. Kallum is truth. Kallum is light. How can you question the creator of all things?"

Leisha let out a short laugh, "He didn't create anything. Coeptus created all things, Dragons, men, dwarves, grongs, and giants, all things. The land we walk on and the air we breathe are the workings of Coeptus. The likes of Kallum and Kaldumahn exist to act as guides, paths to Coeptus."

She wasn't making sense, "Who is Coeptus? Everyone knows Kallum created all things."

Before Leisha could respond, the door burst open. "The city is under attack, my queen," the guard stammered, out of breath, "three hooded riders. They look like men, but our warriors are falling quickly."

"The dead-eyed men!" Leisha stammered.

The three charged out onto the path. Night had fallen. They must have been talking for quite some time. He recognized the attackers immediately. They were Kallum's priests. The riders of Druindahl continuously charged, but they continuously fell. They were no match for the agents of Kallum.

Leisha cried out as she saw Cialia charging into battle, "No!"

Maelich leapt from the path down to the forest floor. He was about twenty feet behind Cialia, but her horse was much too fast for him to catch. She bore down on the monsters firing daggers as she went. They had no effect. She drew her swords as she flipped off Purity's back and slashed at the one in front. He brought his arm up and blocked the blow. Then he smiled as he planted an uppercut under her chin. She sailed through the air and slammed against the ground. The three advanced on her as she tried in vain to crawl away. Maelich reached her first. He stood between her and the priests.

"Stop," he shouted. His voice echoed through the forest as everyone except the priests stood still. Even the archers in the trees held back their arrows.

While the priests' attention was on Maelich, the warriors who hadn't fallen slipped back into the trees to regroup. The dead-eyed men continued to advance, undaunted by Maelich's warning. Maelich remembered what Ymitoth had told him about hesitation. He didn't know what to believe right at that moment. However, he certainly was not about to let any harm befall his newfound family.

He shouted again, "I command you to stop. Your rage is unwelcomed here and will be repaid with violence tenfold."

The three stopped. The leader spoke, "You have done well, my son. The dragon is crafty and has hidden this place from my sight. You have shown me the way. You stand tall in your Lord's eyes on this day. Now, make way. This city has broken my first law and must be punished."

Maelich paused. It suddenly occurred to him he wasn't simply challenging dead-eyed men, but Kallum himself. When first he faced the priests, they were merely adversaries. They were simply men. Since Kallum spoke through them in the temple at Havenstahl, he now knew they acted according to his will. Doubt suddenly clouded his mind. How could he stand against his Lord?

The hero spoke, "I need time. I have been told many things that trouble my mind. Please, my Lord, don't force me to react in my confused state."

The three men removed their hoods in unison, their appearance as menacing as Maelich remembered. The leader grinned. However, the expression wasn't friendly. His wild orange hair and black, dead eyes gave him an evil, maniacal appearance. He continued, "My son, confused or no, do not stand against me for any cause. I created you. I created everything. To stand with this vile, treacherous people is to break my law along with them. You put yourself in a place lower than the vermin creeping among the dirt and dark places. Stand aside and remain within my grace, or face oblivion."

Silence rumbled in all ears on the field that day as Maelich thought hard about his next words. Staring at the man's dead eyes, he raised his head high and with courage in his voice said, "Forgive me, Lord. I cannot."

The warriors of Druindahl had already begun evacuating the city. Using Maelich's distraction to shuffle the women and children deeper into the forest toward the caves. The caves had been used many times in the history of Druindahl to protect her people from those who would do her harm. Those times were long, long ago. They hadn't cause to use the caves for centuries, but on this eve, they would once again prove useful as shelter in the face of a storm.

The leader's face grew grim at Maelich's refusal to submit. He clenched his hands into fists and beat them against his own head as he let out a raspy shout. His rage quickly mounted as he began stomping about and launching rapid, wild curses at Maelich. The two behind him followed suit, stomping and cursing. They pointed their fingers at him and up toward the sky. Maelich held his ground. The last time he had faced them, he was but a swordsman. He figured to have much less to fear from them now.

Meanwhile, Daritus had crept up and dragged Cialia to safety. He sent her away with Leisha, a small group of soldiers, and the rest of the folk of Druindahl toward the caves. The balance of Druindahl's army remained in position to defend them. Should Maelich fall or turn on them, they would fight. They would lay down their lives if necessary. The archers in the trees readied their bows while the soldiers on the ground readied their swords. They watched, and they waited.

Maelich stood his ground as the leader suddenly stopped his stomping and cursing and lunged toward him. Before Maelich could react and present any kind of defense, two fists like stone pounded him in the chest. The canopy raced by overhead as Maelich sailed a solid fifteen feet through the air before slamming into the forest floor. By the time he scrambled to his feet, his eyes glowed red fire.

The three continued to advance. Leery of attacking his Lord, Maelich stood fast. The leader lashed out him with both fists again. This time Maelich reacted by grabbing hold of the dead-eyed man's wrists.

"Enough," Maelich pleaded, "please don't force me into a choice I am not ready to make."

"You have already chosen," the leader hissed, as he smashed the center of his forehead into Maelich's nose.

Maelich stumbled backward, losing his grip on the man's arms. His knees buckled, but he kept his feet. Blood poured from his battered face, saturating what little beard he had. Rage slithered through Maelich's body causing him to tremble slightly. As it slipped down his spine like a snake, that trembling grew until Maelich's body was tense and shaking. Servant of God or no, Maelich was finished with dead-eyed men.

Flames swirled around Maelich's forearms up to his elbows. The muscles in his face bulging as he clamped his jaws down tight. Raising his arms and pointing his fists at the three, he barely noticed the smell of his sleeves burning. Then, hiss, two perfect spheres of fire raced toward the three, exploding against the leader and engulfing him in the flame of Maelich's rage. The concussion from the blast rocketed the dead-eyed man through the air. The remaining two instantly charged, their dead eyes wide and unyielding. Maelich fired again and sent them sailing. They landed near the leader. Three fires became one.

The fire burned for a time. Maelich's breaths came rapid and heavy, as he watched the three writhing in agony. So focused was he on the result of his rage, he didn't notice the shocked looks of hardened warriors staring at his display of power. The fire of the Dragon was an incomparable, mythical force that, according to the traditions of Druindahl, had never been released. That is, until now. Any among those shocked witnesses who had doubted the savior's identity instantly became believers.

As the flames and moans gradually subsided, so did Maelich's rage. Suddenly, the stinging in his nose jumped to the front of his awareness. He turned back toward the city. Hopefully, there was someone who could help him tend to that. However, it seemed everyone had gone. He was alone. Of course, that couldn't be the case. From what he'd seen, the warriors of Druindahl would never stop. They should still be at their posts, hiding among the trees, watching. He started off in the direction he imagined the caves would be. Then he heard another moan.

Maelich spun around in time to see the three rising again, completely unscathed. His confidence sank as they floated toward him with their feet hovering just above the ground. He took one step back and considered flight. Ymitoth's voice in his head stayed his feet, 'Stay strong, son. There be no man or no beast who can sway ye from your path.' Maelich let the fire come again.

Then a growl from deep in the forest, far behind Maelich, shook the very ground on which they stood. The three stopped. They didn't retreat, but Maelich thought he saw the slightest hint of fear on their faces. Maelich advanced. The ground rumbled as if a herd of tubber was stampeding through The Forgotten Forest. Maelich turned toward the sound.

A brilliant, silver light filled the forest, blinding Maelich. He had no idea what was coming but it had to be immense and powerful. He strained his eyes, squinting through the blaze to try and make out a shape. It was no use. The glare was too great, like staring at the sun. The thunderous rumble increased in volume as the violence with which the ground shook steadily increased. Though he couldn't make out what was coming, the danger of staying put was undeniable. He dove behind a tree a moment before a silver streak shot passed him. Within that blazing streak of silver light, he faintly made out powerful legs and jaws.

The three stood their ground as the beast charged through them and continued into the trees without slowing at all. Just as quickly as they had arrived, they were gone, whisked away by a charging beast in a silver light.

Maelich collected himself as the warriors of Druindahl who had stayed behind appeared from among the trees. Excitement buzzed through the crowd. Hardened soldiers hugged and congratulated each other. One even danced a jig.

"On my honor, that was the Lion himself," a voice among the crowd called out.

Another answered, "Bless your eyes. They serve you well. That was Kaldumahn indeed."

"The great silver Lion who stalks the skies," added still another.

Maelich had no idea what to make of all the cheering and singing. He was completely confused. These were the very warriors he had been taught were evil and bent on the destruction of all that is good. The happy group before him didn't fit that description at all. They continued to sing and celebrate as they filtered out toward the caves.

Once the others had gone, only Daritus and Maelich remained in the clearing. Daritus spun and stalked toward Maelich. His eyes mere slits, and his scowl pure fury. Nothing on the king's face remotely resembled the sheer giddiness on the faces of his men as they had tromped off toward the caves. His face pulsed with vengeance.

"You brought Kallum's wrath upon our city?" the king roared.

"I would never," surprise dripped from Maelich's voice "I had no idea they would come. I was drawn to this place, not sent. In fact, I was forbidden to journey anywhere but to the dragon. I disobeyed. They...they must have followed me."

"Bind your lips lest they spew more vile poison upon this sacred ground," Daritus' voice echoed through the forest. However, his demeaner calmed almost instantly before he continued, "You are the queen, my wife's, son, and she has forbidden me from striking you down. I remain unconvinced you are worthy of mercy, but I must honor her judgment. Yours is a task which must be carried out. She will wish to have an audience with you before you depart. Follow me."

Maelich thought to argue his point further, but he kept his tongue. Though he battled the three, he had to concede their appearance immediately after his in a place hidden for so long would appear to be much more than coincidence. Even more than that, he reckoned much of Daritus' anger was caused by sorrow for his lost men.

The journey to the caves was long and wound through woods so dark, Maelich may as well have had his eyes closed. He could barely see Daritus a few inches in front of him. Were it not for the random splash of moonlight penetrating the canopy, he would have been all but blind. Despite the darkness, Daritus guided him through as if it were midday.

A chill crept over Maelich as he did his best to match Daritus' movements, turning to avoid and stepping over obstacles he couldn't see. Twice he stumbled over a root or stump, or some other thing he couldn't hope to identify. Those random bits of moonlight were a blessing, but they cast odd shadows about. Was that a face howling with rage? No, just a knot in an old pine. Maelich wasn't quite afraid, but there was something eerie about the forest. Perhaps it was his presuppositions of the people who inhabited the place. Perhaps it was the howling wind whistling through the trees like a witch whistling to her enchanted. He couldn't be sure. Nonetheless, he gathered his cloak tighter about his shoulders.

Finally, one more turn, and torches blazed. It took Maelich a moment to realize they weren't merely approaching a cave, but already in it. That was a trick. None of the torchlight bled through the loose covering of moss behind him. Maelich barely had time to examine his surroundings before the place echoed with cheers and folks began patting his back.

"Sing me a cheer for the great warrior of the Lake," someone shouted.

Two women quickly ran to Maelich with wet cloths and attended to his shattered nose, while someone from the crowd belted out a tune:

When the vile priests they came to call
They did bite and smash and men did fall

Great soldiers ground beneath the feet
Of dead and soulless beasts

Great Mother cried, her heart did break
When she saw her people's lives at stake
As one after one lay down his life
She pitied for our strife

A savior from the Lake she sent
To save us...

"Stop," Daritus' roared, his voice echoing like thunder through the cave. "You sing praises and offer adoration to this vile thing, this slithering traitor who would bring the weight of Kallum's fury down on our beloved city? Druindahl has been hidden from Kallum's sight for thousands of years and suddenly he stumbles across her only after this fiend has discovered her? Kallum's soldier, his bringer of death, appears immediately before his priests. Is this coincidence? I say no. I say this devil of a man brought Kallum's rage with him to our fair city. I say he is bound to destroy us and then the Dragon."

"But sire, look at him," a voice called out from the crowd. "He stood firm against those monsters and protected us. They battered him for it. That's proof enough for me."

"Ah, you're a simple twit," another voice rang out. "Listen to your king. The treacherous bastard led those beasts right to our door."

"Come now, think about this logically," still another voice begged. "Had the man wished us dead, why not burn our city down with his flame? It makes no sense to bring Kallum to this place when the man is walking around this world with the power of Dragon's flame."

Daritus glared at Maelich as the crowd's arguments turned into pushing and shoving. It wasn't long before fists were flying. One man held his brother's arms back so another man could punch his face. It was all more than Maelich could take. He faced the crowd and raised up his hands to them. He spoke no words with his mouth, but his message was clear in their minds. The fighting slowly diminished and abruptly ended as he soothed them, filling their heads with pleasant thoughts.

As Daritus watched Maelich enchant the people of Druindahl, he slowly realized what was happening. He charged at him, planting his shoulder squarely into Maelich's back. The blow nearly knocked the lad off his feet.

Maelich spun to face his attacker, "Why do you attack me when I bring peace to these people?"

"You enchant them!" Daritus hissed. "You would control them. You would turn their faces toward your god, the king of lies, the father of hate."

Maelich was incredulous, "I don't wish to change their faith. They're destroying each other. I'm calming them, filling them with thoughts of peace and love. Perhaps I am enchanting them, but not for my own good, for theirs. Does your hatred for me blind you to the good in what I'm trying to do?"

"There is nothing good about your cause. You are evil. Your cause is evil," Daritus scowled as he drew his sword. "Leave us now, before your demons return to finish us off."

Leisha's voice deflated the tension, "Daritus, my love, why do you fire these daggers at my son? His mind is confused. His path has been twisted for him throughout his entire life, and now he's trying to find his way. What could he possibly know but what he's been taught? Had you been raised as he was, you would share the same faith as he and harbor the same hatred for the Dragon." She moved toward them through the crowd.

"I know this," Daritus spat, his anger still seething, "but he brought the fury of Kallum upon us. He led them to us to destroy us!"

She shook her head, "Had he truly wanted to destroy us, he could have done that himself. You saw his power. That's all these people can talk about now. He wields Dragon's fire. He could have burned our city and our forest to the ground if he saw fit. Is there a warrior among your army who could challenge him? I think not."

"Then how did Kallum find us?" his eyes never left Maelich.

"Before you arrived, I was in quite a state. I became faint and the Lion took me. He stood with me on a mountaintop, high among the clouds. He told me we must not hinder Maelich in his quest. Whatever path he chooses, he must be allowed to choose. No matter the outcome. Kallum's power grows and the time is now." She turned to Maelich, "Son, you must go now. You must face the Dragon. You must search your heart for truth and trust what you find there. You must push away everything anyone else has told you, even me, and decide which path is yours."

Daritus looked to his wife, and then back to Maelich. The scowl never left his face as he shook his head and stormed through the crowd and out of the cave.

Maelich went to Leisha and embraced her. As he did, images of her life flashed through his head. All the years he had missed, would he ever see her again? Right at that moment, he wished to be a lad again. He wished she would pick him up and take him off to lead a normal life. If only he could turn back time and find her sooner. Instead, he kissed her cheek and pulled away. It was time to go.

A tear trickled down Leisha's check as she watched he and his smile walk away. She wished for the same. Her boy was a man, and she missed him becoming one. Those were years she would never get back. Would she ever see him again? That was something she couldn't know. No one could, not even Kaldumahn or Kallum.

Suddenly an arm from the crowd reached out and grabbed what was left of the sleeve of Maelich's cloak. He turned to see Cialia, a big swollen bruise on her chin, but a wide happy smile on her lips. She threw her arms around her brother and squeezed him.

"You would have left without saying good-bye, brother?" she whispered.

"Not intentionally," he replied quietly, as he returned the embrace.

Of course, she was completely correct. The idea he had a sister at all was so new, it wasn't something he consciously realized. Suddenly, he was overcome with a strange elation, like a tingling in his soul. He had a sister, and she was going to miss him.

"I'm sorry we spent the little time we had together arguing," Cialia's voice still a whisper.

He chuckled, "Me too. If ever again we meet, let's leave our swords in their scabbards."

She nodded as she pulled away, leaving him with a kiss on the cheek. He wiped a tear from hers and kissed her forehead. Then he turned, walked to the mouth of the cave, paused a moment, and was gone.

CHAPTER 23
THE OLD MAN

Once Maelich had left the cave, a sharp whistle brought Validus charging to him. Maelich mounted and they trotted into darkness. The horse must have done quite a bit of exploring while Maelich acquainted himself with his family. He seemed quite accustomed to the forest's paths and runs. Traveling by moonlight wouldn't be nearly the challenge Maelich expected.

As they approached Druindahl, a terrifying thought crept into Maelich's head. The dead-eyed priests knew where Druindahl was. The warriors of the city were no match for them. What would they do without him to protect them? Then a voice eased his mind. He couldn't tell if it was among the trees or in his head, but it spoke to him.

The voice said, "I have bound this place again from the lord of The Lost Forest. Druindahl is once again safe from his rage."

"Who's there," Maelich asked, unable to place the direction from which the voice came.

There was no answer. Perhaps it was the one they called Kaldumahn. Whomever it was, he felt he could trust this voice. By the time they passed the city proper—far up in the trees above them— Maelich's concern had completely fled. However, when the path turned back toward The Edge Mountains, logic took over. This forest borders The Lost Forest. Why go back across the mountains, back the way they had come? Why go all the way back to the path that would take them across Galgooth and back to The Lost Forest when they were already near it? He decided to follow along its edge instead.

Days poured into weeks as the forest gave way to swamps which eventually gave way to rolling hills. Time didn't matter much. They were beyond it. Feeling constantly refreshed, as if they continually ate and slumbered despite taking pause for neither. The only disturbance they met was an odd loneliness seeping out of The Lost Forest. They only felt it when they got too close to the thick tangle of branches marking its edge. There was sadness muddled in with all that loneliness. It was strong, tangible. Something crying out to Maelich without a voice that desperately wanted to be heard for its silence, to be known. That silent cry was like a call for help Maelich was powerless to answer. Despite his best efforts to offer soothing, calming thoughts to whomever suffered such great distress, the forest refused to submit. It surged against his blessings and pushed back against his thoughts. The voiceless cries continued, haunting his journey.

Finally, Validus crested a hill, and Maelich could see the path they would have taken in the valley below him. They had arrived. The path led right into The Lost Forest. There was something else though, something he hadn't been expecting. Across the road, at the edge of the forest was a small hut. It looked old but solid. The wooden planks loosely clinging to the frame of the structure looked weathered but sturdy. They carried the grime and scars of countless years. The place had no windows, only a solitary door directly in the center of the hut's face. He would have thought the place deserted if not for the light wisps of smoke rising out of the chimney. Maelich's curiosity awakened. What type of man or creature would occupy such a place, so far from anything but the loneliness of The Lost Forest?

They charged down the hill. Perhaps they could water and get a meal before attacking the forest. Maelich knew he could sustain them, but a nice meal would be a welcome distraction. He dismounted Validus and pounded on the ancient looking door, careful not to strike too hard for fear it may crumble. Surprisingly, it was quite solid. He pounded harder. There was a slight commotion inside. A few moments later, the door slowly creaked open.

The vision standing in the doorway was perhaps the oldest looking creature Maelich had ever seen. It was a man to be certain. His skin though, it was so leathery. If not for all the wrinkles covering all the wrinkles on his face, he would have looked like a grong. Of course, that only counts what could be seen of the man's face behind his wild beard springing up all here and there. It completely covered his mouth and cheeks before plummeting all the way to his feet.

Maelich considered the wild, ridiculously long beard for a moment. Had it been well cared for it would be quite a magnificent thing. However, in its current state of disrepair it looked rather silly. It perfectly matched the unbelievable white tangle above the man's eyes which must have been eyebrows. Maelich could barely tell where one tangle stopped and the other began. Above all that snarly nonsense was a stark white, billowing fluff of hair that filled the doorway and even escaped its borders. The only thing keeping the man's hair somewhat under control was a tall, cone shaped hat as bright a yellow as the man's cloak. The cloak itself looked like it had been sewn for a man eight times this fellow's size.

Maelich did all he could to remain respectful. He hoped to be a guest, and all guests should be gracious. However, it took everything he had to keep from laughing at the man. He completely lost his composure when the bloke finally spoke.

In a high-pitched, squeaky cackle of a voice the man said, "Wumph waca ida faya?"

Maelich couldn't speak. He fell victim to a mad fit of chortle snorting guffaws. The old man obviously missed the joke as he raised his eyebrows. Not with the muscles in his forehead. No, he literally raised his eyebrows. He took his hands, grabbed them and lifted so he could get a look at the buffoon who was laughing at him. This pushed the laughing idiot further over the edge as he fell to the ground.

The old man tried again. This time taking his left hand and lifting his mustache, "Well what do you want you giggling idiot?"

The man's anger helped calm Maelich's laughter slightly. He choked his reply out amid the giggles, "F…Forgive me…heh, heh. Your ah…your presence…he, he…here startled me." Maelich's laughter finally subsided as the old man continued to glare with exceptionally keen eyes for one of such obviously advanced age. "I didn't realize anyone lived this far to the south and east."

"Well I do," the man snapped, his voice still a raspy squeak. "What of it?"

Maelich began to feel a bit remorseful about laughing at the old man's appearance, "Nothing, nothing at all. I'm just a weary traveler, excited at the idea of a bit of company."

The man sneered, but Maelich couldn't see it, "Or a free meal maybe? Well you can forget it! I don't give hand-outs to beggars."

"I'm no beggar," he was slightly offended, "I'm a warrior of Havenstahl and even more. I mean to conquer that forest. Please forgive the intrusion. I meant you no disrespect. It's just that, the road is lonely, and the thought of a little companionship before I attack the desperation those trees have to offer was quite attractive to me. I'll be on my way."

The man's eyes widened, "You intend to go in there? No one goes in there. I should say, no one goes in there and comes out alive. Perhaps you should rethink this plan of yours."

Maelich shook his head, "No, that's where my path leads. I must go. Good evening to you." He bowed his head slightly, "I'll be on my way."

"Wait a moment," the man stepped toward him, as his voice became a whisper, "a bit of advice for a traveler. Never go drinking with dwarves. Their king is a giant, fifteen feet tall, eyes like fire, teeth like spears. If he catches you inebriating his minions, he'll rip the head from your body and suck your insides out before your brain even realizes you are dead."

Maelich chuckled, "The king of the dwarves? The giant? Do you mean Maomnosett Ahm, the king of the dwarves of Alhouim? I suppose news doesn't make it this far very often does it? I killed Ahm when I was a lad of but twelve summers, just into my thirteenth year. I cut off his head and presented it to the king of Havenstahl on the giant's own spear. You can get the dwarves as drunk as you'd like."

The old man's eyes narrowed, "Who are you, lad?"

"I am Maelich of Havenstahl. And who might you be?"

"My name?" The old man thought for a moment, "You know, lad, I've been out here alone for so long I can't remember what it is they used to call me. You know what? I don't know what my name is. Why don't you call me…old man? That seems an accurate description. Don't you suppose?"

Maelich smiled, "Yes, I suppose, old man. That name suits you better than any other I could think of. Well, good evening, old man. I'll be on my way."

The old man's eyes softened, "Why don't you water your horse and offer him some oats? Then you could step in and share a bit of stew with me. Have a bit of rest before again you hit the trail. That forest can overcome you."

Maelich obliged the man and led Validus to a trough full of water.

Then he filled a feedbag with oats and gave it to his horse before going into the old man's hut. Validus obviously felt the same way about real nourishment, as the horse vigorously attacked the feedbag. Some stew would be nice. Maelich went inside.

The interior of the hut was just as ancient and plain as the outside. There was one table, two chairs, one of which looked to be very seldom, if ever, used. There was a fireplace that was nothing more than a hole in the wall and a stove. What a lonely man this old man must be. Two steaming bowls rested on the table. Maelich took the chair across from where the old man sat.

"You're the one," the old man said as Maelich sat down.

Maelich took up his spoon and tested the stew. It was quite hot, but quite savory. "Which one would that be?" he mused. Then he noticed the old man had tied off his mangle of eyebrows and bush of a mustache to free his hands up for eating. The sight of it almost sent Maelich right back over the edge. This time, however, he managed to contain himself.

"Aw piss off then," the old man had waited long for company and found no humor in Maelich's jest.

"Forgive me," he began. "It's just that…as of late, my idea of who I am has become quite confused for me. I thought I knew my task. In fact, I was sure of it. All I know for sure is I was born of The Lake of Dragons, and I must now face the dragon. Beyond that, I know nothing."

Maelich could see the old man's mouth now. He could also see the smile it wore. "I knew it! You're the lad of the Lake! You're the one who will slay that dragon. Humph, somehow I thought you'd be bigger."

"That's what I thought. Then…" Maelich paused for more than a few moments as he looked off into nothing, "…then my path was confused for me. My whole life I had been led to believe things my own eyes now tell me weren't true. Even the man I trusted most, the one I call father, lied to me. If he lied about my heritage, how can I believe anything else he taught me?"

The old man brushed back his crazy eyebrows that had again fallen over his eyes and tucked them behind his ears. There was knowledge in those eyes. Maelich could see this man knew things about him. Perhaps he was another who knew more about him than he knew about himself. There seemed an abundance of those types on Ouloos.

What's one more?

The man stared into Maelich's eyes, "Ymitoth told you your mother had died, but he never told you how. Then Brerto told you she flung herself off a cliff into the river Galgooth. It is true that neither of these descriptions is completely accurate, but they're not lies. After your birth, your mother was seduced by the dragon. She was enamored by his fire and his power. It was then the pure, innocent young girl who was your mother became the queen of those who worship the vile, winged demon that reigns the sky behind his pulpit of fear. Therefore, when Ymitoth told you she had died, he spoke the truth. She has died. Her spirit has died. Furthermore, when Brerto told you she flung herself off a cliff, he spoke the truth. His description was symbolic. She was flung into a great abyss, the evil fire of the dragon. She did this of her own accord. The river Galgooth that flows far below the cliffs at Havenstahl was symbolic of that abyss. Brerto knew if you met what she had become, she would try to seduce you. He was correct. She did that, and now you are in a state of utter confusion. That is why he forbade you to go anywhere but to the dragon."

Maelich shook his head, "Did you refer to the dragon as he? Those of Druindahl refer to it as her. Its femininity seemed quite important to them."

The old man humphed again, "That's part of the seduction. That vile beast masquerades as a vulnerable, helpless, feminine creature. Those who follow him assist in the masquerade. They are just as evil as the demon they worship. Don't let them or that winged monster fool you. The dragon is powerful. Never let your guard down."

"But I didn't sense evil in those people. They seemed righteous and pure," Maelich continued shaking his head slowly as he spoke.

The old man pointed, "Aha, more of the seduction. Leisha knew you would recognize her. She knew you would want her love with all your being. A lad without a mother has a vast, empty void within him. She used your desire to trick you. She is a witch, and you've been enchanted by her spell. Don't let her illusions sway you from the path of truth, Maelich. She is deceit, just as is the dragon."

Maelich's head swirled again, "All the feeling and emotion I received from her told me she was pure and true. And what about Cialia?"

"Ah, the twin," the old man smiled, "she was lost along with her mother. They tried to save her too when they rescued you, but they were unsuccessful. She has been too long in the dragon's presence. You can't save her. She was destined to accompany you on your quest, but now it can't be. She would seek to defend the vile beast and frustrate your mission. All would be lost. Alas, this task is yours and yours alone."

"Again," Maelich countered, "I saw none of that. We shared a connection, she and I. It was like I could see into her soul. There was no evil, no ill intent."

"She believes it, like they all do," the old man fired back quickly around a mouth full of stew, swallowing before adding, "The dragon's seduction is deep. They don't see the evil in him, so they don't understand their worship of him is evil. Why would you sense evil when they don't know what they're doing is wrong?"

"I suppose," Maelich shrugged, wolfed down some stew, and continued, "Shouldn't I try to save them then?"

"You will when you kill that dragon," the old man shrugged right back at him. "They will all pay for their insolence, but Kallum is fair. They will eventually find peace."

Maelich stared into his bowl. He had so many more questions, but it seemed the answers only served to confuse him more. Finally, he asked, "How can you know so much about me, about everything? Furthermore, what proof do I have I should trust you over anyone else?"

The old man only snored in response.

"Are you sleeping?" Maelich asked.

The hairy, old fellow was deep in it, chin in his chest, sawing logs like he hadn't slept in weeks. Maelich reached across the table and gave his shoulder a tug. Nothing. The old man was out.

"I guess that's it then," he whispered.

Sleep wasn't anything Maelich needed nor desired. He finished up his stew in the company of the old man's snoring. Then he left the hut in silence. Hopefully, he'd find some answers on the other side of that forest.

CHAPTER 24
THE LOST FOREST

The sun had already dipped below the horizon leaving the sky with only the faint memory of its brilliance by the time Maelich roused his sleeping horse. It was almost a shame to wake the slumbering beast. He toyed with the idea of letting his horse have a solid night's rest before attacking that dark place and its terrifying reputation. How many frightful, nightmare inducing yarns had he heard as a lad? He couldn't even guess at a number, but it would be a grand number indeed. Nevertheless, the horse didn't really need the sleep, and Maelich was ready.

It took Maelich the entirety of ten minutes to decide all those horrifying stories he'd heard had been accurate, if not a bit tamer than reality. It wasn't so much the darkness, nor was it even the deafening quiet of the damnable place. Maelich no longer needed the aid of light to see when his mind was clear, nor did he despise the prospect of a quiet trot through the woods. It was more like sadness, not from within, but from the place itself. It oozed from the trees like sap and permeated the air.

Maelich hummed a few bars of some tune he remembered Ymitoth whistling about on the trail during simpler days. He longed for that bygone time when all he had to worry about was following his mentor's orders and minding his tongue. Those days were long gone, and the tune wasn't helping. It seemed as if that sadness had reached right into Maelich's skull and grabbed hold of his consciousness. Despite his best efforts, he could focus on nothing else.

The deeper into the forest they trekked, the darker that sadness became. It was almost tangible, sliding across his skin before slithering into his pores. As Maelich focused on that feeling soaking into his being, he realized it wasn't mere sadness at all. It was too overwhelming, almost debilitating. Worse than even despair, it was utter hopelessness, like lying in hot sand with no water or food knowing you're going to die.

A thick tangle of trees bordered either side of the trail, as if Kallum had decided this one path was the only way through. Any mysteries held within the trees known only to those gnarly, ancient giants. It was like walking down the hall of an impenetrable dungeon, thick walls on either side offering no escape.

Something suddenly stood out among the silence. It seemed a shout, but without sound. Silent cries of agony mingled and swam about the depression speaking to Maelich's psyche rather than his ears. They sang songs of the most pitiable suffering. Validus suddenly shuddered beneath Maelich, as if the horse was acknowledging his spirit had sunk as low as his master's while trudging through the macabre symphony of sadness. He could sense the great suffering as well. Their spirits sunk as they slowly trotted along.

Simple complacency became a summit too high as Maelich searched his mind for the last time he felt joy. Meeting his mother after believing her dead all those years, that had been real joy, albeit short lived. That fleeting moment of elation had been squashed, replaced by the misery of her once again being dead to him. How could he love a vile witch in service of evil himself? After soaring so high, he'd fallen into a pit deeper than the lowest low he had ever felt. Where was the lie in their brief encounter? Dragon's fire was only one of the powers bestowed upon him by the Lake. How did he miss her deceit?

There were too many voices telling him what to do, who to believe, and how things were. Their voices all mingled together in his mind, cavorting with that desperate song of sorrow. The old man's voice stood out among the rest. The chance encounter didn't seem so strange when he was desperately seeking some company. Now that he had a chance to sift through it all, all he could muster were more questions. Who was the old man, and how did he know so much? Those two questions seemed most relevant. Of course, after considering those two questions, whether the old man could be trusted or not ultimately proved most important.

The man's face suddenly popped into Maelich's head. The ridiculous mustache and brows big enough to fashion a wig for a bald man seemed a farce when taken with those keen eyes. His explanations of why it seemed everyone Maelich had ever trusted lied to him were logical enough. The problem was, how could this lonely, old soul at the edge of the world know anything about anything? It just didn't make sense.

Maelich turned these ideas over and over again in his mind asking himself the same answerless questions he'd been asking himself since he'd left the old man's hut as he and Validus trudged deeper into the forest. Night should have long given way to the bright sunshine of a new day. Maelich couldn't know whether that was the case. The forest wouldn't allow it. The canopy above was at least as thick as the impenetrable wall of trees on either side. Even the mighty sun's rays would be no match. What did it matter anyway? Marching toward an unsure destiny made haste seem the least important thing in the world.

Maelich's spirit continued to sink deeper as each inch of the forest gave way to another which seemed the same. This tree was the same as that tree which looked identical to the next and so on until, something changed. A thin break in the trees offered a glimpse into the impenetrable fortress of trees. Those joyless silent shouts seemed even louder there.

Maelich dismounted and warily approached the opening. The shouts almost had form, meaning. What that meaning might be remained a mystery, but something beckoned. There was a sudden urgency, like life and death. He peered through the slit, but it was just more trees and darkness.

Validus suddenly began whinnying and stomping about distracting Maelich for the briefest of moments. The hair on the back of his neck stood as dread filled him before he even turned back toward the thin break in the trees. It was a song with no musician until Maelich saw the thing. A ghostly glow hovered immediately before him. Not quite an apparition, the translucent and shapeless cloud inched closer.

Maelich fought to hold his ground. The battle was brief. His flesh tightened into bumps as a chill ran from the base of his neck all the way through his toes. The hopelessness he had felt earlier fled in the face of terror like nothing he had ever experienced. His breath quickly got away from him as his heart pounded in his chest. He wanted to run, to leap up on Validus' saddle and flee the nameless dread slowly creeping upon him, but his legs wouldn't obey his commands. Instead, he stumbled back into Validus. The horse's trembling rivaled his own.

Logic failed completely as Maelich spiraled deeper into a fear he couldn't understand. The thing approaching him didn't threaten or menace, it merely approached. Why did it strike him with such terror? Whatever the reason, he failed to gain control of it as he pressed himself harder against his trembling horse.

When the formless mist finally slipped out from between the trees and onto the trail, Maelich gave up his battle against the fear gripping him. He ran, charging down the trail, pumping his legs with everything he had. It took mere moments for Validus to charge past him down the path. A moment of regret for not mounting the animal in the first place flashed across his consciousness as he watched his best means of escape vanish into darkness.

With nothing left to do but run for his life, Maelich did just that. He put his head down and pumped even harder. Loathe to spare a glance over his shoulder to gauge the success of his effort to escape the specter, he had no idea how much distance there might be between them. Somehow, that didn't seem to matter. He could feel the thing gaining on him, gobbling up the space between them like a thirsty giant sucking up a shallow pond.

Despite his efforts, the thing was on him. There was no bump, no push, just a feeling more like an emotion than a triggering of sensory nerves. It felt like a cold stream of water slowly trickling down his back, freezing as it went. A shiver raced through his body shaking him off his stride. He cried out as he slipped, sprawling onto the ground. The echo of his voice off the trees seemed foreign, like cries from another. He hadn't time to think about how odd it was to hear your voice from a different perspective. The thing was directly above him, hovering like a cloud untouched by even the slightest breeze. It sat there like that, motionless for what seemed an eternity.

Maelich's eyes slammed shut as he trembled there in the dirt, but he forced them back open. He needed to see the thing, perhaps understand why it filled him with such monumental dread. It had no features, no limbs, no face, nothing it could attack with, yet he knew the thing meant to do him harm. Then it shifted, almost revolved, and slowly descended on him. Again, he cried out. This time swinging a fist at the thing. His arm passed through unhindered, but he felt something. It was so cold. It washed over him like diving into an icy brook on a snowy morning, but it wasn't quite that at all. This cold wasn't the frosty chill of a mountain wind, nor even the icy water of that brook. This cold was different. It was emptiness and loss, as if those emotions had physical characteristics which could be felt by another.

Maelich gasped, his body convulsing as the thing entered his chest. Somehow, it felt even colder, like his very cells were freezing into thick blocks of ice. The convulsions grew more violent as his vision went dark. Though his eyes were open, it seemed he was looking within, somehow beholding this thing within his body. The thing still had no shape, no form, but he saw it. It was like staring into a black void. Nothing. It wasn't really nothing though. It was something. It was loneliness, fear, sorrow, despair, and so much more. He began to feel these things as if they were his own. It was as if the thing was feeding him these emotions from within like unwanted gifts.

The blackness slowly faded as the emptiness grew. Suddenly, there was light. Two hands stretched before his eyes. They weren't his, but from his perspective they had to be. At the end of them a small girl held on tight. He was spinning her. Her soft, green eyes wide as she laughed. She was young, maybe five or six summers. They were on a hill looking over waves of flowing grass speckled with vibrant, purple wildflowers. Rolling hills surrounded them. Though he didn't recognize the girl's face, he felt a joy so complete. It was as if everything he cared about were holding on to his hands right at that moment spinning lazy circles with him. It was such a feeling of peace, the fear and emptiness which had filled him only moments prior were gone, completely forgotten.

The peace, that carefree feeling of complete joy, didn't last. It was chased away by a growl, deep and guttural. He stopped spinning and quickly shuffled the girl behind him just in time to save her from teeth and claws. The effort proved a brief rescue as he was knocked to the side, sprawled across the grass with a stinging in his jaw and blood trickling down his cheek. The landscape before him dipped and swayed as he stumbled to his feet.

Maelich could hear the girl shrieking, pain-soaked, pitiable screams, but he couldn't see her. He scanned the hillside, whipping his head this way and that, but could find no source for those cries. Then crunching, ripping, and popping sounds mingled in with the girls screams and the beasts' growls. All of them merging into a terrifying song. He ran toward the edge of the hill, toward the horrible chorus of pain.

When Maelich finally reached the edge of the hilltop, the screaming had stopped. Somehow, the song was more horrible without the screaming. What he saw was more horrible still. He watched helplessly as two amatilazo ripped the girl in half, shredded pieces of innocence filling the air as two monsters battled for their share of the kill.

The sting in Maelich's heart at that moment was worse than any pain he could remember. He didn't know the girl. He had no connection to her, yet he felt a deep, unconditional love for her he couldn't explain. The cry that left his lips as he raced toward the beasts was a voice he didn't recognize. Ten steps toward the monsters ripping apart the little girl were all he made before something pounded him in the back and dragged him to the ground. Face down in the grass, he whipped about, struggling, swinging, fighting. It was useless. Sharp points poked into the flesh of his neck. The satisfied growl so close to his ear as meat tore away from his throat was even worse than the pain he felt as it happened. Another poke, another growl, another tear, and then another, he lay there helpless as the thing ate him. His struggles grew weaker until he had nothing left. Everything went black.

Maelich gasped as the chill left him. Back on the trail, he lay shivering as the mist slowly floated away from him, back the way it came. It took a few moments to process the idea he wasn't dead, mauled by horrible beasts. Once he realized that, the voiceless cries of the forest began to make sense. How many souls were trapped in this horrible forest, souls crying out to be freed from the torture of reliving awful memories over and over again until the end of time? That was the anguish and despair of the forest. Lost souls begging any who would listen to set them free. Maelich lay weeping until sleep finally took him.

Sleep proved no reprieve from the terrors of the forest. Teeth and claws, blood and shrieks, the same images flashed repeatedly. That poor soul's tragedy slowly became Maelich's own. The pain, the fear, the hurt, the loss, he shared them with this man who could never escape the horrible memories. Worse than that was the loss of his daughter. As Maelich relived the horrid scene time after time, she became his own. Her death and her pain became his loss and his heartbreak. The helplessness of watching, powerless to stop the carnage, to save her, that might have been the worst thing. Hearing her screams, seeing her helpless body tossed about and knowing he could do nothing to help her, it was a sensation so completely foreign to him. He hated it.

Consciousness was perhaps the best blessing Maelich had ever received, saved from the unrelenting terror of his dream. The images dulled while he was awake, but the pain lingered. No matter how hard he tried to focus his mind elsewhere, those soft, green eyes kept staring, trusting. What would they look like after the terror? Would they accuse him? Why was this world so cruel? How could Kallum let such innocence meet such violence? What kind of god was he?

Time was a tricky thing in the darkness of the forest, the difference between day and night barely perceptible. Maelich had no idea how long he lay there wallowing in the sorrow and pain that lost soul had gifted him. However, as he lay there doing just that, it eventually became clear it wasn't doing him or anyone else any good. It was time to move on. The rest of his journey would be much slower without Validus. He fought through his desperation and struggled to his feet.

As Maelich trudged along, he saw other visions and felt other emotions. It was as if his meeting with the specter on the trail had opened his mind to the plight of all the lost. Those voiceless shouts which had been so muffled were coming through loud and clear screaming to be heard, swirling images of sadness and loss. Some were bloody and tragic, while others were simply sad. Different though they were, all of them took over his senses and planted him in a scene which became his own, a memory as clear as any he had experienced for himself.

Weakness suddenly overcame him. It didn't slow him at all. Instead, he trudged along as if someone else were in control of his movements, someone who wanted his full attention. He could feel his legs moving, but the sensation was far away. The trail had vanished. It was replaced by a thatched roof. The sound of rain pounding the dilapidated thing surrounded him, pierced by the drip…drip…drip of drops it couldn't hold back. A group of teary faces crowded close to him.

A young woman with skin still soft with the beauty of youth and dark eyes whispered, "I love you," pushing the hair back from his forehead as she smiled through her tears.

The old woman next to her shook her fists at the roof above and cried out, "Why? Why would you take me only son?"

A little girl between them grabbed at his shirt and sobbed, "No, Papa. Don't go."

Of course, he knew the pain and weakness in his body was not his own. Neither was the poor family begging him not to leave them. It didn't numb the pain or lesson the sadness. They became his own.

The dead continued to speak directly to his consciousness. Each story told more horrible than the last. He didn't sleep or eat. He just continued along, living the sadness and pain of those who shared their stories with him. They were relentless, and he was full of them.

Suddenly, it was quiet. The voices ceased along with the pain. He was on the trail again, and it was beginning to brighten up. The trees once again had distinguishable forms. They were no longer some dark, featureless mass surrounding him. There was even light up ahead. Could it be? He dared not hope. Could his journey through the horrible, lost place be nearing its end?

Then they were back, louder. Not just feelings or emotions, these were actual sounds. Horrible cries of anguish battering his eardrums. It was as if they sensed his departure was near and refused to be forgotten. How could he forget? Their memories mingled with his own to the point he couldn't differentiate between them. They were part of him.

"I hear you," he shouted at the trees, "You won't be forgotten."

They only cried louder, nothing tangible, only passion and pain.

Maelich threw his hands up over his ears and fell to his knees, curling up until his elbows rested on the ground next to them. It didn't help. They were in his head, shouting at his consciousness or his heart, or who knows what. They were relentless, as if they wanted to keep him and never let him go. Couldn't they understand he couldn't help them if he remained among them? He wasn't certain he could help them either way, but he was completely certain he couldn't help them if he died on the trail saturated with their cries.

He fought against the pain and pounding and raised his head enough to see the light at the end of the trail. It was so close. If only they would give him a moment of peace, but they wouldn't. They had someone to listen, someone alive to share their sorrow. They would never let him go if they could help it, but he couldn't stay. It took every ounce of strength he had to get to his feet, as if they were somehow holding him down. Each step he took toward the light was a struggle, like pushing against a mountain. His knees buckled under the weight of their desire, but he didn't fall.

"Stop," he shouted.

There it was. It was brief, a split second, but in that infinitesimal moment there was peace. In that sliver of time, Maelich's focus sharpened on the light like the razor-edge of a blade ready for battle. All his passion, all his love, all his hate, every shred of feeling and will in his entire being reached out for that light. He sprinted toward it, ignoring the shouts of those lost as much as he could.

The warmth of the sun chased the shouts away as Maelich burst forth from the dark chill of the forest and fell to the ground in a heap at its edge. His last sprint toward the light, fighting against the will of those lost souls, had taken everything from him. He lay there for a moment in the glorious light before sleep took him.

CHAPTER 25
THE DRAGON AND THE LAKE

Maelich slumbered for two full days and nights. He finally woke to early morning sunshine and Validus' wet snout moving all about his face. The horse had apparently stopped fleeing once he found safety.

"How noble is the steed who leaves his master to fend for himself at the first sign of danger?" Maelich chuckled as he scratched the animal behind the ear.

He couldn't really blame the horse for fleeing. Given the opportunity, he would have escaped too. However, sitting in the warm sun finally removed from the terror of that dark place, he was fairly certain he would not have left his companion behind. Even still, Maelich couldn't be mad at Validus. The way the horse nuzzled closer into his chest almost seemed an apology.

"It's okay, boy," Maelich said as he patted the animal's neck. "Thank you for waiting around for me. What say we get back to our journey?"

Maelich stretched two days of sleep out of his muscles as he stood and surveyed the foreign land surrounding him. The trees were the first thing he noticed. There were no pines, oaks, or willows. The trees in this place were like nothing he'd ever seen. The trunks were thin, smooth, and tall. They didn't appear to have any branches, just leaves, but those were fat and long, stretching out and drooping toward the ground. There was no uniformity. They grew haphazardly, a small clump of trees here and another there. It was nothing like a proper forest with tree upon tree.

The warmth of the sun on Maelich's face as he looked up toward the top of one of those trees brought an unconscious smile to his face. He drew in a deep breath through his nose. The air was sweet, like the perfume of wildflowers in the prairie but not quite the same. Maelich closed his eyes and took a few more deep breaths in, reveling in the new smells.

When he opened his eyes back up, he finally noticed all the colors. The ground was alive with them, flowers of the most vibrant purples, yellows, and oranges. The petals of some looked sharp like brightly colored daggers standing tall and ready to strike, while others looked softer, almost droopy, as if they were bowing. Filling in the empty spaces between the trees and the flowers was all manner of greenery mimicking the differences in the flowers' petals with their leaves. Snaking around all of it and tangling among themselves were thick vines laden with fruit. To Maelich it all swirled into a picture of chaotic beauty.

There was no path or anything to suggest which direction he should take, so Maelich walked. Trying to ride Validus through the plant life would have proved a fruitless effort, so he guided the horse instead. The going was slow. There was no rhyme or reason to the trees. Everything was so perfectly random. Things in this place seemed to grow wherever they could find a little room and a little light. Somehow, it didn't bother him that he had to go on foot. He liked this place. The tranquility of it helped ease his mind against the lingering memories of the forest.

The days passed slowly as they walked along, mindful of the life surrounding them. It would be a shame to trample such chaotic perfection under the weight of hurried feet. On top of that, the peacefulness of the place was such a dramatic shift from the sheer weight of the forest it seemed a waste not to soak it in and revel in it. Everything about the place was like a peaceful dream.

By the time Maelich spied a lake he had long lost track of time. How often had they slumbered under the moonlight to wake and walk in glorious sunshine? By this point, he didn't much care. He was looking for a lake, and he had found one. It seemed out of place surrounded by the chaos of the trees and plants and vines. There was nothing chaotic about it. In fact, it was a perfect circle, a small bit of order sitting in contrast to the land surrounding it. Approximately two miles in diameter, it was surrounded by another perfect circle of golden sand roughly fifteen feet wide. The trees and plants stopped abruptly at the edge of the sand.

Maelich walked up to the edge of the water and peered in. It was clear and perfectly still, but he couldn't see the bottom. As he peered down into the bottomless void, it occurred to him he couldn't see his own reflection in it. It should have been like a mirror reflecting him and the sky above, but there was only darkness.

Directly across the lake from Maelich, a rocky hill jutted up from the ground. The sand beneath his feet terminated in that spot on either side as if the small peak were a gemstone encrusted onto the ring formed by the sand. As he examined the formation, he noticed an opening in the stone. Something tugged on his consciousness in that instant. His destiny was buried somewhere in a cave underneath that rock.

Maelich skirted quickly around the left side of the lake, racing toward his destiny. As he advanced on the cave, the voiceless cries of the forest returned. The closer he got to the place, the louder they became. Their increasingly passionate shouts seemed a warning, but to what he couldn't tell. The cries were muddled and confused, drowning each other out as they vied for his attention.

An icy breeze greeted him when he reached the mouth of the cave. The cold seemed odd for the home of the last member of the race of fire. He expected flames and sweaty stone. He drew his cloak up around his neck and entered slowly. The darkness was almost immediate as if it were too strong a force for any light from outside to penetrate the opening. Maelich stuck close to the wall as he walked a path leading downward and veering right. The idea of leaving some markings to find his way back fled from his mind as quickly as it had come. He would never be able to see any markings he may leave. Luckily, there weren't any forks, just one path leading ever downward.

The further Maelich ventured, the colder and darker the place became. Shivering against the chill winds, he pulled his cloak up tighter and drew his sword. The sword began to glow as he slowly let the fire come. As the blade grew brighter, the air grew warmer and the darkness fled its brilliance. Stalactites and stalagmites cast long shadows against the cave's walls and floor. Soon, his sword burned bright and strong with the strength of his flame giving him a clear view of the massive cavern into which he descended.

"I'll need to be strong," he gasped, some small part of him

expecting a response.

There wasn't one, of course. He was quite alone. Even Validus had trotted off to explore the majesty of that wonderful place they had spent days strolling through. If only he could abandon this quest, find his horse, and bask in the warm sun. That would be a life, no duty, no responsibility, just living, exploring an untamed land, sampling the plump sweet fruits that seemed to grow everywhere, just peace. Sadly, that wasn't his lot. His destiny lay coiled somewhere deep in this cave waiting to strike and challenge him flame against flame.

As Maelich trudged along toward his glorious victory or miserable, fiery defeat, it occurred to him the voices from the forest had ceased their cries. They were replaced by a silence, massive, overbearing, and complete. So complete was this quiet, it almost had weight as if it were a tangible, physical thing. Maelich paused and listened to the silence. He strained against it, searching for something among the nothing. Finally, there was something. It was steady, bloop...bloop...bloop.

"A sound like that could drive a man insane," he said, again to no one.

The drips increased in volume as Maelich continued down the trail. They remained steady, bloop...bloop...bloop, as the great cavern grew smaller and the walls around Maelich closed in. There was barely enough room for him to stand upright when he finally found the source of the dripping sound. It was a strange little pool off to his right side. The pool itself wasn't unique. It was just a pool. The remarkable thing about it was it appeared to be on the ceiling of the cave rather than its floor where a pool should be. Even more remarkable was the bloop...bloop...bloop was the sound of water dripping from the floor of the cave into the pool on the ceiling. It would have been strange enough if the pool itself managed to remain on the ceiling while slowly dripping its contents onto the floor.

Avoiding the upside-down water dripping into it, Maelich shook off the awe and crouched beneath the pool. Gazing up into it, he saw his reflection staring back at him looking haggard and rough from the road. As he stared at himself, his image began to morph and redden. His features lengthened as his skin grew leathery and red. It continued like that, redder and rougher until a dragon stared back at him. The reflection mimicked his every move and mocked every face he made. He reached his hand up to the pool and disturbed the water there. Both the image and his reflection disappeared in the ripples. When the surface of the water calmed again there was fire.

Deep within the pool, as far as Maelich could see, a perfect circle of flames swirled slowly around its perimeter. Its movements were precise, slowly gaining speed but remaining perfectly uniform. The faster it moved, the more Maelich felt the pull. It was drawing him in. He grabbed for the top of a stalagmite, but the pull was too strong. It had him. His feet left the ground, his head broke the surface of the water, and he was sucked in.

Falling, spinning, tumbling, he cried out. His eyes told him he was going up, but his body assured him he was falling fast. His speed increased, decreased, and increased again. First darkness surrounded him, then light. He was burning and then freezing. He was soaking and then parched. For every extreme, there was an opposite extreme. His senses reeled as he raced upward, still feeling like he was plummeting down.

Finally, he stopped. There was no hard landing, just an abrupt halt to his movement. Lying prone, he was surrounded again by darkness. An instant later there was light, brilliant light. It had no source yet surrounded him. There were no walls around him, no ceiling, no beginning and no end, just light. Beneath him was water, deep water. Though he lay upon it, he didn't break the surface. Straining to look over his shoulder, he gazed into it and found no bottom.

From the depths, a shape approached. Maelich leapt to his feet, still brandishing his sword. The glow had gone, but his blade was ready. As the shape neared the surface, the dragon's features grew increasingly clearer. The thing was immense, seeming to grow larger and larger as it approached. Maelich stumbled backward when the massive thing burst forth from the water, bracing himself against the massive wave. The mighty splash never happened. The surface of the water remained undisturbed as the entire length of the dragon passed through it.

The fire-red dragon soared high above, stretching its wings as it reached its apex. The thing was massive, far bigger than Maelich had imagined. Its wings must have spanned more than one hundred feet from tip to tip. The beast had a head the size of a small hut that consisted mostly of jaws filled with dagger-like teeth. The neck holding that giant head up was long and thin but rippled with wiry muscle. At the other end of that thin neck was a colossal body, somewhat round but solid. Powerful, squat legs curled up underneath it while thinner arms hung loosely at its front. A thick tail finished the monster, ending in a sharp point.

The gigantic creature hovered there for a moment high above Maelich's head and then dove at him, speeding like a red arrow slicing through the air. Maelich leapt backward to avoid being crushed under the thing or plunged deep into the water beneath his feet. The move proved unnecessary, as the beast stopped just above the water's surface and gently touched down upon it. Then it sat motionless on its legs staring at him with eyes burning the same fire red as its skin.

Maelich's heart pounded against his chest as he lost control of his breathing, gasping for air like a man running for his life. Focusing within himself, he searched for the fire. It wouldn't come. Fear had him all bound up and confused. He couldn't focus his energy. Instead he raised his sword toward the monster.

The dragon merely smiled at the gesture and softly said, "Maelich, you are terribly frightened. What are you afraid of?"

All he could do was stammer about like an oaf, "I…um…ah…"

"You have nothing to fear, my child. I will not harm you," the dragon added in just as soft and feminine a tone.

Maelich finally found his voice, "Bind your tongue, beast. I've been warned of your wiles. You know my name, so I must assume you know why I am here."

Maelich did his best to stand tall and appear fearless before the monster, but it was all a ruse. His soul cried out with fear. One breath from the giant could fill the cavern with fire. Would he burn? Of course, Brerto had told him time and again during training it was an impossibility. The old wizard had even gone so far as to have him create fire and stand within it. But that fire was his own. What if the dragon's fire were different somehow? It was too late for second guessing. The beast was before him, and nothing could turn him away from his destiny. His eyes began to glow a dull red.

"I know why you think you are here. I also know your true purpose. Search your soul and your heart. Can you not feel it? Listen to the lost ones. Focus on their cries one at a time. Let them come through," the beast continued the ruse speaking with an undeniable feminine vulnerability.

"What is your name, beast?" Maelich asked, refusing to be fooled.

"I am Helias, but I believe you know that already. Why do you ask me questions for which you already know the answers? I know you are struggling with your task, but deep down you know what is right. You know who I am. Why do you fight it so?" the dragon persisted.

He shook his head, "No. You are the king of lies. How do you presume to hide your hideous form behind the soft, reassuring voice of a woman? Do you think a soft voice and pleasant words can trick me from my task? I am here to extinguish your fire. That is what I know."

Maelich finally squashed his fear and let the fire come. It swirled about him as his sword glowed ever brighter. Standing tall, he was ready to cut the dragon down and end its reign of terror over the land.

Tears filled her eyes, "It seems they have trained a killer. If you will not look inside yourself and seek the truth, you will destroy me. You have that power just as I do. However, you also harbor enough hate to wield it. That is something I could never do. You must know when you murder me, you destroy innocence and everything else with it."

"Enough tricks, beast," Maelich demanded. "I have been warned of your wiles. You'd have me believe you helpless and let my guard down. That will not happen. You will fight me, or you will die in the same flame with which you would burn this world."

The dragon closed its eyes and wept as Maelich advanced.

He paused and asked, "Why won't you fight me? Are you a coward wary of a fair battle, useless without a horde of angry dragons at your back?"

Helias shook her head, "I cannot. Can you not see past the fear and hatred they taught you? I know what is at stake. You do as well. You just refuse to see it. Your entire life has been filled with questions for which you have been refused answers. Here are those answers standing right before you begging to be heard, yet you reject and deny them. Are you merely a man? You come breathing fire, masquerading as a dragon. Dragon's do not kill, Maelich. We only know love."

Their eyes locked. Maelich tried desperately to look away, but he was trapped in the beast's gaze. This was it. He braced for the attack, but it didn't come. Instead, scenes began flashing before his eyes and filling his head. Were they lies? They had to be. Massive dragons fled from men, even cowering before them. Armies of men marched, relentless killers mercilessly stalking their prey. Helpless dragons cried out as swords, spears, and arrows pierced their skins. A river of blood flowed down a mountain of carcasses. Each scene more violent and horrifying than the last. It became like a sport, murderers growing more efficient and creative with each slaughter.

Finally, the carnage stopped. Still, Maelich remained locked in the dragon's stare. More images flashed before him. Wild looking men cheered as they paraded around towns of cheering people with carcasses held aloft on stakes. The heads of terrified dragons were lopped off and impaled on spears as trophies. Then the last image, a dragon flying amid flaming arrows, it was Helias. He recognized the dragon before him as she darted and dodged. Despite her efforts, her body was riddled with arrows. She plummeted. Spears flew at her as she desperately clawed at the ground trying in vain to escape. The men who would have killed her were nearly upon her when another band of warriors came to her aid. These defenders numbered few, but they fought with such determination and purpose they pushed the horde back. They were protecting the fallen dragon.

Maelich's flame had faded slightly by the time he asked, "Why do you show me only parts of stories? Why do you hide the beginnings where dragons destroy towns, burn men alive, and even eat them? The fate of your kind was sealed by their own actions. Now you use these half-truths to protect your own hide. You cower before me like a scrod, pathetic."

Though Maelich's words were fierce, his mind grew riddled with doubt. She was trying to deceive him. No, that was all wrong. He was trying to deceive him. She was confusing him, enchanting him. He didn't know what to believe. Why wouldn't she fight? He could release his flame or plunge his blade into her heart. She cowered before him begging not to be killed.

"Damn," Maelich muttered quietly, as he shook his head and turned around.

There it was. That was the mistake. The wily beast had waited for just the right moment to attack. Maelich's fire returned in a blaze as he quickly spun to face the dragon. She hadn't moved.

"Why won't you listen?" she cried. "I will not, cannot, harm you. Please, Maelich, if you refuse to listen to me, listen to your own heart. Do not let your human mind drown out its shouts. Can you not here the call?"

He raised his sword and advanced, "All I hear are the lies of a vile demon. My path is clear. Nothing you say can hide it from me."

CHAPTER 26
THE FALLON AND THE DRAGON

The hour was late when Ymitoth finally decided to turn in for the night. He had just returned from a trip to Alhouim. Each year since the fall of Ahm, Alhouim hosted a celebration to commemorate Maelich's bravery in defeating the giant. It was a celebration of the return of their great house. The festivities lasted a week and were filled with music, dancing, plays, and parades. They even staged a reenactment of the battle. It was great fun for Ymitoth. He looked forward to it all year long but was always exhausted upon returning to his throne. The effort was well worth the weariness. Alhouim and Havenstahl had once again become strong allies. The great friendship and trade between the two cities had been rekindled.

As soon as Ymitoth entered his room, his weariness fled. The room was completely dark, but he could sense a presence. He quickly produced a flint and lit a candle. His room looked like it always did. Nothing was out of place.

Then a deep and commanding voice from behind him said, "Ymitoth, king of Havenstahl, mentor of the lad of the Lake, your lord beckons you."

He slowly turned toward the voice. The flickering light from his candle danced eerily across three men in drab cloaks. Quickly bowing to one knee, he stuttered, "Milord, I be unworthy of your presence. I beg ye, heal me with your words."

Ymitoth shook with fear as he cowered on the cold stone. It had been thirteen years since his lord had addressed him through these priests, but it was as if it had happened only yesterday. Kallum had called him a scrod and choked him. Those words still stung. What had he done this time to displease his lord? Worse, what had Maelich done? Did Kallum send the priests to inform him Maelich had failed? Would the prophecy remain unfulfilled?

The priest removed his hood, but Ymitoth kept his head down, "Maelich has proven quite resourceful and found The Forgotten Forest which houses the city of Druindahl, the city of the dragon. He led me to it, but the dragon is wily and has again placed it beyond my reach. The vile creatures who exist there—too low to call themselves men, even lower than the worms which slither about on the ground— must be punished. Your lord needs you to enforce his law, Ymitoth. You must lead your great army against the evil existing in that forest. Burn it to the ground. Kill every creature, every man, woman, child, and beast. Spare only those women and girls who have not been spoiled by the touch of a man. Those you may keep for yourself or for your soldiers. They will be your slaves. Do with them what you see fit. For the rest, show no mercy. You will leave at dawn. You will know the way. Your lord will be with you."

"The city exists?" Ymitoth continued, head down, "I thought it to be myth."

"It exists, and my spirit will guide you there."

Ymitoth prayed, "Thank ye, great and mighty Kallum, for allowing me to serve ye. Oh, almighty lord, I be not worthy of your grace but if ye be seeing fit, please be blessing the work I be doing in your name. All honor and glory be given unto you. Telos."

When Ymitoth raised his head, the priests were gone. His mind was swimming. The book said nothing about him having a role in the prophecy. It was to be Maelich's task alone. Now, Kallum had honored him with a task for himself. He would march with pride on Druindahl. They would crumble before the might of Havenstahl. At the sun's first light, he would blast the great horn of Galgooth that belonged to Havenstahl. Hopefully, the other horn would answer and the dwarves of Alhouim would fight alongside the men of Havenstahl.

By sunrise the next day, the army of Havenstahl was prepared to go on the march. The horn of Havenstahl had blared, and the horn of Alhouim answered. The two armies met at the river. Flags flapped in the breeze high above a great column of soldiers from the two great cities marching off to battle evil in the name of Kallum, motivated by the steady pounding of drums.

The road was long. Weeks on the trail had passed before the fighting men of Havenstahl crested The Edge Mountains to see The Forgotten Forest sprawling before them in the valley below. Ymitoth knew it instantly when it came into view. Kallum was at work in his heart. He could feel his lord's presence urging him on. This would be the greatest battle of his life. Generations would honor his memory as the king who brought the foul creatures in service of the dragon low.

Ymitoth called his army to a halt on the peak, the forest before them forgotten no more. They dug in and built camp, spreading out among the hillside and fortifying their position. The king looked on as men got to the task of carving deep trenches into the earth and fortifying them with rocks and wood. If the battle made it out of the valley, it wouldn't get past the top of that hill.

"Dahltaf," Ymitoth called out to a young soldier, a favorite of his. The lad was strong of body, even more so of mind, quickly moving up the ranks after earning his crest only five years prior. He reminded the king of himself as a young soldier.

"Highness," said the brawny lad as he trotted up and bowed to one knee before the king. "What be your bidding? Say the word and see your will done."

Ymitoth motioned the boy to rise. For as long as he'd been king, he still couldn't get used to all the formality of stout men kneeling before him like he was so far above them. In his soul he still felt as one with them, equal and unchanged. Still, as king it was his role to levy the commands, so he did. "Take nine men and ten dwarves—best ye can find, only the stoutest and bravest among ye—and march on into that wood."

"Highness," Dahltaf nodded as he turned and started away.

"Wait a bit there, lad," Ymitoth chuckled at the young warrior's eagerness. "Ye ain't heard the rest of what I be asking of you."

Dahltaf's cheeks grew almost as red as his wild, flowing hair. "Forgive me, highness. Weeks on the trail be having me ready to get to the business of freeing this world of the wickedness creeping around them trees down there."

Ymitoth smiled wide, "Your father would be proud of the lad standing before me now. Ye of the line of Bahlin, each fiercer than the last. I tell ye lad, ye be living up to that name." Ymitoth's expression grew serious as he continued, "Marching a big force like this down at that forest would be foolish. We ain't be doing that. The twenty of ye will slip into that wood and draw them out. Once ye get them out into that valley, we'll be charging in and helping ye to cut them down."

Dahltaf's emerald eyes sparkled in the sun as he smiled back at his king and replied, "Aye, highness. We won't be letting ye down."

Dahltaf gathered a group of the boldest soldiers and solidas he could find and led them down the hill. Scanning the tree line with eyes so keen his fellow soldiers often joked he could spot a charging fallon at two miles through thick brush without effort. He couldn't quite match that boast, but he was deadly with his bow and even deadlier with his sword. The group following him toward the dark forest would have followed him anywhere.

They moved silently among the trees. The folk of Druindahl should have had no idea they were coming, and Dahltaf saw no good reason to alert them. Stealth was the best option. Not a twig snapped. He had chosen his team well. As eager as they all were to spill the blood of the evil lurking in that dark wood, not one did anything to give up their position.

A swift wind bustled through the trees, rustling the leaves and offering cover to any slight noises being made. The forest grew darker as they advanced, but the darkness was no match for Dahltaf's sharp eyes. His group would strike first. The city would be taken completely by surprise. They would engage the enemy and draw them out, feigning retreat. Once out of the forest, the full strength of Havenstahl and Alhouim would descend upon Druindahl's forces. The poor forest folk wouldn't have a chance.

A rustling above caught Dahltaf's attention. It was out of rhythm with the wind. He raised his right fist to halt his men. Scanning the treetops, he focused on that out of place sound. His eyes failed to spot the source, but he trusted his ears. Something large was creeping around up there. Fwip, a bow was fired from high up in the trees. He found the source immediately as the arrow bore down on his group.

"Scatter," he whispered as his men and dwarves dove behind trees and then readied their bows. He fired back in the direction from which the arrow flew, stepping to the side at the very last moment before being impaled. A low groan assured him his aim had been truer than his adversary's. It was followed by the sound of the dead archer breaking upon the forest floor.

Dahltaf barely had a moment to congratulate himself on his skills with a bow before hundreds of arrows rained down on his group from the trees. The small force did their best to return fire, but they were horribly outnumbered. Maintaining cover became more and more difficult.

Dahltaf crept back in the trees to a position held by a brute of a dwarf named Ghidaan. The surly brawler didn't have much love for bows or the little barbs they flung. In fact, he couldn't stand them. As far as he was concerned, bows were weapons fit for women or young lads. Give him an axe and an army to swing it at. That was a fight. Hiding in the trees and poking your head out to fire little sticks at people was for cowards. Bring on the swords of Druindahl.

"Damn arrows," Ghidaan humphed as Dahltaf approached, "this ain't no kind of battle. Let them worms come out of them trees, and I be showing them a fight." He ran a thick hand through the mange of light brown hair curling up about his head like a thicket of brush.

Dahltaf nodded, "Aye, I be betting ye would. For now, slip back through them trees and tell the king we be pinned down. I sense they be advancing, but not as a unit. They be sending one or two to flank us on either side. We can't advance and we can't retreat without losing men. Tell him we be needing more men to outflank them."

Ghidaan grumbled as he slipped back into the trees. Despite being quite stealthy for a dwarf, he wasn't keen on retreating. Even though it was an order given by the leader of his mission, it still felt too much like running away. He fired off a couple of arrows as he stuck to the shadows. As good as his aim was, they probably didn't have much impact on anything. He fired off a couple more anyway.

Dahltaf threw his bow over his shoulder and quickly climbed up the nearest tree. Once among the branches, he had a much better view of his enemies' positions. He fired arrow after arrow. His aim was impeccable. A soldier fell from the treetops every time he fired. It appeared his foes were having a hard time pinning down his location. A few arrows did fly in his general direction, but none close enough to be concerned with. Then he heard a groan from below. He looked down to see a dwarf struggling to breathe as blood pumped from his throat. The poor solida stumbled around tugging at the arrow that had run him through. As he stumbled to the path, three more arrows pounded him. He took one to the leg, one in his belly and one through his heart. He gurgled out something close to a moan and crashed to the dirt. As Dahltaf watched the dwarf fall, it occurred to him he didn't even know the poor bloke's name. May Kallum rest his soul.

The army atop The Edge Mountains stood at the ready, waiting to pounce as Ghidaan burst forth from the trees at a dead run. Ymitoth called the archers to stand at ease. Though the dwarf looked to be fleeing for his life, there wasn't anyone chasing him. He charged down the hill to meet him.

Ghidaan was quite out of breath when he finally reached Ymitoth. "Ambush...archers everywhere...in the trees," he gasped between raspy, deep breaths. "They must have knew we was coming."

"Have the rest fallen?" Ymitoth remained stone-faced, not allowing the rage boiling in his chest to show.

The dwarf shook his head as he tried to compose himself, "No...no, Dahltaf...Dahltaf sent me...he sent me to get reinforcements."

Ymitoth turned and motioned up the hill. "A hundred men," he shouted, "charge that forest!"

With that, the first wave of soldiers charged down the hill. Ymitoth sent Ghidaan as their guide. Stealth was dropped from the plan as they made haste to the battle. By the time they arrived, three men and another dwarf had fallen. Dahltaf hailed them from the trees. He directed them to move out in both directions into the forest. They spread out. Some took up position behind the cover of the trees while others climbed up into them. They returned fire. Arrows filled the sky flying in all directions.

Back at the palace of Druindahl, Daritus had received word the archers had met resistance in the forest. A small force at first, but reinforcements had arrived, and their positions were compromised. He mounted up a troop of riders and led them to the battle. Cialia desperately wanted to be among them, but Daritus forced her to remain at her mother's side. He charged her with protecting the queen.

The forces of Havenstahl and Alhouim were focusing all their firepower on the treetops from which they were being attacked. The riders of Druindahl knew the forest well and charged at them from all directions. By the time Dahltaf noticed their approach it was too late. The riders bore down on his men on the ground. Most were taken completely by surprise and fell all too easily. Some managed to draw their swords and fight back, but they were confused and unprepared. For the most part, it was a slaughter.

A few of the force of Havenstahl managed to collect themselves and make an honorable battle out of it. Ghidaan did quite a bit of damage with his axe as well. Terribly outmatched, the heroics of the few who displayed them were no match for the riders of Druindahl. Those who survived fled. Except Dahltaf, he remained hidden in the trees. Once his forces had been pushed back, he ceased firing with his bow. Gritting his teeth as he hid among the treetops watching the vile pack of demons savor their victory. They had won the battle, but the war was just beginning.

Dahltaf held his position in silence as the sun faded and the forest darkened. The riders of Druindahl were long gone. They had charged back to their holes shortly after the heat of the brief battle had ended. As far as he could tell, the archers hadn't moved. Then he heard a whistle, short and patterned. It sounded like it could have been made by a bird, but he knew it wasn't. The whistle was answered after a few moments of silence. It had to be some form of communication. The forest was good and dark by this point. They had to know Havenstahl would never consider attacking an unfamiliar forest during the dark of night. The archers were leaving. It was obvious the army of Druindahl wouldn't be drawn out of the safety of their forest. He would have to fight the battle their way.

Once the last bits of light had completely fled the forest, Dahltaf began to make his way through the trees. They were tightly packed, and Dahltaf had no trouble feeling his way through the branches from tree to tree. A lover of the hunt, he felt at home in the forest. Oftentimes, he would go into a hunt with nothing more than a short dagger to test his stealth against creatures with far keener senses than the soldiers he'd hunt on this night. He moved quickly and silently through the trees, following in the general direction he'd watched the riders take when they had left.

Weariness can prove a challenging adversary at times. After a couple hours of traversing branches, Dahltaf found himself locked in quite a battle with that old foe. He'd caught himself nodding more than once when pausing to collect himself before a move from one tree to another. He had almost given up on his hunt when a dim glow caught his eye. At first, he thought it might be a trick played by a tired mind. However, as he gazed through the darkness, focused on the ghostly, almost imperceptible glow, shapes became apparent. This was no sleepy tomfoolery. These were lights, magnificent lights brilliantly engineered to hide them from the forest floor. He had made it. The mythical hidden city was no myth. It lay within his reach. His pace quickened.

As he neared the lights, the outline of Druindahl began to materialize before him. His eyes quickly began to adjust. It was immense and amazing, an entire city suspended high among the treetops. Wooden walkways connected building to building from tree to tree. He paused for a moment as he took in the sight with his jaw slack. Once his excitement died down enough for his brain to focus back on his task, he continued.

Dahltaf was a mere one hundred yards from what appeared to be the very southern edge of Druindahl when he spotted the first victims of his hunt. Two guards occupied a circular platform. They seemed aloof, as if the greatest fighting force of men in all of Ouloos didn't stand poised and ready to attack at the edge of their forest. The cockiness in their casual demeanor got Dahltaf's blood boiling. After a quick scan of the surrounding area, he decided they were alone on their watch. Nocking two arrows onto his bow, he silently drew back.

Dahltaf was an expert marksman, probably the best in Havenstahl, possibly in all of Ouloos. He slowly inhaled. Once his lungs were full, he cleared his head of all thought. He exhaled through his mouth as he fired. With one thwip, two arrows cut through the darkness, separating as they gobbled up the air between them and their targets. They met their marks in unison. The hunter smiled as his first two victims fell in heaps to the platform.

Dahltaf made it to that platform in mere moments, leaping silently upon it. One of the guards was still twitching. Dahltaf drew his dagger and slipped it in between two of the man's ribs, easing his suffering. Then he relieved both guards of their weapons. Surveying the network of walkways connecting all the platforms and buildings high among the trees, he marveled at how well-lit everything was considering none of it could be seen from the ground. The good lighting wouldn't help his cause. Anyone strolling about would see him. Stretching out on his belly, he slipped his head over the side of the walkway. The architects of the fair city had done him a favor. The structure supporting the city would be his path. He slipped over the edge.

He moved slowly across the beams. It was much like moving through the branches of the trees, except that he had to crawl. Still, it was much better than walking about amongst the guards. This was slower but safer. As he moved along, he noticed that other paths were moving in toward the path he was under. They came at angles from either side. It seemed all the paths were moving toward some center point. It seemed his most likely destination.

His assumption proved correct. The paths came together at a massive circular platform. It had to be the palace. He moved toward the edge and peered over the top. He counted three guards and assumed, judging from how they were spaced, there would be seven more hidden from his view. He crept along to the mid-point between the two closest to him. Due to the curve of the structure, there was a good ten feet neither of them could see. He moved to that point and slipped up onto the path.

Once on the walkway, he pressed up against the wall and drew his dagger. From what he could tell, the palace was a perfect circle, and a guard was posted at each one-hundred-and-fifty-foot interval. He moved to the left slowly, creeping along the wall until the first guard was in sight. There was no cover, so he wouldn't be able to sneak up and slit the bloke's throat. He slipped his dagger back in its sheath in favor of a throwing knife. He stepped out and fired the blade.

The blade sliced the air end over end, silently racing toward its victim's throat. The guard must have caught the blade's movement, as he turned toward it and drew his sword. It was too late. Before he could swing his blade or call out an alarm, Dahltaf's knife was jutting angrily from his throat. His eyes bulged as a look of fear mixed with confusion raced over his face. Blood pulsed and sprayed as his arms flailed. Then he fell. His body twitched twice and then lay still.

Dahltaf was swift but silent as he charged up to the fallen guard. He retrieved his knife, wiped it clean, and slipped through the door his fallen foe had been guarding. The light wasn't as good inside. There was just enough to determine he had stumbled into a hallway running the same circle as the path outside. Which way to the king? Left again, back the way he had come. The hunter moved stealthily down the hallway.

He slipped past door after door until he found one open a crack. It was dark inside, but even in the dim lit he could make out the lavish decorations. The place seemed fit for a king. He quietly slipped inside.

Moonlight poured into the room from a window overhead, casting a ghostly glow over everything. It was more than bright enough for Dahltaf to determine the shape in the bed was not the king. It may have been the queen, if not so young. Perhaps he had stumbled upon a princess. He had no idea who made up the royal family of Druindahl, but, based on the grandeur of the room, the slumbering person before him had to be a member. If he were looking at a princess, she would make a fine hostage to help him draw out the king. Getting out of the city alone would be difficult. Getting out with a struggling prisoner would be near impossible. Escape wasn't an option. If he were going to kill the king, he would have to do it now. He had only the loose beginnings of a plan when a sharp pain erupted in his knee. His prisoner was awake.

As Dahltaf doubled over, instinctively grabbing for his throbbing knee, Cialia leapt over his back. She almost made it over the top of him, but he maintained enough of his composure to shoot his hand out and grab her leg. Her shoulder pounded into the floorboards a moment before her had smacked against them. The room dipped and swayed as darkness threatened to choke out consciousness. The heel of her foot hammering into Dahltaf's chin was more instinct than a conscious move intended to disable her adversary. No matter, the big man stumbled back and fell into the bed just the same. Dressed in bed clothes and unarmed, Cialia fled.

She made it just to the door when a sharp stinging blasted her right shoulder. Her back arched with pain, and her knees buckled beneath her. She grabbed at the throbbing spot on the back of her shoulder and found the handle of a knife. She gave it yank. It was deep. Stars swam before her eyes and dizziness swept over her as she tugged until the thing finally let loose. She had barely made it back to her feet when Dahltaf tackled her back to the ground. He was strong. She felt her ribs cracking as he pinned her arms down at her sides and bore his weight down on her. She cried out.

The sound of boots approaching snatched Dahltaf's attention from Cialia. Eight guards with swords drawn had poured into the hallway by the time he struggled back to his feet. With two flicks of his wrist, two knives sliced through the air between him and his new adversaries. The pain throbbing in his knee kept his aim from being as crisp as normal. Still, two guards lay wounded. One fought to pry a blade out of his belly as the other stumbled around with one jutting out of his thigh. Dahltaf drew his sword.

Six guards attacked. Dahltaf made fools of them. Even with an injured knee, they were no match for his skill. He quickly removed one of his head, slashed another from gizzard to gullet, and ran another through. Then a stinging in his arm, twisted his face up. It wasn't an expression of pain squatting above his chin. Sure, the shallow cut came with the burning which typically accompanies split skin. However, the twisted expression on Dahltaf's face just then reflected his anger and surprise. One of the pathetic worms had the gall to cut him. In a flash, he grabbed his dagger with his free hand and slit the guard's throat before limping toward the remaining guards. His movements were like art, slicing, stabbing, cutting, and killing in an exquisite, though bloody, dance of death. By the time he spied the king standing in the doorway at the end of the hall, the only ones left breathing were him, Cialia, and his true target, Daritus, king of this wretched city in the trees.

Dahltaf didn't attack Daritus directly. There was a reason he hadn't killed the princess yet, and it he didn't want to spoil it. Retreating to where Cialia desperately fought to crawl away, he grabbed hold of her collar and dragged her back to her feet. The pained groan that ushered forth from her as he hefted her up brought a smile to his face. Her forehead smashing into his nose—along with the stars dancing before his eyes that followed—surprised him. The waif still had some fight in her. Blood instantly began pouring out of Dahltaf's nose as he tossed Cialia to the side. In that same instant, the king had fired his blade. Dahltaf saw the deadly tool coming as it glinted in the light, but he reacted far too slowly to avoid it. The thing pounded into his chest just below his left collarbone.

Everything slowed for Dahltaf as blood pumped from him far too quickly. This was it, his last chance to get some form of payback on those bastards in the forest who had decimated his crew. They could revel in their brief victory, but they would be short their princess once he was done. The fading soldier looked over at Cialia. Their eyes met. She was struggling to regain her feet as he was stumbling to the ground. Taking a reverse grip on his sword with both hands, he drove it into her heart. Fear danced a wild jig in her eyes until they finally clouded over. He stared into them reveling in every invigorating moment until her body stopped twitching, and he pushed her lifeless carcass off the bloodied blade.

"No!" Daritus cried out as he reached Dahltaf.

Dahltaf managed a laugh as he swung his blade at the approaching king. Too much of his blood saturated the wooden slats of the floor surrounding him for the attack to find its mark. The king easily parried the blow. Then he grabbed a handful of Dahltaf's hair with one hand before slashing through his throat with the other. The smile never left his face as he felt his body fall away from his neck. Daritus's pained expression was the last thing he saw before life left him completely.

CHAPTER 27
CLARITY

Pain exploded in Maelich's head, abruptly halting his advance on the dragon and dropping him to his knees. His sword fell helplessly from his hand as dizziness shifted his equilibrium. Before he had a moment to recover, more pain tore through his shoulder. A moment later, he couldn't breathe. Something was squeezing him, robbing him of air. He struggled against the pressure, but he couldn't move. Some force had him pinned down, and it was far too strong for him to overcome.

"Vile tricks," he choked at the dragon.

Helias' tone remained even as she replied, "I have no tricks, and I am not the cause of your pain."

Before Maelich could respond, a man's face filled his vision. It was a warrior staring into his eyes. Then there was more pain. It felt like his chest was ripping apart as the man's eyes filled with joy. The pain lasted moments before fleeing and leaving Maelich breathless on the ground.

Helias' failure to attack him as he struggled against the invisible force left him confused. Why did she pause? Why didn't she finish him while she had the chance? "Are you toying with me beast?" he asked.

Helias shook her head, "The pain you feel is not your own, but you are bound to its owner."

Maelich suddenly felt as if he were being filled up, like some foreign presence existed within him. "What is this?" he demanded. "I feel stronger, even wiser. What is this game?"

Helias' expression became graven, "Cialia has fallen. You two are one. Your souls are intertwined. Now that she has been relieved of her flesh, she will exist within you."

"Impossible. She worships you like a god. How could I be connected to something so vile? The thought sickens me," Maelich spat.

"No, she completes you. If you are the day, she is the night. Without her you are half. She makes you whole. Why do you cling to the lies you've been taught to believe? Listen to yourself. Listen to her. Ignore the nonsense the fears of men have infected your brain with. You are so much more than what they want you to believe. You must see what you truly are," Helias implored.

Maelich thought of raising his sword, but he couldn't do it. The dragon was making sense. Everything he had been taught was about destruction and death. He had been bred to kill. Why was so much glory given to destruction? How could that be right? When he had returned to Havenstahl, he had brought calm and peace to those he touched. It was as if he brought sweet relief to a painful wound. Yet, Ymitoth had hurried him along as if exercises such as those were unimportant. Isn't that more worthy a purpose? He had been gifted with this great power. Shouldn't it be used to heal rather than destroy? If Kallum created everything, why was he so quick to decimate his creation? Would any reasonable man smash a chair into pieces simply because it held his weight and gave him a comfortable place to sit just exactly as intended? No logical thinking being would do that. Shouldn't one presume to expect at least as much from their god?

"You're finally using your own mind," Helias smiled, slightly exposing her menacing teeth.

Maelich's tone was full of confusion as he replied, "There doesn't seem to be an easy answer to all these questions."

Maelich continued struggling with these ideas, questions challenging the authority, the truth, of everything he'd been taught. Understanding human emotion was no problem. It was, after all, very human. Shouldn't the creator of all be beyond that understanding? Was Kallum just some jealous being who created everything simply to have subjects to grovel before him in all his glory, a great king lounging upon his throne as his subjects are forced to constantly beg his forgiveness for being precisely what he created them to be? The idea sickened Maelich, but the more he thought about it, the more it seemed the only plausible answer. There was no love, no mercy, only vengeance, suffering, and pain. In that moment of singular clarity, Maelich decided he wanted no part in it.

"Tell me. I will listen with my heart." Maelich looked earnestly into the Dragon's eyes as he continued, "Did Kallum create us simply to worship him? Are we a game for him, weak-minded creatures to terrify, torture, and toy with? Do we exist merely to crawl about the dirt at his feet?"

Helias' smile widened as she shook her head, "Kallum, the one you call lord, didn't create anything. He was created, just as the rest of us were, by Coeptus."

He raised an eyebrow, "Coeptus? I've heard that name before. Who or what is Coeptus?"

She chuckled, "Who are Coeptus? That would be the proper question. They are a gathering of what you call souls. They are the creators. Quite simply, Coeptus means the beginning. They are the beginning without end."

Maelich's brow wrinkled, "What does that even mean, a gathering of souls?"

"Even with your mind, Maelich, understanding Coeptus is beyond your ability." Her tone became matter of fact, "No amount of explaining will help you understand what they are. They are everything and nothing. You do not know of them, because they have no desire to be worshipped. They do not shout from mountaintops so all might hear their name. On top of that, they know you could not possibly understand them. They are what you wished Kallum to be, perfection. Kallum's true role is to act as a path to that perfection. Sadly, he has failed in that mission."

He scratched his head, "So...then what is Kallum? Is he just a man or some form of wizard or magician? How does he come to be everywhere and nowhere all at the same time?"

"A man? No." Helias continued, "He is quite what you would refer to as a god. They were created first, the gods. After we Dragons, that is." Recognizing the confusion on Maelich's face, she added, "Yes, I said gods. Kallum is not the only one. They were created to govern this place. They are Kallum, whom you know as the lord, Brerto, who trained you, Kaldumahn, Moshat and Ijilv. Somehow, I feel there was another, but no details remain. I trouble over it at times, but it is not important right in this moment. What is important is you believed Brerto to be some form of immortal man, maybe a wizard. That is merely his guise. His human form allows him to walk among men and spread Kallum's word without diminishing Kallum's power as creator and ruler of everything. Would you have feared and revered Kallum if you knew he was but one of a group of gods?"

Maelich stared far past the rocky walls surrounding him as he digested everything Helias had to say. All he had to say was, "No, I guess I wouldn't have."

"Of course not. I should think the fear of being cast into oblivion had something to do with your belief in him as well. Anyhow, Kallum is very powerful and extremely persuasive. He convinced Brerto that together they would be more powerful and that Brerto should assist him in elevating their power. Therefore, Brerto passed on his bid as the truth, the light, and the way for some group of men in dire need of something to worship, to serve Kallum. I should say that Havenstahl is not alone in her worship of Kallum. In fact, most of Ouloos serves him. Save the city of Druindahl. She worships Kaldumahn and Moshat. They rule together. They are quite similar to Kallum and Brerto in their desire to be worshipped. However, their rule is based more on love and adoration than fear. They also stood against Kallum during the great campaign. If not for them, I surely would have been destroyed and all would have been lost," the dragon's gaze drifted toward the same faraway place as Maelich's.

The Dragon's words were making more and more sense to Maelich. He asked, "What of this Ijilv? You left him out. Who are his subjects?"

"He is something of a mystery. Kallum tried to seduce him, claiming that together they could destroy all the Dragons and topple Coeptus. The idea is completely absurd, but his thirst for power is so great he would destroy everything to satisfy it. His jealously of Coeptus greatly illustrates his complete lack of understanding. Coeptus cannot be destroyed. They are everything. Ijilv was torn. Like any god, power is an aphrodisiac for him. On the other hand, he is great of mind and understanding. He realized that even if Coeptus could be destroyed, that destruction would be his own demise. He chose to bind himself in seclusion and has yet to pledge his allegiance to any cause," she finished with a shrug.

Maelich nodded, "So then, what is my role? My entire life has been training to destroy you, and that your destruction would bring balance to Ouloos. If you are not my destiny, then what?"

The smile returned to Helias' face, "Oh, but I am your destiny. There is no power on Ouloos greater than Dragon's fire. However, we Dragons lack the malice needed to wield that power. Even if you were to plunge your sword all ablaze in your fire into my heart, I would not be able to attack you. We were not meant to destroy. But you, on the other hand, have both the fire of Dragons and the blood of men in you. You have the power and the means to use it. You will need it. Do you remember the souls that touched you in The Lost Forest?"

Again, he nodded, "Yes, they still speak to me, even as I'm speaking to you. What of them?"

"They are trapped in that place, forced to relive their ends over and over again as they haunt that wood. They want to go home."

Confused, he asked, "What does that have to do with me?"

Helias continued, "The power of Dragon's fire held open a portal. Think of it as a road, a road back to the beginning. Every time a Dragon was slain, that road, that portal got smaller. It shrunk. At the same time, a fresh bunch of trees sprung up in The Lost Forest. The trees of that forest house the immortal souls of the fallen Dragons. A Dragon's soul is never meant to return to the beginning. We hold open the portal. That is our role for all eternity. Thus, the souls of those fallen had nowhere to go and were trapped in the trees. I cannot hold the portal open alone, and now it is all but closed. The souls of men are drawn to the forest because they are drawn to the Dragons. They long to return to the beginning. They remain trapped in that dark place, clinging to the power which can no longer end their suffering and send them home. They are prisoners. That is your role. You are their savior."

Palms up, he raised his hands and shrugged, "How do I save them? What good is a savior who doesn't know the way?"

Helias' smile dipped into a shallow frown, "Kallum feeds off of the souls trapped in The Lost Forest. Every nightmare they relive is a feast for him. He grows more powerful every moment. He is the door, you are the key, and I the hand that will place you in the lock. It pains me to say this, but your true destiny is to destroy. Your true purpose is to ride the last Dragon against Kallum. His destruction will bring balance, not just to Ouloos, but also to everything. The souls must be freed so they might return home and continue the cycle. I know there is more, but I am unable to see beyond that point."

Something suddenly scurried into Maelich's awareness. It was barely a thought, more of a feeling, but right at that moment, he knew, "Druindahl is under attack. My mother…we must go."

"They are," Helias agreed, "set upon by the army of the man who raised you."

Maelich scanned the cave, "I have to do something. How do I get out of this place?"

Helias took Maelich's hand and guided him up onto her back. The instant he was seated upon her, he felt power surge through him. It was intoxicating, flowing through his skin and mixing with his own. Doubt. Could he wield a power so great? He felt he might crumble at any moment.

Sensing his struggle, Helias coached, "Do not fight it. You were born of the Lake. This power is yours to wield. This is your destiny."

Helias flew straight up and then dove straight down toward the surface of the water they had been resting on. Maelich wrapped his arms around her neck. She was faster than any creature he had ever known. That water had effortlessly held their weight. They would crumble on impact. If not, he would most certainly drown. With fear gripping his heart, he squeezed tighter and prepared to die.

Helias responded to Maelich's strong embrace, "Relax." The softness of her voice seemed impossible with the great volume she achieved as she continued, "You are the champion of this world. I would not do anything which might damage you in any way."

Their impact was not nearly as spectacular or damaging as Maelich expected. In fact, they passed through completely unhindered. It felt like nothing, like no barrier existed at all. What's more, the water didn't slow them in the least bit. Maelich had barely begun to panic at the idea he couldn't breathe under water when he realized he had no urge to breathe. His lungs didn't burn. He didn't lose his body to convulsions. Slowly beginning to relax, the sheer magnificence of what he was experiencing began to sink in. At the speeds they were traveling, the water should have been a frothy brew. However, there were no bubbles and no wake of any sort. The water remained completely still.

As they soared through the water, Maelich's head filled with images and emotions, gifts from Cialia. He watched her whole life unfold before his eyes. Daritus had trained her to be a warrior—just as Ymitoth had trained him—and, based on what he saw, she was at least his equal with a sword. Then he saw his mother's face. The water surrounding him was a great blessing. It hid the tears. Cialia's gift, these images, these memories of a mother he never got to know, were at once both wonderful and terrible. The pride in those loving eyes and that caring smile had been given to Cialia. He yearned to have her loving, proud looks for himself. Still, these gifts were real. Tangible memories to replace the imaginary ones he had concocted throughout his life.

Maelich was still deep in borrowed memories when he and Helias burst forth from the Lake of Dragons without so much as a splash. The fresh air blasting his face quickly brought him back to the moment. Helias' mighty wings lifted them high above the trees of The Lost Forest. Looking down upon that dark place and remembering the pain of their sad songs filled him with purpose. They needed him. He was their champion.

Looking back over his shoulder, the place where the maps don't go stretched as far as he could see. Trees and rivers gave way to dry, cracked land. He couldn't imagine what might lie beyond that. There weren't even stories about that place. It was farther than Maelich had ever been, and he'd never met anyone who knew more about it than it was the place where the maps don't go.

As Helias carried Maelich higher and higher, racing closer to The Forgotten Forest and Druindahl with every moment, the old man who had counseled Maelich on his way to face the Dragon was in the throes of quite a fit. He shook with rage, stomping about as he cursed Maelich's name.

"Impetuous bastard of a man!" the old man shouted at the ceiling, spit flying from his mouth and frothing about the edges of it. "I should have known he'd end in failure. Humans are so pathetic and unpredictable." Pounding both his fists upon his table, he raged on, "After all I've done for him, showing him the way and giving him his power, he repays me by joining that demon of a witch."

He continued stomping about as his skin reddened. His face twisted in an expression of hatred, rage, fear, and hurt in equal parts. He grew. His body expanded in all directions until he filled his small hut. The walls and ceiling creaked and groaned under the pressure until they finally gave way. The hut erupted.

An explosion off to Maelich's left snatched his attention. There he saw the eagle—giant, powerful, and golden—quickly gaining altitude among the debris that used to be a hut. The great beast was still a good distance away, but Maelich could see the thing's eyes as if they were right before his face. They were black and dead, just like the eyes of Kallum's priests.

As Maelich stared in awe at those horrible eyes of a god, he could almost feel the rage radiating from them. Then the wind, with one mighty flap of wings even greater than the Dragon's, Maelich was struggling to hold on. Latching even tighter onto Helias' neck, it took everything he had to keep from toppling. So strong was that wind, it tossed the Dragon off course, careening through the wide open.

"Kallum," Helias cried, "the eagle is upon us."

Kallum, the great eagle, god of gods, no matter what name one used to describe him, he was awesome to behold. Soaring, racing, straight up into the bright blue, he quickly elevated himself far past where any eye could behold him. He didn't remain out of sight for long. Within moments, he dove down at his prey with sharp talons aching to taste flesh. He moved so quickly he nearly blasted right through them.

A bit of a stranger to wide open skies of late—she'd been hiding under the Lake of Dragons for more hundreds of years than she could number—Helias dodged right and narrowly avoided the assault. She had nary a moment to steady herself before she was spinning out of control with Maelich holding on for dear life. The great eagle's velocity had been so great, and carried such a current, she was sucked into the wake.

Despite his struggles to maintain a grip on his mount, Maelich had focused his thoughts within. His breathing had grown steady. It was time to let the fire come. Too late. Thrown from Helias back, he plummeted toward the trees. Toppling end over end and falling faster and faster, he cried out.

Meanwhile, both Kallum and Helias had recovered from their near collision, and both circled around for another pass. The eagle exploded toward Maelich a mere breath before the Dragon. He was faster, but she was closer. Despite her advantage in distance, the eagle was simply too fast, easily doubling Helias' speed. She would never make it in time.

Maelich's helpless body flailed as he plunged. After all he had been through, the crown at the top of his failure would be his broken carcass splattered among the trees of The Lost Forest. The chill winds blasting him as he fell did more than simply cause his cloak to flap madly all about and behind him. They also had his body quite numb. His skin was as ice as he trembled. He fought to gain control of his mind, to let the fire come. He couldn't. Panic squeezed him like giant fingers balling up into a fist around him. Simply sucking air into his lungs was battle enough. His body turned again, and his back was to the trees below him. Above him, the eagle bore down with sharp talons outstretched, glinting in the bright sun.

Then a screech—mighty and terrible like that of the great eagle, but different somehow—ripped through the air, distracting Kallum from his attack. The moment, brief as it was, was just enough to steal the god's prey. Rather than running the flailing soldier through, he narrowly missed. He barely felt Maelich's body career off his own and flop right into Helias.

The Dragon wasted no time swooping in to snatch Maelich's tumbling body from the sky. Banking hard to the left, she quickly led them away from the eagle. She stole only enough of a glance to catch sight of the ferocious hawk descending on Kallum like madness on a broken mind.

"It is Ijilv," Helias shouted. "The mighty hawk has flown out of the shadows to support our cause."

"The hawk is Ijilv, and the eagle is Kallum? But I thought they were gods," Maelich stammered, trying to make sense of what he was seeing, two massive beasts—gods if Helias were to be believed—tumbling through the sky locked in battle.

"They are gods," Helias continued, still trying to find her breath. "They can present themselves in many forms. When a god goes to battle, he will normally present himself as a great beast. That is a bold move for Ijilv. I fear the hawk cannot defeat the eagle on his own."

"If another god cannot match his strength, how can I?" Maelich marveled at Kallum's might as the great eagle battered the failing hawk.

The mighty hawk suddenly fled, racing across the sky back the way he came. Kallum, in his rage, immediately gave chase. The eagle couldn't hope to match the hawk's speed, but that didn't matter. The slight against him would not go unpunished.

"You must," Helias finally replied. Then—noting the chase—added, "It appears you will have some time to work out how."

CHAPTER 28
WAR

Leisha shook as she cradled her daughter in her arms, weeping over her corpse. Daritus knelt beside her rubbing her shoulders and doing his best to console his queen. He had already ordered a few of his guards to dispose of the assassin who had taken his daughter's life. As customary in Druindahl for traitors—and now spineless assassins— the carcass would be tied to a tree and left for wild scrods of the forest to consume. Daritus damned himself for not being able to save Cialia. How weak were the defenses of Druindahl if a killer could slip in undetected during a time of war? As king and general of Druindahl's armies, he had failed. He had failed his daughter. He had failed his wife and queen. He had failed himself. He would never make that mistake again. Druindahl would not sit idle and wait for the next attack. She would march out in vengeance and take the battle to her enemies.

"I will forget what Kaldumahn said!" Leisha's tearful proclamation ripped Daritus from his own self-loathing. "I will not forgive my son for leading the forces of his city and their hatred to our peaceful home. I will not rest until the people of Havenstahl suffer pain equal to my own. None will be forgiven. None will be spared." She grabbed Daritus' cloak and pulled him close to her. Spit flew from her mouth, as her sobs became a whisper, almost a hiss. "Take your armies, mount up your soldiers, and attack them. Leave none alive. Trample them under the hooves of your horses. Slay the heartless bas..." Her words were lost amid her wails.

Daritus held her face close against his chest and caressed her face,

"Shh. I have heard your command, my love. They will die on their hands and knees like scrods. I will make them grovel and beg forgiveness. If they flee, I will hunt them to the very ends of Ouloos. They will know no peace forever more. I will avenge our daughter's death."

In the darkness, Daritus called together all able-bodied men and boys. He armed them with swords, clubs, and spears. He sent the archers off into the trees. The riders of Druindahl would take the lead. Behind them the trained swordsman would march. And behind them would be those untrained, tasting their first battle. By daybreak, they were ready to march. The archers would already be hidden at the forest's edge, waiting to lay down cover for those on the ground.

Just as the sun broke the horizon, the forces of Havenstahl and Alhouim were formed in columns ready to march on Druindahl. Ymitoth sat astride Rumallah. Despite the steed's age, he was the only horse Ymitoth would consider riding into battle. He trusted the animal more than any man he had ever met. Ymitoth raised his sword toward the forest as a horn blared behind him. The riders of Havenstahl charged down Edge Mountain toward the forest. The foot soldiers marched behind them.

At the same instant, a horn answered from within the forest. Arrows from the trees filled the skies. Riders from Havenstahl fell here and there as the charge continued. Within moments, archers atop Edge Mountain returned fire at the trees. Few bodies fell, but the aim of the arrows from the forest had changed to the hilltop. This gave the riders of Havenstahl clear passage to the tree line. Just as they were about to breech the trees, they were met by the riders of Druindahl. The two forces collided, and the battle began.

The battle at the forest's edge raged for hours. Many dwarves and many men from each side fell. Neither seemed able to gain an upper hand. Both sides boasted heroic warriors fighting for far more than pride alone, and both sides felt as if they were fighting against evil. As the heat of the battle grew, it expanded into the forest and up the mountain.

Ymitoth and Daritus battled through the melee and eventually found each other. There was an instant and mutual recognition. Ymitoth realized that when he had Daritus as a prisoner, he had been imprisoning the king of Druindahl. He should have killed him when he had the chance. Instead, he nursed him back to health only to watch him escape. The battle continued around them, but they were both suddenly unaware of all those surrounding them. In their minds, the battlefield was theirs and theirs alone. Daritus raised his sword, aiming it at Ymitoth's heart.

"Coward!" He grunted through clenched teeth. "You failed to kill me whilst I was in your clutches, so you send an assassin, a snake to slither into my city and kill my daughter. Now you will taste death, but only after I make you suffer as I have."

Ymitoth's response carried just as much anger, "I know nothing of your daughter. But ye be right about me failure. I should have killed ye when I had the chance. That be a mistake I won't be repeating."

With that the two kings attacked each other. Both were expert in their art. The rest of Ouloos seemed to stand still as they focused on each other. In Daritus' mind, Ymitoth shared equal blame in Cialia's death. For Ymitoth, he may as well have been facing the dragon himself. Both felt slaying the other would be a great, heroic feat that would lead toward peace and balance on Ouloos. Neither one proved able to gain an advantage, however. They each matched the other's attacks perfectly. Their stalemate could have lasted eternity, if not for an explosion which caused them both to pause and look skyward.

As Maelich approached The Forgotten Forest, he noticed the disturbance going on at the base of Edge Mountain. He told Helias to bring him in closer. As they neared, he realized Druindahl was locked in battle with Havenstahl and even Alhouim. He looked upon the bloody, fallen warriors decorating the hillside. Sorrow filled him. What a waste. All those lives lost for no other reason than differing beliefs. He finally understood how wrong his beliefs had been. How could he stop this? He let the fire come and released it in a great explosion that rocked the forest and hillside below. The battle quickly stopped as all the warriors from both sides looked skyward. Confusion gripped all at the sight of Maelich astride the Dragon.

Maelich's voice boomed loud enough that all could hear, "What do you hope to gain through destruction? What truth can you find in the killing of your fellow man? There is but one enemy of Ouloos, and he is not among us on this battlefield."

As Maelich spoke, he filled the combatants of both forces with feelings of peace and calm. Swords began falling to the ground as Helias touched down in the center of the battlefield. She was putting a great deal of faith in Maelich's power, as the soldiers of Havenstahl and Alhouim would like nothing more than to strike her down. Maelich dismounted and walked over to where Ymitoth and Daritus stood.

Ymitoth spoke first, "What be the meaning of this? Ye come astride the dragon, that vile deceiver. Ye have failed, seduced by the dragon. Ye have fallen."

Then Daritus, "You led Kallum and these forces to us. Now Cialia is dead, and you are again lost to your mother. I begged her let me slay you, and she refused. Now she wishes for your head. You are as low as this king claims. You are unwelcomed here, except for slaughter."

Maelich knew if he allowed it, either one of these men would run him through. He addressed Daritus first, "Cialia is not dead. She lives on in me. We are one. I felt everything she felt, and I saw the eyes of her murderer as she expired. Please know she does not suffer, and she shares my desire. She wishes peace in this place, and she will help make that peace come to be."

He then turned his attention to Ymitoth, "Father…" he began, but Ymitoth cut him off.

"Don't be calling me that, ye vile scrod!" Ymitoth hissed. "Me son be dead, slain by the dragon. That is what ye be now, dead to me. Me son would never be serving the likes of that beast. Ye are not me son! I deny ye!"

Maelich's expression became resolute, "I understand your anger and all the venom you have for me. It saddens me greatly, but I cannot change it. I am sorry you see me this way, but this is what I must do. It is my destiny. It is Ouloos' destiny. Kallum lied. He has lied since the beginning of time, and his teachings are all you know. They were all I knew until my eyes were opened. I hope we survive this, and you can someday forgive me. When my task is complete, the truth will be revealed to all, and then you can make your judgment on me. Until then, know you have my love, father, and I have not failed you."

"Blasphemy!" Ymitoth shouted. "Ye be a treacherous liar! Kallum be giving us all we have, and ye be trampling on his name! Ye be the most vile, the lowest form of sinner!"

Ymitoth would have continued his ranting accusations against Maelich, but he was interrupted by a mighty roar. The ground shook and battle-hardened warriors trembled like babes. All looked to the crest of Edge Mountain. Atop it stood a ferocious looking beast, blazing white fur striped with black as deep as Kallum's dead eyes.

Once the monster had everyone's attention, it roared again. Its open mouth exposed giant fangs the size of a large man. It crouched on all fours. Daritus thought the beast to resemble the lion that had come to him in his dream, but it was different somehow. This beast was angry and full of hate. Its muscles tensed as it prepared to pounce.

Helias cried out, "It is the tiger, Brerto! Maelich, you must fight!"

Maelich drew his sword and let the fire come. Brerto launched himself down the hill. He landed on a group of soldiers, impaling some with his claws while others were crushed under his weight. Spears flew at him but couldn't penetrate his flesh. They glanced off without effect. He advanced, knocking warriors to the side as he came. Some soldiers retreated into the forest while others attempted to attack the beast. The three cities now fought as one force, as the tiger seemed uninterested in what mark they bore. He killed all he encountered.

Maelich was all ablaze, as was his sword. He pointed it at Brerto. A burst of flame shot from the end of it hitting the tiger squarely on the snout. The concussion blasted the beast backward up the mountain. Incensed by the attack, the beast raised his front paws high into the air and brought them crashing down upon the ground. It rumbled so violently Maelich was swept off his feet, along with everyone else on the battlefield. Brerto charged.

Before the tiger was close enough to attack again, Kaldumahn, the lion, burst forth from the forest. The silver lion met the white tiger halfway down the hill. All the soldiers remaining on the battlefield fled into the forest. The two beasts—gods locked in battle—battered each other up and down the hill, slashing and biting at one another. Brerto raised himself up on his back legs and blasted Kaldumahn with his right paw. The lion crashed to the ground. Before he could regain his feet, the tiger was on him. Claws pierced into his back as fangs sunk into the nape of his neck. His roar dripped with pain, as he threw Brerto off. The tiger attacked again, quickly gaining the upper hand. After eons of subjugation serving Kallum, he was finally able to unleash his fury. He let it out on Kaldumahn. His ferocious assault was a great release.

As Maelich watched, the lion was being ripped to shreds. He fired again, blasting Brerto in the side and sending him sprawling.

Helias called to him, "Maelich, we must go. It will not be long until Kallum returns. He must be alone when we face him. With Brerto's aid he would be difficult to destroy."

Maelich nodded and then fired again at the tiger. Again, the beast sprawled further away from Kaldumahn who did his best to regain his feet. Maelich leapt onto Helias back. She stretched out her wings and with a mighty flap had them soaring again. She led them quickly away, back in the direction which Ijilv had led Kallum.

It took Brerto a moment to recover from Maelich's assault. By the time he regained his feet and prepared to renew his attack against Kaldumahn, pain erupted between his ears. Something had hit him hard and sent him tumbling down the hill. A mighty roar filled the air as he regained his feet only to be slashed across the face by Moshat, the great bear.

Moshat didn't let up. He swatted and clawed at Brerto, battering the tiger's head and slashing his flesh. It happened so quickly, Brerto could barely defend himself.

Moshat's attack on their brother reinvigorated Kaldumahn. The mighty lion fought to his feet and charged Brerto. Together he and Moshat attacked with a fury only gods could muster. They pushed the white tiger back over Edge Mountain and away from The Forgotten Forest.

Maelich nearly felt hope as he watched the tide turning against the great tiger. Helias shouting instructions at him pulled his mind back to his own peril. "You cannot be taken by surprise again. Ijilv is no match for Kallum. I hope the great hawk hasn't fallen. Regardless of his fate, this is it. This will be the final battle. If you fail, all is lost. You have all my power and your own at your disposal. Wield it well. I can take you to battle, but I cannot assist you in your assault. Are you ready?"

Noticing a shape approaching from the skies above the place where the maps don't go, he replied, "It seems I have no choice. I think I know what I must do. I just need you to get me close enough."

As the eagle gobbled up the distance between them, Maelich let the fire come. It swirled all about he and Helias until they were completely engulfed. He released it, sending a giant sphere of flame toward Kallum. The eagle was swift and more agile than his massive size would suggest, easily dodging the attack. Maelich fired again and again, finally finding his mark.

Kallum spun backward out of control for a moment, but quickly regained his flight. Another fireball rocked him, and then another. Tumbling out of control, he called to the winds and sent them swirling toward Maelich and Helias.

Helias raced higher trying to avoid the attack, but fierce gales blasted her from every direction. Careening toward the land below, she could feel Maelich's grip slipping from her neck. There wasn't anything she could do to stop it. Fighting against the furious winds, her wings did nothing to correct her flight.

Maelich maintained control, loosely holding onto Helias' neck. The wind was strong enough to toss the mighty Dragon about like a dry leaf. She was helpless. That gave Maelich an idea. Keeping his eyes on Kallum, he leapt from Helias' back into the open air. The swirling winds swept him up just as he had hoped. He fired a steady barrage of fireballs at the eagle, striking him more often than missing. It slowed the great beast but didn't stop him. Maelich drew his sword. Once Kallum was close enough, he drove it all ablaze into the eagle's heart. They became one and then erupted in a bright white flash that singed the treetops and shook the ground.

Helias had regained control of her flight and watched in horror as Kallum, as well as Maelich, burned up in the explosion. She felt heat upon her as the ball of light grew as if it might never stop. Her ears rung from the sound of it. Then, as quickly as it had expanded, it shrunk to nothing. All that remained was dust, and that was scattered upon the wind. Both Kallum and Maelich were gone.

At the same moment, the hawk returned. He flew to the very spot where Kallum and Maelich had exploded into impossibly bright light and saw Helias hovering alone. Feeling her emotions, he knew how the battle had ended. The villain was destroyed, but so was the hero. It was a day for rejoice but also for lament. There was nothing left for him to do. His task was complete. With a flap of his mighty wings, the noble hawk raced back across the skies above the place where the maps don't go.

On the other side of The Edge Mountains, a great battle among gods came to an abrupt halt at the brilliant flash of the explosion. Then its booming report shook the ground beneath them. Instantly, Brerto knew Kallum was no more. They had failed. His roar was like thunder as he evaporated into the air. Exhausted, Kaldumahn and Moshat looked to each other and then then also made a quick exit. All the gods, save Kallum, returned to their thrones. The battle for the lost souls had ended. The lad of the Lake had defeated the king of the gods.

A deafening silence filled the forest after the last echoes of the thunderous boom which had erupted in the skies above the Lost

Forest dissipated. Men from Havenstahl and dwarves from Alhouim looked to men from Druindahl and the men of Druindahl looked back. They all wondered if they had anything left to fight about. Before Maelich had departed, he had removed their desire to raise swords against each other. What now?

Suddenly, all were filled with truth. The warriors of Havenstahl and Alhouim were treated to images of Ouloos' true history. They all saw men mercilessly hunting down Dragons who were—though menacing to behold—quite defenseless. They saw Dragons weeping and even speaking. They pleaded and begged to be spared for the sake of Ouloos and much more that men didn't and couldn't understand. Their pleas didn't matter as they were chased up mountains and into valleys. Their begging fell on deaf ears as they were tracked and killed.

At the same time, the people of Druindahl were exposed to teachings of Kallum. They saw firsthand how those who fought for Havenstahl and Alhouim had been raised. They felt the fear and hatred for Dragons which had been bred in those men and dwarves. They knew why these cities rode against them. Right at that moment, all in the forest knew truth. That is, at least as much as they could comprehend. Most importantly, they knew the war was over.

Daritus went to Ymitoth and draped an arm across his shoulder, "This war is over. We have all lost, and we have all won. We have all learned much on this day. You are welcome to stay with us until your troops are ready to ride back to your home. We will replenish your supplies, and you can depart in peace."

"Aye," Ymitoth put an arm around Daritus, "much has been learned indeed. I be full of regret for all the things I've done. What I regret most be doubting me pupil, me son. Me last words to him were filled with anger and hate. Me eyes were blind, and when he tried to open them for me, I turned me back on him. Damn me."

"No," Daritus shook his head, "Maelich knew much. Surely, he knew how strong the hold of Kallum's lies. Trust me when I say, his spirit forgives you. Honor his memory and the good work he has done."

Alone in a room in the palace of Druindahl, Leisha wept. Her eyes too had been completely opened. Though she knew of the lies, she was apart from the strength of Kallum's grip on the hearts and minds of his believers. She was torn as emotions battled within her. The war was won. For that she carried great elation. However, the price had been many of her people and both of her children. She missed the sight of the explosion that took her son, but she felt both of her children wail in pain as they were swept up in it. Though she was overcome with pride with what they had done as one, her heart ached for their sacrifice. She knew from the beginning what their roles were, but she never realized it would mean their end. Even worse for her was the knowledge that she had been reunited with her son only to feel him die as she damned his name. He followed his path and completed his journey, and she hated him for it before it was complete. She would never forgive herself for that.

CHAPTER 29
REBIRTH

Helias began back toward the Lake of Dragons. She had known everything that was meant to happen up until that point. Kallum had been destroyed. The war was over. But now what was she to do? Nothing had changed. Everything was the same as it had always been. She expected something, some sign that victory was complete. Yet there was nothing for her.

Suddenly, as she flew over The Lost Forest, the trees—the tombs of her fallen sisters—began to quake. They swayed slightly at first, then violently. They whipped back and forth, slamming against each other and battering the ground. They twisted and pulsed and then started vanishing. Clumps at a time were sucked into the ground. Helias hovered above the trees and watched them disappear. Soon, the entire forest was gone. In its place, a dense fog clung close to the ground. It slowly began moving toward the lake.

The lake bubbled into a frothy brew as the ground surrounding it rumbled. Then came Dragons. They poured out of the lake toward the sky. Thousands of them squeezed through the opening that was the Lake's shore. Body on body, they rose like a column into the heavens. The Lake was alive once again. Helias raced to join them.

The column raised up one thousand feet before dragons poured out in all directions like water bursting forth from a geyser. They circled the Lake as they slowly dipped toward the ground. Then, once all the Dragons had been released, a pure, white column of light reached up from out of the Lake to the sky until its end could no longer be seen. Brilliant balls of light, much brighter than the column itself moved together skyward. Tears came to Helias' eyes as she joined her sisters and watched all the souls who had been trapped in The Lost Forest for so long make their journey home. They were free just as the Dragons were free. No longer would they suffer the prison of their pain.

Elsewhere, in a plane that existed not in the physical, two young saviors quite literally met their maker. Maelich and Cialia walked amid a thick, waist high mist which resembled clouds. All that surrounded them was light and the mist they walked through. Neither had any idea where they were or what was happening on Ouloos.

"Could you feel me inside of you? Did you know I was there?" Cialia broke the silence.

Maelich smiled, "Yes, I can barely explain the sensation. Your whole life unfolded before my eyes. You let me see our mother when she was younger, all those years I missed. I can't thank you enough for sharing those memories with me. An empty part of me has been filled. It's like I lived all those missed moments. Did you feel anything from me?"

She looked at the ground, "Yes, yes I did. I am sorry for all the venom I had for you when first we met. I guess I viewed your belief in Kallum as some sort of choice you made. I realize now Kallum's word was pounded into your head from the time you were old enough to understand. Even before that, you were surrounded by it. It wasn't a choice. It was truth for you. How could I hold that against you? Please forgive me."

Maelich embraced his sister, "There's nothing to forgive. We both misunderstood the other's motives, and we were both doing what we knew to be right. Holding your actions against you would be akin to damning the trees for not bearing fruit out of season. You simply did what you were supposed to do. How can you tell someone they are wrong when they know they are right? That is where we both were when we met." He looked around, "But where are we now? Is this it? Is this the end? What do we do now?"

Before Cialia could answer her brother, someone else did. "This is not the end. Your work is not done." A striking old man dressed in a simple white robe appeared before them.

Both Maelich and Cialia were startled at the old man's sudden appearance, but they weren't afraid. Somehow, they knew he meant them no harm. They both considered him. His hair was long and wavy. It was pulled back from his face and poured over his shoulders to his waist. It was as bright and white as his robe. His beard matched them perfectly. All were brighter than the sun, but somehow didn't hurt to look at. Looking at the sun could burn the eyes from your head but beholding the brilliance of this man was quite painless. Despite the age the color of his hair would have suggested, his face was youthful. His skin was smooth and taught. He was beautiful.

The old man chuckled, "Both your heads are so full of thought. Haven't you anything to say? Surely you have questions. Maybe just one?"

Maelich began first, "Who are you, and where are we? There, that's two questions."

"Excellent," the old man boomed, "Who am I? Stay with us now, this is going to be a bit confusing to you. We'll do our best to help you keep up. Who are we? That is the correct question. We are Coeptus. We are many, though we are one. We created all you know. That is our role. We are creators. We create worlds and fill them with all manner of plant and creature."

The old man—they according to him—paused to give what they had said a chance to sink in with their guests.

The brief pause didn't help Maelich or Cialia. They remained completely lost. The old man was obviously insane. He was one being but spoke as if he were legion.

Coeptus continued, "Where are you? That question may be a little easier for you to digest. You are in a realm apart from the physical world which you know. You wouldn't realize this except we saved your consciousness, as your time in the physical is not yet complete."

Cialia shook her head and wrinkled up her brow, "Why do you speak of yourself in the plural as if you were a group of men? I see one man before me. And your second reply makes just as little sense as your first. What of consciousness and physical?"

"Forgive us. We tend to forget the limits of human understanding," they replied. Though their words seemed to carry a note of condescension, it was absent from their tone as they continued, "What you understand to be your spirit or your soul is merely the energy which animates your physical being, or your body. The physical representation of yourself is merely your energy or consciousness presenting itself in the physical realm. Your physical existence occurred on Ouloos. That is your world. The realm you occupy now is non-physical. Your body is not with us, merely your energy or consciousness. As for what we are, the best way to explain that so you can understand is to say we are many people working together as one being. Of course, we are not people, but it may be easier for you to understand us in that way. We are a great gathering of what you think of as spirits. You see us as a man because that is what you can understand. An old godly looking man is what your human mind can accept. Is this making any more sense?"

Maelich nodded, "As much sense as it needs to make. So, you are the Coeptus Helias spoke to me about. She tried to explain you to me, but I believe her understanding of you to be limited as well. Now, you said our work was not done. What have we left to do? I was led to believe my role was to destroy the last Dragon. Then I was convinced it was to ride the last Dragon against Kallum. Did I choose wrong? Has Ouloos been destroyed?"

"No," Coeptus looked quite pleased, "you chose wisely. We are quite impressed with both of you. Know this Maelich, you could never have done what you did without the help of both Helias and Cialia. That was how we intended it. You didn't reach your destination on the exact path we had laid out for you, but luckily you found your way. Ouloos has not been destroyed. Neither has Kallum. A god cannot be destroyed, but his consciousness has been scattered. He can no longer cause Ouloos any harm. When we say your work is not done, we mean your work on Ouloos. You must return to the physical and record what you know. The two of you will write the story future generations of Ouloos will use to learn how to travel 'The great journey of life', as your mentor Ymitoth calls it. You can record the truth and what you've learned about us, or you can make something up. It really doesn't matter. The important thing is the people of Ouloos have something to believe in, a reason to exist. We ask only that your teachings do nothing to disrupt the cycle of life of which we are all a part."

Maelich was shocked, "Make something up? Doesn't truth matter? With all due respect to you, or all of you, that sounds ridiculous to me."

Coeptus' expression became somber, "Maelich, you are part of something so much bigger than you could ever comprehend. What is truth but what you believe it to be? The actual events which occur throughout the history of men are not nearly as important as what they are believed to be. Take you, for example, up until a few of your weeks ago you believed Kallum to be creator of everything. Did that belief keep you from finding your end? No. Your belief gave you reason to continue down your path, and that is what matters. The physical exists merely to strengthen your spirit. All your experiences, good or bad, make you stronger. As you grow and learn, you get smarter. Don't you? That is your consciousness growing stronger. That strength returns to the beginning and is used like your physical body uses food. That is the one reason Kallum had to be scattered. He was in the way of that cycle."

Cialia piped in, "So what you're saying is that we exist merely as food for some other creatures in some other realm? What happens to us doesn't matter at all. Are we simply playing pieces in some game played by beings greater than ourselves?"

Coeptus humphed, "That is quite a rudimentary explanation, but not far from the truth. Your feelings right now are not incorrect. It is natural for you to feel the way you feel right at this moment. It's part of what you are, what you must be. Humans tend to cling to the physical as if that is all there is. You are designed that way. Your desire to cling to the physical is very necessary. If you did not believe in this importance, the events in your lives would not have a strong enough impact on your consciousness. The cycle would eventually cease. Your consciousness is the important thing. The physical is simply a means to gather experiences."

"Then why do we need gods?" Cialia fired back, still slight angered at the idea that people were so miniscule in the grand scheme of things.

Coeptus spoke calmly, "Human beings need to believe they are the center of everything. That is the main reason you are having such a difficult time accepting the true nature of the physical experience. Coupled with that belief is the need to worship something of a parental nature. You need to believe someone—some great, all powerful being—is watching over and protecting you. In exchange for that protection and guidance, you offer worship and praise. Thus, the need for gods, they fill that role. Through the worship of this almighty creator, pick the one you like best, you believe you propel yourselves body and soul into some greater plane of consciousness, a place where you experience eternal bliss and exist in proximity to that which you worship. You believe that to be your purpose. When you think about what we are presenting to you now, your belief is not far from the truth. The only difference being that you are not the main purpose of everything. You are just a part of it all. You have a role as have we and everything else in the cycle. The gods charged with governing physical realms merely give you that fatherly, creator figure to worship. You form a perfect, symbiotic relationship with them, as they have an unquenchable desire to be worshipped and glorified. It all makes perfect sense. Ouloos would have been left unchecked were it not for Kallum's jealousy and desire to expand outside of his role."

Cialia pondered these new ideas in silence as Maelich picked up the conversation, "Where does this cycle exist, and how does it strip us of our consciousness?"

Coeptus stroked their beard, "Well, do you remember the visions you received from the souls lost in the forest?"

Maelich nodded.

"Those visions were memories which belonged to the souls who shared them with you. They only shared the terrifying ones with you, but they were filled with so much more you didn't get to see. Those memories are the strength of the souls they cling to. There are many worlds with beings just like the people of Ouloos. Their souls all carry the same energy from experiences. Upon the death of their physical being, their consciousness is released and returned to the beginning. Imagine a lake with many rivers flowing to and from it. This lake is the beginning. The rivers flowing to it are the portals such as the one you opened by scattering Kallum and freeing the Dragons. These portals, or rivers, carry the spirits or consciousness of humans, and other creatures for that matter, back to the beginning. When they arrive, the energy they carry is returned to the beginning and they are mixed in with the greater spirit which swirls there in the lake. When new consciousnesses form from this mixture and are ready to present themselves, they are carried through portals or rivers flowing back to the various worlds existing among the physical. Then they are born into whatever world they happen to be born to as whatever creature they are meant to be, and the cycle continues. Now, we understand that for you this makes your existence seem quite unimportant, but it's not. Without the experiences, the energy your spirits possess, the cycle would cease. All would be lost."

Cialia was beginning to accept what Coeptus had to say, "I think I understand. Though nothing is what we believed it to be, what it is isn't as important for us as what our belief is. Our beliefs are what drive us, our experiences make us strong, and that is our role. The fact we are merely a small part of something greater doesn't diminish our importance. It simply changes our role. For Maelich and I, it changes our role even more as we are to return and begin a new chapter in Ouloos' history. We are to create a new story, something Ouloos can believe in. Truth will be what we make it."

Coeptus smiled, "Exactly! There are still four gods and a whole race of Dragons at your disposal. They will fill whatever role you write them into. The belief of people is for those people who believe in it. Give them something to believe in."

Maelich looked confused, "All of that is fine and good, but why all of the evil and despair? Why do Amatilazo hunt men for food? Why are men plagued by disease? What is the point of suffering?"

"We will explain this and then you must return." Again, Coeptus became the teacher, "Earlier we told you experiences were what made the spirit strong. Those can be good or bad. Many times, a good scare is much more powerful than a bit of joy, much more memorable too. That is not the only reason. One of the great things about humanity is also one of its greatest flaws. The race of men, and women," they winked at Cialia, "never seem to find a workable balance with their physical surroundings. You are unbelievably adept at using every little bit of your environment to make your physical experience more comfortable and more rewarding. This fact is wonderful in that invention and discovery do marvelous things to strengthen a soul. However, many of these inventions and discoveries are designed to prolong the physical experience much longer than it was meant to be. This coupled with the natural human desire to procreate would, if unchecked, cause great overpopulation. Furthermore, you use up your resources much faster than they can be replenished. Imagine if there were nothing to challenge humanity. Men would eventually live to be hundreds, even thousands, of your years old. They would continue to spawn more and more offspring. It wouldn't be long before there was no food to eat, no resources for building shelters, no room to live, and, in time, humanity would die out. You might be amazed to hear this, but it's always the same with human beings. No matter what environment we place them in, they always seem to conquer their surroundings. Finally, your time away from the beginning would be too long. These...evils you describe exist merely to keep humankind in check."

Coeptus turned and pointed toward a light behind them, "Now, we bid you farewell. Good luck, Maelich, Cialia. Your task is great, but we know you are fit to it."

CHAPTER 30
THE RETURN

Two weeks had passed since the great explosion which marked the end of Kallum and a new beginning for Ouloos. The Dragons had returned to their posts, and balance had returned to their world. The sky all around the Lake was full of Dragons stretching their wings after centuries of imprisonment. Those not flying were catching up with those they had been missing. There was an energy there, an energy which had been missing for far too long. Among the crowd was Helias. She shared the story of Ouloos with all those of her sisters who listened. She filled them in on what they had missed. Often during her story, she wept. She lost the most tears for Maelich and Cialia and the sacrifice they made to save their world. What a brave act that was, especially for two with human blood.

Helias was deep in describing the great battle with Kallum when she felt something strange, a disturbance in the Lake. It felt unnatural. Her sisters felt it too. The feeling grew stronger and stronger. It felt as if something were coming through the portal the wrong way. The Lake grew brighter and brighter still. Then two shapes looked to be walking on the water of the Lake amid the light. The light was brighter around them. Before long, they were at the shore. When they reached it, the light from the portal shone like the sun around their silhouettes. Then in a brilliant flash, two people stood at the edge of the Lake.

Helias looked to the two who had come backward through the portal. Instantly she recognized one of them. "Maelich!" she cried out.

He raced to her, Cialia following close behind. When they reached the Dragon, Maelich flew into her outstretched arms. They had formed a connection, a bond in their short time together. There was a part of Helias in Maelich and a part of him in her. After a moment, Cialia joined the embrace. She was also a part of this union. The three of them stayed in that embrace for some time. As they did, they drew strength from each other. The reunion may have lasted eternity were it not for the group of curious Dragons who began surrounding the trio.

Without verbalizing, Dragons began expressing their gratitude to Maelich and Cialia, even to Helias. Whole conversations went on without so much as a word being spoken. The Dragons shared a bond. Though they were all individuals, they belonged to one whole. What one felt, they all felt and what one knew, they all knew. Due to the Dragon blood flowing through their veins, Maelich and Cialia were a part of that greater consciousness the Dragons shared.

As the conversations continued, Maelich learned his efforts had indeed proved quite successful. The war and been stopped, Brerto had been banished to his throne, and the people of Druindahl stood side by side with those of Havenstahl and the dwarves of Alhouim. He further learned that Helias had been deemed queen of all Dragons for her efforts. Not only for her bravery during the final battle, but for carrying on the race of Dragons alone for so many centuries. She was a hero among her sisters.

The praise and adoration went on for the better part of the day. Finally, Helias spoke with her mouth instead of her mind, "We must get you two weary heroes home to the rest of your family. I will take you there."

Neither Maelich nor Cialia responded. They simply smiled, shared one more embrace with Helias and then climbed upon her back. In an instant they were in flight. One mighty flap of Helias' powerful wings had them air born, and a few more had them high above Lake. The journey to Druindahl would be a quick one.

The armies of Havenstahl and Alhouim were forming up in the forest, preparing for the journey home, when one of the scouts of Druindahl called an alarm, "A Dragon approaches."

Just a few weeks ago, that would have been cause for the warriors of Havenstahl and Alhouim to beat the drums of war. It would also have been cause for those of Druindahl to race to her protection. On this day, it merely gave them cause to wonder what she might want.

Ymitoth, Doentaat, Daritus, and Leisha rode to the edge of the forest to greet her.

When the small group reached the forest's edge, Helias had already touched down. Immediately, Leisha saw her two children astride the Dragon. Her eyes welled up as she cried out thanking, Coeptus, Kaldumahn, Moshat, the Dragons, and everything else on Ouloos. Fighting through knees weakened by emotion, she ran to them. Both of her children leapt from Helias' back and raced to meet her. When they reached each other, they collided in an embrace full of wet eyes and kissed cheeks. Leisha poured apologies on Maelich and praises on both of her children.

"Oh, my sweet babes," she cried. "I thought you were lost to me forever. Maelich, please forgive me for the way I damned your name."

Maelich soaked up his mother's affection and replied very simply, "There's nothing to forgive."

"We're all together now," Cialia added. "As we always should have been."

Then Maelich's tone became very sober, "Alas, it can only be but for a short time. Cialia, you and I have much work left for us to tend to. Our home will be the road, maybe for all of our days."

"Well then, that is where my home shall be," Leisha replied, cheeks full of tears.

"As well as mine," Daritus had walked up to join the embrace.

"What about your kingdom?" Cialia asked. "What about Druindahl?"

"They'll have to be governing themselves," Ymitoth piped up, "just as the people of Havenstahl."

Maelich turned and hugged his father. He didn't say a word and neither did Ymitoth. Both knew what the other had to say. No words were necessary. As they embraced, Maelich noticed Doentaat, looking quite lonely all by himself, away from the love fest. Maelich put an arm around him and pulled him into the group.

"We've always room for the great king of the mightiest city of dwarves," Maelich chuckled as he planted a kiss on Doentaat's head.

Doentaat chuckled as he pulled his head away from the less than masculine display of affection. "Knock it off, you big oaf."

The conversation ended just as the sun dipped below the horizon. They decided the cities of Havenstahl and Alhouim would stay one more night in Druindahl. In the morning they would depart for their homes. Maelich would join them. Leisha would pass down her crown and make sure all was right in her city, and then she, along with Daritus and Cialia, would meet them in Havenstahl a few weeks later. Beyond that, none of them new what the future would bring for them. Maelich and Cialia had been charged with the task of leading Ouloos into her future. The rest would follow them on that path.

CHAPTER 31
A NEW BEGINNING

Hagen addressed a great gathering in the courtyard at Havenstahl. He stood at the top of the steps where Maelich had received his crest so many years ago. Maelich stood before him, dressed in similar princely garb to what he had worn on that day. Horns blared out a triumphant song in the background. From the crowd, Perrin appeared adorned in a long, flowing white gown. A veil covered her face and frilly bows decorated her dress. She clung to Kendal's arm as he led her toward the man she would spend the rest of her days with. Haleen stepped from the crowd and lifted Perrin's veil to kiss her cheek. Leisha did the same on her other side. Then Cialia kissed the bride's hand while Daritus and Ymitoth shook Kendal's. They mounted the stairs. Maelich descended meeting them halfway up the staircase. He shook Kendal's hand as he took Perrin's. He and his bride took the rest of the stairs together and stood before Hagen.

Hagen spoke, "Love is an emotion which has no equal. Love is an emotion which must be shared. When two people find each other and become one, that love consumes them. The two become one. Today we celebrate the love Maelich and Perrin share. On this day, these two make a vow to share their love and their lives with each other. On this day, they become one."

He looked to Maelich, "Maelich, do you vow to care for Perrin, to love her, to cherish her, to share with her in all your experiences? What say you?"

Maelich smiled, "I do."

Hagen looked to Perrin, "Perrin, do you vow to care for Maelich, to love him, to cherish him, to share with him in all your experiences? What say you?"

A lone tear trickled down her cheek, "I do."

He addressed them both, "Maelich, Perrin, you have made a vow to each other before all of Havenstahl. You have made a vow which shall bind your destinies for the rest of your days. It is a duty you share to honor this union and nurture your love for one another. Now you may seal this vow with a kiss, a symbol to all of the love you share for one another."

Maelich stepped closer to Perrin. He gently raised her veil and pulled her into his embrace. She fell into him as they kissed. The crowd cheered as the kiss lasted perhaps a bit longer than it should have. They both were filled with dreams and plans, ready to begin their life together.

Hagen looked to the crowd, "We have all witnessed the union of this man and this woman. Let no man or woman interfere with the vow they have made to each other."

The crowd spilled up onto the steps to congratulate the new couple. All in Havenstahl looked on this union as the beginning of something new, not only for the bride and groom, but for all Ouloos as well. It was a brand new world.

The End

ABOUT THE AUTHOR

E. Michael Mettille is the author of Kallum's Fury (Lake of Dragons Book 2), Kill the Gods (Lake of Dragons Book 3), and Hell and the Hunger (as Mike Reynolds). He has also written numerous short stories and poems. Mike has spent the last twenty years in direct marketing, print, and communication. He is fascinated by history, belief systems, the human condition and how all of those things work together to define who we are as a people. The world is a wonder and, based on the history of us, it is a wonder we have a world left to wonder about. Mike lives in Milwaukee, WI with his wife, Shelia.

www.ingramcontent.com/pod-product-compliance
Lightning Source LLC
Chambersburg PA
CBHW060947120726
47910CB00002B/518